W9-BWI-548

The RED *and the* BLACK

STENDHAL'S
The RED and the BLACK

in a new translation by JOAN CHARLES

and Illustrated by FREDE VIDAR

INTERNATIONAL COLLECTORS LIBRARY

AMERICAN HEADQUARTERS

Garden City · New York

TO THE HAPPY FEW

CONTENTS ✦ ✦ ✦

Volume One

Volume Two

TRANSLATOR'S NOTE

Because Stendhal felt his style to be lacking in elegance, because he was never entirely satisfied with anything he had written and was continually adding phrases and emendations in an attempt to produce what his times thought of as polished prose, no two editions of *Le Rouge et le Noir* are exactly similar. This translation has been made from the French text published by Editions de Cluny in 1937, which seems to include the majority of Stendhal's own marginal notes in the body of the text rather than as footnotes.

The publisher's abridgment of this edition has eliminated almost entirely the lengthy discussions of political and religious intrigue which serve rather as counterpoint than as an integral part of Julien Sorel's life in the original. Inevitably this abridgment has resulted in the loss of some entire chapters, and the combining of others so that the chapter numbers no longer agree with those of the original edition, but the text has not been altered or rearranged in any other way.

J. C.

Volume 1

CHAPTER 1

A Small Town

THE small town of Verrières must rank among the loveliest of Franche-Comté. Its white houses with their pointed red-tiled roofs climb the slope of a hill, each least curve of which is marked by clumps of flourishing chestnut trees. The Doubs flows past a few hundred feet below fortifications built long ago by the Spanish and now in ruins.

On the north side, Verrières is protected by a high mountain, a spur of the Jura range. The broken peaks of the Verra are covered with snow from the earliest October frosts. A torrent rushing down from the mountain flows through Verrières before plunging into the Doubs, and supplies power to a large number of sawmills—an easy form of industry which insures a certain prosperity to the greater part of a population more peasant than bourgeois. Yet it is not the sawmills that have enriched this small town. The general affluence—which, since Napoleon's fall, has made it possible for almost all of Verrières' houses to have their front faces rebuilt—is due to the manufacture of printed cotton materials.

Upon first entering the town one is stunned by the clamor of a machine both noisy and hideous. Twenty heavy mallets, which fall with a noise that makes the pavement shudder, are raised by a wheel that the water of the mountain stream turns. Each of these mallets produces in a day I do not know how many thousand nails. Bits of iron which are speedily converted into nails are presented to these enormous hammers by fresh, pretty girls. If, upon entering Verrières, the traveler asks whose property is that fine nail factory which deafens people walking up the main street, he is told in a drawling accent: "Oh, that's the mayor's."

Should the traveler but pause for a few moments on the main street of Verrières, which leads up from the bank of the Doubs nearly to the top of the hill, the chances are a hundred to one that he will see a tall man with a busy and important air appear.

At sight of him, all hats are quickly raised. His hair is graying, and he is dressed in gray. He is a knight in several Orders; he has a broad forehead, an aquiline nose, and his face as a whole is not without a certain regularity: it even seems, on first glance, to join the dignity of a village mayor to that sort of charm which may still be recognizable at forty-eight or fifty years of age. But soon the visitor from Paris is shocked by a certain air of self-satisfaction, of self-sufficiency mingled with something narrow and lacking in flexibility. One receives the impression that this man's talent is limited to seeing to it that he is paid precisely what is owing him, and to putting off payment of his own debts as long as possible.

Such is the mayor of Verrières, Monsieur de Rênal. Having crossed the street at a sober gait, he enters the town hall and is lost to the traveler's sight. But a few hundred yards farther on, should one continue walking, one sees a rather handsome house and, through the wrought-iron gates leading to the house, a magnificent garden. Beyond lies the horizon line traced by the hills of Burgundy, as if made expressly for the eye's pleasure. The view helps the visitor forget the atmosphere, poisoned by petty money concerns, by which he is beginning to be stifled.

He is told that the house is the property of Monsieur de Rênal. It is to the profits from his great nail factory that the mayor of Verrières owes the fine freestone mansion which is now being completed. His family is said to be Spanish, ancient and, so they claim, established in this region long before Louis XIV's conquest.

Since 1815, being an industrialist has been embarrassing to him: 1815 made him mayor of Verrières. The terraced walls that retain the various levels of his magnificent garden, which slopes, step by step, down to the Doubs, are also the reward of Monsieur de Rênal's competence in the iron industry.

Do not look, in France, for those picturesque gardens that surround the factory towns of Germany: Leipzig, Frankfort, Nuremberg and the rest. In Franche-Comté the more walls one builds, the more one's property bristles with stones laid one upon the other, the more right one has to the respect of one's neighbors. Monsieur de Rênal's gardens, littered with walls, are admired all the more because he bought the small plots of earth upon which they stand for their weight in gold. That sawmill, for example, whose singular location on the bank of the Doubs struck you upon entering Verrières, and on which you noticed the name SOREL in gigantic letters on a board surmounting the roof: six years ago it stood upon the spot where the wall of the fourth terrace of Monsieur de Rênal's garden is now being constructed.

Despite his pride, the mayor was obliged to make many an offer to old Sorel, a hard and stubborn peasant; he had to count out a good number of gold pieces to get him to move his mill elsewhere. As for the community watercourse that turned the mill wheel, Monsieur de Rênal made use of his influence in Paris to have its course altered.

He gave Sorel four acres for one, five hundred yards downstream on the Doubs. And, although this situation was far more advantageous for his trade in pine boards, Père Sorel, as he has been called since he became rich, contrived so to play upon his neighbor's impatience and his eagerness for the property as to pry out of him the sum of six thousand francs.

It is true that this transaction was criticized by the sound business heads of the town. One time, on a Sunday four years later, Monsieur de Rênal, returning from church in his mayorial garb, saw old Sorel some distance away, surrounded by his three sons, look at him and smile. The smile was fatal to Monsieur de Rênal's peace of mind; from that day on he has thought that he could have got a better bargain out of the exchange.

To achieve public respect in Verrières it is essential, while building a great many walls, not to adopt any of the plans brought from Italy by the masons who cross the Jura passes in the spring on their way to Paris. Such an innovation would earn the imprudent builder an eternal

3

reputation for eccentricity, and he would be lost forever in the opinion of the wise and moderate folk who distribute respect in Franche-Comté.

As a matter of fact, these wise folk exercise the most burdensome *despotism* there; it is because of that ugly word that a visit in such small towns is insupportable to anyone who has lived in the great republic called Paris. Tyranny of opinion—and such opinion!—is as stupid in the small towns of France as in the United States of America.

CHAPTER 2

A Mayor

Fortunately for Monsieur de Rênal's reputation as an administrator, an immense retaining wall was required for the public promenade that skirts the hill a hundred feet above the course of the river. To this location it owes one of the most picturesque views in France; but every spring the rains flood the promenade, washing out great crevices and rendering it impassable. This inconvenience, felt by everyone, placed Monsieur de Rênal under the happy necessity of immortalizing his administration by means of a wall twenty feet high and five or six hundred feet long.

The parapet of this wall, topped with slabs of gray-blue freestone, rises some four feet above ground level. The sun is quite hot in these mountains; when it shines directly down, the traveler dreaming upon the terrace is sheltered by magnificent plane trees. Their rapid growth and their beautiful blue-green foliage are owing to the soil that the mayor had brought to fill in behind his immense retaining wall, for despite the municipal council's opposition he broadened the terrace by more than six feet, which is why in his opinion—and in that of Monsieur Valenod, the prosperous director of Verrières' poorhouse—this terrace can support comparison to that of Saint-Germain-en-Laye.

As for me, I have but one fault to find with the Cours de la Fidélité, and that is the barbarous fashion in which the authorities have these flourishing plane trees clipped and pruned within an inch of their lives. But the mayor's will is despotic, and twice a year all trees belonging to the community are pitilessly amputated. An old surgeon major of the Army of Italy, retired to Verrières, who according to the mayor was once a Jacobin and a Bonapartist during his lifetime, dared one day to complain to him of the periodic mutilation of these beautiful trees.

"I like shade," Monsieur de Rênal answered with the suggestion of arrogance suitable when speaking to a surgeon, a member of the Legion of Honor, "and I do not see that a tree has any other purpose except when, like the useful walnut, it brings in revenue."

There is the great phrase which settles everything in Verrières: *bring in revenue*. In itself, it represents the habitual thought processes of three quarters of the inhabitants.

It was a fine autumn day, and Monsieur de Rênal was pacing the Cours de la Fidélité, his wife upon his arm. While she listened to her husband speaking with a sober air, Madame de Rênal's eye was uneasily following the activities of three small boys. The eldest, who might have been about eleven, kept going over to the parapet and making as if to climb upon it. Then a gentle voice would call "Adolphe!" and the boy would abandon his ambitious project. Madame de Rênal appeared to be a woman of thirty, but still quite attractive.

"It's quite possible that he'll regret it, this fine gentleman from Paris," Monsieur de Rênal was saying with an offended air, his cheek even a bit paler than was normal. "I have one or two friends at the Château."

But I am not so barbarous as to inflict upon you the lengthiness and the knowing circumspection of a provincial dialogue.

This fine gentleman from Paris, so odious to the mayor of Verrières, was none other than Monsieur Appert, who two days earlier had contrived to insinuate himself not only into Verrières' prison and poorhouse, but also into the hospital administered without recompense by the mayor and the principal landowners of the district.

"But," Madame de Rênal said timidly, "what harm can this gentleman from Paris do you, since you supervise the welfare of the poor with the most scrupulous honesty?"

"He came here purely for the sake of finding fault, and later on he'll get articles printed in the liberal papers."

"You never read them, my dear."

"But people tell us about these Jacobin articles; all that sort of thing distracts us and hinders us in our good works."

Monsieur de Rênal was upon the point of flying into a rage when his wife cried out. Her second son had climbed up onto the parapet of the terrace wall and was running along it, although the wall stood some twenty feet above the vineyard that lies upon its other side. The fear of startling her son and causing him to fall prevented Madame de Rênal from speaking a word to him. At length the boy, laughing over his exploit, glanced at his mother, noticed her pallor, jumped down to the path and ran to her. He was soundly scolded.

The small event changed the course of the conversation.

"I have definitely made up my mind to have Sorel, the sawmill owner's son, come to live at the house," Monsieur de Rênal said. "He will take charge of the children, they're getting to be too much of a handful for us. He's a young priest, or something of the sort, a sound Latinist; and he will see to it that the boys make progress, for the curé says he has a firm character. I'll give him three hundred francs and his board. I should never have dreamed of putting a carpenter's son in charge of our children, but the curé was telling me just the other day that this Sorel has been studying theology for the past three years, with the idea of entering the seminary; so he isn't a liberal and he is a Latin scholar.

"It will be a desirable arrangement in more ways than one," Monsieur de Rênal went on, glancing at his wife with the air of a diplomat. "That Valenod is bursting with pride over the fine pair of Norman horses he just bought for his barouche. But he has no tutor for his children."

"He'd be quite capable of taking this one away from us."

"Then you approve of my plan?" Monsieur de Rênal said, thanking his wife with a smile for having had so excellent an idea. "Well, then, that's settled."

"Heavens, my dear, you do make up your mind quickly!"

"That's because I'm a man of character. Let's not delude ourselves, we're surrounded by liberals here. All these cloth merchants are envious of me, I'm certain of it; two or three of them are getting to be rich men. Well, I'd rather like them to see Monsieur de Rênal's children pass by on their way for a walk, accompanied by their tutor. It will impress them. My grandfather often used to tell us that he had a tutor

7

when he was young. It may cost me a hundred écus, but that can be classed as an expense necessary for maintaining our social position."

This sudden decision left Madame de Rênal very thoughtful. She was a tall, well-proportioned woman who had been the beauty of the district. She had a certain air of simplicity and of youth in her bearing. To a Parisian, that artless grace, full of innocence and vivacity, might even have suggested a gentle sensuality. If she had become aware of this sort of success, Madame de Rênal would have been thoroughly ashamed of it. Neither coquetry nor affectation had ever been part of her nature. It was said that Monsieur Valenod, the wealthy director of the poorhouse, had made advances to her, but without success, which added a pronounced luster to her virtue, for Monsieur Valenod, a tall young man, well built, with a high color and heavy black sideburns, was one of those coarse, bold, blustering creatures who, in the provinces, are called fine handsome men.

Madame de Rênal, being very shy and apparently very indecisive in character, was predominantly shocked by Monsieur Valenod's incessant restlessness and the loudness of his voice. The distaste she had for what is called entertainment in Verrières had earned her the reputation of being overproud of her birth. That never occurred to her; but she was perfectly content to see the townspeople come less frequently to visit her. We will not conceal the fact that she was considered stupid, in the eyes of the ladies, because, without regard for her husband's political position, she passed up the most wonderful opportunities for having exquisite hats brought to her from Paris or Besançon. So long as she was left alone to wander in her beautiful garden, she never complained.

She was an innocent soul who had never even arrived at the point of judging her husband and admitting that he bored her. She supposed, without ever putting the thought into words, that there was no more agreeable relationship between husband and wife. She was particularly fond of Monsieur de Rênal when he spoke of plans for their children, of whom he intended one for the army, the second for the bench, the third for the church. On the whole she found Monsieur de Rênal far less boring than any other man of her acquaintance.

This wifely opinion was a reasonable one. The mayor of Verrières owed a reputation for wit, and more particularly for good breeding, to a half-dozen amusing anecdotes which he had inherited from an uncle. Before the Revolution old Captain de Rênal had served in the Duc d'Orléans' infantry regiment and, when he went to Paris, had been received in the prince's drawing-rooms. There he had seen Madame de Montesson, the famous Madame de Genlis, Monsieur Ducrest, the designer of the Palais-Royal. There was a time when these personages appeared only too often in Monsieur de Rênal's conversation. But, little by little, recalling things so delicate to put into words had become a chore for him, and for some time past he had been repeating his anecdotes about the House of Orléans only on great occasions. As he was, in addition, extremely courteous except when discussing money matters, he was reputed, and accurately so, to be the most aristocratic person in Verrières.

CHAPTER 3
Father and Son

MY WIFE is really most intelligent, the mayor of Verrières thought, the next morning at six o'clock, walking down toward old Sorel's sawmill. Although I told her that I had—in order to preserve my rightful superiority—I had not realized that if I do not hire this young priest Sorel who, they say, knows Latin like an angel, the poorhouse director, impulsive as he is, might very well have the same idea and take him away from me. The self-satisfied tone he would use for talking about his children's tutor! . . . This tutor, once I get him, will he wear a cassock?

Monsieur de Rênal was absorbed in this question when he saw at a distance a peasant, a man nearly six feet tall who, in the dawn light, seemed to be very intent upon measuring some pieces of wood laid out on the towpath along the Doubs. The peasant seemed none too pleased at seeing the mayor approach, for his lengths of wood were obstructing the path and had been laid out there in contravention of the law.

Père Sorel, for it was he, was greatly surprised and even more pleased at the unexpected proposal Monsieur de Rênal made for his son, Julien. He listened to it, however, with that air of gloomy dissatisfaction and lack of interest which the shrewdness of these mountain dwellers is so readily able to assume. Slaves in the time of the Spanish dominion, they still retain this facial characteristic of the Egyptian fellah.

Sorel's first response was no more than the lengthy recital of all the respectful formulas which he knew by heart. While he repeated these empty words with an awkward smile that accentuated the air of falseness, almost of mockery, natural to his features, the peasant's agile mind was searching for some reason that might lead so eminent a man to take that worthless son of his into his home. He was greatly dissatisfied with Julien, and yet Monsieur de Rênal was offering the miraculous wage of three hundred francs a year for him, and his food and even his clothing besides. That last condition, which old Sorel had been clever enough to bring up immediately, had been granted at once by Monsieur de Rênal.

The demand made an impression upon the mayor. Since Sorel is not overwhelmed and delighted by my proposal, as he naturally ought to be, he thought, it is obvious that he has received offers from another source; and from whom could they have come if not from Valenod? In vain Monsieur de Rênal urged Sorel to come to an agreement on the spot; the old peasant's cunning obstinately refused to do so; he wished, he said, to consult his son—as if a rich provincial father ever consulted a penniless son, except as a formality.

A sawmill consists of a shed on the bank of a stream. The roof is supported by a framework which rests on four thick wooden pillars. In the middle of the shed, at a height of eight or ten feet, one sees a saw that moves up and down while a very simple mechanism pushes a length of wood against the blade. A wheel turned by the stream operates this double mechanism, the vertical action of the blade and the device that pushes the wood gently against the saw, which cuts it into boards.

Approaching his mill, the elder Sorel shouted for Julien in his stentorian voice; no one answered. He saw only his older sons, giants who, armed with heavy axes, were squaring up the pine-tree trunks which they would then take to the saw. Completely absorbed in following exactly the black line drawn on the log, each ax stroke splitting off enormous chips, they did not hear their father's voice. He turned toward the shed; entering, he looked in vain for Julien in the place where he was supposed to be, beside the saw. He caught sight of him five or six feet farther up, astride one of the roof beams. Instead of attentively supervising the action of the machinery, Julien was reading. There was

11

nothing more irritating to old Sorel. He might perhaps have forgiven Julien his slender build, unsuited to heavy labor and so different from that of his older boys, but that mania for reading was abominable to him: he himself did not know how to read.

He called Julien two or three times without result. The young man's concentration upon his book, far more than the noise of the saw, prevented him from hearing his father's terrible voice. At length, despite his age, the old man leaped agilely upon the tree trunk which was being sawed and from there to the transverse beam that supported the roof. A violent blow sent the book Julien was holding spinning into the mill race; a second blow, as violent as the first, this time aimed at his head as a box on the ears, made him lose his balance. He was about to fall twelve or fifteen feet below among the levers of the moving machinery, which would have crushed him, but his father caught him back with his left hand as he was falling.

"Well, lazybones! So you'll read your damned books, will you, even when you're supposed to be minding the saw? Read them in the evening when you go to waste your time at the priest's, why don't you!"

Julien, although dazed by the force of the blow, and covered with blood, returned to his official post beside the saw. He had tears in his eyes, less because of the physical pain than because of losing the book which he adored.

"Come down here, stupid, while I talk to you."

Again the noise of the machinery prevented Julien from hearing the order. His father, who had climbed down, not wishing to take the trouble of clambering up again, went to get a long pole used for gathering nuts and struck him on the shoulder with it. Julien had no more than reached the ground when old Sorel, driving him roughly before him, shoved him toward the house. God knows what he is going to do to me! the young man thought. In passing he glanced sorrowfully at the mill race into which his book had fallen; it was the one he loved best of all: *Le Mémorial de Sainte-Hélène*.

His cheeks were scarlet, his eyes lowered. He was a slight young man of eighteen or nineteen, frail looking, with irregular but delicate features and an aquiline nose. Great black eyes, which in moments of tranquillity spoke of meditation and of ardor, were at present alive with an expression of the fiercest hatred. Dark chestnut hair, growing low, gave him a narrow forehead, and, in moments of anger, a wicked look. Among the innumerable variations of the human physiognomy, there is perhaps none distinguished by a more startling peculiarity. A slender and well-knit body suggested greater agility than robustness. In his earliest childhood his extremely pensive air and his pronounced pallor had given his father the idea that he would not live, or would live only to be a burden upon his family. An object of dislike to the whole household, he hated his brothers and his father; in the Sunday games in the public square he was always beaten. It was less than a year, now, since his attractive face had begun to earn him a few friendly voices among the girls. Despised as a feeble creature by everyone, Julien had adored the old surgeon-major who once had dared to speak to the mayor about the plane trees.

Sometimes the surgeon had paid old Sorel for a day of his son's time, and had taught him Latin and history: that is, what he knew of history, the Italian campaign of 1796. Dying, he had left Julien his Cross of the Legion of Honor, the arrears of his pension, and thirty or forty volumes, the most treasured of which had just tumbled into the public stream whose course had been altered through the mayor's influence.

Scarcely had Julien entered the house, when he felt his shoulder grasped and held by his father's powerful hand; he trembled, expecting further blows.

"Answer me and don't lie," the old peasant's harsh voice shouted at his ear, while one hand turned him about as a child's hand turns a lead soldier. Julien's great black eyes, filled with tears, met the old carpenter's small, mean, gray eyes which seemed to be trying to search the depths of his soul.

CHAPTER 4
Negotiation

Answer me and don't lie, for once, you fool bookworm. Since when have you known Madame de Rênal? When have you talked to her?"

"I've never talked to her," Julien replied. "I've never seen her, except in church."

"But you must have looked at her, you ugly impudent rascal?"

"Never. You know that in church I see only God," Julien said with a mild hypocritical air nicely calculated to avert another beating.

"There's something behind it, just the same," the shrewd peasant said, and was silent a moment; "but I'll never find out from you, you damned hypocrite. Well, I'm going to be rid of you, and my sawmill will run all the better for that. You've made a hit with the priest, or somebody, and he's got a fine job for you. Go pack your things and I'll take you to Monsieur de Rênal's. You're going to be the children's tutor."

"What will I get for that?"

"Board, clothing and three hundred francs a year."

"I don't want to be a servant."

"Stupid! Who's talking about your being a servant? Would I let my own son be a servant?"

"Well, but with whom will I take my meals?"

The question disconcerted old Sorel, he felt instinctively that by speaking he might commit some imprudence; he flew into a rage with Julien, heaping him with abuse, accusing him of greed, and then left him, to go and consult with his other sons.

Julien saw them soon after, each leaning upon his ax, holding council. Having watched them for a long time, Julien, realizing that he could not find anything out that way, went and sat down on the other side of the sawmill, to avoid being discovered. He wanted to think over this unexpected development that was about to change the course of his life; but his whole imagination was engaged in picturing what he would see in Monsieur de Rênal's fine house.

I must renounce all that, he thought, rather than allow myself to be reduced to eating with servants. My father would like to force me into it; I'd rather die. I have fifteen hundred francs and eight sous saved up, I'll run away tonight; in two days I can get to Besançon by back roads where there's no fear of police; there I'll join up as a soldier and, if necessary, cross over into Switzerland. But then, no more achievement, no more ambition for me, no more of this fine ecclesiastical career that leads to all things.

This horror of taking his meals with servants was not natural to Julien; as a means to success he would have done other things quite as distasteful. He had borrowed the repugnance from Rousseau's *Confessions*. It was the only book that enabled his imagination to form a picture of the social world. The collected bulletins of Napoleon's Grand Army and the *Mémorial de Sainte-Hélène* completed his Koran. He would have died for these three books. He never believed in any others. Influenced by a remark of the surgeon-major's, he regarded all other books in the world as falsehoods written by impostors to gain advancement.

Along with his intense nature, Julien had one of those amazing memories so often found combined with low intelligence. To win favor with old Monsieur Chélan, upon whom he was quite convinced that his future circumstances depended, he had memorized the entire New Testament in Latin; he also knew Monsieur du Maistre's *Du Pape*, and believed in one as little as the other.

As if by mutual agreement, Sorel and his son avoided speaking to one another that day. At dusk Julien went to the priest's house for his theology lesson, but he felt it unwise to say anything about the strange

15

proposal that had been made to his father. Perhaps it is a trap, he thought. I must pretend to have put it out of my mind.

Early the next morning Monsieur de Rênal sent for old Sorel, who after having kept him waiting an hour or two, at length arrived, beginning at the door with a hundred excuses mingled with as many expressions of respect. By bringing up all sorts of objections, Sorel reached the understanding that his son would take his meals with the master and mistress of the house and, on days when there were guests, alone with the children in a separate room. Always more disposed to raise difficulties in proportion to the definite eagerness he perceived on the mayor's part, Sorel demanded to see the room where his son was to sleep. It was a large room, very comfortably furnished, but the beds of the three children were already being moved into it.

This circumstance opened the old peasant's eyes; at once, with assurance, he asked to see the clothing his son was to be given. Monsieur de Rênal opened his desk and took out a hundred francs.

"Have your son take this money to Monsieur Durand, the clothier, and pick out a black suit, all black."

"And even when I take him back again," said the peasant, who had suddenly discarded all his respectful manners, "will this black suit still be his?"

"Of course."

"Very well," Sorel said in a drawling tone of voice, "then all we have to do is settle one thing: the money you're going to give him."

"What!" Monsieur de Rênal cried, outraged. "We agreed yesterday: I'll pay him three hundred francs. I think that's enough, perhaps too much."

"That was your offer, I don't deny that," old Sorel said, speaking even more slowly; and, with a flash of intuition which will astonish only those who are not familiar with the countryfolk of Franche-Comté, he added, staring fixedly at Monsieur de Rênal: "We can do better somewhere else."

At these words the mayor's face fell abruptly. He regained control of himself, however, and after a shrewd conversation that lasted two full hours, in the course of which not a word was spoken at random, the peasant's craft triumphed over that of the rich man, who did not depend upon it for his living. All the many conditions that were to govern Julien's new existence were agreed upon; not only were his wages set at four hundred francs, but they were to be paid in advance, the first of each month.

"Very well, I'll give him thirty-five francs," Monsieur de Rênal said.

"Just to make it a round sum, a rich and generous man like our mayor would surely go as far as thirty-six francs," the peasant said in a wheedling tone.

"All right," Monsieur de Rênal said, "but that's the end of it."

Anger gave him, for once, a decisive tone. The peasant saw that he must go no farther. Then Monsieur de Rênal, in his turn, gained ground. He absolutely refused to hand over the first month's thirty-six francs to old Sorel, who was more than willing to accept them for his son. Monsieur de Rênal began to think that he must tell his wife about the part he had played throughout the negotiations.

"Give me back that hundred francs I gave you," he said coldly. "Monsieur Durand owes me some money. I'll go with your son to buy the black suit."

After this display of forcefulness, Sorel wisely returned to his respectful formula; it took a good quarter hour. In the end, seeing that he certainly had nothing further to gain, he withdrew. His last obsequious speech ended with the words: "I'll send my son to the château."

This was the manner in which the mayor's underlings referred to his house when they wished to please him.

Upon his return to the mill, Sorel hunted in vain for his son. Distrustful of what might happen, Julien had gone out in the middle of the night. He had wanted to put his books and his Cross of the Legion of Honor in safekeeping. He had taken them all to the home of his friend, a young woodcutter named Fouqué, who lived up in the high mountain that rises above Verrières.

When he returned: "God knows if you'll ever be honest enough to pay me back for the food I've been giving you all these years, you damned lazy oaf," his father said. "Take your traps and get on over to the mayor's."

Julien, astonished at not being beaten, hastened to leave. But when barely out of sight of his terrible father, he slowed his pace. He decided that it would be a useful bit of hypocrisy to go and say a prayer at the church.

You find the word surprising? Before arriving at that hideous word the young peasant's soul had had a long road to travel.

In his earliest childhood, the sight of certain dragoons of the Sixth Regiment, returning from Italy with their long white cloaks and their black-crested helmets, whom Julien had seen tethering their horses to the barred window of his father's house, had roused in him a fever for the military life. But when he was fourteen, Verrières had begun construction of a church that could well be called magnificent for so small a town. Among other things it had four marble columns, the sight of which was most impressive to Julien.

All at once Julien ceased talking about Napoleon; he let it be known that he intended to become a priest, and he was constantly to be seen in his father's sawmill, intent upon memorizing a Latin Bible which the curé had lent him. This good old man, marveling over his progress, devoted whole evenings to teaching him theology. Julien expressed only devout sentiments in Monsieur Chélan's presence. Who could have guessed that those girlish features, so pale and so gentle, concealed an implacable determination to expose himself to a thousand deaths rather than fail to make a fortune?

For Julien, to make a fortune was first to leave Verrières; he loathed his native countryside. All that he saw there chilled his imagination.

Since childhood he had been given to moments of exaltation. At such times he dreamed exultantly of how, one day, he would be presented to the beautiful women of Paris, and how he would contrive to attract their attention by some brilliant exploit. Why should he not be loved by them as Napoleon, while yet a poor man, had been loved by the radiant Madame de Beauharnais? For many years Julien had probably not let one hour of his life go by without reminding himself that Bonaparte, an obscure lieutenant with no fortune, had made himself master of the world with his sword. That idea consoled him for his misfortunes, which seemed great to him, and redoubled his joys when he had any.

The building of the church brought him a sudden illumination: an idea that obsessed him for several weeks, and at length took possession of him with all the potency of an intense spirit's first discovery.

"When Bonaparte made his name for himself, France was afraid of being invaded; military ability was vital and timely. Today one sees forty-year-old priests receiving a hundred thousand francs a year, three times the pay of Napoleon's famous generals. A priest is the thing to be."

Once, in the midst of his new piety, when Julien had been studying theology for two years, he was betrayed by a sudden eruption of the fire that was devouring his spirit. It happened at Monsieur Chélan's, during a dinner for some churchmen to whom the good priest had introduced Julien as a prodigy of learning, that he was moved to praise Napoleon with fervor. Afterwards he strapped his arm across his chest, pretended to have dislocated it moving a pine-tree trunk, and kept it in that uncomfortable position for two months. After that self-inflicted punishment he pardoned himself. This, then, was the young man of nineteen, but so slight-looking that one would have credited him with no more than seventeen years, who, carrying a small bundle under his arm, entered the magnificent Verrières church.

He found it dim and deserted. All the windows of the edifice had been covered with crimson cloth for some feast day. The result was to give the sunlight an effect of dazzling luminosity, most impressive and most religious in nature. Julien shivered. Alone in the church, he sat down in the finest looking pew. It bore Monsieur de Rênal's arms.

Kneeling, Julien noticed a scrap of printed paper lying there as if on purpose for him to read. He fixed his eyes upon it and read:

Details of the execution and last days of Louis Jenrel, executed in Besançon on . . .

The paper was torn. On the back of it the first few words of a line could be read; they were: *The first step.*

Who could have left this paper here? Julien wondered. Poor unlucky soul, he added with a sigh, his name has the same last syllable as mine. . . . And he crumpled the paper.

Going out, Julien thought he saw blood beside the font; it was holy water which had been spilled: the reflection from the red draperies over the windows made it look like blood.

Presently Julien felt ashamed of his secret terror.

What kind of coward am I? he thought. To arms! The phrase had a heroic sound to him. He rose and walked rapidly toward Monsieur de Rênal's house.

In spite of his fine resolutions, as soon as he came within sight of it, some twenty yards away, he was assailed by an unconquerable timidity. The wrought-iron gate stood open; to him it looked magnificent; he had to go through it.

Julien was not the only one whose spirit was troubled by his coming to the house. Madame de Rênal's extreme shyness was tormented by the thought of this stranger who, by the nature of his duties, would constantly be coming between her and her children. She was accustomed to having her sons sleep in her bedroom. That morning many tears had fallen when she had seen their small beds moved into the room assigned to their tutor. In vain she begged her husband to have the bed of Stanislaus-Xavier, the youngest, brought back to her room.

In Madame de Rênal, feminine delicacy was carried to an extreme. She drew herself a most disagreeable picture of a coarse and unkempt individual, hired to scold her children simply because he knew Latin, a barbarous language for the sake of which her sons were to be whipped.

CHAPTER 5
Boredom

WITH the vivacity and grace which were natural to her when she was away from masculine eyes, Madame de Rênal was leaving the house by the French doors of the drawing-room that overlooked the garden when she saw near the front door the figure of a young peasant, still little more than a child, extremely pale, who had been crying. He wore a very clean white shirt and carried under his arm a neat jacket of purple frieze.

This young peasant's complexion was so white, his eyes so soft, that Madame de Rênal's rather romantic mind first conceived the notion that he might be a young girl in disguise, come to ask some favor of the mayor. She felt pity for that poor creature hesitating before the front door, evidently not daring to raise his hand to the bell. Madame de Rênal went closer, momentarily diverted from the bitter sorrow induced by the tutor's arrival. Julien, turned toward the door, did not see her approach. He jumped when a gentle voice, close to his ear, said:

"What do you want here, my child?"

Julien turned quickly and, struck by Madame de Rênal's look of graciousness, lost a part of his shyness. Then, astonished by her beauty, he forgot everything, even what he had come here to do. Madame de Rênal repeated her question.

"I've come to be a tutor, Madame," he said at length, thoroughly ashamed of his tears which he wiped away as well as he could.

Madame de Rênal remained speechless; standing quite close together they looked at one another. Julien had never seen anyone so well dressed, certainly not a woman with so exquisite a complexion, speaking to him with so charming a manner. Madame de Rênal was looking at the great tears which still stood on the young peasant's cheeks, at first so pale and now so flushed. Presently she began to laugh with all the simple gaiety of a young girl; she was laughing at herself, unable to conceive of such happiness. So this was the tutor whom she had pictured as a dirty, untidy priest who would scold her children and whip them!

"What, Monsieur," she said at last, "do you know Latin?"

The word monsieur astonished Julien so, that he had to think for a moment.

"Yes, Madame," he said shyly.

Madame de Rênal was so happy that she ventured to say to Julien, "You won't scold those poor children too much?"

"I, scold them?" Julien said, dumfounded. "Why?"

"You will be good to them, won't you, Monsieur?" she said after a small silence and in a voice in which emotion grew with every moment. "You'll promise me that?"

Hearing himself called "monsieur" again, in all seriousness, by so well dressed a woman, was beyond all Julien's expectations: in all his youthful castles in the air he had assured himself that no well-bred woman would ever condescend to speak to him until he had on a fine uniform. Madame de Rênal, for her part, was completely deceived by the beauty of Julien's coloring, his great black eyes and his attractive hair, which was curlier than usual because he had just dipped his head into the basin of the public fountain to cool himself. To her great joy she recognized the timid manner of a girl in this dreaded tutor whose harshness and bad-tempered air she had so feared for her children. To so tranquil a nature as Madame de Rênal's, the contrast between her fears and what she now saw was a great event. At last she recovered from her surprise. She was astonished to find herself standing thus at the door of her house with a young man almost in his shirt sleeves, and so close to him.

22

"Let us go in, Monsieur," she said to him with a slightly embarrassed air.

In all her life no purely agreeable sensation had so deeply stirred Madame de Rênal, never had so grateful a reality followed upon more disturbing apprehensions. So those lovely children, watched over so lovingly by her, were not to fall into the hands of some cross uncleanly priest. Scarcely had she entered the vestibule than she turned back to Julien, who was timidly following her. His look of wonder at sight of so fine a home was a further charm in Madame de Rênal's eyes. She could hardly believe her eyes; above all it seemed to her that the tutor should be wearing a black suit.

"Is it really true, Monsieur?" she said, pausing again, and in mortal terror of having made a mistake, for belief in it made her so happy. "You do know Latin?"

The words offended Julien's pride and dissipated the spell under which he had been living for the past quarter of an hour.

"Yes, Madame," he said, trying to assume a cold manner. "I know Latin as well as Monsieur Chélan, and he is even kind enough sometimes to say I know it better."

Madame de Rênal thought Julien's manner very menacing; he had stopped a few feet away from her. She went closer to him and said in a low voice, "The first few days you won't whip my children, will you, even if they don't know their lessons?"

This tone of voice, so gentle and almost suppliant, coming from so beautiful a woman, made Julien suddenly forget all that he owed to his reputation as a Latinist. Madame de Rênal's face was close to his, he smelled the fragrance of a woman's summer garments, a thing so full of wonder to a poor peasant. Julien blushed vividly and said with a deep breath and in an unsteady voice:

"Do not worry, Madame. I shall obey you in everything."

It was only at this moment, when her uneasiness for her children was completely set at rest, that Madame de Rênal was struck by Julien's extraordinary good looks. The almost feminine cast of his features and his air of embarrassment seemed not in the least ridiculous to a woman who was, herself, extremely timid. The masculine manner commonly considered essential to a man's charm would have frightened her.

"How old are you, Monsieur?" she asked Julien.

"Almost nineteen."

"My oldest son is eleven," Madame de Rênal said, now altogether reassured. "He will be almost a friend for you, you will be able to reason with him. Once his father tried to give him a spanking and the child was ill for a whole week, although it was just a light blow."

How different for me, Julien thought. Just yesterday my father beat me. How lucky rich people are!

Already Madame de Rênal had reached the point of noticing the slightest indications of what was going on in the tutor's mind; she took his expression of sadness for timidity, and tried to encourage him.

"What is your name, Monsieur?" she asked him with an accent and a graciousness of which Julien could feel all the charm without being able to define it.

"I'm called Julien Sorel, Madame. I am frightened, coming into a strange house for the first time in my life; I need your protection, and you will have to forgive me for many things, the first few days. I never went to college, I was too poor; I've never talked to any men but my cousin the surgeon-major who was a member of the Legion of Honor, and Monsieur Chélan, the curé. He will give you a good account of me. My brothers have always beaten me, you mustn't believe them if they speak ill of me. Excuse my faults, Madame, I shall never have bad intentions."

Julien was reassuring himself during this long speech; he was examining Madame de Rênal. Such is the effect of perfect grace when it is a natural attribute, and particularly when the person whom it distinguishes is unconscious of it, that Julien, who was rather an expert on feminine beauty, would have sworn in that moment that she was no more than twenty years old. Instantly he had a rash impulse to kiss her hand. Immediately afterwards the idea frightened him; a second later he told himself: It would be cowardly of me not to perform a gesture that might be useful to me, and lessen the scorn this fine lady probably has for a poor laborer only just released from the saw.

Perhaps Julien was a little encouraged by the words "good-looking fellow," which he had been hearing some of the girls repeat on Sundays for the last six months. During this inner debate, Madame de Rênal was giving him one or two instructions on how to start off with her children. The violence of his internal struggle turned Julien very pale again; he said with an air of constraint:

"I shall never strike your children, Madame; I swear it to God."

And speaking these words he dared to take her hand and raise it to his lips. She was astounded at the gesture and, upon second thought, shocked. As the weather was very warm, her arm was completely bare beneath her shawl, and Julien's action in raising her hand to his lips had entirely uncovered it. A few instants later she scolded herself; it seemed to her that she had not become indignant quickly enough.

Monsieur de Rênal, who had heard the sound of voices, came out of his study; with the same majestic and paternal air that he assumed when he performed marriage ceremonies at the town hall, he said to Julien:

"It is essential that I speak to you before the children see you."

He showed Julien into a room and detained his wife, who was about to leave them alone together. The door being closed, Monsieur de Rênal gravely sat down.

"Monsieur Chélan has told me that you are a conscientious young man. Everyone here will treat you honestly, and if I am pleased with you, later on I'll help you to set up a little business of your own. From now on, I do not want you to see either your family or your friends, their manners would not be suitable for my children. Here are thirty-six francs for the first month but I want your word of honor not to give a penny of this money to your father."

Monsieur de Rênal was offended with the old man for having been, in this case, more cunning than himself.

"Now, *Monsieur*—for my orders are that everyone here is to call you monsieur and you will be aware of the advantages of living among well-bred people; now, Monsieur, it is not proper that the children see you in a jacket. Have the servants seen him?" Monsieur de Rênal asked his wife.

"No, dear," she said with a profoundly abstracted air.

"That's good. Put this on," he said to the young man, giving him one of his own frock coats. "Now we'll go to Monsieur Durand, the clothier."

More than an hour later when Monsieur de Rênal returned with the new tutor dressed all in black, he found his wife still sitting in the same spot. She felt comforted by Julien's presence; studying him, she forgot to be afraid. Julien was not thinking of her at all; despite all his distrust of destiny and of men, his spirit at that moment was no more than a child's; it seemed to him that he had lived years since the instant, three hours before, when he had stood trembling in the church. He observed Madame de Rênal's frigid manner and assumed that she was angry with him for having dared to kiss her hand. But the feeling of pride lent him by the touch of clothes so different from those he was accustomed to wearing was so stimulating, and he was so anxious to hide his delight, that all his actions had in them something abrupt and exaggerated. Madame de Rênal gazed at him with astonished eyes.

"A little dignity, Monsieur," Monsieur de Rênal said, "if you want my children and my servants to respect you."

"Monsieur," Julien replied, "I'm not at ease yet in these new clothes; I'm a poor peasant, I have never worn anything but short jackets. With your permission, I'll go to my room."

"What do you think of this new acquisition?" Monsieur de Rênal asked his wife.

Obedient to an instinctive reaction of which she was certainly not conscious, Madame de Rênal concealed the truth from her husband. "I'm not nearly so delighted as you are with this little peasant. Your kindness will make him impertinent and you'll have to dismiss him inside of a month."

"Well, then, we'll dismiss him. It won't cost me more than a hundred francs or so, and Verrières will be used to seeing Monsieur de Rênal's children with a tutor. It wouldn't have served that purpose at all if I had left Julien in laborers' clothes. When I dismiss him, naturally, I'll keep the black suit I've just ordered for him from the tailor. All he'll keep will be the ready-made one I bought for him at the clothier's and had him put on."

The hour Julien spent in his room seemed but a moment to Madame de Rênal. The children, having been told of the tutor's arrival, overwhelmed her with questions. At length Julien appeared. He was a changed man. It would be an understatement to say that he was sober; he was the incarnation of sobriety. He was introduced to the children and spoke to them with an air that astounded even Monsieur de Rênal.

"Young gentlemen," he said at the end of his address, "I am here to teach you Latin. You know what it is to recite a lesson. Here is the Holy Bible," he went on, showing them a small volume bound in black. "It is, above all else, the story of Our Lord Jesus Christ, it is the part known as the New Testament. I am often going to make you recite lessons, this time you make me recite mine."

Adolphe, the eldest of the boys, had taken the book.

"Open it anywhere," Julien continued, "and tell me the first words of a paragraph. I will recite from memory the sacred text that governs all our conduct, until you stop me."

Adolphe opened the book, read a word or two, and Julien recited the whole page with as great ease as if he had been speaking in French. Monsieur de Rênal glanced at his wife with an air of triumph. The children, seeing their parents' amazement, opened their eyes wide. A servant came to the drawing-room door, Julien continued to speak Latin. The servant at first stood transfixed, then vanished. Soon Madame de Rênal's maid and the cook appeared at the door; by then Adolphe had already opened the book at eight places, and Julien was still reciting with the same fluency.

"Lord, what a nice little priest!" the cook, a good and very pious girl said aloud.

Monsieur de Rênal's vanity was pricked; far from thinking of testing the tutor, he was completely absorbed in searching his memory for a few words of Latin; at last he produced a verse from Horace. Julien knew no Latin other than his Bible. He answered, frowning:

"The holy calling to which I am dedicated forbids me to read so secular a poet."

Monsieur de Rênal quoted quite a number of alleged lines of Horace. He explained to his children who Horace was; but the children, spellbound with admiration, paid not the slightest attention to what he was saying. They were staring at Julien.

The servants were still at the door; Julien felt obliged to prolong the test.

"Monsieur Stanislaus-Xavier must choose a passage from the Holy Book for me," he said to the youngest child.

Little Stanislaus, very proud, read as well as he could the first word of a paragraph, and Julien recited the whole page. To complete Monsieur de Rênal's triumph, while Julien was reciting, Monsieur Valenod, the owner of the fine Norman horses, and Monsieur Charcot de Maugiron, subprefect of the district, came in. That scene earned Julien the title of monsieur; even the servants did not dare refuse it to him.

That evening all Verrières flocked to Monsieur de Rênal's house to see the marvel. Julien answered everyone with a somber air that kept people at a distance. His fame spread so rapidly throughout the town that, a few days later, Monsieur de Rênal, fearing lest someone take him away, suggested signing a two-year contract.

"No, Monsieur," Julien answered coldly. "If you wish to discharge me, I shall be obliged to go. An agreement which binds me without putting you under any obligation is not at all fair. I will not sign it."

Julien was able to conduct himself so well that, less than a month after his arrival at the house, Monsieur de Rênal himself respected him. The curé having quarreled with Messieurs de Rênal and Valenod, no one could now betray Julien's old passion for Napoleon, of whom he now spoke only with horror.

CHAPTER 6
Elective Affinities

THE children adored him, he was not even fond of them; his thoughts were elsewhere. Nothing these boys could do ever made him impatient. Cold, just, impassive, and yet well liked because his coming had somehow dispelled the monotony of the house, he made a good tutor. As for him, he felt nothing but hatred and horror for the high society into which he had been admitted—literally at the foot of the table, which perhaps explains the hatred and horror. There were certain ceremonial dinners at which he was scarcely able to contain his aversion for everyone about him. On Saint-Louis' day, among other occasions, when Monsieur Valenod was pontificating in Monsieur de Rênal's drawing-room, Julien was upon the point of betraying himself; he took refuge in the garden, upon pretext of watching the children. "What hymns to honesty!" he exclaimed to himself. "One would think it was the only virtue; and at the same time what esteem, what base respect for a man who has obviously doubled or tripled his fortune since he has been administering the pauper's welfare! I'll bet he even makes something out of the funds set aside for foundlings, those poor souls whose distress is an even holier thing than that of the others. Oh, the monsters, the monsters! And I'm a sort of foundling, myself, hated by my father, my brothers, my whole family."

Several days before, Julien, walking alone and saying his breviary in a small woods called the Belvedere which overlooks the Cours de la Fidélité, had tried in vain to avoid his two brothers whom he saw at a distance coming toward him down a lonely path. The jealousy of these coarse laborers had been so aroused by the fine black suit, by their brother's extremely neat appearance, by the sincere contempt he had for them, that they had beaten him until they left him bleeding and unconscious. Madame de Rênal, out for a walk with Monsieur Valenod and the subprefect, happened to come to the little woods; she saw Julien flung down on the ground and thought him dead. The violence of her reaction was such as to make Monsieur Valenod jealous.

He took alarm too soon. Julien considered Madame de Rênal a very beautiful woman, but he hated her for her beauty; it was this obstacle which had almost put an end to his good fortune at the start. He spoke to her as little as possible, to avoid recalling the impulse that had led him, that first day, to kiss her hand.

Elisa, Madame de Rênal's maid, had lost no time in falling in love with the young tutor; she spoke of him frequently to her mistress. Elisa's love had earned Julien the hatred of one of the footmen. One day he heard the man say to Elisa, "You won't even talk to me now that that filthy tutor has come into the house." Julien did not deserve that epithet; but with the instinct of a handsome young man he redoubled his care of his appearance. Monsieur Valenod's dislike redoubled in proportion. He observed publicly that such worldly ways were unbecoming to a young priest. Except for the cassock Julien's costume was as close as possible to clerical.

Madame de Rênal noticed that he was speaking more often than usual to Mademoiselle Elisa; she discovered that these interviews were occasioned by the poverty of Julien's very small wardrobe. He had so little linen that he was obliged to send it out to be washed very frequently, and it was in such small services that Elisa was useful to him. This extreme poverty, of which she had had no idea, touched Madame de Rênal; she wanted to make gifts to him but did not dare; this inner resistance was the first painful feeling Julien caused her. Until that time Julien's name had been synonymous with a pure and entirely intellectual joy. Tormented by the thought of Julien's poverty, Madame de Rênal spoke to her husband about making him a present of linens.

"What nonsense!" he said. "Give presents to a man we're perfectly satisfied with and who serves us well? If he neglected himself, then would be the time to stimulate his zeal."

Madame de Rênal was humiliated by this attitude; she would not even have noticed it before Julien's arrival. She never saw the extreme neatness of the young tutor's dress, simple as it was, without thinking: Poor boy, how can he do it?

Little by little, instead of being shocked by all that Julien lacked, she began to pity him.

Madame de Rênal was one of those provincial women very easily mistaken for fools in the first fortnight's acquaintance. She had no experience of life and cared nothing for conversation. Endowed with a fastidious and distant nature, and responsive to that instinct for happiness natural to all human beings, she paid for the most part no attention to the behavior of the crude people among whom chance had cast her.

She would have been distinguished by the sincerity and quickness of her mind if she had received any sort of education. But as an heiress she had been brought up at the convent of the Sacred Heart of Jesus, a fanatically religious order animated by a violent hatred for the French enemies of the Jesuits. Madame de Rênal had considered all that she had learned at the convent absurd, and had forgotten it; but she put nothing else in place of it and ended by knowing nothing. The precocious flattery of which she had been the object, as heiress of a large fortune, and a decided tendency toward passionate devotion had induced in her a wholly inward way of living. For all her air of perfect compliance and submission, which the husbands of Verrières held up as an example to their wives and which was a source of pride to Monsieur de Rênal, her normal inner attitude was actually a reflection of the most arrogant disposition. The princess famous for her haughtiness pays infinitely more attention to what the gentlemen about her are doing than this woman, so gentle and outwardly so modest, paid to anything her husband said or did. Until Julien's arrival she had paid real attention only to her children. Their small illnesses, their sorrows, their little joys absorbed all the emotion of a heart which, in all its existence, had loved only God, when she was at the Sacred Heart.

Although she had never been willing to admit it to anyone, an attack of fever in one of her sons sent her into almost the same state as if the child had died. Her upbringing had designed her for unhappiness. Too proud to speak of this sort of trouble even to her friend Madame

Derville, she assumed that all men were like her husband, Monsieur Valenod and the subprefect Charcot de Maugiron. Coarseness, the most brutal insensibility to all that did not concern money, advancement or honors, and a blind hatred for any point of view that opposed theirs seemed to her to be natural attributes of the sex, like wearing boots and a felt hat.

Hence the success of the young peasant, Julien. She found a gentle pleasure alight with the charm of novelty in the sympathy of that proud and noble spirit. She had soon forgiven him his extreme ignorance, which was an added grace, and his uncultivated manners, which she succeeded in correcting. She found that it was worth while to listen to him even when the talk was of the most everyday matters, even when it was a case of a poor dog run down, as it crossed the street, by a peasant's cart going at a trot. That painful sight had moved her husband to loud laughter, whereas she saw Julien's fine, arched black eyebrows contract. Little by little it began to seem to her that generosity, nobility of spirit and humanity existed nowhere but in this young abbé. For him alone she had all the sympathy and even admiration that these virtues arouse in people of breeding.

In Paris, Julien's relationship to Madame de Rênal would speedily have been resolved; but in Paris love is born of fiction. The young tutor and his shy mistress would have found the solution of their position in three or four novels and even in the verses of the Gymnase. The novels would have outlined the part to play, set up the model to imitate; and sooner or later, although without any pleasure and perhaps against his will, vanity would have forced Julien to follow it.

In a small town of Aveyron or the Pyrenees, the smallest incident would have been made decisive by the heat of the climate. Under our more gloomy skies a poor young man, ambitious only because the vulnerability of his spirit causes him to need some of the gratifications that money brings, may continue to associate daily with a woman of thirty, sincerely good, absorbed in her children and taking none of her standards of behavior from novels. Everything moves slowly, everything happens by degrees in the provinces, things happen more naturally.

Sometimes, thinking of the young tutor's poverty, Madame de Rênal was moved to the point of tears. Julien came upon her one day, actually crying.

"Oh, Madame, something must have happened to make you sad!"

"No, my friend," she said. "Call the children, and let us take a walk."

She took his arm and leaned upon it in a manner that seemed odd to Julien. For the first time she had called him "my friend."

Toward the end of the walk Julien noticed that she was very much flushed. She slowed her pace.

"You have probably heard," she said without looking at him, "that I am the only heir of a very rich aunt who lives in Besançon. She's forever sending me presents . . . my sons' progress is so—astonishing —that I'd like to ask you to accept a little present as a sign of my gratitude. Just a few louis so that you can get some linen. But—"she added, blushing even more, and stopped.

"What, Madame?" Julien said.

"There would be no point," she continued, lowering her head, "in mentioning this to my husband."

"I may be small, Madame, but I am not low," Julien said, pausing, his eyes brilliant with anger, and summoning all his arrogance. "That is something you haven't considered. I should be lower than a common servant if I put myself in the position of hiding anything to do with *my money* from Monsieur de Rênal."

Madame de Rênal was dumfounded.

"The mayor," Julien went on, "has paid me thirty-six francs five times since I have been living in his house; I'm prepared to show my accounts to Monsieur de Rênal or anybody else, even Monsieur Valenod, who hates me."

After this tirade, Madame de Rênal was left pale and trembling, and the walk came to an end before either of them could find a pretext for resuming the conversation. Love for Madame de Rênal became more and more impossible to Julien's proud spirit; as for her, she respected him, she admired him: he had scolded her. Ostensibly in order to make up for the humiliation she had involuntarily caused him, she permitted herself the most affectionate attentions. The novelty of such conduct made Madame de Rênal happy for a week. Its effect upon Julien was to appease his anger somewhat; he was far from seeing in it anything resembling personal fondness.

"That's how rich people act," he thought. "They humiliate you, and then they think they can make up for everything with a few pats on the back."

In spite of her resolutions Madame de Rênal's heart was too full, and still too innocent to allow her not to tell her husband about the offer she had made to Julien and the manner in which she had been refused.

Monsieur de Rênal, acutely irritated, reproved her: "How could you tolerate such a refusal from a servant?"

And as Madame de Rênal protested the word:

"My dear woman, I speak as the late Prince de Condé did, presenting his chamberlains to his new wife: 'All those people,' he said, 'are our servants.' I read you the passage from Besenval's Memoirs that establishes rules of precedence. Anyone who is not a gentleman, lives in your house and receives a salary, is a servant. I am going to say a word or two to this Monsieur Julien and give him a hundred francs."

"Oh, my dear," Madame de Rênal said, trembling, "please not in front of the servants!"

"Yes, it may make them jealous, and with good reason," her husband said and moved away, considering the magnificence of the sum.

Madame de Rênal fell into a chair, almost faint with sorrow. He is going to humiliate Julien, and it is all my fault! She felt horror for her husband and hid her face in her hands. She made herself a firm promise never to make confidences.

When she saw Julien again she was shaking in every limb, her chest so contracted that she was unable to pronounce a single word. In her confusion she took his hands and pressed them.

"Well, my friend," she said to him at length, "are you pleased with my husband?"

"Why wouldn't I be?" Julien answered with a wry smile. "He gave me a hundred francs."

Madame de Rênal gazed at him uncertainly.

"Give me your arm," she said presently, with an accent of courage which Julien had never before seen in her.

She was bold enough to go into the bookstore in Verrières, in spite of its shocking reputation for liberalism. There she picked out ten louis' worth of books which she gave to her sons. But these books were the ones she knew Julien wanted.

Thus Julien's life was composed of a series of petty negotiations; and the success of these interested him far more than the feeling of pronounced favor that he could scarcely help recognizing in Madame de Rênal's attitude.

The ethical position he had occupied all his life was reinforced in the home of the mayor of Verrières. There, as in his father's sawmill, he was profoundly contemptuous of the people among whom he lived, and was disliked by them. Daily he saw in statements made by the subprefect, by Monsieur Valenod, by other friends of the family commenting upon things that had recently happened right before their eyes, how little their ideas resembled reality. If an action seemed admirable to him, it was sure to be the one that called forth the censure of the persons about him. His inner reply was always: What monsters! or: What fools! The amusing thing was that, with all his pride, he frequently understood absolutely nothing about the subject of which they were speaking.

In his life, he had spoken with sincerity only to the old surgeon-major; the few ideas he had were related to Bonaparte's campaigns in Italy, or to surgery. His youthful courage took pleasure in the circumstantial description of the most painful operations; he used to tell himself: I should not have winced.

The first time Madame de Rênal tried to start a conversation with him about something other than the children's education, he began to talk of surgical operations; she turned pale and begged him to stop.

On other subjects Julien had no knowledge. So, as he passed his days with Madame de Rênal, the most curious silence settled down between them whenever they were alone. In the drawing-room, however humble his attitude might be, she found in his eyes a look of intellectual superiority to all who came to visit her. She was troubled by it, for her feminine instinct made her realize that this was not a sentimental embarrassment.

Whenever a silence fell while he was with a woman, Julien felt humiliated as if the silence were his own particular fault. This sensation was a thousand times more disagreeable during private conversations. His imagination, filled with the most exaggerated, the most Spanish notions of what a man should say when he is alone with a woman, offered him in his trouble only inadmissible ideas. His spirit was in the skies, and yet he could not emerge from the most shameful silence. So his stern manner, during his long walks with Madame de Rênal and the children, was intensified by the cruelest torments. He despised himself abysmally. If by some unlucky chance he forced himself to speak, he was inspired to say the most ridiculous things. To top off his misery, he saw his own absurdity and exaggerated it to himself; but what he did not see was the expression in his eyes; they were so beautiful and revealed so ardent a spirit that, like accomplished actors, they sometimes gave a charming meaning to what had none. Madame de Rênal noticed that, alone with her, he never managed to speak eloquently except when, diverted by some unforeseen occurrence, he was not thinking of turning a graceful compliment. Since the friends of the family did not precisely spoil her by offering new and brilliant ideas, she took delight in Julien's flashes of intellect.

Madame de Rênal, the wealthy heiress of a devout aunt, married at sixteen to a suitable gentleman, had never in her life experienced anything in the least resembling love. No one but her confessor, the good curé Chélan, had ever spoken to her of love and he, speaking in connection with M. Valenod's advances, had drawn her so repellent a picture of it that to her the word represented only the most abject lust. Love, as she had found it in the very few novels that chance had brought to her eyes, she regarded as an exception or even as an abnormality. Thanks to such ignorance Madame de Rênal, completely happy, constantly absorbed in Julien, was far from reproaching herself in the smallest measure.

CHAPTER 7
Minor Events

THE angelic sweetness that Madame de Rênal owed to her character and to her present happiness was slightly altered only when she happened to think of her maid Elisa. This girl came into a little money, went to Monsieur Chélan for confession and declared to him that she planned to marry Julien. The priest was genuinely delighted at his friend's good fortune; but his surprise was unbounded when Julien told him with a determined air that Mademoiselle Elisa's offer did not appeal to him.

Madame de Rênal was astonished that her maid's new fortune did not make the girl happier; she saw her going incessantly to the curé, and returning with tears in her eyes. At length Elisa spoke to her about her marriage.

Madame de Rênal thought that she must have been taken ill: a sort of fever prevented her from finding rest; she lived only when she had her maid or Julien before her eyes. She could think of nothing but them, and the happiness they would find in their marriage. The poverty of that small house in which one must live with an income of fifty louis, appeared to her in ravishing colors. Julien might very well become a lawyer in Bray, the subprefecture two leagues from Verrières; in that case she would see him sometimes.

Madame de Rênal sincerely believed that she was going out of her mind; she told her husband so, and at last she did fall ill. That same evening, as her maid was serving her, she noticed that the girl was crying. She detested Elisa at that moment, and had just spoken harshly to her; she asked her pardon. Elisa's tears flowed more freely; she said that if her mistress would permit her to, she would tell her all about her unhappiness.

"Tell me," Madame de Rênal answered.

"Well, Madame, he won't have me; some wicked people must have told him bad things about me, and he believes them."

"Who won't have you?" Madame de Rênal said, scarcely able to breathe.

"Monsieur Julien, who else?" the maid said, sobbing. "Even Monsieur Chélan couldn't get him to give in—for Monsieur Chélan doesn't think he has any right to turn down an honest girl just because she's a maid. After all, Monsieur Julien's father is nothing but a carpenter; and how did he, himself, make his living before he came to Madame?"

Madame de Rênal was no longer listening; the sudden access of happiness had almost deprived her of the use of her wits. She had the assurance repeated several times that Julien had refused in a positive manner which precluded a change to a more sensible decision later on.

"I'll make one more effort," she said to her maid. "I shall speak to Monsieur Julien."

The next day, after luncheon, Madame de Rênal gave herself the exquisite pleasure of pleading her rival's cause and of seeing Elisa's hand and fortune firmly rejected for the whole of an hour.

Bit by bit Julien abandoned his stilted answers and at length was making spirited replies to Madame de Rênal's wise remonstrances. She was unable to withstand the torrent of happiness that flooded her spirit after so many days of despair. She found herself literally ill. When she was restored and comfortably settled in her room she sent everyone away. She was deeply astonished.

"Can I be in love with Julien?" she wondered at last.

This discovery, which at any other moment would have plunged her into remorse and violent agitation, seemed to her nothing but a spectacle, curious but rather impersonal. Her spirit, exhausted by all that it had recently experienced, had no feeling left for the uses of passion.

Madame de Rênal tried to study the question, and fell into a deep sleep; when she awoke she was not so much alarmed as she ought to have been. She was too happy to be offended by anything. Simple and innocent, this good provincial woman had never tormented her soul in order to try to force from it a little reaction to some new shade of sentiment or sorrow. Entirely absorbed, before Julien's arrival, in that mass of work which is the portion of a good housewife anywhere but in Paris, Madame de Rênal thought of passions as we think of a lottery: a sure disappointment, a happiness sought by fools.

The dinner bell rang; Madame de Rênal blushed violently when she heard Julien's voice as he brought the children in. With the ingenuity acquired since she had fallen in love, she complained of a frightful headache to explain her flush.

"That's women for you," Monsieur de Rênal said with a loud laugh. "There's always something in their machinery that needs repairing."

Although accustomed to this sort of wit, Madame de Rênal was shocked by the tone of voice. As a diversion, she gazed at Julien's face; had he been the ugliest of men, at that instant she would have found him charming.

In the first fine days of spring Monsieur de Rênal, always diligent in following the customs of Court circles, removed his household to Vergy, the village made famous by Gabrielle's tragic adventure. A few hundred yards from the picturesque ruins of the ancient Gothic church, Monsieur de Rênal owned an old château with four towers and a garden laid out like that of the Tuileries, with a great many boxwood hedges and paths lined with chestnut trees which were trimmed twice a year. A near-by apple orchard served as a promenade. Eight or ten magnificent walnut trees grew at the far end of the orchard; their huge branches rose to a height of perhaps eighty feet.

"Each of those damned walnuts," Monsieur de Rênal used to say when his wife admired them, "costs me a half-acre's harvest; wheat can't grow in their shade."

The whole countryside looked new to Madame de Rênal; her admiration approached ecstasy. The emotion stirring in her gave her spirit and resolution. The day after their arrival in Vergy, Monsieur de Rênal having returned to town on official business, Madame de Rênal hired laborers at her own expense. Julien had given her the idea of a little sandy path that would wander about the orchard and under the great walnut trees, and would permit the children to go for morning walks without getting their shoes wet with dew. This idea was put into execution less than forty-eight hours after its conception. Madame spent the whole day with Julien, gaily directing the laborers.

When the mayor of Verrières returned from town, he was greatly surprised to find the path all laid out. His arrival was as surprising to Madame de Rênal: she had forgotten his existence. For the next two months he spoke crossly of the audacity of making so great an alteration without consulting him, but Madame de Rênal had accomplished it at her own expense, which consoled him a little.

She spent her days roaming the orchard with her children and chasing butterflies. They had made large nets of thin gauze with which to catch the poor *lepidoptera*. This was the barbarous term Julien taught Madame de Rênal; for she had sent to Besançon for Monsieur Godart's fine work, and Julien told her about the curious habits of these unfortunate creatures. Pitilessly they fastened them with pins to a large cardboard square, also constructed by Julien.

At last there was a subject for conversation between Madame de Rênal and Julien. He was no longer subjected to fearful torment which moments of silence caused him.

They talked together constantly, and with intense interest, although always on quite innocent subjects. This active life, busy and gay, contented everyone except Mademoiselle Elisa, who found herself overburdened with work. "Even at carnival time," she said, "even when there was a ball in Verrières, Madame never took so much trouble with her clothes; she changes her dress two or three times a day."

As it is not our intention to flatter anyone, we will not deny that Madame de Rênal, who had exquisite skin, ordered made for her only dresses that left her arms and bosom quite uncovered. She had a lovely figure, and this style of dress was remarkably becoming to her.

"You've never looked younger, Madame," friends from Verrières told her when they came to dine at Vergy.

One odd thing, which will find little credence among us, is that it was without any direct intention that Madame de Rênal indulged in all these attentions. She found pleasure in it; and without any other thought than that, she spent all her time—when she was not chasing butterflies with the children and Julien—making dresses with Elisa. Her one trip to Verrières was brought about by a wish to buy some new summer dresses that had just been brought from Mulhouse.

She brought back to Vergy a young woman, one of her relatives. Since her marriage, Madame de Rênal had gradually become very much attached to Madame Derville, who had been a friend of hers in the old days at the Sacred Heart.

Madame Derville laughed heartily at what she called her cousin's wild ideas: "Left to myself, I'd never have thought of such things," she would say. When she was with her husband, Madame de Rênal was ashamed of these unexpected fancies which in Paris would have been called inspirations; but Madame Derville's presence gave her self-confidence. At first she told her thoughts in a hesitant voice; but after these ladies had spent some time alone together Madame de Rênal's wit would quicken, and a long lonely morning passed like an instant, leaving the two friends very gay. During this visit, the practical Madame Derville found her cousin much less gay and much happier.

Julien, for his part, had lived like a real child since coming to the country, as happy running after butterflies as his students were. After so much constraint and clever politics, alone, removed from men's eyes and instinctively having no fear of Madame de Rênal, he gave himself up to the pleasure of living, so intense at his age, and in the midst of the most beautiful mountains in the world.

From the moment of Madame Derville's arrival, it seemed to Julien that she was his friend; he hastened to show her the view from the far end of the new path beneath the walnut trees; as a matter of fact it is equal, if not superior, to the finest views Switzerland or the Italian lakes can offer. If one ascends the abrupt slope that begins a few yards farther on, one soon comes upon great precipices fringed with oak tree groves, which lean out over the river. It was to the summit of these rocks, with the sheer drop below, that Julien, happy, free, and even something more, king of the household, led the two friends, and gloried in their admiration for that magnificent view.

"To me, it's like Mozart's music," Madame Derville said.

His brothers' jealousy, the presence of a despotic and bad-tempered father, had spoiled the countryside about Verrières for Julien's eyes. In Vergy he found none of these bitter memories; for the first time in his life he saw no sign of an enemy. When Monsieur de Rênal was in town, as often happened, he dared to read; soon, instead of reading at night, and even then being careful to hide his lamp under a vase turned upside down, he could give himself up to sleep; in the daytime, in the interval between lessons, he came to these rocks with the single book which was the guide of his behavior and the object of his passions.

In it he found at once happiness, ecstasy and, in moments of discouragement, consolation.

Certain things that Napoleon says about women, a number of observations on the merit of novels popular during his reign, gave Julien, for the first time, several ideas that any other young man of his age would have had long before.

The hot weather settled down. They fell into the habit of spending the evenings under an immense linden a few yards from the house. There the darkness was profound. One evening Julien was speaking with gestures, delighting in the pleasure of speaking fluently to two young women; gesticulating, he touched Madame de Rênal's hand which rested on the back of one of the painted wooden chairs which are used in gardens.

The hand was very quickly withdrawn, but Julien thought he owed it to himself to insure that that hand was not withdrawn when he touched it. The idea of a duty to be accomplished, and ridicule, or rather a sense of inferiority to be incurred if he did not succeed, immediately banished all pleasure from his heart.

CHAPTER 8

An Evening in the Country

His glances the next day when he saw Madame de Rênal again were very strange; he eyed her like an enemy with whom he was going to have to fight. These glances, so different from those of the day before, caused Madame de Rênal to lose her head: she had been kind to him, and he seemed angry. She could not tear her eyes from him.

Madame Derville's presence permitted Julien to talk less and to concentrate more upon what was going on inside his mind. His only concern during that entire day was to fortify himself by reading from the inspired book that refreshed his spirit.

He curtailed the children's lessons considerably, and later, when Madame de Rênal's presence recalled him to complete anxiety for his honor, he decided that this evening she must absolutely allow her hand to remain in his.

The setting sun, bringing closer the decisive moment, made Julien's heart beat in a most erratic manner. Night fell. He noticed, with a relief that lifted an immense weight from his chest, that it would be a very dark one. The sky, obscured by heavy clouds driven by a hot wind, seemed to prophesy a storm. The two ladies prolonged their walk until quite late. Everything they did that evening seemed strange to Julien.

They exulted in this weather which, for certain sensitive natures, seems to augment the joy of loving.

At last they sat down, Madame de Rênal at Julien's side, and Madame Derville beside her friend. Preoccupied with what he was about to attempt, Julien found nothing to say. The conversation languished.

Shall I be as miserable and tremulous as this faced with the first duel that comes my way? Julien wondered, for he had too much contempt both for himself and for others not to recognize the mental state he was in.

In his extreme anguish, any other danger would have seemed preferable to him. How many times he hoped to see some errand occur to Madame de Rênal that would oblige her to leave the garden and go into the house! The violence to which Julien was forced to subject himself was too extreme not to alter his voice greatly; presently Madame de Rênal's voice, too, became unsteady, but Julien was not in the least aware of it. The frightful struggle to which duty condemned timidity was too painful to let him observe anything external. The château clock had just struck the quarter hour before ten, and still he had not dared make any move. Shocked by his own cowardice, Julien told himself: At the exact moment when ten o'clock strikes I shall do what I have been promising myself all day to do this evening, or I shall go up to my rooms and blow my brains out.

After one last instant of suspense and anxiety, during which the acuteness of his emotion set Julien almost beside himself, ten o'clock sounded from the clock tower above his head. Each fatal stroke of the clock reverberated in his chest and caused a sort of physical reaction.

At last, while the last stroke of ten was still reëchoing, he stretched out his hand and took Madame de Rênal's, which she instantly snatched away. Julien, not entirely conscious of what he was doing, grasped it again. Although thoroughly shaken himself, he was struck by the icy coldness of the hand he held; he pressed it with convulsive force; there was one last effort to withdraw it, but at last the hand remained in his.

His spirit was flooded with happiness, not because he loved Madame de Rênal, but because the frightful ordeal was over. So that Madame Derville should suspect nothing, he felt obliged to talk; his voice was now loud and assured. Madame de Rênal's, on the other hand, so betrayed her emotion that her friend thought she had been taken ill and proposed that they return to the house. Julien sensed danger: If

Madame de Rênal returns to the drawing-room, I shall be replaced in the horrible position in which I have been all day. I've held this hand too short a time for it to count as an advantage won.

Just as Madame Derville reiterated her suggestion that they return to the house, Julien forcefully clasped the hand which had been yielded to him.

Madame de Rênal, already in the act of rising, sat down again, saying in a faint voice, "As a matter of fact I do feel a little ill, but the fresh air is doing me good."

These words confirmed Julien's happiness which at that moment was excessive: he talked, he forgot to pose, he seemed the most likable of men to the two friends who listened to him. Nevertheless, there was still a slight lack of courage behind this eloquence that suddenly came to him. He was mortally afraid that Madame Derville, tiring of the wind which was beginning to rise and which heralded the storm, would return to the drawing-room, leaving him alone with Madame de Rênal. It was almost by chance that he had found enough blind courage to act; but he was aware that it was quite beyond his strength to say the simplest word to Madame de Rênal. Gentle as her reproaches might be, he would be beaten, and the advantage he had just gained reduced to nothing.

Fortunately for him, that evening his moving and emphatic speech found favor with Madame Derville, who quite often found him awkward as a child and not particularly amusing. As for Madame de Rênal, with her hand in Julien's, she was not thinking at all; she was absorbed in living. The hours passed under this great linden, which local tradition said had been planted by Charles the Bold, were for her a time of happiness. She listened with rapture to the moaning of the wind in the dense foliage of the linden and the sound of a few scattered raindrops which were beginning to fall upon the lower leaves. Julien did not notice one circumstance that would greatly have reassured him: Madame de Rênal, who had been obliged to withdraw her hand in order to rise and help her cousin right a vase of flowers that the wind had just upset at their feet, had scarcely sat down again when she gave him back her hand almost without hesitation, as if it had already become an accepted thing between them.

Midnight had long since sounded; at last they must leave the garden; they separated. Madame de Rênal, carried away by the joy of loving, was so heedless of all else that she scarcely reproached herself at all. Happiness kept her from sleep. A profound slumber overcame Julien, utterly worn out by the conflicts which timidity and pride had waged all day long in his heart.

The next morning he was awakened at five o'clock; and—a fact that would have hurt Madame de Rênal cruelly had she known it—he hardly gave her a thought. He had done his duty, a heroic duty. Filled with well-being by this sensation, he locked the door of his room and gave himself up, with a wholly new pleasure, to reading of his hero's exploits.

By the time the bell sounded for lunch he had forgotten, in reading the bulletins of the Grand Army, all about the advantages he had gained the evening before. As he went down to the drawing-room he told himself unconcernedly: I must tell that woman that I love her.

In place of those affectionate glances which he expected to encounter, he found the stern face of Monsieur de Rênal, who, having arrived from Verrières at two o'clock, took no trouble to conceal his displeasure over the fact that Julien had spent the whole morning without attending to the children. Nothing could have been more offensive than this pompous man, in a bad temper and considering himself licensed to show it.

Each of her husband's harsh words pierced Madame de Rênal's heart. As for Julien, he was so submerged in ecstasy, still so absorbed in the great events that for several hours had been passing before his eyes, that he was hardly able to lower his attention to the point of listening to the sharp words Monsieur de Rênal was addressing to him.

At last he said, somewhat abruptly, "I was sick."

The tone of this reply would have irritated a far less susceptible man than the mayor of Verrières; he had a notion to answer Julien by dismissing him instantly. He was only restrained by his own maxim against acting upon issues too hastily.

This young blockhead, he thought presently, has made a sort of reputation for himself in my household; Valenod might hire him, or he might marry Elisa, and in either case he'll be able to laugh up his sleeve at me.

In spite of the wisdom of these reflections, Monsieur de Rênal's displeasure continued to vent itself unabated in a succession of coarse phrases which, little by little, annoyed Julien. Madame de Rênal was upon the point of bursting into tears. The moment luncheon was finished she asked Julien to give her his arm for a walk, she leaned upon it affectionately. To all that Madame de Rênal said to him, Julien could only reply in a low voice:

"That's rich people for you!"

Monsieur de Rênal was walking quite near them; his presence augmented Julien's anger. Suddenly he noticed that Madame de Rênal was leaning on his arm in an obvious manner; this behavior filled him with horror, he pushed her violently away and disengaged his arm.

Fortunately Monsieur de Rênal did not see this further impertinence, only Madame Derville noticed that her friend burst into tears. Just then Monsieur de Rênal began flinging stones at a little peasant girl who was trespassing by crossing a corner of the orchard.

"Monsieur Julien, please, restrain yourself; remember that we all have moments of ill-humor," Madame Derville said swiftly.

Julien looked at her coldly out of eyes in which was portrayed the most supreme contempt.

This expression startled Madame Derville, and would have surprised her even more if she had guessed the true impulse behind it; she would have read in it a sort of vague yearning for the most atrocious revenge. Very likely it is such moments of humiliation that make a Robespierre.

"Your Julien certainly is violent; he frightens me," Madame Derville said very softly to her friend.

"He has every right to be angry," Madame de Rênal answered. "After the amazing progress the children have made with him, what difference does it make if he spends a morning without speaking to them? You must admit that men are very hard."

For the first time in her life Madame de Rênal felt a kind of desire for revenge against her husband. The excessive hatred for the rich which filled Julien was about to break out. Fortunately Monsieur de Rênal summoned his gardener and remained with him, engrossed in barring the trespassers' path across the orchard with thorny branches. Julien did not answer by so much as a word the kind remarks addressed to him during all the rest of the walk. Scarcely had Monsieur de Rênal moved away when the two friends, feigning weariness, asked to take his arms.

Between the two women with their cheeks flushed by embarrassment and extreme uneasiness, Julien's grim and determined air offered a strange contrast. He despised these women and all gentle emotions. Oh, he was thinking, how I'd like to send her about her business!

Absorbed by these harsh reflections, he found what little he condescended to hear of the two friends' gracious speech displeasing, devoid of sense, silly, weak: in a word, *feminine*.

In the course of talking for the sake of talking, and of trying to keep the conversation alive, Madame de Rênal happened to mention that her husband had come from Verrières because he had struck a bargain with one of his farmers for some corn husks. (In these parts, mattresses are filled with corn husks.)

"My husband won't be joining us again," Madame de Rênal added. "He and his manservant and the gardner are going to be busy refilling all the mattresses in the house. This morning he put corn husks in all the first-floor beds, now he is about to do the second floor."

Julien changed color; he stared at Madame de Rênal in a strange manner and presently drew her aside, after a fashion, by quickening his step. Madame Derville let them go on ahead.

"Save my life," Julien said to Madame de Rênal, "you are the only one who can, because you know that manservant has a deadly hatred for me. I have to confess, Madame, that I have a portrait hidden in the mattress of my bed."

At these words Madame de Rênal turned pale in turn.

"Only you can go into my room right now, Madame. Without letting anyone see you, feel in the corner of the mattress nearest the window, and you'll find a little box made of smooth black cardboard."

"With a portrait in it!" Madame de Rênal said, scarcely able to stand.

Her air of despondency was not lost upon Julien, who at once took advantage of it.

"I have a second favor to ask, Madame. I beg you not to look at the portrait, it's my secret."

"It's a secret," Madame de Rênal echoed in a faint voice.

But although she had been brought up among people proud of their wealth and sensitive only to the appeal of money, love had already given rise to generosity in her spirit. Cruelly hurt, Madame de Rênal asked Julien, with an air of the simplest devotion, the questions that would enable her to accomplish her mission successfully.

"So," she said, moving away, "a little round box, black cardboard, very smooth."

"Yes, Madame," Julien answered with the hard look danger gives to men.

She went upstairs to the second floor of the château, pale as if she were going to her death. To crown her misery, she felt that she was upon the point of being ill; but the necessity of rendering a service to Julien restored her strength.

"I must get that box," she thought, hastening her steps.

She heard her husband speaking to the manservant, actually in Julien's room. Fortunately they moved on to the children's room. She raised the mattress and plunged her hand into the straw with such violence that she scraped skin from her fingers. But, although very sensitive to such minor hurts, she was not conscious of this one, for almost simultaneously she felt the shiny surface of the cardboard box. She seized it and fled.

She was barely relieved of the fear of being intercepted by her husband when the horror with which the box inspired her began to make her feel literally ill.

So Julien is in love, and I have here the portrait of the woman he loves!

Seated on a chair in the outer room of her apartments, Madame de Rênal was assailed by all the horrors of jealousy. Her extreme ignorance was again of use to her in that moment; astonishment tempered her pain. Julien appeared, seized the box without thanking her, without uttering a word, and ran into his room where he made a fire and instantly burned it. He was pale, prostrated; he exaggerated to himself the danger he had just run.

Napoleon's portrait, he thought, shaking his head, found hidden in the room of a man who professes such hatred for the usurper, found by Monsieur de Rênal, so violently Royalist and so antagonistic! And to top off the indiscretion, those lines in my handwriting on the white cardboard in back of the portrait! They couldn't leave any doubt of the extent of my admiration, and each one of those transports of love is dated, one of them yesterday!

My whole reputation collapsed, wiped out in one moment! Julien thought, watching the box burn, and my reputation is all I have, I can make a living only through it . . . and even at that, what a living, my God!

An hour later, fatigue and the pity he felt for himself had made him feel inclined to tenderness. He met Madame de Rênal and took her hand, kissing it with more sincerity than he had ever shown her. She flushed with happiness and, almost at the same instant, pushed Julien away with the anger of jealousy. Julien's pride, so recently wounded, made a fool of him at that moment. He saw Madame de Rênal only as a wealthy woman; he dropped her hand disdainfully and walked away. He went to stroll thoughtfully in the garden; presently a bitter smile came to his lips.

Here I am, strolling about as tranquilly as a man whose time is his own! I'm not attending to the children. I am exposing myself to Monsieur de Rênal's insults, and he would be in the right!

He hurried to the children's room. The caresses of the youngest, of whom he had become very fond, eased his smarting pain a little.

He doesn't despise me yet, Julien thought. But soon he reproached himself for his new weakness in having allowed his pain to be eased. These children caress me the way they caress the hound puppy they bought yesterday, he thought.

CHAPTER 9

A Big Heart and a Small Fortune

Monsieur de Rênal, who was going through all the bedrooms of the château, returned to the children's room with the servants who brought back the mattresses. The sudden entrance of the man was, for Julien, the drop of water which makes the vase overflow.

Paler, more somber than usual, he strode toward him. Monsieur de Rênal paused and glanced at the servants.

"Monsieur," Julien said, "do you think that your children would have made the same progress with any other tutor as they have made with me? If you answer no," Julien continued without giving Monsieur de Rênal time to speak, "how can you reproach me with having neglected them?"

Monsieur de Rênal, recovering from his first alarm, deduced from the extraordinary tone this young peasant used that he had some advantageous proposal up his sleeve and that he was going to give notice. Julien's anger increasing in proportion as he talked:

"I can get along without you, Monsieur," he added.

"I'm very sorry to find you so stirred up," Monsieur de Rênal said, stammering a little. The servants were some ten steps away, intent upon arranging the beds.

"That won't do, Monsieur," Julien said, beside himself. "Think of the degrading things you said to me, and in front of women too!"

Monsieur de Rênal understood only too well what it was that Julien wanted, and a painful conflict was torturing his soul. It happened that Julien, utterly insane with fury, cried out, "I know where to go, Monsieur, wher I leave your house!"

At these words, Monsieur de Rênal saw Julien established in Monsieur Valenod's home.

"Very well, Monsieur," he said at last with a sigh, and in the tone in which he would have called a surgeon to perform the most agonizing operation, "I agree to your demand. Starting day after tomorrow, which is the first of the month, I will pay you fifty francs a month."

Julien had a desire to laugh, and was left dumfounded: all his anger had evaporated.

I didn't despise this animal enough, he reflected. That is without a doubt the handsomest apology a nature as low as his knows how to make.

The children, who were listening open-mouthed to this scene, ran to the garden to tell their mother that Monsieur Julien was in a terrible rage, but that he was to have fifty francs a month. Julien followed them out of habit, without even glancing at Monsieur de Rênal whom he left deeply irritated.

That makes a hundred and sixty-eight francs Monsieur Valenod is costing me, the mayor thought. I must absolutely say a firm word or two to him about his contract for supplies to the foundlings home.

A moment later Julien found himself once more face to face with Monsieur de Rênal:

"I have things on my conscience to talk over with Monsieur Chélan; I have the honor to let you know that I shall be gone several hours."

"Why, my dear Julien!" Monsieur de Rênal said, laughing in the falsest manner, "take the whole day, if you like, and all day tomorrow, my friend. Take the gardener's horse to ride to Verrières."

There he goes, Monsieur de Rênal thought, to take his answer to Valenod. He didn't promise me anything, but I must let his raw young head cool down.

Julien quickly took his departure and climbed up into the great woods through which one can make one's way from Vergy to Verrières. He was in no hurry whatsoever to reach Monsieur Chélan. Far from eager to subject himself to a new scene of hypocrisy, he felt a need to come to an understanding of his own soul, and to give audience to a host of emotions that were tormenting him.

I have won a battle, he thought, as soon as he found himself in the woods and remote from all eyes, so I've won a battle!

The word cast a flattering light over his whole position, and restored a measure of tranquillity to his spirit.

Here I am, with a salary of fifty francs a month; Monsieur de Rênal must have been very much afraid of something, but of what?

Meditation upon what could have inspired fear in the fortunate and powerful man against whom, an hour earlier, he had been boiling with anger, completed the restoration of Julien's serenity. For a moment he was almost aware of the extraordinary beauty of the woods through which he was walking. Enormous masses of bare rock had fallen long before from the mountainside into the midst of the forest. Great beech trees rose almost to the height of these rocks whose shadow offered a delightful coolness three yards from places where the heat of the sun's rays would have made it impossible to stand still.

Julien paused briefly for breath in the shadow of these great rocks and then began to climb again. Presently, by way of a narrow and barely discernible path used by gamekeepers, he found himself standing upon an immense crag, and entirely sure of being set apart from all men. That physical situation made him smile, it represented the intellectual position he was burning to attain. The pure air of these lofty mountains imparted serenity and even joy to his spirit. The mayor of Verrières clearly remained the representative, in his eyes, of all the rich and all the insolents of the earth; but Julien felt that the hatred which had lately shaken him, despite the violence of its reactions, had not been of a personal nature. If he had ceased associating with Monsieur de Rênal, he would have forgotten him in a week, himself, his château, his hounds, his children and his entire family.

I have forced him, I do not know how, to make the greatest sacrifice of all. What! More than fifty écus a year! And an instant before, I had extricated myself from the greatest danger. That makes two victories in one day; the second one has no merit, one would have to know the why and wherefore of it. But troublesome investigations can wait until tomorrow.

Standing upon his great rock, Julien gazed at the sky, ablaze with

August sunlight. Cicadas shrilled in the field below the rock; when they were still, all about him was silence. He saw at his feet sixty miles of countryside. From time to time a hawk from the great cliffs above his head caught his eye, soaring in vast silent circles. Julien's eye followed the bird of prey mechanically.

Its calm and powerful motion impressed him, he envied that strength, he envied that isolation.

It had been Napoleon's destiny; would it one day be his?

CHAPTER 10
Evening

NEVERTHELESS he must make an appearance at Verrières. As he was leaving the presbytery, Julien had the good luck to encounter Monsieur Valenod, to whom he hastened to tell the story of his rise in salary.

Returning to Vergy, Julien did not go down to the garden until night had closed in. His spirit was exhausted by the many potent emotions that had troubled it throughout the day. What shall I say to them? he wondered uneasily, thinking of the ladies. He was far from realizing that his inner state was precisely on the level of those small circumstances that normally absorb all of women's interest. Frequently Julien was unintelligible to Madame Derville and even to her friend, and, for his part, understood no more than half of all they said. Such was the effect of the power and, if I may venture to use the word, the grandeur of the passionate impulses that were throwing this ambitious young man's soul into disorder. In this singular being, it was almost always stormy weather.

Coming into the garden that evening, Julien felt disposed to devote his whole attention to the ideas of the lovely cousins. They were waiting for him with impatience. He took his usual place, beside Madame de Rênal. Soon the darkness became profound. He tried to take the white hand that had for some time been resting on the back of a chair close to him. There was a slight hesitation, but in the end it was withdrawn from his in a fashion that indicated displeasure. Julien's inclination was to let the matter rest there and to continue talking cheerfully, when he heard Monsieur de Rênal approaching.

Julien still had in his ears the boorish words of that morning. Wouldn't it, he thought, be a way of mocking that fellow, rich as he is in all the advantages of fortune, to take possession of his wife's hand right in front of him? Yes, I'll do it; I, the man for whom he showed such contempt.

In that moment the tranquillity so foreign to Julien's character was rapidly dispelled; he desired with anxiety, and without being able to think of anything else, that Madame de Rênal should leave her hand in his.

Monsieur de Rênal was wrathfully talking politics: two or three of Verrières' industrialists were becoming decidedly richer than he was, and were trying to override him in the elections. Madame Derville listened to him. Irritated by his speech, Julien moved his chair closer to Madame de Rênal's. The darkness hid all his movements. He ventured to rest his hand very close to the lovely arm left bare by the dress. He was agitated, he was no longer able to control his thoughts, he brushed his cheek against that lovely arm, he made so bold as to touch it with his lips.

Madame de Rênal quivered. Her husband was no more than four steps away, she hastened to give Julien her hand and at the same time to push him away a little. As Monsieur de Rênal continued his abusive remarks against the nobodies and Jacobins who were making fortunes, Julien covered the hand which had been given him with passionate kisses, or at least they seemed so to Madame de Rênal. Nevertheless, the poor woman had seen proof, that terrible day, that the man she adored without admitting it to herself loved someone else! All during Julien's absence she had been in the grip of a violent unhappiness that had made her reflect.

What! she thought, can I be in love, is love what is the matter with me? I, a married woman, in love! But, she thought, I have never felt for my husband this dark obsession that makes me unable to tear my thoughts from Julien. After all, he is only a child full of respect for me! This obsession will be a passing thing. What difference could the feeling I may have for this young man make to my husband? Monsieur de

Rênal would be bored by the conversations I have with Julien about intellectual matters. He himself thinks only of business. I am not taking anything from him to give to Julien.

No trace of hypocrisy came to adulterate the purity of that innocent soul, distracted by a passion such as she had never experienced. She was deluded, but unconsciously, and yet an instinct of virtue was alarmed. Such was the conflict that had been tormenting her when Julien appeared in the garden. She heard him speak, and almost at the same moment saw him sit down beside her. It was as if her spirit was lifted by this enchanting happiness which for two weeks had been astonishing her even more than it charmed her. It all came as a revelation to her. After a few moments, however: So Julien's presence, she thought, is enough to erase all his faults? She was frightened; that was when she drew her hand away from him.

Those kisses filled with passion such as she had never experienced before made her suddenly forget that he was perhaps in love with another woman. Soon he no longer had any faults in her eyes. The cessation of the poignant anguish born of despair, the presence of a happiness such as she had never even dreamed, inspired in her transports of love and foolish gaiety. That evening was a delightful one for everyone but the mayor of Verrières, who was unable to forget his newly rich industrialists. Julien thought no more of his black ambition nor of his plans, so difficult to put into execution. For the first time in his life he was carried away by the power of beauty. Lost in a vague and gentle reverie, so foreign to his nature, gently pressing that hand which charmed him with its perfect grace, he half listened to the rustle of linden leaves teased by the soft night wind and the dogs from a mill on the Doubs, baying in the distance.

But this emotion was pleasure, not passion. Returning to his room, he was looking forward to only one delight: that of taking up his favorite book; at twenty, ideas of the great world and the effect to be made upon it triumph over everything.

Even so, he soon put down the book. In contemplating Napoleon's victories he had discovered something new in his own. Yes, I've won a battle, he thought, but now I must profit by it, I must destroy this proud gentleman's pride while he is in retreat. That's exactly Napoleon's way. I must ask for three days off to go and see my friend Fouqué. If he refuses to let me go, I'll threaten to break off our bargain again, but he won't refuse.

Madame de Rênal could not close her eyes. It seemed to her that she had never lived until now. She could not distract her mind from the delight of feeling Julien cover her hand with ardent kisses.

Abruptly the hideous word: adultery, occurred to her. Every revolting suggestion that the vilest debauch can impress upon the conception of sensual love crowded into her imagination. These suggestions threatened to tarnish the tender and beatific image of Julien and of the joy of loving him which she had constructed. The future clothed itself in terrible colors. She saw herself as contemptible.

It was a horrible moment; her soul reached out into unknown territory. During the evening she had tasted an unparalleled happiness; now she found herself abruptly plunged into excruciating despair. She had no idea that such suffering existed; it disordered her mind. For an instant she had an impulse to confess to her husband that she was afraid she loved Julien. It would have been a chance to talk about him. Fortunately she recalled a maxim once given her by her aunt, on the eve of her marriage. It concerned the danger of confiding in a husband, who is, after all, a master. In the excess of her grief she wrung her hands.

She was driven this way and that by contradictory and agonizing images. Now she was in terror of not being loved; now the hideous thought of sin tortured her as if she were to be exposed in the pillory the next day, in the public square at Verrières with a placard describing her adultery to the populace.

Madame de Rênal had no experience of life; even fully conscious and in command of all her mental faculties she would not have made any distinction between being guilty in the eyes of God and being publicly heaped with the most blatant tokens of general scorn.

When the loathsome thought of adultery and all the ignominy which, she believed, this sin brings as a consequence left her briefly at peace, and she began to dream of the pleasure of living with Julien innocently and, as it were, in the past, she found herself confronted with the horrid possibility that Julien loved another woman. She saw again his pallor when he had been afraid of losing his portrait, or of compromising the woman by letting it be seen. For the first time, she had caught a look of fear on those features, usually so calm and so noble. He had never shown himself so disturbed about her or about the children. This aggravation of torment reached the utmost intensity of pain that it is given the human spirit to be able to endure. Without being in the least aware of it, Madame de Rênal uttered whimpering sounds, which roused her maid. Suddenly she saw the light of a lamp at her bedside and recognized Elisa.

"Are you the one he loves?" she cried out in her frenzy.

The maid, appalled by the frightful anguish in which she found her mistress, fortunately paid no attention to this odd remark. Madame de Rênal was aware of her indiscretion. "I have a fever," she said. "Stay with me."

Thoroughly roused by the necessity of controlling herself, she felt less wretched; reason regained the command of which it had been deprived in her half-conscious state. To escape from the fixed stare of the maid, she ordered her to read the newspaper, and it was to the monotonous sound of the girl's voice reading a long article from the *Quotidienne* that Madame de Rênal made the virtuous resolution to treat Julien with the utmost coldness when next she saw him.

CHAPTER 11
A Journey

B<small>Y FIVE</small> o'clock the next morning, before Madame de Rênal came down, Julien had obtained a three-day leave of absence from her husband. Contrary to his expectations, Julien found himself desiring to see her again, he thought of her hand, and how pretty it was. He went down to the garden. Madame de Rênal kept him waiting a long time, but if Julien had loved her, he would have discovered her behind the closed shutters of the first floor, her forehead pressed against the glass. She was watching him. At last, despite her resolutions, she made up her mind to appear in the garden. Her normal pallor had given way to the most vivid color. This extremely innocent woman was obviously disturbed: a feeling of constraint, even of anger, impaired that expression of serenity, profound and as if above all the vulgar considerations of life, which gave so much charm to that angelic face.

Julien went to her quickly; he admired the beautiful arms, exposed to view by a shawl hastily flung on. The coolness of the morning air seemed to heighten even more the radiance of a complexion which the night's agitation had made more responsive than ever to all impressions. That beauty, modest and touching, and yet thoughtful, which one will never find among the lower classes, seemed to reveal to Julien a faculty of his nature of which he had been quite unaware before. Utterly absorbed in admiration of charms that captivated his eager glances, Julien did not give a thought to the friendly greeting he expected to receive. He was all the more astonished by the icy coldness she tried to display, and thought that he distinguished behind it the intention of putting him in his place again.

The smile of pleasure died on his lips; he remembered the position he held in society, and particularly in the eyes of a rich and well-born heiress. A moment later there was nothing upon his face but arrogance and anger against himself. He felt violently annoyed with himself for having delayed his departure more than an hour in order to receive so humiliating a greeting.

Only a fool, he told himself, loses his temper with others: a stone falls because it is heavy. Shall I always be a child? When shall I have mastered the good habit of selling my soul to these people merely for their money? If I want to be respected by them and by myself, I must show them that it is my poverty which deals with their wealth, but that my heart is a thousand leagues removed from their insolence and inhabits too high a sphere to be touched by their petty gestures of disdain or of favor.

While these emotions seethed in the young tutor's mind, his expressive features took on a look of wounded pride and ferocity. Madame de Rênal was utterly confused by it. The virtuous coolness that she had tried to infuse into her greeting gave way to an expression of interest, an interest quickened by complete surprise at the abrupt change she had just witnessed. The empty words that people address to one another in the morning, about the state of their health, the beauty of the day, fell silent upon both their lips. Julien, whose perception was not dulled by any sort of passion, speedily found a means of showing Madame de Rênal how little he considered himself to be on friendly terms with her; he said nothing to her about the little journey he was about to undertake, bowed to her and left.

As she watching him go, overwhelmed by the gloomy arrogance which she read in his glance, so friendly the previous evening, her eldest son came running from the end of the garden, kissed her and said:

"We have a holiday, Monsieur Julien is going on a trip."

At these words Madame de Rênal felt overcome by a deadly coldness; she was made wretched by her virtue, and even more wretched by her weakness.

This new event took possession of her entire imagination; she was carried away, far beyond the wise resolutions which she owed to the terrible night she had just passed. It was no longer a question of resisting so appealing a lover, but of losing him forever.

She had to take her place at breakfast. To crown her misery, Monsieur de Rênal and Madame Derville could talk of nothing but Julien's departure. The mayor of Verrières had noticed something unusual in the firm tone in which he had asked for his days off.

"Beyond a doubt that young fellow has an offer from someone else up his sleeve. But this someone else, if it's Monsieur Valenod, should be a bit discouraged by the sum of six hundred francs, which is what he'll have to raise the annual outlay to, now. Yesterday, in Verrières, this other person must have asked for three days to think it over; and this morning, rather than be obliged to give me an answer, the young gentleman set off for the mountains. Being forced to reckon with the insolence of a common laborer; that's what we've come to!"

Since my husband, who has no idea how deeply he hurt Julien, believes that he is going to leave us, Madame de Rênal thought, what am I to think? Oh, it's all settled!

In order to be able at least to weep in peace and not answer Madame Derville's questions, she mentioned a severe headache and went to bed.

"That's a woman for you," Monsieur de Rênal said. "Always something out of order in those complicated machines." And he went out grinning.

While Madame de Rênal was beset by the cruelest effects of the terrible passion in which chance had involved her, Julien was cheerfully pursuing his course in the midst of the most beautiful scenes that mountain landscapes can offer. He had to cross the great ridge north of Vergy. The path he was following, rising gradually among vast beech woods, wound in endless zigzags up the slope of the high mountain that forms the north side of the Doubs valley. Soon the traveler's gaze, passing over the lesser hills that confine the Doubs on its southern side, reaches out over the fertile plains of Burgundy and Beaujolais. Insensitive as this ambitious young man's spirit was to this sort of beauty, he could not resist pausing from time to time to look at a spectacle so vast and so imposing.

At last he gained the summit of the great mountain, near which one must pass, by this crossing, to reach the lonely valley where his friend, the woodcutter Fouqué, lived. Julien was in no hurry to see him, him or any other human being. Hidden like a bird of prey among the bare rocks that crowned the huge mountain, he could catch sight at a great distance of any man who might approach. He discovered a small grotto halfway up the almost vertical face of one the cliffs. He picked his way up, and soon was settled in this retreat. Here, he thought, his eyes blazing with triumph, men would never be able to harm me. He had an impulse to abandon himself to the pleasure of writing down his thoughts, a pleasure so dangerous for him anywhere else. A square stone served him as a desk. His pen flew; he saw nothing of his surroundings. At length he noticed that the sun was setting behind the far-away mountains of Beaujolais.

Why shouldn't I spend the night here? he thought. I have some bread, and I am *free!* At the sound of this splendid word his soul exulted, his hypocrisy convinced him that he was not free even at Fouqué's. His head resting in his two hands, Julien sat in the grotto, happier than he had ever been in his life, vibrant with dreams and with the joy of liberty. Heedless, he watched the last glow of twilight die away. In the midst of that immense dark, his spirit wandered in contemplation of what he anticipated finding, some day, in Paris. First, a woman far more beautiful and far more highly developed intellectually than any he could have found in the provinces. He loved her passionately, he was loved. If he left her side for a few moments, it was only in order to go and cover himself with glory, and so deserve to be loved by her even more.

Even supposing him gifted with Julien's imagination, a young man brought up among the sorry realities of Parisian society would have been awakened at this point in his romanticizing by chilly irony; the great achievements would have vanished along with the hope of attaining them, to give place to the so familiar axiom: Anyone who leaves his mistress' side runs the risk, unfortunately, of being deceived two or three times a day. To the young peasant, nothing lay between himself and the most heroic exploits except lack of opportunity.

But deep night had replaced daylight, and he had still six miles to go to reach the village where Fouqué lived. Before leaving the little grotto, Julien lighted a fire and carefully burned all that he had written.

He utterly astonished his friend by rapping on his door at one o'clock in the morning. He found Fouqué engaged in writing up his accounts. He was a young man of tall stature, rather ungainly, with big hard features, an enormous nose, and a great deal of good nature hidden beneath this forbidding exterior.

"So have you quarreled with your Monsieur de Rênal, that you come to me like this without warning?"

Julien told him, but in his own way, the events of the previous day.

"Stay with me," Fouqué said. "I see that you understand Monsieur de Rênal, Monsieur Valenod, the subprefect Maugiron, Father Chélan; you've found out what sly characters those people have; now you're all ready to put yourself up on the auction block. You're better at arithmetic than I am, you can keep my books. I'm making a good bit out of my business. Every day I'm prevented from accepting excellent contracts because it's impossible for me to do everything myself and yet I'm afraid anyone I might hire as an assistant may turn out to be a cheat. Less than a month ago I turned over six thousand francs worth of business to Michaud of Saint-Amand, whom I hadn't seen for six years until I ran into him at the Pontarlier auction. Why shouldn't you have earned that six thousand francs, or at least three thousand?— for if I had had you with me that day I would have bid higher for that cutting, and everybody would soon enough have let me have it. Be my partner."

This proposal angered Julien; it clashed with his obsession. All during supper, which the two friends, like Homer's heroes, prepared themselves, for Fouqué lived alone, he showed Julien his account books and proved to him how many advantages his trade in timber offered. Fouqué had the highest opinion of Julien's insight and of his character.

When Julien was at length alone in his small room built of pine logs: It is true, he thought, I can earn a few thousand francs here and then return with profit to being a soldier or a priest, whichever is by then the fashion in France. The little nest egg I'll have saved will remove all the petty difficulties. Alone in this mountain, I shall have overcome to some extent the frightful ignorance I have about so many matters that interest these influential gentlemen. But Fouqué has renounced marriage, and he keeps telling me that solitude makes him unhappy. It's obvious that if he takes a partner who has no money to invest in his business, it is in the hope of having a companion who will never leave him.

Am I to deceive my friend? Julien asked himself angrily. This being, to whom hypocrisy and the absence of all sympathy were the normal avenues to security, was unable this time to endure the slightest suggestion of a lack of scrupulous honesty toward a man who liked him.

But suddenly Julien was relieved: he had a reason for refusing. Why, I should be indolently wasting seven or eight years! At that rate, I'd be twenty-eight years old; but at that age Bonaparte had made his greatest achievements. After I've earned some money in this obscure fashion, attending timber sales and currying favor with a few subordinate swindlers, who is to say that I shall still have this sacred fire with which one makes a name for oneself?

The next morning Julien answered Fouqué, who considered the matter of the partnership settled, with the greatest composure, saying that his vocation for the holy ministry would not permit him to accept. Fouqué could not believe his ears.

"But think," he said, "I'll make you my partner or, if you'd rather, I'll pay you four thousand francs a year. And you want to go back to your Monsieur de Rênal, who despises you like the mud on his shoes! What's to prevent you from entering the seminary after you've got two hundred louis put by? I'll tell you something else: I'll undertake to get the best benefice in the country for you. Because," Fouqué added, lowering his voice, "I furnish firewood to at least three very influential gentlemen . . . I let them have the best grade of oak for the price of softwood, but there was never a better investment."

Nothing could overcome Julien's vocation. In the end Fouqué came to the conclusion that he was a little mad. The third day, early in the morning, Julien took leave of his friend in order to spend the day among the rocks of the great mountain. He found his small grotto again, but he no longer had peace of mind, his friend's offers had destroyed it. Like Hercules, he found himself, not between vice and virtue, but between mediocrity attended by certain prosperity and all the heroic dreams of youth. Apparently I have no real constancy, he thought; and it was that misgiving that gave him the most pain. I am not made of the stuff of which great men are made, since I am afraid that eight years spent in earning my bread will rob me of that sublime energy which leads to extraordinary achievements.

CHAPTER 12
Openwork Stockings

WHEN Julien came in sight of the picturesque ruins of the ancient Vergy church, he realized that he had not once thought of Madame de Rênal since two days before. The other day as I was leaving, that woman reminded me of the infinite distance that lies between us, she treated me like a laborer's son. She undoubtedly wanted to show me her regret for having let me hold her hand the previous evening . . . Just the same, it's very pretty, that hand! And what charm, what breeding in that woman's glances!

The possibility of making a fortune with Fouqué gave Julien's reasonings a certain flexibility; they were no longer so often impaired by irritation and an acute consciousness of his poverty and his humbleness in the world's eyes. As if raised to a high promotory, he was able to use judgment, and he took a more distant view, so to speak, of extreme poverty and the comfort he still called wealth. He was far from taking a philosophical attitude toward his position, but he had enough perspicacity to feel that he was *different* after this little journey to the mountains.

He was struck by the extreme uneasiness with which Madame de Rênal listened to the little story of his trip, which she had asked him for.

Fouqué had at one time had marriage plans, an unhappy love affair;

long confidences on this subject had filled the two friends' conversation. Having found happiness too soon, Fouqué had discovered that he was not the only lover. All these tales had amazed Julien; he had learned many things new to him. His solitary life, all imagination and distrust, had kept him apart from all that might have enlightened him.

During his absence, life for Madame de Rênal had been no more than a succession of torments, varying, but all intolerable; she was genuinely ill.

"Surely," Madame Derville said to her when she saw Julien return, "you will not go to the garden this evening, sick as you are. The damp air would make you feel a great deal worse."

Madame Derville saw with amazement that her friend, eternally criticized by Monsieur de Rênal for the excessive simplicity of her dress, had just put on openwork stockings and exquisite little shoes newly arrived from Paris. For the past three days, Madame de Rênal's only diversion had been to design and to have Elisa make, in the greatest haste, a summer dress of a pretty light material that was all the fashion. This dress was not finished until a few moments after Julien's return; Madame de Rênal put it on at once. Her friend had no further doubts. She loves him, poor woman! Madame Derville thought. She understood all the strange symptoms of her illness.

She saw her speak to Julien. Pallor succeeded the most vivid flush. Anxiety was plainly displayed in her eyes, which clung to those of the young tutor. Madame de Rênal was expecting that at any moment he would make his intentions known and announce that he was going to leave or stay. Julien had nothing to say on this subject; it did not enter his mind. After a frightful struggle, Madame de Rênal at last plucked up courage to say, in an unsteady voice that betrayed all her passion:

"Are you going to leave your pupils and take another position?"

Julien was struck by Madame de Rênal's uncertain voice and by the look in her eyes. That woman loves me, he thought; but after this passing moment of weakness which is an affront to her pride, and as soon as she no longer fears that I may leave, she will recover her arrogance. This view of the respective position came to Julien swift as a lightning flash; he answered hesitantly:

"It would make me very unhappy to leave such likable and such *well-born* children, but perhaps I shall have to. One has duties toward oneself too."

In speaking the words *well-born* (it was one of the aristocratic words Julien had recently learned), he was overwhelmed by a profound sensation of antipathy.

In this woman's eyes, he thought, I myself am not well-born.

Madame de Rênal, listening to him, marveled at his intelligence, his beauty; her heart was wrung by the possibility he let her glimpse of his departure. All her friends from Verrières who had come to dine at Vergy during Julien's absence had complimented her almost enviously upon the remarkable man her husband had been fortunate enough to unearth. Not that they knew anything about the children's progress. The feat of having learned the Bible by heart, and in Latin besides, had impressed the inhabitants of Verrières with an admiration that will probably last a century.

Julien, having spoken to no one, was ignorant of all this. If Madame de Rênal had had any presence of mind whatever, she would have complimented him upon the reputation he had acquired, and Julien, his vanity soothed, would have become gentle and pleasant to her, especially since the new dress seemed charming to him. Madame de Rênal, also pleased with her pretty dress, and with what Julien said to her about it, had wanted to walk around the garden; soon she admitted that she was in no condition for walking. She had taken the returned traveler's arm and, far from reënforcing her strength, the contact of this arm deprived her of it altogether.

Night fell; scarcely had they sat down when Julien, availing himself of his former privilege, ventured to touch his lips to his lovely neighbor's arm, and take her hand. He was thinking of the boldness which Fouqué had evidenced with his mistresses, and not of Madame de Rênal; the words *well-born* still weighed upon his mind. His hand was pressed, it gave him not the slightest pleasure. Far from being proud, or at least grateful for the emotion which Madame de Rênal betrayed that evening by only too obvious signs, he was left almost unmoved by her beauty, her elegance, her freshness. Purity of spirit, the absence of any hateful sentiment undoubtedly prolongs youth. It is the features that age first in most pretty women.

Julien was sullen all evening. Until now he had raged only against chance and society; since Fouqué had offered him an ignoble way of achieving prosperity he had been angry with himself. Absorbed in his thoughts, although from time to time he said a few words to the ladies, Julien ended by relinquishing Madame de Rênal's hand without even realizing that he had done so. That occurrence threw the poor woman's soul into despair; she saw it as the manifestation of her destiny.

If she had been certain of Julien's affection, perhaps her virtue would have found defenses against him. Trembling at the thought of losing him forever, her passion drove her to the point of reaching out for Julien's hand which, in his perturbation, he had left resting on the back of a chair. That gesture roused the ambitious young man: he would have liked it to be witnessed by all those proud gentlemen who, at table where he sat at the far end with the children, looked at him with so condescending a smile. It can't be that this woman despises me any longer, he thought; in that case, I ought to be responsive to her beauty; I owe it to myself to become her lover. Such an idea would never have occurred to him before the artless confidences made him by his friend.

The sudden determination which he had just formed made an agreeable distraction. He thought: I must have one of these two women; he came to the conclusion that he would have much preferred making love to Madame Derville, not that she was more attractive, but she had always seen him as a tutor honored for his learning, and not as a carpenter, a laborer with a frieze jacket folded under his arm, as he had appeared to Madame de Rênal.

It was exactly so: as a young laborer, blushing to the whites of his eyes, hesitating at the door of the house and not daring to ring, that Madame de Rênal pictured him with the most pleasure.

Pursuing the analysis of his position, Julien saw that he must not contemplate the conquest of Madame Derville, who probably noticed the fondness Madame de Rênal showed for him. Forced to revert to the latter: What do I know of that woman's character? Julien thought. Only this: before I went away I took her hand, she drew it away; today I draw my hand away, she grasps it and squeezes it. A fine opportunity to pay her back all the contempt she used to have for me. God knows how many lovers she has had! Perhaps she is deciding in my favor only because of the ease of arranging meetings.

Such, unfortunately, is the evil of excessive civilization! At twenty, a young man's nature, if he has any education, is a thousand leagues from that spontaneity without which love is often no more than the most tedious of duties.

I owe it to myself all the more to succeed with this woman, Julien's petty vanity continued, because if I never make a fortune, and if any-

one taunts me with my mean position as a tutor, I can let it be understood that love has brought me to this pass.

Again Julien moved his hand away from Madame de Rênal's, then
he grasped hers once more and pressed it. As they were returning to
the drawing-room, about midnight, Madame de Rênal asked him
softly:

"Are you leaving us, are you going away?"

Julien answered, sighing: "I absolutely must go, because I love you
passionately. That is a sin . . . and what a sin for a young priest!"

Madame de Rênal leaned upon his arm, and with such abandon
that her cheek felt the warmth of Julien's cheek.

The nights these two human beings spent were very different.
Madame de Rênal was exalted by transports of the most exquisite
mental sensation. A young flirt who falls in love early in life becomes
accustomed to the disturbances of love; when she reaches an age for
real passion, the charm of novelty is lacking. As Madame de Rênal had
read very few novels, all the fine details of her happiness were new to
her. No sordid reality came to chill her, not even the specter of the
future. She saw herself as happy in ten years as she was at this moment.
Even the thought of virtue and of the fidelity sworn to Monsieur de
Rênal, which had distressed her a few days before, came to her in vain
and was sent away like a tiresome guest. I shall never grant Julien
anything, Madame de Rênal assured herself; we will live in the future
as we have lived for the past month. He will be a friend.

CHAPTER 13
The English Scissors

For Julien, Fouqué's offer had literally destroyed all happiness; he was unable to adhere to any one decision.

Alas, perhaps I am lacking in character; I should have made a bad soldier for Napoleon. At least, he added, my little affair with the mistress of the house will divert me for a while.

Happily for him, even in this minor instance, his inner nature was in poor accord with his cavalier language. He was afraid of Madame de Rênal because of her beautiful dress. That dress was, in his eyes, the vanguard of Paris. His pride would not leave anything to chance and the inspiration of the moment. According to Fouqué's confidences and the little he had read about love in his Bible, he made a most detailed plan of campaign. Since he was very much disturbed, although he did not admit it to himself, he wrote this plan down.

The next morning Madame de Rênal was alone with him for an instant in the drawing-room:

"Is Julien the only name you have?" she asked him.

To this highly flattering question, our hero did not know what to reply. This situation was not foreseen in his plan. If it had not been for the foolishness of making a plan, Julien's quick wits would have served him well, surprise would merely have added to the acuteness of his perception.

He was awkward, and exaggerated his awkwardness to himself. Madame de Rênal forgave him for it at once. To her it seemed the effect of a charming ingenuousness. And the one thing she found lacking in this man, to whom so much intelligence was attributed, was the look of ingenuousness.

"I don't think I trust your little tutor," Madame Derville sometimes said to her. "He looks to me as if he were always calculating and never did anything except from policy. He's a sly one."

Julien remained deeply humiliated by the misfortune of not knowing how to answer Madame de Rênal.

A man like me owes it to himself to make up for that setback . . . and, seizing the moment when passing from one room to the other, he thought it his duty to give Madame de Rênal a kiss.

Nothing could have been less anticipated, nothing less agreeable both for him and for her, nothing more imprudent. They were upon the point of being seen. Madame de Rênal thought him mad. She was terrified, and even more shocked. That foolishness reminded her of Monsieur Valenod.

What would happen to me, she wondered, if I were alone with him? All her virtue returned, love being eclipsed.

She arranged matters so that one of her children stayed with her at all times.

The day was tedious to Julien, he spent the whole of it awkwardly putting his plan of seduction into execution. He did not once glance at Madame de Rênal without the glance's being full of meaning; yet he was not so stupid as to fail to see that he was not succeeding in being at all agreeable, much less seductive.

Madame de Rênal could not recover from her astonishment at finding him so awkward and at the same time so bold. It's the timidity of love in a man of perception! she thought at last, with inexpressible joy. Could it possibly be that he has never been loved by my rival!

After luncheon, Madame de Rênal returned to the drawing-room to receive Monsieur Charcot de Maugiron, the subprefect of Bray, who came to call. She was working at a small, raised, tapestry frame. Madame Derville was at her side. It was under such conditions, and in broad daylight, that our hero saw fit to advance his boot and press the graceful foot of Madame de Rênal, whose openwork stocking and charming Parisian shoes were obviously attracting the gallant sub-prefect's eyes.

Madame de Rênal was terrified; she let fall her scissors, her ball of wool, her needles, so that Julien's action might be taken for an awkward attempt to prevent the scissors, which he had seen slip, from falling. Luckily the small scissors of English steel broke apart, and Madame de Rênal wasted no time in regretting that Julien had not been closer to her.

"You noticed before I did that they were about to fall, you could have prevented it; instead, your zeal succeeded only in giving me a fine big kick."

All this deceived the subprefect, but not Madame Derville. This handsome boy has very unseemly manners! she thought; the good breeding of a provincial capital does not pardon errors of this sort. Madame de Rênal found an opportunity to say to Julien: "Be discreet, I order you to."

Julien was aware of his blunder, he was irritated. He deliberated for a long time over whether he ought to become angry at that phrase: *I order you*. He was stupid enough to think: She could have said *I order* if it were something to do with the children's education, but in responding to my love she implies equality . . . ; and his whole mind became absorbed in making truisms on the subject of equality. He repeated to himself, angrily, those lines from Corneille which Madame Derville had taught him several days earlier:

. . . . Love
Creates equalities, and does not seek them.

Julien insisted upon playing the rôle of a Don Juan, he who had never in his life had a mistress; he was unendurably stupid all that day. He had only one sensible idea; bored with himself and with Madame de Rênal, he looked forward with dismay to the approach of evening when he would be sitting beside her in the garden, in the dark. He told Monsieur de Rênal that he was going to Verrières to see the priest; he left after dinner and did not return until late at night.

CHAPTER 14
Cockcrow

HAD Julien possessed a little of the dexterity which he so gratuitously attributed to himself, he could have congratulated himself the next morning upon the effect produced by his trip to Verrières. His absence had caused his blunders to be forgotten. He was still somewhat sullen that day; just at evening a ridiculous idea came to him, and he communicated it to Madame de Rênal with rare temerity.

Scarcely had they seated themselves in the garden when, without waiting for sufficient darkness, Julien leaned close to Madame de Rênal's ear and, at the risk of compromising her horribly, said:

"Madame, at two o'clock tonight I shall come to your room, I have something I must tell you."

Julien trembled for fear that his demand might not be granted; his rôle of seducer weighed so frightfully upon him that if he could have followed his own inclination he would have retired to his room for several days and not seen these ladies again. He realized that by his masterly conduct the day before he had spoiled all the fine possibilities of the preceding day, and he literally did not know which way to turn.

Madame de Rênal responded with genuine, unexaggerated indignation to the impertinent announcement Julien had dared to make to her. He was convinced that he detected contempt in her short answer.

It is certain that in that answer, spoken in a very low voice, the words *for shame* had been uttered. Upon pretext of having something to say to the children, Julien went to their room, and on his return sat down beside Madame Derville and at some distance from Madame de Rênal, thus removing any possibility of taking her hand. The conversation was serious, and Julien acquitted himself very well in it, except for several moments of silence during which he wracked his brain. If only I could devise some fine maneuver, he thought, to force Madame de Rênal to show me again those unequivocal signs of affection which made me think, three days ago, that she was mine!

Julien was completely disconcerted by the almost desperate state into which he had thrown his affairs. On the other hand, nothing would have embarrassed him more than success.

When they separated at midnight, his pessimism convinced him that he had earned Madame Derville's scorn, and that probably he was no better off with Madame de Rênal.

In a very bad humor, and deeply humiliated, Julien did not sleep at all. Nothing was farther from his mind than the idea of renouncing all pretense, all plan, and living from day to day with Madame de Rênal, being satisfied, like a child, with the happiness each day brought.

He exhausted his brain inventing clever moves; an instant later he found them absurd; he was, in a word, very wretched by the time two o'clock sounded from the clock tower.

This sound aroused him as the crowing of the cock aroused Saint Peter. He felt himself to be upon the brink of the most painful experience. He had thought no more about his impertinent proposal since the moment he had made it; it had been so unfavorably received!

I told her that I would come to her room at two o'clock, he thought, rising. I may be inexperienced and crude as befits a peasant's son: Madame Derville has let me see that clearly enough, but at least I shall not be weak.

Julien had every reason to glory in his courage, never had he imposed a more difficult obligation upon himself. As he opened his door he was trembling so that his knees gave way beneath him, and he was obliged to lean against the wall.

He had not put on slippers. He went to listen at Monsieur de Rênal's door, and heard him snoring. He was desolated by the sound. He had, then, no further excuse for not going to her room. But good God! what would he do there? He had no plan, and by the time he made one he felt so upset that he would have been in no state to follow it out.

At length, suffering a thousand times more than if he had been going to his death, he entered the small corridor that led to Madame de Rênal's room. He opened the door with a trembling hand, making a frightful noise.

There was light, a night light burned on the mantel; he had not expected this new misfortune. Seeing him enter, Madame de Rênal sprang quickly out of bed. "You wretched creature!" she cried. There was a little confusion. Julien forgot his vain projects and returned to his natural rôle; not to please so charming a woman seemed to him the greatest of disasters. His only answer to her reproaches was to fling himself at her feet and embrace her knees. As she continued to speak extremely harshly to him, he burst into tears.

Several hours later, when Julien left Madame de Rênal's bedroom he had, to put it in the style of a novel, nothing further to desire. As a matter of fact, he owed to the love he had inspired and to the unexpected effect made upon himself by seductive charms, a victory to which all his clumsy ingenuity would never have led him.

But, even at the most gratifying moments, the victim of an eccentric pride, he still pretended to play the part of a man accustomed to subjugating women: he made incredible conscious efforts to destroy everything that was most likable in himself. Instead of being attentive to the passion he aroused and to the remorse that heightened its violence, he never ceased to see the word *duty* before his eyes. He dreaded a fearful regret and eternal ridicule if he deviated from the ideal model he set up for himself to follow. In a word, it was precisely what made Julien a superior being that prevented him from enjoying the happiness that offered itself so freely to him. He was like the young girl of sixteen who has exquisite color and who, to go to a ball, is foolish enough to put on rouge.

Mortally frightened by Julien's appearance, Madame de Rênal was soon beset by the cruelest alarm. Julien's tears and despair troubled her acutely.

Even when she had no longer anything to refuse him, she pushed Julien away from her with genuine indignation, and then flung herself into his arms. No coherence appeared in all this behavior. She believed herself damned beyond remission, and sought to hide from the sight of hell by heaping Julien with the most ardent caresses. In short, nothing would have been lacking to our hero's happiness, not even an intense sensitivity on the part of the woman he had just possessed, if he had been able to enjoy it. Julien's leaving her did not put an end to the transports which shook her in spite of herself, and her struggles with the remorse which was tearing her.

My God! to be happy, to be loved, is that all it is? was Julien's first thought upon returning to his own room. He was in that state of amazement and uneasy disquiet into which the soul falls when it has just obtained what it has long desired. It is accustomed to desiring, finds nothing further to desire and has as yet no memories. Like the soldier who returns from parade, Julien was exclusively absorbed in going over all the details of his conduct. "Did I miss anything I owe to myself? Did I play my part well?"

And what part? That of a man accustomed to shining with women.

CHAPTER 15
The Day After

FORTUNATELY for Julien's glory, Madame de Rênal had been too agitated, too astonished to perceive the idiocy of the man who, in one moment, had become everything in the world to her.

As she was urging him to leave, seeing day about to break: "Oh, dear Lord!" she said. "If my husband heard any sound, I am lost."

Julien, who had time to compose phrases, remembered this one: "Should you regret your life?"

"Ah, very much, just now! But I shall never regret having known you."

Julien found it necessary to his dignity to return to his room by broad daylight and without caution.

The constant attention with which he studied his own smallest actions, with the senseless idea of appearing to be a man of experience, had but one advantage; when he saw Madame de Rênal again at luncheon, his behavior was a masterpiece of discretion.

As for her, she was unable to look at him without blushing up to her eyes, and unable to live an instant without looking at him; she was aware of her trouble, and her efforts to hide it intensified it. Julien raised his eyes to her only once. At first Madame de Rênal admired his discretion. Presently, seeing that this one glance was not repeated, she became alarmed: Can it be that he doesn't love me any more? she wondered. Alas, I'm so old for him; I am ten years older than he is.

Passing from the dining room to the garden, she pressed Julien's hand. In the surprise which so extraordinary a sign of love caused him, he gazed at her with passion, for she had seemed very lovely to him at luncheon and all the time he had kept his eyes lowered he had been passing the time enumerating her charms. This glance reassured Madame de Rênal; it did not remove all her uneasiness, but her uneasiness almost entirely removed her remorse toward her husband.

At luncheon this husband had noticed nothing; he was not even as alert as Madame Derville: She thought Madame de Rênal about to collapse. All during that day her hardy and incisive friendship did not let her miss one of the half-hints destined to reveal to her, in hideous colors, the danger her friend was running.

Madame de Rênal was burning to be left alone with Julien; she wanted to ask him if he still loved her. Despite the unalterable gentleness of her character, she was upon the point several times of telling her friend how unwelcome she was.

That evening, in the garden, Madame Derville arranged matters so deftly that she was placed between Madame de Rênal and Julien. Madame de Rênal, who had formed a delightful picture of the pleasure of holding Julien's hand and pressing it to her lips, was unable even to say a word to him.

This disappointment augmented her agitation. She was devoured by one regret. She had so soundly scolded Julien for the indiscretion he had committed by coming to her room the night before that she was trembling for fear he might not come this night. She left the garden early and went to her room to prepare for bed. But unable to contain her impatience, she went to press her ear against Julien's door. In spite of the uncertainty and the passion that were consuming her, she dared not enter. That action seemed to her the ultimate in baseness, for it serves as the subject of a provincial adage.

The servants had not all gone to bed. Prudence at last obliged her to return to her room. Two hours of waiting were like two centuries of torment.

But Julien was too faithful to what he called duty to fail to execute, step by step, the course of action he had set himself.

As one o'clock was striking he slipped softly from his room, made sure that the master of the house was sleeping deeply, and went to Madame de Rênal's room. That night he found more happiness with his mistress, for he thought less constantly of the part to be played. He had eyes to see and ears to hear. What Madame de Rênal said to him about his age helped to give him some assurance.

"I am ten years older than you, how can you love me!" she kept repeating purposelessly, because the idea oppressed her.

Julien could not fathom her distress, but he saw that it was genuine, and he forgot almost all his fear of being ridiculous.

The foolish apprehension of being considered an inferior lover because of his humble birth also disappeared. In proportion as Julien's ardent response reassured his timid mistress, she recovered something of her happiness and of the faculty of judging her lover. Fortunately, on this occasion he had almost none of that borrowed air which had made the previous evening's encounter a victory but not a pleasure. If she had become aware of his concentration upon playing a rôle, that melancholy discovery would have destroyed all her happiness forever. She could have seen it only as a sad effect of disparity in ages.

Although Madame de Rênal had never given thought to theories of love, difference in age is second only to difference in fortune as a subject for common provincial jesting, whenever love is in question.

In a very few days Julien, restored to all the ardor normal to his age, was desperately in love.

It must be admitted, he thought, that she has an angelic goodness of spirit, and no one is any prettier.

He had almost entirely lost the idea of playing a part. In one moment of abandon he even confessed all his apprehensions to her. That confidence raised the passion he inspired to its peak. So I have not had any successful rival! Madame de Rênal thought with intense joy. She ventured to ask him about the portrait upon which he set such importance; Julien swore to her that it was a man's.

When Madame de Rênal retained enough composure to reflect upon it, she could not recover from her astonishment that such happiness existed, and that she had never suspected it.

Oh, she thought, if only I had known Julien ten years ago, when I still had some claim to prettiness!

Julien was very far from thoughts such as these. His love was still ambitious in character; it sprang from the joy of possessing, poor unfortunate creature as he was, and so despised, a woman so well-born and so beautiful. His gestures of adoration, his raptures at sight of his mistress' charms, eventually reassured her a little about the difference in their ages. If she had been gifted with a little of the worldly wisdom which any woman of thirty, in more civilized localities, has long since acquired, she would have trembled for the permanence of a love that seemed to live only on surprise and the gratification of vanity.

In the moments when he forgot ambition, Julien passionately admired even Madame de Rênal's hats, even her gowns. He could never tire of their scent. He would open her mirrored wardrobe and stand for hours on end marveling over the beauty and order of all that he found within. His mistress, leaning against him, gazed at him; as for him, he gazed at those jewels, those exquisite fabrics which are showered upon a bride on the eve of her marriage.

I might have married a man like this, Madame de Rênal thought at times; what fiery spirit! how enchanting life would be with him!

Julien, for his part, had never found himself so close to these terrible instruments of feminine artillery. It is impossible, he thought, that anyone in Paris has anything finer; so he saw no drawback to his happiness. Often his mistress' sincere admiration and her ecstasies made him forget the empty theory which had turned him so rigid, so nearly ridiculous, in the first moments of this affair. There were instants when, in spite of his habits of hypocrisy, he found immense comfort in admitting to this great lady who admired him his ignorance of a host of small social customs. His mistress' rank seemed to raise him above himself. Madame de Rênal, on her side, took the tenderest satisfaction from thus instructing, in a score of minor issues, this young man so full of intelligence and regarded by everyone as likely to go so far. Even the subprefect and Monsieur Valenod were unable to refrain from admiring him; for that they seemed less stupid to her. As for Madame Derville, she was far from having a like opinion to express. In despair over what she believed was to come, and seeing that her wise counsel was becoming detestable to a woman who had quite literally lost her head, she left Vergy without giving an explanation, which was carefully not asked for. Madame de Rênal shed a few tears over this, but very soon it seemed to her that her happiness redoubled. Owing to this departure, she was left alone with her lover almost all day long.

Julien abandoned himself all the more eagerly to the pleasant companionship of his mistress since every time he was too long alone with himself, Fouqué's disastrous proposal came again to torment him. In the first days of this new life there were times when he, who had never loved and never been loved by anyone, found so exquisite a pleasure in being sincere that he was on the verge of confiding in Madame de Rênal the ambition which up to that time had been the very essence of his existence. He would have liked to be able to consult her about the strange temptation which Fouqué's offer represented, but a small event put an end to all frankness.

CHAPTER 16
The Chief Deputy

ONE evening at sundown, sitting beside his mistress at the lower end of the orchard, far from intruders, he was deep in contemplation. Will such pleasant times last forever? he wondered. His mind was utterly absorbed in the difficulty of attaining a position of consequence, he deplored this excessive misfortune that puts an end to childhood and spoils the first years of youth for those oppressed by poverty.

"Ah!" he cried, "Napoleon was certainly sent by God to young Frenchmen. Who will replace him? Without him, what will become of the poor fellows—even the ones richer than I am—who have just the few écus it takes to get a good education, and not enough money, at twenty, to buy favor and start out upon a career? No matter what we do," he added with a heavy sigh, "this fatal memory will forever prevent us from being happy!"

Suddenly he saw Madame de Rênal frown, she assumed a cool and disdainful air; to her, this manner of thinking seemed to be what one would expect of a servant. Brought up in the knowledge that she was very wealthy, she felt that it should be tacitly assumed that Julien was too. She loved him a thousand times more than life and had no esteem whatever for money.

Julien was far from guessing at these thoughts. The frown recalled him to earth. He had sufficient presence of mind to compose phrases and explain to this aristocratic lady seated so close beside him on the grassy bank that the words he had just repeated were some he had heard during his visit to his old friend the woodcutter. It was the reasoning of the ungodly.

"Well, don't have anything more to do with such people," Madame de Rênal said, still retaining something of the frigid air which, all at once, had replaced an expression of the most ardent tenderness.

That frown, or rather remorse for his indiscretion, was the first damaging blow to the illusion which was carrying Julien away. He thought: She is kind and gentle, her fondness for me is intense, but she was brought up in the enemy camp. They must be particularly afraid of that class of ambitious men who, after a good education, have not enough money to start a career. What would become of these aristocrats if it were given us to fight them with equal weapons! Myself, for example, mayor of Verrières, well-intentioned, honest as Monsieur de Rênal is at bottom! How I'd get rid of the vicar, Monsieur Valenod and all their schemes! How justice would triumph in Verrières! It isn't their talents that would be any obstacle to me. They're always groping about for their way.

That day Julien's happiness was close to becoming permanent. Our hero lacked the courage to be sincere. He needed the courage to give battle, but *at once;* Madame de Rênal had been shocked by Julien's pronouncement because the men of her circle kept reiterating that Robespierre's return was especially possible on account of these young men of the lower classes educated above their station. Madame de Rênal's frigid manner continued for some time, and seemed pronounced to Julien. As a matter of fact, the fear of having indirectly said something disagreeable to him had replaced her displeasure at his unfortunate remark. This distress was vividly reflected upon her features, so pure and so artless when she was happy and at a distance from dull people.

Julien no longer dared to dream with abandon. More tranquil and less enamored, he decided that it was indiscreet to go to see Madame de Rênal in her room. It would be better for her to come to his; if a servant caught sight of her moving about the house, twenty different excuses could explain her errand.

But this arrangement, too, had its inconveniences. Julien had received from Fouqué some books which he himself, a theology student, could never have asked for in a bookshop. He dared open them only at night. Frequently he would have been highly relieved not to be interrupted by a visit anticipation of which, up to the time of the little scene in the orchard, would have put him in no frame of mind for reading.

He owed to Madame de Rênal a wholly new comprehension of books. He had ventured to question her about a host of small matters, ignorance of which is an insuperable obstacle to the intelligence of a young man born outside of cultivated circles, whatever natural talents may be attributed to him.

This education in love, given by an extremely ignorant woman, was a great asset. Julien acquired a direct insight into society as it is today.

The time flew. The memory of his mistress' charms distracted Julien from his dark ambition. The necessity of not speaking to her of sober and realistic matters, since they were on opposite sides, added, without his suspecting it, to the happiness he owed to the influence she was acquiring over him.

At times when the presence of overalert children reduced them to speaking only the language of cold reason, Julien, gazing at her out of eyes alight with love, listened with the utmost docility to her explanations of how the world goes. Often, in the midst of telling about some clever bit of trickery connected with a contract or with the building of a road, Madame de Rênal would forget herself to the point of utter folly; Julien would have to scold her, she permitted herself the same intimate gestures with him as with her children. Actually there were days when she had the illusion of loving him as if he were her child. Was she not constantly having to answer his ingenuous questions about a thousand simple things which any well-born child has grasped by the time he is fifteen? An instant later she would be looking up to him as to a master. His intellectual powers came close to frightening her; every day she seemed to see more clearly the great man of the future in this young priest. She saw him as Pope; she saw him as prime minister, like Richelieu.

"Shall I live long enough to see your triumph?" she would say to Julien. "There is a place ready for a great man; the monarchy and the Church have need of one."

CHAPTER 17

A King in Verrières

ON THE third of September, at ten o'clock in the evening, a police-
man aroused all Verrières by riding at a gallop up the main
street; he brought the news that His Majesty the King of . . . would
arrive the following Sunday, and it was now Tuesday. The prefect
authorized—that is to say, demanded—the formation of a guard of
honor; all possible pomp must be displayed. A courier was dispatched
to Vergy. Monsieur de Rênal arrived during the night and found the
whole town in an uproar. Everyone had a claim to put forward; the
less consequential citizens were renting balconies from which to watch
the king's entrance. There was barely time to refurbish the uniforms
which had seen service seven years before when a prince of the blood
had passed through town.

At seven o'clock Madame de Rênal arrived from Vergy with Julien
and the children. She found her drawing-room full of liberal ladies who
were urging that the parties unite, and had come to beg her to induce
her husband to grant theirs a place in the guard of honor. One of
them insisted that if her husband were not appointed, he would go
bankrupt out of sheer disappointment. Madame de Rênal promptly
got rid of all these people. She seemed very much engrossed.

Julien was amazed and even more irritated by her making a mystery of what was troubling her. I foresaw it, he thought bitterly, her love is eclipsed by the joy of receiving a king in her home. All this splendor dazzles her. She'll love me again when her caste consciousness stops distracting her mind.

An astounding fact: he loved her the more for it.

The decorators were beginning to overrun the house; for a long time he watched in vain for an opportunity to speak to her. At last he encountered her coming out of his own room carrying one of his suits. They were alone. He tried to talk to her. She hurried away, refusing to listen. I'm the worst kind of fool, he thought, to love such a woman; ambition makes her as senseless as her husband.

She was even more so: one of her greatest desires, which she had never confessed to Julien for fear of shocking him, was to see him leave off his gloomy black clothes if only for one day. With an adroitness really remarkable in so artless a woman, she had contrived that Julien should be appointed to the guard of honor in preference to five or six young men, sons of very prosperous manufacturers, at least two of whom were known for exemplary piety. Monsieur Valenod, who was counting upon lending his barouche to the prettiest women of the town and showing off his fine Norman horses, consented to let Julien, the human being he most disliked, have one of them for a saddle horse. But each member of the guard of honor owned or had borrowed one of the handsome sky-blue uniforms, with a colonel's insignia in silver on the shoulders, which had glittered seven years earlier. Madame de Rênal wanted a new suit, and she had only four days left in which to send to Besançon and get back the jacket, the side arms, the cap and all the rest that goes to make a guard of honor. The amusing thing is that she considered it indiscreet to have Julien's uniform made in Verrières. She wanted to surprise him, him and the town.

From morning on, on Sunday, thousands of peasants from the near-by mountains thronged the streets of Verrières. There was the most brilliant sunshine. At last, toward three o'clock, the great crowd stirred, a large fire had been sighted on a cliff two leagues from Verrières. This signal announced that the king had just entered the territory of the department. At once the clamor of all the bells and the repeated firing of an old Spanish cannon belonging to the town bore witness to its joy at this great event. Half the population clambered up to the roofs. All the women were on the balconies. The guard of honor began to advance. The splendid uniforms were admired, everyone recognized a relative, a friend. But one observation eclipsed all others: the first horseman of the ninth rank was an exceedingly handsome and very slender youth whom no one recognized at first. Presently a cry of indignation from some, a silence of astonishment from others signaled a general sensation. They realized that this young man, riding one of Monsieur Valenod's Norman horses, was young Sorel, the carpenter's son. Particularly among the liberals, all voices were lifted as one against the mayor. What, because this common laborer disguised as a priest was tutor to his brats, he had the audacity to appoint him to the guard of honor, to the detriment of such wealthy manufacturers as Messieurs This and That! Those gentlemen, a banker's wife said, ought to put that young guttersnipe in his place, once and for all.

"He's sly and he's wearing a saber," the woman next her replied. "He'd be treacherous enough to cut up their faces."

The comments of the aristocratic circles were more dangerous. The ladies wondered among themselves if it was the mayor alone who was responsible for this extreme impropriety. In general, he was given credit for his contempt of the lowborn.

While the object of so much comment, Julien was the happiest of men. Naturally daring, he sat a horse better than most of the young men of this mountain village. He saw in the women's eyes that he was the center of attention.

His epaulettes were the most dazzling because they were new. His mount pranced skittishly at every step, he was on a pinnacle of joy.

His happiness was unbounded when, as they passed the ancient ramparts, the noise of the small cannon made his horse shy out of line. By great good luck, he did not fall off; from that moment on, he felt himself a hero. He was Napoleon's artillery officer, charging an emplacement.

One person was happier than he was. At first she had watched him pass from one of the windows of the town hall; then, getting into a barouche and rapidly making a wide detour, she arrived in time to shudder when his horse sprang out of the ranks. Finally, her carriage going at a fast gallop out through another of the town's gates, she was able to rejoin the road by which the king was to travel, and follow the guard of honor at a distance of some twenty yards in the midst of a noble cloud of dust. Ten thousand peasants shouted: "Long live the king!" when the mayor had the honor of haranguing His Majesty.

One hour later, when, having listened to all the speeches, the king was about to enter the town, the small cannon began to fire again in hasty explosions.

His Majesty alighted at the fine new church which was decked out for this occasion in all its crimson draperies. The king was to dine, and immediately afterwards return to his carriage for a pilgrimage to the famous shrine of Saint Clément. Scarcely had the king entered the church when Julien galloped off toward Monsieur de Rênal's house. There, sighing, he took off his beautiful sky-blue uniform, his saber, his epaulettes, to resume his everyday suit of rough black cloth. He remounted, and a few instants later was in Bray-le-Haut, which stands upon the summit of a lofty hill. Enthusiasm is multiplying these peasants, Julien thought. One can't move in Verrières, and here are more than ten thousand of them around this old abbey. Half destroyed by revolutionary vandalism, it had been magnificently rebuilt since the Restoration, and there was beginning to be some talk of miracles. Julien joined Monsieur Chélan, who scolded him soundly and gave him a cassock and a surplice. He dressed quickly and followed Monsieur Chélan, who was about to take his place beside the young Bishop of Agde, recently appointed, who had been entrusted with showing the relic of Saint Clément to the king. But the bishop could not be found.

Twenty-four priests had been assembled to represent the ancient chapter of Bray-le-Haut which, up to 1789, had been composed of twenty-four canons. After having spent three-quarters of an hour deploring the bishop's youth, the priests thought it proper for the Dean to approach Monseigneur and inform him that the king was about to arrive and that it was time to come to the chancel. Monsieur Chélan's great age had made him Dean; despite the ill-humor he had shown Julien, he signed to him that he was to follow. Julien looked very well in his surplice. By means of some secret ecclesiastical process he had made his handsome curls lie quite flat; but through an oversight which redoubled Monsieur Chélan's wrath, below the long folds of his cassock the spurs of the guard of honor could be seen.

At the bishop's apartments the tall resplendent lackeys barely condescended to answer the old priest that Monseigneur could not be seen. They mocked him when he tried to explain that, as Dean of the noble Order of Bray-le-Haut, he was privileged to be admitted to the presence of the officiating bishop at all times.

Julien's arrogant nature was shocked by the lackeys' insolence. He began to prowl the dormitories of the ancient abbey, shaking every door he came to. One very small one yielded to his efforts, and he found himself in a cell, surrounded by Monseigneur's menservants, dressed in black and with chains about their necks. From his urgent manner these gentlemen assumed that he had been sent for by the bishop, and let him pass. He took a few steps and found himself in an immense Gothic chamber, extremely gloomy and paneled throughout in black oak; with one single exception the pointed windows had been bricked up.

At the far end of the room, near this one source of daylight, he saw a portable mirror framed in mahogany. A young man in purple robe and lace surplice, but bareheaded, was standing a few paces from the mirror. Julien thought that the young man had an irritable look; with his right hand he was solemnly making signs of benediction in the direction of the mirror.

What can be the meaning of this? he thought. Is it some preparatory ceremony this young priest is performing? Perhaps he's the bishop's secretary . . . he'll be as insolent as the lackeys . . . well, no matter, we'll have to try.

He started forward and walked the length of the room rather slowly, keeping his gaze turned toward the single window and watching the young man who continued to make signs of benediction, executed deliberately but in infinite number and without an instant's pause. The young man caught sight of him in the glass, turned, and abruptly discarding his irritable air, said in the pleasantest manner:

"Well, Monsieur, is it fixed at last?"

Julien was dumfounded. As the young man turned toward him, he saw the pectoral cross on his chest: this was the Bishop of Agde! So young, Julien thought; six, or at most eight, years older than me! . . .

And he was ashamed of his spurs.

"Monseigneur," he answered timidly, "I'm sent by the Dean of the chapter, Monsieur Chélan."

"Ah, yes, he is very highly spoken of," the bishop said in a courteous tone that redoubled his charm in Julien's eyes. "But I beg your pardon, Monsieur, I took you for the person who is supposed to bring back my miter. It was carelessly packed in Paris; the silver brocade is horribly crushed on top. It will make the most hideous effect," the young bishop added with a mournful air, "and besides, they're keeping me waiting."

"Monseigneur, I will go and look for your miter, if Your Lordship will allow me."

Julien's fine eyes had their effect.

"Do, Monsieur," the bishop answered with charming courtesy; "I need it this minute. I'm more than sorry to keep the gentlemen of the chapter waiting."

When Julien had reached the middle of the room, he turned back toward the bishop and saw that he had once more begun to make signs of benediction. What can be the point of that? Julien wondered; very likely it's a ritual preparation required for the ceremony that is going to take place. When he came into the cell where the attendants were, he saw the miter in their hands. These gentlemen, yielding in spite of themselves to Julien's imperious look, delivered the miter to him.

He felt proud, carrying it; crossing the room he walked slowly; he held it respectfully. He found the bishop seated before the mirror; but from time to time his right hand, although weary, still made the sign of benediction. Julien helped him assume his miter. The bishop shook his head.

"Good! It will stay on," he said to Julien with a gratified air. "Will you move back a little?"

Thereupon the bishop walked very quickly to the center of the room, then returning toward the mirror with slow steps he resumed his stern look and gravely gave benedictions.

Julien was motionless with astonishment. He was tempted to explain this to himself, but did not dare. The bishop paused and, glancing at him with an expression that was rapidly losing its gravity:

"What do you think of my miter, Monsieur? Does it look well?"

"Very well, Monseigneur."

"It isn't too far back? That would look a bit silly; but it shouldn't be worn over the eyes like an officer's cap, either."

"It looks very well to me."

"The King of . . . is accustomed to a venerable, and probably very sober-minded clergy. Particularly because of my age, I wouldn't like to look frivolous."

And once more the bishop began to walk about, making signs of benediction.

Obviously, Julien thought, daring at last to understand, he is rehearsing.

After a few moments:

"I am ready," the bishop said. "Go and let the Dean and the gentlemen of the Chapter know, Monsieur."

Soon Monsieur Chélan, followed by the two eldest priests, entered through a massive door, magnificently carved, which Julien had not noticed before. But this time he remained in his regular position, the last of all, and could see the bishop only over the shoulders of the churchmen who crowded forward to the door.

The bishop crossed the room slowly; when he reached the threshold the priests formed a procession. After a brief instant of confusion the procession began to move, chanting a psalm. The bishop walked last, between Monsieur Chélan and another very aged priest. Julien was spellbound with awe at so beautiful a ceremony. The ambition aroused by the bishop's youth, the delicacy and the exquisite courtesy of this prelate contended for possession of his heart. This courtesy was quite another thing than that shown by Monsieur de Rênal, even on his good days. The higher one goes in the social order, Julien thought, the more charming the manners one encounters.

They entered the church by a side door; suddenly an appalling noise made its ancient vaults shudder; Julien thought that they were collapsing. It was the small cannon again; drawn by eight horses at the gallop, it had just arrived, and it was no sooner arrived than, manned by the gunners of Leipzig, it began firing five rounds a minute as if the Prussians were in front of it.

The king entered.

After the bishop's address and the king's response, His Majesty took his place below the dais; then he knelt devoutly on a cushion near the altar. There was a *Te Deum*, clouds of incense, countless bursts of musket and artillery fire; the peasants were drunk with delight and piety. A day such as this undoes the work of a hundred issues of the Jacobin papers.

Julien was within six paces of the king, who was praying with genuine fervor. For the first time he noticed a small man of intelligent appearance, wearing a suit almost without embroideries. But he wore a sky-blue ribbon across this very simple costume. He stood closer to the king than many other gentlemen whose coats were so heavily trimmed with gold braid that, as Julien put it, one could not see the cloth. Sometime later he learned that this was Monsieur de la Mole, the bishop's uncle. He thought his manner lofty, even insolent.

That marquis would not be polite like my nice bishop, he thought. Oh, the clerical vocation makes one gentle and wise!

Monsieur de la Mole had ten thousand bottles of wine distributed among the peasantry. That evening, in Verrières, the liberals saw fit to illuminate their houses a hundred times more brightly than the royalists.

CHAPTER 18
To Think Is to Suffer

A WEEK after the king's visit to Verrières, the question that super-
seded the innumerable lies, idiotic interpretations, ridiculous
arguments and so forth—the objects of which had been, successively,
the king, the Bishop of Agde, the Marquis de la Mole, the ten thousand
bottles of wine—was the utter indecency of having insinuated Julien
Sorel, the son of a carpenter, into the guard of honor. In this connection the wealthy calico manufacturers were to be heard morning and
evening at the café, shouting themselves hoarse with preaching equality. The arrogant woman, Madame de Rênal, was the author of that
abomination. The reason? Young Abbé Sorel's fine eyes and smooth
cheeks told the whole story.

Shortly after the return to Vergy, Stanislaus-Xavier, the youngest of
the children, came down with a fever; at once Madame de Rênal was
plunged into appalling remorse. For the first time she reproached herself in a coherent fashion for her love; she seemed to realize, as if by a
miracle, the enormity of the sin into which she had let herself be
drawn. Although of a profoundly religious nature, she had not until
now thought of the magnitude of her crime in the eyes of God.

Long ago, at the convent of the Sacred Heart, she had loved God
passionately; in this situation she feared Him as passionately. The con-

flicts that ravaged her spirit were all the more terrible for the lack of logic in her fear. Julien discovered that, far from calming her, the slightest attempt to reason with her made her irritable; she saw in such reasoning the language of hell. However, as Julien himself was very fond of little Stainslaus, he was better received when he talked to her about the child's illness, which rapidly became serious. Then incessant remorse deprived Madame de Rênal even of the possibility of sleeping; she refused to emerge from a hostile silence; if she had opened her mouth, it would have been to confess her sin to God and to the world.

"Don't speak to anyone, I beg you," Julien said to her when they were left alone. "Let me be the only one in whom you confide your troubles. If you still love me, don't speak out; your words couldn't cure our Stanislaus' fever."

But his offers of consolation had no effect; he did not know that Madame de Rênal had taken it into her head that, to appease the wrath of a jealous God, she must hate Julien or see her son die. It was because she felt herself unable to hate her lover that she was so grief-stricken.

"Go away from me," she said to Julien one day. "For the love of God, get out of this house; it's your presence here that is killing my boy."

"God is punishing me," she added softly. "He is just; I worship his justice; my sin is frightful, and I was living without remorse! That was the first sign of God's forsaking me: I ought to be doubly punished."

Julien was deeply moved. He could see neither hypocrisy nor exaggeration here. She believes that she is killing her son by loving me, and yet the poor soul loves me more than her son. That is the source of the remorse that is destroying her, beyond a doubt; that is real greatness in emotion. But how can I have inspired such a love, I who am so poor, so ill-bred, so ignorant, so coarse, sometimes, in my manners?

One night the child was at his worst. At about two o'clock in the morning, Monsieur de Rênal came to see him. The child, consumed by fever, was greatly flushed and did not recognize his father. Suddenly Madame de Rênal flung herself at her husband's feet: Julien saw that she was about to tell all and destroy herself forever.

Fortunately this extraordinary behavior antagonized Monsieur de Rênal. "Good night, good night!" he said, moving away.

"No, listen to me," his wife cried, on her knees before him and trying to hold him back. "You must know the truth. I am the one who is killing my son. I gave him life, and I am taking it from him. Heaven is punishing me, in God's eyes I am guilty of murder. I must destroy myself, abase myself; perhaps this sacrifice will appease the Lord."

If Monsieur de Rênal had been a man of imagination, he would have understood everything.

"Romantic notions," he snapped, thrusting his wife aside as she tried to embrace his knees. "All these romantic notions! Julien, at daybreak send for the doctor."

And he returned to his bed. Madame de Rênal fell to her knees, half fainting, and repulsing Julien with a convulsive gesture when he would have aided her.

Julien was dumfounded.

So that is adultery! he thought. Is it possible that these priests are right? Can they, who commit so many sins, be privileged to understand the true theory of sin? How strange . . .

For twenty minutes after Monsieur de Rênal had left the room, Julien watched the woman he loved, her head resting against the child's small bed, motionless and almost unconscious. There, he thought, is a woman of superior intellect reduced to the depths of despair because she has known me.

The hours are passing quickly. What can I do for her? Now it's no longer a question of me. What do men and their dull pretenses matter to me? What can I do for her . . . leave her? But I'll be leaving her to suffer the most frightful torments, alone. That automaton of a husband hurts her more than he helps her. He'll say something ugly to her, just to be crude; she might go mad and throw herself out of the window.

If I leave her, if I cease watching over her, she will confess everything to him. And who knows, perhaps he'll make an open scandal in spite of the fortune she must be worth to him. Good God, she might tell everything to that b—— Abbé Maslon, who is using the illness of a six-year-old child as a pretext for never stirring from the house, and not without his own reasons! In her distress and her fear of God she forgets everything she knows about the man; she sees only the priest.

"Go away," Madame de Rênal said abruptly, opening her eyes.

"I'd give my life a thousand times over to know what would be the best thing to do for you," Julien answered. "I have never loved you so much, my darling—or rather, it is only now that I am beginning to adore you as you deserve to be adored. What will become of me far away from you, and knowing that you are unhappy because of me!

But let's not take my suffering into account. I'll go away, yes, my love. But if I leave you, if I cease watching over you, putting myself constantly between you and your husband, you'll tell him everything, you'll destroy yourself. Think how ignominiously he'll drive you out of his house; all Verrières, all Besançon will be talking about the scandal. You'll be given all the blame; you will never live down the shame."

"That's what I want," she cried, rising to her feet. "I shall suffer, so much the better."

"But by this atrocious scandal you'll be making unhappiness for him too."

"But I'll be humbling myself, debasing myself; and perhaps that way I shall save my son. Won't that humiliation count as a public act of contrition in other people's eyes? As far as I can judge, in my weakness, isn't it the greatest sacrifice I can make to God? . . . Perhaps He will be willing to accept my humiliation and leave me my son! Show me another sacrifice more painful and I'll hurry to make it."

"Let me be the one to punish myself. I am guilty too. Would you like me to enter the Trappist monastery? The austerity of that life ought to appease your God . . . Oh, heaven! If only I could take Stanislaus' sickness upon myself . . ."

"Oh, you do love him," Madame de Rênal said, flinging herself into his arms.

In the same instant she pushed him away with horror.

"I believe you! I believe you!" she went on, having dropped once more to her knees. "Oh, my only friend; oh, why aren't you Stanislaus' father? Then it wouldn't be a terrible sin to love you better than your son."

"Will you let me stay and love you only as a brother from now on? That is the only logical expiation, it might appease the Almighty's anger."

"And what about me?" she exclaimed, rising and taking Julien's head between her two hands, holding it before her eyes, a little away from her. "Am I to love you like a brother? Is it in my power to love you like a brother?"

Julien burst into tears.

"I will obey you," he said, falling at her feet, "whatever you command, I will obey you; it is the only thing left for me to do. My brain is struck blind, I can't see what course to take. If I leave you, you tell your husband everything, you ruin yourself and him too. After being made so ridiculous he'll never be appointed deputy. If I stay, you'll believe me to be the cause of your son's death, and you will die of sorrow. Would you like to try the effect of my leaving you? If you want, I will punish myself for our sin by going away from you for a week. I'll spend it wherever you say. At the abbey of Bray-le-Haut, for example: but swear to me that during my absence you won't confess anything to your husband. Remember that I can never come back if you speak."

She promised. He left, but was recalled at the end of two days.

"Without you, it is impossible for me to keep my vow. I shall speak to my husband if you are not constantly here to command me, by your glances, to keep silent. Every hour of this abominable life seems to me to last a day."

At last heaven took pity on that grief-stricken mother. Little by little, Stanislaus advanced out of danger. But the ice had been broken, her mind had recognized the extent of her sin; she was unable to recover her equilibrium. Remorse remained, and it was what it must be in so guileless a heart. Her life was heaven and hell: hell when she did not see Julien, heaven when she was at his feet. "I'm not deluding myself any more," she would tell him, even at those times when she dared abandon herself to love: "I am damned, irremediably damned. You are young, you yielded to my seductions, heaven may pardon you; but I am damned. I can tell by a sure sign. I am afraid; who wouldn't be afraid at the sight of hell? But deep down I am not a bit repentant. If I had my sin to commit again, I should commit it. If heaven only doesn't punish me in this world, through my children, I shall have more than I deserve. But you, my Julien," she cried at other times, "are you at least happy? Do you think I love you enough?"

Julien's distrust, and his suffering pride which needed, above all else, a self-sacrificing love, could not withstand the sight of so great, so unquestionable a sacrifice, constantly renewed. He adored Madame de Rênal. Even if she is an aristocrat, and I am the son of a laborer, she loves me . . . To her I'm not just a manservant charged with the duties of a lover. That fear removed, Julien fell into all the unreasonableness of love, into its mortal uncertainties.

"At least," she cried, seeing his doubts of her love, "let me make you very happy during the few days we have to spend together! We must hurry; tomorrow, perhaps, I shan't be yours any longer. If heaven strikes at me through my children, it will be useless for me to try to live only to love you, to try not to see that it is my crime that kills them. I will not be able to survive that blow. Even if I wanted to, I could not; I should go mad.

"Oh, if only I could take your share of the sin upon myself, as you so generously wanted to take that raging fever of Stanislaus'!"

This great moral crisis changed the nature of the emotion that attached Julien to his mistress. His love was no longer simply admiration for beauty, the pride of possessing it.

Their happiness from that time on was of a far superior quality, the flame which was consuming them was more intense. They experienced moments of ecstasy close to madness. Their happiness would have appeared greater to other eyes; but they no longer found the delightful serenity, the cloudless felicity, the easy contentment of the early stage of their love when Madame de Rênal's only fear was that Julien did not love her enough. Sometimes their pleasure took on the features of crime.

In the happiest and, apparently, the most tranquil moments: "Oh, dear God! I can see hell," Madame de Rênal would suddenly cry out, grasping Julien's hand with a convulsive pressure. "What horrible agonies! I have certainly earned them." She would clasp him in her arms, clinging to him like ivy to a wall.

Julien tried in vain to quiet that tormented spirit. She took his hand to cover it with kisses. Then, relapsing into gloomy revery: "Hell would be a blessing for me," she said. "I should still have a few days to spend with him on earth; but hell on earth, my children's death . . . Still, at that price my sin might be forgiven . . . Oh, God, don't grant me my absolution at that price! These poor children have never offended against You; I, I alone am guilty: I love a man who is not my husband."

Presently Julien saw Madame de Rênal regain a state of apparent tranquillity. She tried to control herself, she did not want to poison the life of one she loved.

In the midst of this recurrent cycle of love, remorse and pleasure, the days passed for them with the rapidity of lightning. Julien lost the habit of brooding.

Mademoiselle Elisa went to oversee the progress of a minor lawsuit she was bringing in Verrières. She found Monsieur Valenod highly incensed with Julien. She hated the tutor and frequently talked about him to Monsieur Valenod.

"You would have me thrown out, Monsieur, if I told you the truth," she said to him one day. "Masters all stick together when it comes to important things. We poor servants are never forgiven for telling about some things . . ."

After these customary phrases, which Monsieur Valenod's impatient curiosity found means to cut short, he learned certain facts extremely mortifying to his self-esteem.

That woman, the most distinguished in the whole region, whom he had surrounded with so many attentions during the past six years—and, unfortunately, in full sight of everyone—that woman, so high and mighty, whose disdain had so often caused him to blush, had taken for her lover a young laborer disguised as a tutor. And finally, that nothing might be lacking to the discomfiture of the poorhouse director, Madame de Rênal adored this lover.

"And," the maid added with a sigh, "Monsieur Julien didn't go to any trouble at all to make this conquest, he hasn't even left off his usual coldness for Madame."

Elisa had felt certain only in the country, but she believed that the affair dated from much farther back.

"That's undoubtedly why he refused to marry me that time," she added spitefully. "And I, like an imbecile, went to consult Madame de Rênal and begged her to speak to the tutor."

That very evening Monsieur de Rênal received from town, along with his newspaper, a long anonymous letter which informed him in the greatest detail of what was going on in his house. Julien saw him grow pale and cast malignant glances at him while reading that letter, written on bluish paper. All evening long the mayor did not recover from his uneasiness; it was in vain that Julien paid court to him by asking for explanations of the genealogy of the best Burgundian families.

CHAPTER 19

Anonymous Letters

As THEY were leaving the drawing-room at midnight, Julien had an opportunity to say to his mistress:

"We won't meet this evening, your husband is suspicious; I'd swear that long letter he has been reading and sighing over is an anonymous letter."

Luckily Julien locked the door of his room. Madame de Rênal had the insane idea that this warning was merely an excuse for not visiting her. She lost her head completely, and at the usual hour went to his door. Julien, hearing a sound in the corridor, instantly blew out his lamp. There was an effort to open his door; was it Madame de Rênal, was it a jealous husband?

Very early the next morning the cook, who had a liking for Julien, brought him a book on the cover of which he read these words written in Italian: *Guardate alla pagina 130.*

Julien shuddered at the imprudence, looked up page 130 and found pinned to it the following letter, hastily written, drenched with tears and shockingly misspelled. Ordinarily Madame de Rênal spelled very well, he was touched by this detail and a little more inclined to overlook the frightful indiscretion.

"You wouldn't let me in last night? There are moments when I think that I have never seen into the depths of your heart. Your eyes frighten me. I am afraid of you. Good God, can it be that you have never loved me! In that case, let my husband discover our love affair, let him shut me up in an eternal prison, in the country, away from my children. Maybe that is God's will. I shall die soon. But you will be a monster.

"Don't you love me? Are you tired of my foolishness, my remorse, you traitor? Do you want to destroy me? I'm giving you an easy way of doing it. Go and show this letter all over Verrières—or rather, just show it to Monsieur Valenod. Tell him that I love you—but no, don't speak such blasphemy, tell him that I adore you, that life didn't begin for me until the day I saw you; that in the maddest moments of my girlhood I never even dreamed of such happiness as I owe to you; that I have sacrificed my life to you, that I am sacrificing my soul. You know that I am sacrificing much more.

"But what does he know about sacrifices, that man? Tell him, just for the sake of irritating him, tell him that I defy all evil people, that there is only one sorrow left in the world for me, and that is to see a change of heart in the one man who makes life worth living to me. What a blessing it would be for me to lose this life, to offer it as a sacrifice, never again to fear for my children!

"You need have no doubt, my dear, that if there is an anonymous letter it comes from that odious person, who, for six years, has been pursuing me with his coarse voice, with tales of his horsemanship and the eternal enumeration of all his superior qualities.

"Is there an anonymous letter? That is what I wanted to talk over with you, you wicked man; but no, you did the right thing. Clasping you in my arms, perhaps for the last time, I could never have thought things out coolly, as I do when I am alone. From now on our happiness will no longer be so easily arranged. Will that be a disappointment to you? Yes, on the days when you haven't received an interesting book from Monsieur Fouqué. The sacrifice is made. To-morrow, whether there is or is not an anonymous letter, I am going to tell my husband that I too have received an anonymous letter, that he must instantly make you a present of money, find some honest pretext and send you back to your parents without delay.

"Alas, my dear, we are going to be separated for two weeks, perhaps a month! Never mind, I do you justice, you will suffer as much as I . . . Anyway, this is the only way to undermine the effect of that anonymous letter; it is not the first my husband has received, and about me too. Oh, how I used to laugh at them!

"The whole aim of my behavior is to make my husband think that the letter comes from Monsieur Valenod; I have no doubt that he is the author of it. If you leave this house, do not fail to go and settle down in Verrières. I shall arrange matters so that my husband takes it into his head to spend a fortnight there, to prove to those fools that there is no coldness between himself and me. Once in Verrières, be friendly with everyone, even the liberals. I know that all the women will seek you out.

"Do not go and quarrel with Monsieur Valenod, nor cut his ears off as you said you would one day; on the contrary, show him every sign of cordiality. The essential thing is to make the people in Verrières think that you are going to take employment with the Valenods, or with anybody else, to educate the children.

"That is something my husband will never stand for. If he should become resigned to it, well, at least you will be living in Verrières and I shall see you sometimes. My children who are so fond of you will go to see you . . . Dear God! I feel that I love my children more because they love you. What remorse! What will be the end of all this? . . . I am wandering . . . Anyway, you understand how you must act; be gentle, polite, not scornful with those coarse people, I ask you on my knees: they are going to be the arbiters of our future. Don't doubt for an instant but that my husband will conform to what *public opinion* demands of him in your case.

"You are the one who is going to provide me with the anonymous letter; arm yourself with patience and a pair of scissors. Cut the words you will see below out of a book; then stick them down with glue on the sheet of blue paper I am sending you; I got it from Monsieur Valenod. Be prepared for a search of your room, burn the mutilated pages of the book. If you don't find the words ready-made, be patient enough to form them letter by letter. To spare you trouble, I have made the anonymous letter too short. Alas, if you do not love me any more, as I fear, how long mine must seem to you!

ANONYMOUS LETTER

"Madame:

All your little secrets are known; but the persons whose concern it will be to put a stop to them have been warned. Because of a

remnant of friendship for you, I advise you to cut yourself off entirely from the little peasant. If you are wise enough to do so,
your husband will believe that the information he has received is
false, and he will be allowed to remain in error. Remember that
I have your secret; tremble, wretched woman; now you must
walk the straight and narrow path, I will be watching."

"As soon as you have finished gluing the words that make up this
letter (did you recognize the director's turns of speech?), come out of
your room and walk about the house, I shall meet you.

"I will go to the village and come back with a troubled face; as a
matter of fact I shall be very much troubled. Dear God! What risk
am I running? and all because you *thought you guessed* at an anonymous
letter. At last, with a stunned look, I shall give my husband a letter
which was handed to me by a stranger. You, meanwhile, go for a
walk on the path through the big woods with the children, and don't
come back until dinnertime.

"From the top of the cliffs you can see the dovecote tower. If our
affairs go well, I'll put a white handkerchief there; in the opposite case
there will be nothing there.

"Ingrate, will your heart not make you find a way to tell me that
you love me before you go for that walk? Whatever may happen, be
sure of one thing: I shall not survive our final separation by so much
as a day. Oh, I am a bad mother! Those are empty words that I have
just written, dear Julien. I do not feel them; I can think of nothing but
you at this moment, I wrote them only so that you would not find fault
with me. Now that I find myself on the point of losing you, what is the
use of pretending? Yes, even though my soul may seem revolting to
you, I do not lie to the man I adore! I have already practiced only too
much deceit in my life. Well, I forgive you if you no longer love me.
I have not time to reread my letter. To me it seems a small thing, to
pay with my life for the happy days I have passed in your arms. You
know that they will cost me more than that."

A KING AT VERRIÈRES

CHAPTER 20

Conversation with a Master

IT WAS with a childish pleasure that Julien spent the next hour assembling words. As he was leaving his room he met his pupils and their mother; she took the letter with a simplicity and courage whose tranquillity startled him.

"Is the glue dry enough?" she asked him.

Is this the woman who was so crazed by remorse? he thought. What are her plans now? He was too proud to ask her; but never, perhaps, had she seemed more desirable to him.

"If this turns out badly," she added with the same coolness, "everything will be taken from me. Bury this case somewhere in the mountains; someday it may be my only resource."

She handed him a glass-topped casket of red morocco leather, filled with gold and a few diamonds.

"Now go," she told him.

She kissed the children, and the youngest twice. Julien stood immobile. She left him with a rapid step and without glancing at him.

Since the instant when he had opened the anonymous letter, Monsieur de Rênal's existence had been a torment. He had not been so disturbed since a duel that he had almost fought in 1816 and, to do him justice, the prospect of receiving a bullet then had made him less wretched. He studied the letter from every aspect: Isn't this a woman's writing? he thought. In that case, what woman wrote it? He reviewed all his feminine acquaintances in Verrières without being able to pin his suspicions upon any. Could a man have dictated that letter? What man? An equal uncertainty here; he was envied and very likely hated by the majority of the men he knew. I must consult my wife, he thought out of habit, rising from the armchair into which he had sunk.

No sooner risen than: Good God! he thought, slapping his forehead, she is the one above all whom I must distrust; right now she is my enemy. And tears of anger started into his eyes.

As just compensation for that barrenness of heart which passes for practical common sense in the provinces, the two men whom Monsieur de Rênal most dreaded at that moment were his two most intimate friends.

'Was there ever a misery like mine!" he cried out in rage. "What loneliness!" He passed a hideous night; but fortunately it did not occur to him to spy upon his wife.

I am accustomed to Louise, he thought, she knows all my business; even if I were free to marry again tomorrow, I should not find anyone to take her place. Then he comforted himself with the conviction that his wife was innocent; that point of view relieved him of the necessity of showing strength of character and suited him far better; how many unjustly slandered wives has one not seen!

"But look here!" he cried suddenly, pacing about with a convulsive step. "Am I to suffer as if I were a nobody, a barefoot beggar, that she mocks me with her lover? Is all Verrières to be allowed to make a laughingstock of my softness? What didn't they have to say about Charmier (this was a husband notoriously deceived in that locality)? When his name comes up, isn't there a smile on everyone's lips? He is a good lawyer, but who ever mentions his oratorical talent? 'Ah, Charmier!' they say, 'Bernard's Charmier,' designating him thus by the name of the man who is responsible for his disgrace."

"Thank heaven," Monsieur de Rênal said at other times, "I have no daughter, and the manner in which I am going to punish the mother will in no way prejudice my children's future; I can catch this little peasant with my wife and kill them both; in this case the tragic aspect of the affair will perhaps overshadow the ridiculous." That notion appealed to him; he worked it out in every detail. "The penal code is on my side, and no matter what happens, our congregation and my friends on the jury will save me." He examined his hunting knife, which was well sharpened; but the thought of blood frightened him.

"I can give this insolent tutor a sound thrashing and drive him out of my house; but then what an uproar in Verrières, and even throughout the department! An aristocratic man who keeps up his social position as I do is detested by the common folk. I'll see myself in those beastly Paris newspapers. Oh, my God, what a catastrophe! To see the ancient name of Rênal sunk in the mire of ridicule! . . . If I ever travel, I'll have to change my name. What! Leave off this name which is my pride and my strength? That would be the last straw.

"If I do not kill my wife, and if I throw her out in disgrace, she has her aunt in Besançon who will give her her entire fortune, right into her hands. My wife will go to live in Paris with Julien; it will be known in Verrières and I'll still be taken for a fool." At this juncture the wretched man perceived by the fading of the lamplight that day was beginning to break. He went to the garden for a breath of fresh air. At that moment he had almost resolved not to make any overt gesture, particularly because of his conviction that a scandal would fill his friends in Verrières with joy.

His walk in the garden quieted him somewhat. "No," he exclaimed, "I will most certainly not deprive myself of my wife, she is too useful to me." He imagined with horror what his home would be without his wife; his only relative was the Marquise de R . . . , ancient, half-witted and malicious.

One very intelligent idea came to him, but its execution required strength of character far superior to the little the poor man possessed. If I keep my wife, he thought, I know that someday when she irritates me I will reproach her with her sin. She is proud, we will have a quarrel, and all this will happen before she has inherited her aunt's fortune. Then how they'll jeer at me! My wife loves her children, the money will all go to them in the end. But I shall be the laughingstock of Verrières. "What!" they'll say, "couldn't he even punish his own wife!" Wouldn't it be better to keep my suspicions to myself and not verify anything? That way I tie my hands, I can never reproach her with anything later on.

An instant later Monsieur de Rênal, once more assailed by wounded vanity, recalled minutely all the circumstances described at the billiard tables of the Casino or the Cercle Noble in Verrières when some good story-teller interrupted the game to make jokes at the expense of a cuckold husband. How cruel these witticisms sounded to him at this moment!

God, if only my wife were dead! Then I should be impervious to ridicule. If I were only a widower! I would go to Paris and spend six months mingling with the best social circles. After this brief access of happiness brought by the notion of being a widower, his imagination returned to methods of ascertaining the truth. If at midnight, after everyone had gone to bed, he should sprinkle a light film of sawdust in front of Julien's door, the next morning at daybreak he would see footprints.

"But that's no good," he cried out suddenly in anger. "That hussy Elisa would see it, and pretty soon everybody in the house would know that I'm jealous."

In another tale told at the Casino, a husband had made sure of his misfortune by fastening a hair with a bit of wax like a seal across his wife's door and her lover's.

After so many hours of uncertainty, this means of clarifying his position seemed to him decidedly the best, and he was thinking of employing it when, at a turn in the path, he met the woman whom he had been wishing to see dead.

She was returning from the village. She had been to hear Mass at the Vergy church. A tradition completely unsubstantiated to the coldly philosophical view, but one in which she firmly believed, claimed that the small church in use today was once the chapel of the lord of Vergy's château. This idea had obsessed Madame de Rênal all during the time which she had intended to spend praying in that church. She kept imagining, over and over, her husband killing Julien, as if by accident while out hunting, and then in the evening forcing her to eat his heart.

My whole destiny, she thought, depends upon what he is going to think when he hears what I have to say. After this crucial quarter hour it may be that I shall never have another opportunity to speak to him. He is not a wise person, guided by reason. If he were, I could foresee, by the light of my own feeble reason, what he will say or do. He will be the one to determine our common fate, he has the authority. But the outcome depends upon my ingenuity, upon the art of influencing the reactions of this erratic creature whom anger blinds, making him incapable of seeing even half clearly. Dear God, I need cunning, coolness! Where am I to get them?

She recovered her composure as if by magic upon entering the garden and seeing her husband from a distance. His disordered hair and clothes proclaimed that he had not slept.

She handed him a letter which had been opened but replaced in its envelope. Without opening it, he stared at his wife with frantic eyes.

"Here is an abominable thing," she said, "that an unpleasant-looking man who claimed that he knew you and owed you a debt of gratitude handed to me as I was passing the notary's garden. I have one thing to demand of you, and that is that you send this Monsieur Julien back to his parents, and without delay." Madame de Rênal hastened to utter this phrase, a little before the right time, perhaps, in order to be rid of the appalling prospect of having to say it.

She was overwhelmed with joy at sight of the joy she gave her husband. From the intentness of the stare he fixed upon her she realized that Julien had guessed accurately. Rather than being distressed by this very real calamity: What intuition! she thought. What perfect subtlety! And in a young man still quite without experience. What may he not achieve later on? Alas, then his success will make him forget me.

This little impulse of admiration for the man she adored relieved her entirely of her apprehension.

She congratulated herself upon her artifice. I was not unworthy of Julien, she thought with a soft intimate pleasure.

Without uttering a word, for fear of compromising himself, Monsieur de Rênal studied the second anonymous letter composed, if the reader remembers, of printed words glued to a blue-tinted paper. They're making game of me in every possible way, Monsieur de Rênal thought, overcome by fatigue.

Again new insults to examine, and always because of my wife! He was about to heap her with the most offensive epithets; the prospect of the Besançon inheritance was barely able to restrain him. Consumed by a need to expend his anger on something, he crumpled the paper of the second anonymous letter and began to walk with great strides, feeling that he must get away from his wife. A few moments later he returned to her in a calmer frame of mind.

"The only thing to do is take a firm stand and dismiss Julien," she said to him at once. "After all, he's only a laborer's son. You can give him a few écus as compensation, and besides he is intelligent and will easily find a new post: with Monsieur Valenod, for instance, or the subprefect de Maugiron, both of them have children. So you won't be doing him any injury . . ."

"There you go talking like the fool you are," Monsieur de Rênal cried in a terrible voice. "What good sense can one expect of a woman? You never pay any attention to what is reasonable; how could you know anything? Your heedlessness, your laziness allow you only enough energy for chasing butterflies, you feeble creatures; it's our misfortune that we have to have you in our families! . . ."

Madame de Rênal let him have his say, which he did at great length; he talked out his anger, as the local phrase goes.

"Monsieur," she answered him at last, "I speak as a woman whose most precious possession, her honor, has been outraged."

Madame de Rênal maintained an unalterable coolness throughout this disagreeable conversation upon which depended the possibility of continuing to live beneath the same roof as Julien. She searched for considerations most likely to influence her husband's blind anger. She had been unmoved by all the offensive remarks he had addressed to her, she did not listen to them, she was thinking of Julien. Will he be pleased with me?

"This young peasant whom we've showered with privileges and even with gifts may be innocent," she said at length, "but just the same he is the cause of the first insult I have ever received. . . . Monsieur, when I read this vile paper I promised myself that either he or I should leave your house!"

"Do you want to make a scandal that will disgrace me and you too? You'll be doing a favor for a good many people in Verrières."

"That's true, most people do envy the prosperity your wise administration has brought to you, your family and the town . . . Well, then, I am going to persuade Julien to ask you for a month's leave to go to the mountains and visit that woodcutter—a suitable friend for a young laborer."

"You are not to do anything," Monsieur de Rênal returned, quietly enough. "Above everything else, I require that you do not speak to him. You would antagonize him and stir up trouble between him and me, you know what a touchy young fellow he is."

"The man has no tact whatever," Madame de Rênal said. "He may be intelligent, you know more about that, but underneath he's nothing but a real peasant. For my part, I haven't had a good opinion of him since he refused to marry Elisa, a wealthy match for him; and all because he claimed that sometimes she visits Monsieur Valenod in secret."

"Oh," Monsieur de Rênal said, raising an eyebrow in an exaggerated manner. "What? Julien told you that?"

"No, not exactly; he always talked to me about the vocation he has for the holy ministry; but believe me, the most urgent vocation for these common people is to get food. He made it plain enough that he wasn't ignorant of those secret visits."

"And I, I was ignorant of them!" Monsieur de Rênal shouted, recovering all his fury and heavily emphasizing his words. "Things go on in my house that I know nothing about . . . What! There was something between Elisa and Valenod?"

"Mercy, that's ancient history, my dear," Madame de Rênal said, laughing, "and very likely there was nothing wrong with it. That was in the days when your good friend Valenod wouldn't have minded letting people in Verrières think that he and I were having a little love affair—quite platonic, of course."

"I had that idea once!" Monsieur de Rênal cried, slapping his forehead in a frenzy and progressing from discovery to discovery. "And you didn't say anything about it to me?"

"Start a quarrel between two friends over a little fit of vanity on our dear director's part? Show me the society woman who hasn't received a few extremely sprightly, not to say amorous, letters from him."

"Has he written to you?"

"He writes a great deal."

"Show me his letters this instant, I order you!" And Monsieur de Rênal grew fully six feet taller.

"I shall do nothing of the sort," she answered with a gentleness that amounted almost to indifference. "I'll show them to you someday when you're in a more rational mood."

"This very instant, damn it!" Monsieur de Rênal shouted, drunk with rage and yet happier than he had been for twelve hours.

"Will you swear to me," Madame de Rênal said very gravely, "that you will never have a quarrel with the poorhouse director over those letters?"

"Quarrel or no quarrel, I can take the foundlings away from him; but," he added furiously, "I want those letters right now. Where are they?"

"In a drawer of my desk, but I am certainly not going to give you the key to it."

"I can break it open," he cried, hurrying toward his wife's room. He actually did break open, with an iron poker, a valuable dark mahogany secretary from Paris which he was in the habit of rubbing with his coattail when he thought he noticed a mark on it.

Madame de Rênal had gone running up the hundred and twenty steps to the dovecote; she tied the corner of a white handkerchief to one of the iron bars at the small window. She was the happiest of women. Tears in her eyes, she gazed out toward the great woods on the mountainside. From beneath one of those clustered beech trees, she thought, Julien undoubtedly sees this joyful signal. For a long time she strained her ears, then she cried out bitterly against the monotonous chant of crickets and the singing of birds. Without these intervening sounds, a cry of joy rising from the great rocks might reach this far. Her hungry eyes searched that vast slope of foliage, dark green, unbroken, like a meadow made of treetops. Why doesn't he think of inventing some signal, she thought with the utmost tenderness, to let me know that his happiness is as great as mine? She did not leave the dovecote until she became afraid that her husband might come there in search of her.

She found him in a fury. He was perusing Monsieur Valenod's soothing phrases, which had probably never been read with so much emotion.

Seizing a moment when her husband's exclamations allowed her a possibility of making herself heard:

"I still think my idea was right," Madame de Rênal said. "It would be best for Julien to take a little trip. Whatever talent he may have for Latin, he's nothing but a peasant, after all, and often coarse and lacking in tact; every day, under the impression that he's being polite, he pays me exaggerated and tasteless compliments which he must learn by heart out of some novel . . ."

"He never reads them," Monsieur de Rênal said sharply, "of that I'm certain. Do you think I'm a blind master who doesn't know what goes on in his home?"

"Well, if he doesn't read these ridiculous compliments anywhere, then he makes them up, and that's even worse. He may have spoken about me in that manner in Verrières . . . for that matter, without going so far," Madame de Rênal said with the air of having made a discovery, "he may have talked like that in front of Elisa, which is practically the same as if he had talked in front of Monsieur Valenod."

"Hah!" Monsieur de Rênal shouted, shaking the table and, indeed, the whole room with one of the mightiest blows ever given by any fist, "the printed letter and Valenod's letters are written on the same paper."

At last! Madame de Rênal thought; she seemed appalled by this discovery, and without courage to add a single word, went and sat down at a distance from him, on the couch at the far end of the drawing-room.

From that moment, the battle was won; she had all she could do to prevent Monsieur de Rênal from going to have words with the supposed author of the anonymous letter.

"Why can't you see that to make a scene with Monsieur Valenod without sufficient proof would be the most awful blunder? You are envied, Monsieur, and what is to blame for that? Your talents: your wise administration, your good taste in architecture, the dowry I brought you and, above all, the inheritance we can expect from my good aunt, a heritage whose size they greatly exaggerate: these are the things that have made you the most important man in Verrières."

"You're forgetting good birth," Monsieur de Rênal said, smiling a little.

"You're one of the most distinguished men of the province," Madame de Rênal went on hastily. "If the king were free to do justice to good birth, you would undoubtedly have a place in the Chamber of Peers, and all the rest. And in a magnificent position like that, you want to give envious tongues food for gossip?

"If these letters you have just unearthed should prove to you that I responded to Monsieur Valenod's love, you ought to kill me, I should deserve it a hundred times over, but not to show him your anger. Remember that all your neighbors are only waiting for a chance to be revenged for your superiority."

"I don't believe you have either respect or friendship for me," Monsieur de Rênal cried with all the bitterness aroused by an unpleasant reminder. "So I'm not a peer!"

"I think, my friend," Madame de Rênal returned, smiling, "that I am going to be richer than you are, that I have been your companion for twelve years and that by these tokens I ought to have a voice in our affairs, especially this one today. If you prefer a Monsieur Julien to me," she added with thinly disguised malice, "I'm prepared to go and spend a winter with my aunt."

This last phrase was spoken *happily*. There was in it the firmness that seeks to cloak itself with courtesy; it convinced Monsieur de Rênal. But, obedient to provincial habit, he continued to talk for some time, reviewing all the arguments; his wife let him talk, there was still an angry note in his speech. At length two hours of ineffectual chatter exhausted the forces of a man who had suffered all night long from excessive anger. He determined upon the line of conduct he intended to follow toward Monsieur Valenod, Julien and even Elisa.

Once or twice during this great scene Madame de Rênal was upon the point of feeling some sympathy for the quite genuine distress of this man who for twelve years had been her husband. But true passions are egotistical. In addition, she was momentarily expecting an admission of the anonymous letter he had received the day before, and that admission did not come. Not knowing what ideas might have been suggested to the man upon whom her future circumstances depended, Madame de Rênal could not feel entirely secure. For in the provinces the husbands control public opinion. A husband who complains of his wife covers himself with ridicule, a consideration which daily becomes less dangerous in France; but his wife, if he does not give her money, is reduced to the level of a houseworker at fifteen sous a day, and even so, virtuous people hesitate to employ her.

A concubine in a harem may deeply love the sultan; he is omnipotent, she has no hope of stealing his authority from him by a series of little artifices. The master's revenge is terrible, bloody, but military and generous: a dagger stroke settles the whole matter. A nineteenth-century husband kills his wife with public disgrace, by closing all drawing-rooms to her.

Consciousness of danger was sharply reawakened in Madame de Rênal upon her return to her room; she was shocked by the disorder in which she found it. The locks of all her pretty little boxes had been broken open; several of the floor boards had been torn up. He would have had no pity for me! she thought. To have ruined in this way the colored parquet flooring he loves so much; when one of the children comes in here with damp feet he turns red with anger. And there it is, spoiled forever! The sight of this violence speedily dispelled the last remnants of her self-reproach for too easy a victory.

Shortly before the dinner bell Julien returned with the children.

Over dessert, when the servants had withdrawn, Madame de Rênal said very distantly:

"You informed me that you wished to go and spend a fortnight in Verrières. Monsieur de Rênal is willing to let you have a leave of absence. You may go whenever it suits you. But in order that the children shall not lose time, their themes will be sent you every day for you to correct."

"I shall certainly not let you have more than a week," Monsieur de Rênal added in a sharp tone.

Julien saw in his face the distress of a man profoundly troubled.

"He hasn't yet settled on the course he should take," he said to his mistress during the instant they had alone in the drawing-room.

Madame de Rênal hastily recounted to him all that she had done since morning. "The details can wait until tonight," she added, laughing.

The perversity of women! Julien thought. How delightedly, how instinctively they turn to deceit.

"You seem to me to be both illuminated and blinded by your love," he said to her with some coolness; "today your behavior has been admirable, but is it discreet to try to meet tonight? This house is full of enemies; think how passionately Elisa hates me."

"Her hatred has a strong resemblance to the passionate indifference you seem to have for me."

"Even indifferent, I owe it to you to save you from the danger I have got you into. If Monsieur de Rênal just happened to speak to Elisa, she could tell him everything in one word. What is to prevent him from hiding near my room, well armed . . . ?"

"What, not even courage!" Madame de Rênal said with all the arrogance of noble birth.

"I shall never lower myself to discussing my courage," Julien said frigidly, "that is vulgar. Let the world judge by the facts. But," he added, taking her hand, "you have no idea how much I care for you, and what joy it will give me to be able to take leave of you before this cruel absence."

CHAPTER 21
Social Customs in 1830

BARELY arrived in Verrières, Julien began to reproach himself for his injustice toward Madame de Rênal. I would have scorned her as a silly spineless creature if, through weakness, she had failed in her scene with Monsieur de Rênal! She acquitted herself like a diplomat, and I sympathize with the vanquished, who is my enemy. It's the middle-class pettiness in me: my vanity is offended, because Monsieur de Rênal is a man, one of that vast and illustrious corporation to which I have the honor of belonging! I'm nothing but a fool.

Monsieur de Rênal had instructed Julien to stay at the Rênal town house. No one had any suspicion of what had happened. The third day after his arrival, Julien saw no less a personage than the subprefect, Monsieur de Maugiron, come up to his room. It was only after two long hours of aimless talk and lengthy jeremiads on man's wickedness, the lack of probity in men charged with the administration of public funds, the perils of poor France and so on and so forth, that Julien at last glimpsed the purpose of the visit. They were already upon the staircase landing, and the poor, half-disgraced tutor was escorting to the door, with suitable respect, the future prefect of some fortunate department, when that gentleman was pleased to show an interest in Julien's circumstances, to praise his moderation in selfish concerns, and so on at great length. Finally Monsieur de Maugiron, taking him into his arms in the most paternal manner, suggested that he leave Monsieur de Rênal and enter the home of an official who had children worth educating and who, like King Philippe, thanked heaven not so much for having given them to him as for having seen to it that they were born in the vicinity of Monsieur Julien. Their tutor would enjoy a salary of eight hundred francs payable not monthly—which was ignoble, Monsieur de Maugiron said—but quarterly, and always in advance.

Now it was the turn of Julien who, for the past hour and a half, had been awaiting, with boredom, his chance to speak. His reply was perfect, and above all long, like a bishop's mandate; it let everything be understood and yet said nothing definitely. In it could be found at once respect for Monsieur de Rênal, veneration for Verrières' populace and gratitude for the illustrious subprefect. The said subprefect, astonished at finding someone more hypocritical than himself, tried in vain to extort something in the nature of a precise answer. Julien, enchanted, seized the opportunity for practice and repeated his response in other words. Never has any minister, endeavoring to monopolize the last moments of a meeting when the Chamber shows signs of coming to life, said less in more words. Scarcely had Monsieur de Maugiron left when Julien began to laugh uncontrollably. By way of profiting by his hypocritical artistry he wrote a nine-page letter to Monsieur de Rênal, in which he recounted everything that had been said to him and humbly asked for advice. The sneak, he didn't even tell me the name of the person the offer comes from! It must be Monsieur Valenod, seeing my exile in Verrières as the effect of his anonymous letter.

His dispatch sent off, Julien, as happy as a hunter who, at six o'clock of a fine autumn morning, comes suddenly upon a plain abounding with game, set out to go and ask Monsieur Chélan for his advice. But before he reached the good curé's house, heaven, intent upon preparing fresh joys for him, caused his path to cross that of Monsieur Valenod, from whom he did not conceal the fact that his heart was broken; a poor young fellow like himself should devote himself utterly to the vocation which heaven had planted in his heart, but vocation was not everything in this base world. In order to cultivate the Lord's vineyard properly and not be completely unworthy of all his learned fellow laborers, he needed instruction; he needed to spend two very costly years at the Besançon seminary; it was, therefore, indispensable that he save money, which was much more easily done on a salary of eight hundred francs, paid quarterly, than on six hundred which one ate up from month to month. On the other hand, did it not seem that heaven, by placing him with the young Rênals and particularly by inspiring in him an unusual fondness for them, was indicating that it was not time for him to abandon that course of education for another . . . ?

Julien achieved such a degree of perfection in this sort of eloquence, which has replaced the Empire's swiftness of action, that he ended by boring himself with the sound of his words.

Returning to the house, he found one of Monsieur Valenod's footmen, in full regalia, who was searching the town for him with an invitation to dinner for that very evening.

Julien had never been to the man's home; only a few days before he had been thinking only of how to give him a sound thrashing without getting himself embroiled with the police.

Nevertheless, obedient to Madame de Rênal's instructions, he was obliged to attend several dinners of the same sort; Julien was the fashion; he was forgiven for his guard of honor uniform—or, rather, that indiscretion was the true cause of his success. Soon the only matter of absorbing interest in Verrières was to see who would triumph in the struggle for possession of the learned young man, Monsieur de Rênal or the director of the poorhouse. In a word, he was well on the way toward restoring his reputation when, one morning, he was greatly surprised at being awakened by two hands laid over his eyes.

It was Madame de Rênal, who had made a trip to town and who, running up the stairs four at a time and leaving her children absorbed with a favorite rabbit which they had brought along, had reached Julien's room an instant before them. The moment was delightful, but very short; Madame de Rênal had vanished by the time the children arrived with the rabbit, which they wanted to show to their friend. Julien welcomed them all, even the rabbit. To him it was like being reunited with his family; he felt that he loved these children, that he took pleasure in chattering with them. He was amazed by the gentleness of their voices, the simplicity and dignity of their behavior; he had to wash his imagination clean of all the vulgar mannerisms, all the disagreeable thoughts in the midst of which he had been living in Verrières. Always the fear of missing something, always luxury and poverty at one another's throats. The people at whose homes he dined gave utterance, over the roast, to confidences humiliating to themselves and nauseating to their listeners.

"You have every reason to be proud, you aristocrats," he said to

Madame de Rênal. And he told her about all the dinners to which he had been subjected.

"Why, you're the fashion!" she laughed delightedly.

Luncheon was a pleasant time. The children's presence, although it might seem an obstacle, actually increased their shared happiness. These poor boys did not know how to express their joy at seeing Julien again. The servants had not failed to tell them that he had been offered two hundred francs a year more to "educate" the young Valenods.

In the midst of luncheon, Stanislaus-Xavier, still pale from his severe illness, suddenly asked his mother how much his silver place setting and the goblet from which he was drinking were worth.

"Why do you want to know?"

"I want to sell them and give the money to Monsieur Julien, so that he won't be *sold* for staying with us."

Julien embraced him, tears in his eyes. His mother wept outright while Julien, taking Stanislaus up on his knees, explained to him that he should not use the word *sold* which, used in that sense, was a servant's expression. Seeing the pleasure he was giving Madame de Rênal, he tried to explain further, with picturesque examples which amused the children, what it was to be tricked in that sense.

"I understand," Stanislaus said, "it's like the crow who was silly and dropped his cheese and the fox picked it up and he was a flatterer."

Madame de Rênal, beside herself with happiness, covered her children with kisses, which she could not possibly do without leaning a little upon Julien.

Suddenly the door opened; it was Monsieur de Rênal. His stern and resentful face contrasted strangely with the gentle happiness which his presence dissipated. Madame de Rênal paled; she felt that she was in no state of mind to deny anything. Julien took command and, talking loudly, began to tell the mayor the tale of the silver goblet which Stanislaus wanted to sell. He was sure that the story would not be well received. At first Monsieur de Rênal frowned simply out of habit at the mention of money. "That subject," he said, "always comes as a preface to some demand upon my purse."

But in this case there was more at stake than money; there was the intensification of his suspicions. The air of happiness that animated his family in his absence was not designed to reassure a man whose dominant characteristic was such sensitive vanity. As his wife was praising the graceful and intelligent manner in which Julien presented new ideas to his students: Yes, yes, I know, he's making me seem detestable to my children! It's very easy for him to be a hundred times pleasanter to them than I who am, after all, the master. In these times the tendency is all toward throwing odium upon *legitimate* authority.

Madame de Rênal wasted no time analyzing the reception her husband gave her. She had just glimpsed the possibility of spending twelve hours with Julien. She had a score of errands to do in town, and declared that she absolutely insisted upon going to the cabaret for dinner; no matter what her husband could say or do she clung to her idea. The children were enchanted merely by the word cabaret, which modern prudery utters with so much pleasure.

Monsieur de Rênal left his wife in the first shop she entered, to go and pay a few visits. He rejoined her more morose than ever; he was convinced that the whole town was talking of nothing but himself and Julien. As a matter of fact, no one had yet allowed him even to suspect the offensive side of the public comments. All that had been repeated to the mayor dealt exclusively with the question of whether Julien would remain with him at six hundred francs or accept the eight hundred offered by the poorhouse director.

Never has vanity, in conflict with all the bitterest and most sordid elements of avarice, placed a man in a more pitiful state than that in which Monsieur de Rênal found himself on entering the cabaret. Never, on the other hand, had his children been gayer and more joyous. The contrast added the finishing touch to his irritation.

"I am an unwelcome addition to my own family, as far as I can see!" he said as he joined them, in a tone which he tried to make impressive.

For an answer, his wife took him to one side and explained to him the necessity for dismissing Julien. The hours of happiness that she had just lived through had restored to her the ease and assurance necessary for following the course of action she had been meditating for the past fortnight. What completed the mayor's thorough annoyance was the knowledge that the townsfolk joked publicly about his fondness for cash. Monsieur Valenod was as generous as a thief, and he himself had responded in a manner more prudent than brilliant in the last five or six collections for the Brotherhood of Saint Joseph, the Congregation of the Blessed Virgin, the Congregation of the Holy Sacrament and all the rest.

CHAPTER 22
Sorrows of an Official

IMMEDIATELY after dinner the family left for Vergy again; but early the next morning Julien saw them return to Verrières.

One thing was astonishing to him: the solitary weeks spent in Verrières, in Monsieur de Rênal's house, had been for him a time of happiness. He had experienced disgust and melancholy impulses only at the dinners that had been given him; in this deserted house, could he not read, write, reflect without being disturbed? He was not constantly being diverted from his brilliant daydreams by the bitter necessity of studying the activities of a mean spirit in order to delude it once more by some contrivance or by hypocritical speech.

Can happiness be so close within my reach . . . ? The expense of such a life is small; I could take my choice of marrying Elisa or becoming Fouqué's partner . . . But the traveler who has just climbed a steep mountainside sits down at the summit and finds complete pleasure in resting. Would he be happy if he were forced to rest forever?

Madame de Rênal's mind had turned to a disastrous train of thought. She would without hesitation have sacrificed her life to save her husband's, had she seen him in peril. Hers was one of those noble and romantic natures for which seeing the possibility of a generous action, and yet not performing it, is a source of remorse almost equal to that of having committed a crime. At the same time, there were hideous days when she was unable to rid herself of the thought of the excessive happiness that would be hers if, suddenly widowed, she could marry Julien.

He cared more for her sons than their father did; despite his rigorous justice they adored him. She realized perfectly that marrying Julien must mean leaving Vergy, whose very shadows were so dear to her. She imagined herself living in Paris, continuing to give her sons that education which compelled everyone's admiration. Her children, herself, Julien, all utterly happy.

The curious effect of marriage as the nineteenth century has made it! The tedium of married life inevitably causes the death of love, when love has preceded marriage. And at the same time, as a philosopher might say, among people wealthy enough not to have to work, it quickly brings a profound boredom with all uneventful pleasures. And, among women, it is only the barren spirits that it does not predispose toward love-affairs.

The philosopher's observation excuses Madame de Rênal in my eyes, but she was not excused in Verrières, and without her suspecting it, the whole town was obsessed with the scandal of her love affair. Because of that great scandal life was less boring than usual that autumn.

Autumn and part of the winter passed very quickly. It was time to leave the woods of Vergy. The good people of Verrières began to resent the fact that their anathemas made so little impression upon Monsieur de Rênal. Within less than a week, several sober persons who compensated for their habitual solemnity by their pleasure in fulfilling missions of this sort, had imparted to him the cruelest suspicions, but all through the medium of the most subtle hints.

Monsieur Valenod, who was playing safe, had found a position for Elisa in an aristocratic and highly respected family in which there were five women. Elisa, fearing—so she said—that she might not find a place during the winter, had asked of this family only about two-thirds of the wages she received at the mayor's. Of her own accord the girl had had the excellent idea of going to confess to the old curé Chélan and at the same time to the new one, in order to tell both of them the details of Julien's love affair.

The day after his arrival, before six o'clock in the morning, Monsieur Chélan sent for Julien:

"I am not asking you any questions," he said, "I beg you—order you if necessary—not to tell me anything. I insist that within three days you leave either for the seminary in Besançon or for the home of your friend Fouqué, who is still disposed to offer you a splendid future. I have foreseen everything, arranged everything, but you must go and not return to Verrières for at least a year."

Julien made no reply; he was considering whether or not his honor should feel itself insulted by the pains Monsieur Chélan, who after all was not his father, had taken on his behalf.

"I shall have the honor of seeing you again tomorrow at this same time," he said at length to the curé.

Monsieur Chélan, who counted upon influencing so young a man by sheer will power, said a great deal. Julien, maintaining the most submissive attitude and expression, did not open his mouth.

He escaped at last, and hurried to warn Madame de Rênal, whom he found in despair. Her husband had just been speaking to her with a certain amount of frankness. The natural weakness of his character combined with the prospect of the Besançon inheritance had persuaded him to regard her as completely innocent. He had just informed her of the strange state in which he found public opinion in Verrières. The public was wrong, it had been led astray by jealous tongues, but still, what was to be done?

For a moment Madame de Rênal had the illusion that Julien could accept Monsieur Valenod's offer and remain in Verrières. But she was no longer that artless and timid woman of the year before; her disastrous passion, her remorse had enlightened her. Presently, even while listening to her husband, she came to the painful conclusion that at least a temporary separation had become unavoidable. And away from me, Julien will relapse into those ambitious projects, so natural when one has nothing. And I, dear God, I am rich! so uselessly rich, when it comes to my own happiness. He will forget me. Attractive as he is, he will be loved, he will fall in love. Oh, I am miserable! . . . What have I to complain of? Heaven is just, I hadn't virtue enough to put an end to my sin, it destroyed my judgment. All I had to do was win Elisa over with a little money, nothing would have been easier. I didn't take the trouble to think a moment, the insane fancies of love absorbed all my time. Now I am destroyed.

Julien was struck by one thing in breaking the terrible news of his departure to Madame de Rênal: he met with no selfish objections. She was evidently making an effort not to cry.

"We must be resolute, my dear."

She cut off a lock of his hair.

"I don't know what I shall do," she said, "but if I die, promise me that you will never forget my children. Near to them or far, try to make honest men of them. If there's another revolution, all the aristocrats will be slaughtered, their father will probably leave the country because of that peasant killed on the roof. Watch over the family . . . Give me your hand. Good-by, my dear. These are our last moments. Once this great sacrifice is made, I hope that in public I shall have the courage to think of my reputation."

Julien had expected despair. The simplicity of this farewell touched him.

"No, I won't say good-by to you like this. I will go; they wish it; you wish it, yourself. But three days after I go, I'll come back at night to see you."

Madame de Rênal's whole existence was changed. Julien really loved her, then, since he had of his own accord thought of seeing her again! Her frightful sorrow changed to one of the most acute spasms of joy she had ever experienced. Everything became easy. The certainty of seeing her lover again removed all the anguish from these last moments. From that instant on, Madame de Rênal's bearing, as well as her expression, was noble, firm and perfectly controlled.

Monsieur de Rênal returned shortly after; he was beside himself. At last he spoke to his wife of the anonymous letter received two months before.

"I'd like to take it to the Casino to show everybody that it's the work of that scoundrel Valenod, whom I took from beggary to make him one of the richest citizens in Verrières. I'll shame him with it publicly, and I may even fight him. This is too much!"

Dear God, I might become a widow! Madame de Rênal thought. But almost in the same instant she reflected: If I don't prevent this duel, as I certainly can, I shall be my husband's murderess.

Never had she played upon his conceit so adroitly. Within less than two hours she had made him see, and always by means of arguments he himself brought up, that he must show more friendship than ever to Monsieur Valenod, and even take Elisa back into service. It took courage for Madame de Rênal to make up her mind to see that girl again, the cause of all her misfortunes. But that idea came from Julien.

At length, after having been started on the right path two or three times, Monsieur de Rênal came independently to the financially distressing conclusion that the most disagreeable thing that could happen, from his point of view, would be Julien's remaining as tutor to Monsieur Valenod's children, in the midst of the ferment and excited gossip of all Verrières. Obviously it would be to Julien's advantage to accept the poorhouse director's offer. On the other hand, it would reflect to Monsieur de Rênal's glory if Julien left Verrières to enter the seminary in Besançon or in Dijon. But how was he to be persuaded to do so, and once there, what was he to live on?

Monsieur de Rênal, seeing the imminence of a monetary sacrifice, was more in despair than his wife. In the end she succeeded in transforming the courage required for giving Monsieur Valenod a box on the ears into that required for offering Julien six hundred francs for his year's expenses at the seminary. Monsieur de Rênal, with a thousand curses for the day he had had the disastrous idea of taking a tutor into his home, forgot the anonymous letter.

Madame de Rênal found it somewhat more difficult to persuade Julien that, having saved appearances for her husband by sacrificing the eight hundred francs a year which the poorhouse director publicly offered him, he could without shame accept a present of money.

"But," Julien kept insisting, "I never even for a moment considered accepting that offer. You've made me too accustomed to gracious living, the crudity of those people would kill me."

Bitter necessity, with its iron hand, broke Julien's resistance. His pride offered him the illusion of accepting only as a loan the sum given him by the mayor of Verrières, and of giving him a note providing for repayment with interest in five years.

Madame de Rênal still had several thousand francs hidden in the small mountain grotto.

She offered them to him hesitantly, knowing only too well that she would be refused with anger.

"Are you trying to make the memory of our love revolting?" Julien asked her.

At last Julien left Verrières. Monsieur de Rênal was in excellent humor: at the ultimate moment, when it came to accepting his money, the sacrifice proved too great for Julien. He refused outright. Monsieur de Rênal flung his arms around his neck, tears in his eyes. Julien having asked for a testimonial of satisfactory service, he was unable in his enthusiasm to find phrases magnificent enough to praise the tutor's behavior. Our hero had five louis saved, and intended to ask Fouqué for an equal sum.

He was deeply moved. But by the time he had gone three miles from Verrières, where he was leaving so much love, he was thinking only of the pleasure of seeing a capital, a great military town like Besançon.

During that short, three-day separation, Madame de Rênal was betrayed by one of love's cruelest disappointments. Her life was endurable; between her and the ultimate tragedy lay that last meeting she was to have with Julien. She counted the hours, the minutes that divided her from it. At last, during the night of the third day, she heard far away the signal agreed upon. Having run a thousand dangers, Julien appeared before her.

From that moment she had but one thought: I am seeing him for the last time. Far from responding to her lover's ardor, she was like a corpse, scarcely alive. When she forced herself to tell him that she loved him, it was with an awkward manner that seemed almost to prove the reverse. Nothing could distract her from the cruel consciousness of eternal separation. The distrustful Julien thought for an instant that he had already been forgotten. His resentful comments on this conviction were greeted only by great tears falling in silence, and almost convulsive grippings of his hand.

"But my God, what am I supposed to think!" Julien replied to his mistress' chilly protestations. "You would show a hundred times more genuine fondness to Madame Derville, to a mere acquaintance."

Madame de Rênal, paralyzed, could only answer:

"It's impossible to be any more miserable—I hope I am going to die—I can feel my heart freezing . . ."

These were the longest answers he was able to get from her.

When approaching daylight made his departure inevitable, Madame de Rênal's tears ceased entirely. Without a word, without returning his kisses, she watched him attach the knotted rope to the window. In vain Julien kept repeating:

"Now we're in the position you've been hoping for so long. From now on you will have no cause for remorse. When your children come down with the least little illness you won't see them in their graves."

"I'm sorry you can't give Stanislaus a kiss," she said coldly.

In the end Julien was deeply impressed by the apathetic embraces of that living corpse; he could think of nothing else for several miles. His heart was torn, and until he crossed the mountain, as long as he could see the belfry of the Verrières church, he turned often to look.

CHAPTER 23

A Capital

A<small>T LAST</small>, on a distant mountain, he caught a glimpse of black walls; it was the citadel of Besançon. How different for me, he thought, sighing, if I were arriving in that noble fortress to act as lieutenant in one of the regiments detailed to defend it!

Besançon is not merely one of the most picturesque towns in France, it abounds in spirited and intelligent citizens. But Julien was only a humble peasant and had no way of approaching distinguished persons.

At Fouqué's he had put on laymen's clothes, and it was in this costume that he crossed the drawbridges. Steeped in the history of the siege of 1674, he wanted to see the ramparts and the citadel before burying himself in the seminary. Two or three times he was on the point of getting himself arrested by the guards; he made his way into places that the military authorities close to the public, in order to make twelve or fifteen francs a year selling hay.

The height of the walls, the depth of the moats, the terrifying aspect of the cannons had been absorbing him for some hours when he passed the great café on the boulevard. He stood motionless in admiration; in spite of the word *café*, which he could read in bold letters above the two immense doors, he could not believe his eyes. He made an effort to conquer his timidity; he ventured to go in, and found himself in a room some thirty or forty feet long, with a ceiling at least twenty feet high. That day everything was a miracle to him.

Two billiard games were in progress. The attendants cried out the scores; the players moved quickly about the tables crowded with spectators. Waves of tobacco smoke, blown from every mouth, enveloped them in a blue cloud. The tall stature of these men, their rounded shoulders, their heavy steps, their tremendous sideburns, the long frock coats they wore, all caught Julien's attention. These aristocratic children of old Bisontium spoke only in shouts; they affected the air of redoubtable warriors. Julien, unmoving, marveled; he was contemplating the immensity and the magnificence of a great capital such as Besançon. He certainly did not feel courage enough to ask one of these haughty looking gentlemen who were calling out the billiard scores for a cup of coffee.

But the young lady at the counter had noticed the charming face of this young country boy who, hesitating three feet from the stove with his little bundle under his arm, was studying the fine white plaster bust of the king. This young lady, a robust Franc-Comtoise with a fine figure and dressed in a manner calculated to increase her value to the café, had already said twice, in a low voice intended to be heard only by Julien: "Monsieur! Monsieur!" Julien became aware of great tender blue eyes, and realized that it was to him she was speaking.

He went eagerly over to the counter and the pretty girl, as he would have marched against the enemy. Approaching so beautiful a young lady who had condescended to speak to him: I must tell her the truth, Julien thought, acquiring courage through conquered shyness.

"Madame, I've come to Besançon for the first time in my life; I should like to get a roll and a cup of coffee, and pay for it."

The young lady smiled a little, and then blushed; she dreaded the ironic notice of the billiard players for this attractive young man. He would be frightened away and never return.

"Sit down over here, near me," she said, pointing out a marble-topped table almost completely hidden by the huge mahogany counter that thrust out into the room.

She leaned over the counter, which gave her an opportunity to display a superb figure. Julien observed it; all his ideas changed. She placed before him a cup, sugar and a small roll. She hesitated over calling a waiter for coffee, realizing that upon the waiter's arrival her private talk with Julien would end.

Julien, pensive, was comparing this blond and vivacious beauty with certain memories that frequently disturbed him. The thought of the passion of which he had been the object removed almost all of his shyness. The pretty young lady had only a moment; she read Julien's eyes.

"All this pipe smoke makes you cough. Come and have breakfast tomorrow morning before eight; I'm almost alone then."

"What is your name?" Julien asked, with the caressing smile of timidity reassured.

"Amanda Binet."

"Would you let me send you, in about an hour, a little package the size of this one?"

The beautiful Amanda reflected a moment. "I am watched: what you are asking might compromise me; still, I'll write my address on a card that you can attach to your package. Send it to me openly."

"My name is Julien Sorel," the young man said. "I have no relatives or acquaintances in Besançon."

"Oh, I see!" she said happily. "You've come to the law school?"

"Unfortunately, no," Julien answered. "They're sending me to the seminary."

The most complete disappointment clouded Amanda's features; she called a waiter: now she had courage. The waiter poured Julien's coffee without looking at him.

Amanda was receiving money at the counter; Julien was proud of having dared to speak: there was a quarrel going on at one of the billiard tables. The shouts and contradictions of the players, reverberating in that vast room, made an uproar that appalled Julien. Amanda was thoughtful, her eyes lowered.

"If you like, mademoiselle," he said abruptly and with assurance, "I'll say that I am your cousin."

The suggestion of authority pleased Amanda. This is no insignificant young man, she thought. She said very quickly, not looking at him, for her eye was engaged in watching to see if anyone came near the counter:

"I come from Genlis, near Dijon; say that you're from Genlis, too, and my mother's cousin."

"I surely will."

"Every Thursday, in summer, the seminarists pass by the café here at five o'clock."

"If you're thinking of me, have a bunch of violets in your hand when I pass."

Amanda looked at him with an astonished air; this look changed Julien's courage to boldness; he blushed deeply, however, as he said:

"I feel that I love you with the most violent love."

"Speak lower, then," she said in a frightened manner.

It occurred to Julien to recall some phrases from an odd volume of the *Nouvelle Héloïse* which he had found at Vergy. His memory served him well: for ten minutes he recited *Nouvelle Héloïse* to Mademoiselle Amanda, who was enraptured; he was congratulating himself upon his gallantry when suddenly the lovely Franc-Comtoise assumed a frigid air. One of her lovers had appeared at the door of the café.

He strode to the counter, whistling and swaggering; he glanced at Julien. Instantly Julien's imagination, forever flying to extremes, was filled with nothing but the thought of a duel. He became quite pale, pushed his cup aside, assumed a look of assurance and stared attentively at his rival. As this rival turned his head while unceremoniously pouring himself out a glass of brandy at the counter, Amanda ordered Julien, with a glance, to lower his eyes. He obeyed, and for the next two minutes sat motionless in his place, pale, resolute and thinking only of what was about to happen; he was really superb at that instant. The rival had been astonished by Julien's glare; having swallowed his glass of brandy at one gulp, he said a word to Amanda, thrust his two hands into the side pockets of his bulky frock coat and strolled over to one of the billiard tables, whistling and glancing at Julien. Julien rose, transported with anger; but he did not know how to go about being insolent. He laid down his little bundle and, with the most swaggering air he could manage, stalked toward the billiard table.

In vain prudence insisted: But after a duel on first arrival in Besançon, the ecclesiastical career is finished.

"No matter, it shan't be said that I overlooked an insult."

Amanda recognized his courage; it made an attractive contrast with the ingenuousness of his manner; at that instant she preferred him to the fine young man in the frock coat. She rose and, pretending to be completely absorbed in watching someone passing in the street, moved quickly between him and the billiard table.

"Stop glaring at that gentleman that way, he is my brother-in-law."

"What do I care? He stared at me."

"Do you want to make me unhappy? Very likely he did look at you, maybe he'll even come and speak to you. I told him you were a relative of my mother's, and that you had just come from Genlis. He's a native of Franche-Comté himself, and has never been farther than Dôle on the way to Burgundy, so you can say anything you like and not be afraid of anything."

Still Julien hesitated; she added rapidly, her barmaid's imagination supplying her with falsehoods in plenty:

"No doubt he did look at you, but that was when he was asking me who you were; he's the kind of man who is insolent with everybody, he didn't mean to insult you."

Julien's eye followed the so-called brother-in-law; he saw him buy a ticket for the pool game that was being played at the farther of the two tables. Julien heard his coarse voice call out in a threatening tone: "Count me in!" He moved quickly past Mademoiselle Amanda and took a step toward the table. Amanda caught him by the arm:

"Come and pay me first," she said.

That's right, Julien thought; she's afraid I'll leave without paying. Amanda was as disturbed as he was, and quite flushed; she gave him his change as slowly as she could, meanwhile repeating in a low voice:

"Leave the café this instant, or I shan't like you any more; and I do like you very much."

Julien did leave, but reluctantly. Isn't it my duty, he kept asking himself, to go back to that big boor and take my turn at staring and whistling? This uncertainty kept him hanging about for an hour on the boulevard in front of the café; he watched to see if his man came out. As he did not appear, Julien moved away.

He had been in Besançon only for a few hours, and already he had found something to regret. The retired surgeon-major, in spite of his gout, had once given him a few fencing lessons; that was the only skill Julien possessed to vindicate his anger. But this obstacle would not have mattered if only he had known any other way of starting a quarrel than by hitting out with his fist; and, if it came to a fist fight, his rival, a tremendous man, would have beaten him and stretched him out full length.

For a poor devil like me, Julien thought, without protection and without money, there's no great difference between a seminary and a prison; I've got to take off my lay clothes in some inn, and put my black suit back on. If ever I manage to escape from the seminary for a few hours, I can perfectly well go back to see Mademoiselle Amanda, as long as I have these clothes. This reasoning was inviting, but Julien walked on past all the inns, not daring to enter any of them.

At last, as he was repassing the Hôtel des Ambassadeurs, his uneasy eyes met those of a stout woman, still quite young, with vivid coloring and a pleasant merry expression. He approached her and told her his story.

"Why certainly, my nice little priest," the hostess of the Ambassadeurs said, "I'll keep your lay outfit for you, and even have it brushed now and again. In this weather it's bad to leave a wool suit without care." She took a key and led him, herself, to a room, advising him to write a list of what he was leaving.

"Oh, Lord, how nice you look like that, Father Sorel!" the stout woman said when he came down to the kitchen. "I'm going to have them serve you a good dinner; and," she added in a low voice, "it won't cost you but twenty sous, instead of the fifty everybody else pays, for you've got to be careful with your little nest egg."

"I have ten louis," Julien said with a certain amount of pride.

"Oh, Lord!" the hostess said, alarmed, "don't talk so loud; there are plenty of rogues in Besançon. They'll steal it from you in less than no time. Especially don't ever go into the cafés, they're full of wicked people."

"Really!" Julien said, made thoughtful by this statement.

"Don't ever go any place but here, I'll have them make coffee for you. Remember that you will always find a friend here, and a good dinner for twenty sous; that's plain talk, I hope. Go and sit down at the table, I'm going to serve you myself."

"I can't eat," Julien said, "I'm too upset. I am going into the seminary when I leave here."

The good woman would not let him go until she had filled his pockets with provisions. At length Julien set forth toward the terrible place; the hostess, standing in her doorway, pointed out the way.

CHAPTER 24
The Seminary

FROM a distance he saw the gilded iron cross on the door; he approached slowly; his legs seem to be melting beneath him. Here, then, is that hell on earth from which I will not be able to escape! At last he made up his mind to ring. The sound of the bell reëchoed as if in a deserted place. After ten minutes a pallid young man dressed in black came to open the door for him. Julien glanced at him and at once lowered his eyes. This porter had an extraordinary face. The prominent green pupils of his eyes were rounded like those of a cat, the unvarying contours of his eyelids proclaimed the absence of all sympathy; his thin lips drew up into a half circle over protuberant teeth. His features, however, did not so much suggest criminal tendencies as that utter insensibility which inspires youth with far greater terror. The only emotion Julien's rapid glance could discern on that elongated face was a profound contempt for anything one might mention that was not concerned with heaven.

Julien raised his eyes again, and in a voice made unsteady by the beating of his heart, explained that he wished to speak to Monsieur Pirard, the director of the seminary. Without a word, the man in black signed to him to follow. They climbed two flights of a wide staircase with a wooden bannister, the warped steps of which slanted precipitously away from the wall and seemed about to collapse. A small door surmounted by a huge graveyard cross of black-painted wood was opened with difficulty, and the porter ushered him into a low-ceilinged and gloomy room whose whitewashed walls were hung with two great time-blackened pictures. Here Julien was left alone; he was overcome, his heart hammered violently; it would have comforted him if he had dared to cry. A deathly silence reigned throughout the house.

At the end of a quarter hour which seemed a day to him, the sinister-looking porter reappeared upon the threshold of a door at the other end of the room and, without condescending to speak, signed to him to come forward. He entered a room even larger than the first, and very poorly lighted. These walls, too, were whitewashed, but undecorated. Near a small window with yellowed panes, flanked by vases of dusty flowers, he saw a man seated at a table, dressed in a threadbare cassock; he looked angry, and was engaged in picking up, one by one, a mass of little squares of paper that he spread out on his table after having written a few words on each. He did not notice Julien's presence. Julien remained motionless, standing in the center of the room where the porter had left him.

Ten minutes passed in this fashion, the poorly dressed man continuing to write. Julien's emotion and terror were such that he felt himself to be upon the point of collapse. A philosophical observer might have said, and perhaps erroneously: This is the violent effect of ugliness upon a spirit designed to love the beautiful.

The man who was writing raised his head; Julien did not notice this for a moment, and even after he became aware of it he still stood transfixed, as if struck dead by the terrible glance directed at him. His dazed eyes were barely able to make out a long face speckled all over with red spots except on the forehead which stood out in ghastly pallor. Between the red cheeks and white forehead glittered two small black eyes designed to terrify the bravest spirit. The vast expanse of the forehead was outlined by heavy hair, flat and jet black.

"Will you come here, yes or no?" the man said at last, impatiently.

Julien moved closer with an unsteady step and at length, upon the point of falling, and paler than he had ever been in his life, he stopped three feet from the small white wooden table covered with bits of paper.

"Closer," the man said.

Julien took another step, holding out his hand as if seeking to lean upon something.

"Your name?"

"Julien Sorel."

The man in black had half risen and was irritably searching for a letter in his table drawer which opened with a creak. He found it, sat down slowly, and once more stared at Julien in a manner calculated to squeeze out what little life was left in him.

"You have been recommended to me by Monsieur Chélan, who was the best priest in the diocese, a good man if ever there was one, and my friend for the past thirty years."

"Oh, then it's to Monsieur Pirard I have the honor of speaking," Julien said in a faint voice.

"Apparently," the director of the seminary replied, looking at him ill-temperedly.

There was a sudden increase of brilliance in his small eyes, followed by an involuntary twitching of the muscles at the corner of his mouth. It was the face of a tiger tasting in advance the pleasure of devouring its prey.

"I have here three hundred and twenty-one aspirants to the holiest of callings," the Abbé Pirard said at last in a stern, but not malignant tone of voice. "Only seven or eight of them are sent to me by men such as Monsieur Chélan; so you will be ninth among the three hundred and twenty-one. But my protection does not mean favoritism nor weakness, it means redoubled vigilance, redoubled severity toward vice. Go and lock that door."

Julien made an effort and succeeded in walking without falling down. He noticed that a small window near the entrance door looked out over the countryside. He looked at the trees; the sight of them helped him, as if he had seen old friends.

"*Loquerisne linguam latinam?*" (Do you speak Latin?) Abbé Pirard asked as he returned.

"*Ita, pater optime*" (Yes, excellent Father), Julien answered, somewhat restored to himself. Certainly no man in the world had ever seemed less excellent to him than the Abbé Pirard, for the past half hour.

The interview continued in Latin. The expression in the abbé's eyes became milder; Julien recovered some composure. How weak I am, he thought, to let myself be taken in by these outward signs of virtue! This man will be nothing but a cheat, like Monsieur Maslon; and Julien congratulated himself upon having hidden almost all of his money in his boots.

Monsieur Pirard examined Julien in theology and was surprised by the extent of his knowledge. His astonishment grew when he questioned him particularly upon the Holy Scriptures.

"If you had not been recommended to me by a man such as Monsieur Chélan," the Abbé Pirard said, "I should speak to you the vain language of the world to which, it seems, you are too much accustomed. I should tell you that the scholarship you are applying for is the most difficult thing in the world to obtain. But the Abbé Chélan has earned very little by his fifty-six years of apostolic labors if he cannot have the disposition of one scholarship at the seminary."

After these words, the Abbé Pirard advised Julien not to become a member of any society or secret congregation without his consent.

"I give you my word of honor on that," Julien said with the open-hearted sincerity of an honest man.

The director of the seminary smiled for the first time.

"That is an expression we do not use, here," he said. "It is too reminiscent of the vain honor of worldly folk which leads to so many sins, and often even to crimes. You owe me devout obedience by virtue of paragraph seventeen of Pope Pius V's Bull, *Unam Ecclesiam*. I am your ecclesiastical superior. In this house, my dear son, to hear is to obey. How much money have you?"

Now we're getting to the point, Julien thought. This is what was behind that "my dear son."

"Thirty-five francs, father."

"Write down carefully what you do with your money; you will have to account to me for it."

This distressing interview had lasted three hours. Julien summoned the porter.

"Put Julien Sorel in cell number 103," the Abbé Pirard instructed the man.

As a great mark of favor he was assigning Julien a private room.

All the violent reactions which he had experienced in the short time he had been in Besançon had utterly exhausted Julien's strength. He sat down near the window on the cell's one wooden chair, and fell at once into profound sleep. He did not hear the supper bell nor the bell for Benediction; he had been forgotten.

When the first rays of sunlight awakened him the following morning, he found himself lying on the floor.

"YES, MADAME, I AM LEAVING YOU FOREVER."

CHAPTER 25

Procession

W ITH the reader's kind permission, we will give very few clear
and precise details of this period of Julien's life. Not that they
are lacking, quite the contrary; but it may be that what he saw at the
seminary is too black for the temperate colors we have tried to preserve
in these pages. Those of our contemporaries who have suffered certain
things can recall them only with a horror that paralyzes all impulses
of pleasure, even that of reading a story.

In vain Julien made himself act humble and dull-witted, he was
unable to find favor with anyone, he was too different. Still, he
thought, all these professors are very clever, chosen among thousands;
why do they not like my humility? Only one of them seemed to him to
take advantage of his willingness to believe anything and to act as a
universal dupe. This was the Abbé Chas-Bernard, Director of Ceremonies at the cathedral, in which, for the past fifteen years, he had been
allowed to hope for a post as canon; while waiting he taught sacred
eloquence at the seminary. During the time of his blindness, this course
was among those in which Julien habitually excelled.

One evening in the midst of armed drill, Julien was summoned to the
Abbé Pirard, who said to him:

"Tomorrow is the feast of Corpus Domini. The Abbé Chas-Bernard
needs you to help him decorate the cathedral; go and obey."

Monsieur Pirard called him back and added with an air of compassion, "If you want to profit by the opportunity to take a little walk through the town, that's up to you."

"*Incedo per ignes*," Julien answered, indicating that he was watched by unfriendly eyes.

The next day, early in the morning, Julien made his way to the cathedral, his eyes lowered. The sight of the streets and the activity that was beginning to spread through the town did him good. On every side, housefronts were being decorated for the procession. All the time he had spent in the seminary seemed no more than an instant to him. His thoughts went to Vergy, and to that pretty Amanda Binet whom he might meet, for her café was not far away. From a distance he caught sight of the Abbé Chas-Bernard at the door of his beloved cathedral; he was a stout man with a cheerful face and open manner. That day he was triumphant:

"I've been waiting for you, my dear son," he cried as soon as Julien came within sight. "I'm glad to see you. This day's labor will be long and hard, let's fortify ourselves with a first breakfast; we'll have a second one at ten o'clock, during High Mass."

The Abbé Chas had been right in saying that the work would be hard. On the previous day there had been a great funeral service at the cathedral; it had not been possible to make any preparations; in a single morning, therefore, all the Gothic pillars that formed the nave had to be reclothed in a sort of sheath of red damask up to a height of thirty feet. The bishop had sent to Paris for four upholsterers to come by mailcoach, but these gentlemen were unable to attend to everything, and far from making allowances for their Besançon assistants' clumsiness, they redoubled it by making fun of them.

Julien saw that he would be obliged to climb up on a ladder himself; his agility was of good service to him. He undertook to direct the local upholsterers. The Abbé Chas, delighted, watched him leap from ladder to ladder. When all the pillars had been swathed in damask, it was a question of climbing up to place five huge clusters of feathers on the great canopy over the main altar. A crown of wood, lavishly carved and gilded, was supported by eight tall twisted columns of Italian marble. But to reach the center of the canopy, above the tabernacle, one must walk along an ancient wooden cornice, possibly worm-eaten, and forty feet above the floor.

The aspect of this perilous undertaking had extinguished all the gaiety of the Parisian decorators, so brilliant up to that moment; they looked up at it from below, argued a great deal and did not ascend. Julien snatched up the clusters of feathers and ran up the ladder. He arranged them most attractively upon the ornament shaped like a crown in the center of the canopy. As he came down the ladder, the Abbé Chas-Bernard flung his arms about him. "*Optime,*" cried the good priest, "I shall tell Monseigneur about that."

The ten-o'clock breakfast was very gay. Never had the Abbé Chas seen his church look so beautiful.

"My dear disciple," he said to Julien, "my mother used to rent chairs in this ancient basilica, so I was suckled in this great edifice. Robespierre's Terror ruined us; but when I was eight years old I was already serving at private Masses, and they used to give me my meals on Mass days. Nobody could fold a chasuble better than I could, the gold braid never got broken. Since Napoleon reinstated religion, I have had the good fortune to be in charge of everything in this venerable mother-church. Five times a year my eyes see it decked out in such splendor, but never has it been so resplendent, never have the strips of damask been so well adjusted as today, so closely wrapped on the pillars."

As he finished speaking, the quarter hour before twelve sounded, and at once the great bell tolled. It rang out full peal; the sound, so deep and so solemn, stirred Julien. His imagination soared.

The odor of incense, and of rose petals strewn before the Blessed Sacrament by small boys dressed as Saint John, completed his exaltation.

While the procession wound slowly through Besançon, on the most beautiful day in the world, and paused before the gleaming stations which all the authorities had competed in erecting, the church was left in deep silence. A half-darkness, a pleasant coolness pervaded it; it was still haunted by the fragrance of flowers and incense.

The silence, the profound solitude, the coolness of the long nave enhanced the pleasure of Julien's reverie. He had no fear of being disturbed by the Abbé Chas, who by now was busy in another part of the building. His spirit had almost abandoned its mortal envelope, which was walking at a slow pace up and down the north aisle intrusted to his supervision. He was even more at ease for knowing that there was no one in the confessionals except for a few pious women; his eyes looked without seeing.

His abstraction, however, was half interrupted by the sight of two very well-dressed women who were kneeling, one in a confessional and the other quite close to her, beside a chair. He glanced at them without actually noticing them; some impulse, however, whether a vague recollection of his duties, or admiration for the simple and aristocratic bearing of these ladies, reminded him that there was no priest in that confessional. Odd, he thought, that these fine ladies aren't kneeling at one of the stations, if they are devout; or, if they're worldly, in an advantageous spot on some balcony. How becoming that dress is, what grace! He slowed his step, trying to see their faces.

The one who was kneeling in the confessional turned her head a little, hearing the sound of Julien's footsteps in the midst of that vast stillness. Suddenly she cried out and seemed overcome.

Losing her strength, the kneeling lady fell backward; her friend, who was near her, sprang up to help her. At the same time, Julien saw the shoulders of the one who had fallen. A twisted rope of exquisite large pearls, very familiar to him, caught his eye. To his stupefaction, he recognized Madame de Rênal's hair, it was she! The lady who was attempting to support her head and prevent her from falling altogether was Madame Derville. Julien, scarcely knowing what he did, leaped forward; Madame de Rênal's collapse would probably have dragged her friend to the floor if Julien had not supported them. He saw Madame de Rênal's head, the face colorless, drained of all consciousness, drooping against his shoulder. He helped Madame Derville lean that lovely head against the back of a wicker chair; he was on his knees.

Madame Derville turned and recognized him:

"Go away, Monsieur, go away this minute!" she said to him with an accent of the most vehement anger. "Whatever happens, she mustn't see you. The sight of you would really be horrible for her, she was so happy before you came! Your behavior is unspeakable. Go away; leave us, if there is any decency in you."

It was said with so much authority, and Julien was at that moment so weakened, that he moved away. She has always hated me, he reflected, thinking of Madame Derville.

At the same time the nasal chanting of the first priests in the procession resounded in the church; the procession was returning. The Abbé Chas-Bernard called several times to Julien, who at first did not hear: at length he came to the pillar behind which Julien had taken refuge, half dead, and took him by the arm. He wanted to present him to the bishop.

"You're not feeling well, my son," the abbé said, seeing him so pale and almost incapable of walking. "You worked too hard." The abbé gave him his arm. "Come, sit down on the little seat by the font, here, behind me; I'll hide you." They were then beside the great door. "Rest yourself, we still have a good twenty minutes before Monseigneur will arrive. Try to get over it; when he comes past I'll help you up, for I'm strong and hardy in spite of my age."

But when the bishop passed, Julien was shaking so that the Abbé Chas gave up the idea of presenting him.

"Don't be too disappointed," he said, "I'll find another opportunity."

That evening he sent to the seminary chapel ten pounds of wax tapers saved, he said, by Julien's solicitude and the rapidity with which he had seen to it that they were extinguished. Nothing could have been less true. The poor boy had been extinguished himself; he had not had one conscious thought after having seen Madame de Rênal.

CHAPTER 26

Promotion

Julien had still not emerged from the profound abstraction into which the episode in the cathedral had plunged him, when one morning the stern Abbé Pirard sent for him.

"It seems the Abbé Chas-Bernard has written me a favorable account of you. I am quite pleased with your conduct on the whole. You are extremely incautious, even rash, without its being apparent; however, so far your heart seems to be good, I might even say generous: your mind is superior. All in all, I see in you a spark that should not be neglected.

"After fifteen years of labors, I am about to leave this house: my crime is having left the seminarists to their own devices, and having neither protected nor countenanced their secret society. Before I go, I want to do something for you. I am going to appoint you instructor in the Old and New Testaments."

Julien, overwhelmed with gratitude, had the appropriate idea of dropping to his knees and thanking God; but he yielded to a more genuine impulse. He approached the Abbé Pirard and took his hand, which he raised to his lips.

"What's this?" the director cried, looking displeased; but Julien's eyes were even more expressive than his gesture.

The Abbé Pirard stared at him in astonishment, like a man who, over long years, has lost the habit of encountering delicate emotions. This attention penetrated the director's defenses; his voice changed.

"Well, yes, my son, I am fond of you. Heaven knows that it's in spite of my best efforts. I should be just, and have neither hatred nor love for anyone. Your career will be a difficult one. I see something in you that offends the vulgar. Jealousy and slander will pursue you. Wherever Providence sees fit to place you, your associates will never look at you without hating you; and if they pretend to like you it will be in order to betray you the more surely. For that there is only one remedy: have recourse only to God, who has given you that inevitable faculty of making yourself hated as punishment for your presumption; let your own behavior be faultless, that is the only resort I see for you. If you cling to truth with unalterable tenacity, sooner or later your enemies will be confounded."

It had been so long since Julien had heard a friendly voice that he must be pardoned for one weakness: he burst into tears. The Abbé Pirard opened his arms; it was a very comforting moment for both of them.

Julien was wild with joy; this promotion was the first he had secured; the advantages were tremendous. To understand them, one must have been condemned to spend months on end without an instant of privacy, and in immediate contact with companions at least unwelcome, and for the most part intolerable. Their blatant voices alone would have been enough to throw a sensitive organism into disorder. The bursting enthusiasm of these peasants, well fed and well clothed, could not be contained, found expression only when they were shouting at the top of their lungs.

Now Julien dined alone, or almost alone, an hour after the other seminarists. He had a key to the garden and could go to walk there at times when it was deserted.

It was the hunting season. Fouqué was inspired to send a stag and a boar to the seminary in the name of Julien's parents. The dead animals were hung in the passage between the kitchen and the refectory. There all the seminarists came to see them, on the way to dinner. They were objects of great curiosity. The boar, dead as he was, frightened the younger boys; they fingered his tusks. For more than a week they talked of nothing else.

This gift, which classed Julien's family in that division of the social order which must be respected, dealt jealousy a mortal blow. This was a superiority sanctified by wealth. The most distinguished of the seminarists made advances to him, and all but reproached him for not having let them know the extent of his parents' fortune and thus having exposed them to the danger of failing to respect money.

The time for examinations came. The first day, the examiners appointed by the illustrious Grand Vicar de Frilair were highly displeased at having to place first, or at least second, on every list the name of this Julien Sorel, who had been described to them as the Abbé Pirard's favorite. In the seminary, the betting was that, on the general examination list, Julien would hold first place, which entailed the honor of a dinner at the bishop's home. But at the end of one session that had dealt with the Fathers of the Church, an ingenious examiner, having questioned Julien upon Saint Jerome and his passion for Cicero, went on to mention Horace, Virgil and other profane authors. Unknown to his classmates, Julien had memorized a large number of passages from these authors. Carried away by his success, he forgot where he was and, at the repeated requests of the examiner, enthusiastically recited and paraphrased several of Horace's odes. Having let him spend twenty minutes digging a pit for himself, the examiner abruptly changed expression and rebuked him sharply for the time he had wasted on these profane studies and for the useless or criminal notions with which he had filled his head.

"I have been a fool, Monsieur, you are right," Julien said, recognizing the clever stratagem of which he had been the victim.

This trick of the examiner's was considered filthy, even at the seminary, but this did not prevent Monsieur Frilair, that shrewd man whose reports to Paris caused judges, prefects and even general officers of the garrison to tremble, from writing with his powerful hand the number 198 beside Julien's name. He took joy in thus mortifying his enemy, the Jansenist Pirard.

For the past ten years he had been concentrating upon removing him from the directorship of the seminary. The abbé, following on his own account the line of conduct he had prescribed for Julien, was sincere, devout, uncalculating, devoted to his duties. But heaven in its wrath had endowed him with that bilious temperament designed to feel injuries and hatred deeply. No outrage directed against him was lost upon that fiery spirit. A hundred times he would have handed in his resignation, but he believed himself to be useful in the position where Providence had placed him.

At the time of the examinations it had been perhaps two months since he had spoken to Julien, and yet he was ill for a week when, receiving the official announcement of the results, he saw the number 198 written against the name of that student whom he had considered the glory of his institution. The only consolation for this stern character was in concentrating upon Julien all his powers of observation. It was with delight that he found in him neither anger, plans for revenge nor discouragement.

Several weeks later Julien was shaken by the receipt of a letter; it bore the Paris postmark. At last, he thought, Madame de Rênal is remembering her promises. A gentleman who signed himself Paul Sorel, and called himself a relative, was sending him a letter of credit for five hundred francs. The writer added that if Julien continued to make progress in his studies of the sound Latin authors, a like sum would be sent him every year.

It is from her, it is her kindness, Julien thought, touched. She wants to console me; but why not a single word of friendship?

He was mistaken about the letter; Madame de Rênal, under the guidance of her friend Madame Derville, was entirely dedicated to her remorse. In spite of herself she often thought of the strange being who had thrown her whole life into disorder, but she had taken great care not to write to him.

If we spoke the language of the seminary, we might acknowledge a miracle in this present of five hundred francs, and say that it was Monsieur de Frilair himself who was employed by heaven to make this gift to Julien.

Twelve years earlier the Abbé Frilair had arrived in Besançon with the lightest of suitcases which, so the story ran, contained all his worldly possessions. Now he was one of the wealthiest landowners of the department. In the course of his rise to prosperity, he had purchased half of an estate, the other half of which fell to Monsieur de la Mole by inheritance. Hence a great lawsuit between these two gentlemen.

Despite his brilliant social position in Paris and the influence he had at Court, Monsieur le Marquis de la Mole felt it dangerous to carry on a fight, in Besançon, with a grand vicar who had a reputation for making and breaking prefects.

Constantly in correspondence with the Abbé Pirard over a matter in which both of them were passionately interested, the marquis at length came to appreciate the abbé's turn of mind. Little by little, notwithstanding the vast distance between their social positions, their correspondence took on a note of friendship. The Abbé Pirard told the marquis that an effort was being made to force him, by means of indignities, into giving his resignation. In the anger which the infamous trick, as he called it, practiced upon Julien aroused in him, he told the story to the marquis.

Although very wealthy, this great nobleman was by no means grasping. He had never been able to induce the Abbé Pirard to accept even repayment for the postage he spent in the interests of the lawsuit. He seized upon the idea of sending five hundred francs to the abbé's favorite pupil. Monsieur de la Mole went to the trouble of writing the covering letter with his own hand. It made him think of the abbé.

One day Monsieur Pirard received a note requesting him to go without delay, on a most urgent matter, to an inn on the outskirts of Besançon. There he found Monsieur de la Mole's steward.

"Monsieur le Marquis instructed me to bring you his carriage," this man said. "He hopes that after having read this letter you will find it convenient to leave for Paris in four or five days. I am to use the time, meanwhile, inspecting Monsieur le Marquis' estates in Franche-Comté. After that, whenever you tell me that you are ready, we will leave for Paris."

The letter was short:

"My dear sir, rid yourself of all those provincial bickerings, come and breathe a more tranquil air in Paris. I am sending you my carriage, which has orders to wait four days for your decision. I myself shall wait for you in Paris until Tuesday. All I need is your assent, Monsieur, to accept in your name one of the best livings in the neighborhood of Paris. The wealthiest of your future parishoners has never met you but is more devoted to you than you can conceive; he is the Marquis de la Mole."

Without ever having suspected it, the Abbé Pirard loved this seminary, peopled by his enemies, to which for the past fifteen years he had dedicated all his thoughts. Monsieur de la Mole's letter was to him like the arrival of a surgeon intrusted with performing a brutal but necessary operation. His dismissal was inevitable. He arranged with the steward to meet him three days later.

CHAPTER 27
Ambition

THE Marquis de la Mole received the Abbé Pirard without any of a great aristocrat's petty mannerisms, so courteous but so insolent to those who understand them. It would have been a waste of time, and the marquis had enough weighty matters on hand to have no time to waste.

For the past six months he had been intriguing to secure the acceptance both by the king and by the nation of a certain minister who, out of gratitude, would make him a duke.

The marquis had, for many long years, vainly been asking his attorney in Besançon for a clear and precise statement of the lawsuit in Franche-Comté. How was the famous lawyer to explain it to him, if he did not understand it himself?

The small sheet of paper which the abbé handed him explained everything.

"My dear abbé," the marquis said, having compressed into less than five minutes the whole formula of courtesy and interrogation upon personal matters, "my dear abbé, in the midst of my so-called prosperity I lack time to attend seriously to two minor matters which are nevertheless rather important: my family and my business affairs. I go to

147

great lengths in taking care of my family's fortune, I may carry it far; I take care of my pleasures, that's a primary consideration, at least in my opinion," he added, catching a look of astonishment in the Abbé Pirard's eyes. Although a reasonable man, the abbé was astonished at hearing an elderly man speak so frankly of his pleasures.

"No doubt help exists in Paris," the nobleman went on, "but roosting on the top floors; and as soon as I approach a man he takes an apartment on the second floor, his wife starts a salon, and consequently no more work, no more effort except to be or seem to be a man of the world. That's their only interest, once they've got food.

"For my own lawsuits and also for each lawsuit undertaken in my name I have lawyers who work themselves to death; one of them died of consumption just the day before yesterday. But for my affairs in general, will you believe it, Monsieur, three years ago I gave up hoping to find a man who, while writing letters for me, would condescend to give a little serious thought to what he was doing. However, all this is just a preamble.

"I respect you and, I may venture to add, although I am meeting you for the first time, I like you. Would you consent to be my secretary at eight thousand francs a year, or twice that, if you like? I'll gain more than that by it, I assure you; and I'll make it my business to keep your fine parish for you, against the day when we no longer agree."

The abbé refused, but toward the end of the conversation his appreciation of the marquis' genuine dilemma suggested an idea to him.

"Back in my seminary I left a young man who, if I'm not mistaken, is going to be cruelly persecuted. If he were nothing but a simple friar, he would already be *in pace*.

"So far this young man knows only Latin and the Holy Scripture; but it is not impossible that someday he will display great talent either for preaching or for spiritual guidance. I do not know what he will do; but he has the sacred spark, he may go far. I intended to put him in the hands of our bishop, if ever we should get one with something of your way of looking at men and circumstances."

"Where does your young man come from?" the marquis said.

"They say he's the son of a carpenter from our mountains, but I should be more inclined to believe him the illegitimate son of some rich man. I noticed that he received a letter, unsigned or signed with a fictitious name, with a letter of credit for five hundred francs."

"Oh, it's Julien Sorel," the marquis said.

"How do you know his name?" the abbé asked, astonished; and, as he was blushing for the question:

"That's something I won't tell you," the marquis said.

"Well," the abbé resumed, "you might try to make a secretary out of him, he has energy, he's intelligent; in a word, it's worth trying."

"Why not?" the marquis said. "But is he the kind of man to let his palm be greased by the prefect of police or by anyone else, to spy on me? There's my whole objection."

After favorable reassurances from the Abbé Pirard, the marquis took out a thousand-franc note:

"Send this to Julien Sorel for his traveling-money; have him come to me."

"It's easy to see that you live in Paris," the Abbé Pirard said. "You don't realize the tyranny that weighs on us poor provincials, and particularly on priests who are not friends of the Jesuits. They won't be willing to let Julien Sorel go, they will find ways to cover themselves with the most artful excuses, they'll answer that he is ill, that the letters have gone astray in the mail, all that sort of thing."

"One of these days I'll get a letter from the minister to the bishop," the marquis said.

"I forgot one warning," the abbé said: "this young man, although he's of very low birth, has an independent spirit; he will be of no use to you if his pride is injured; you would make him stupid."

"I like that," the marquis said. "I'll make him my son's companion, will that do?"

Sometime later Julien received a letter in a strange handwriting and bearing the Chalon postmark; in it he found a draft on one of Besançon's shopkeepers, and instructions to set out for Paris without delay. The letter was signed with an assumed name, but in opening it Julien had trembled; the leaf of a tree had fallen at his feet; it was the sign he and the Abbé Pirard had agreed upon.

Less than an hour after this, Julien was summoned to the bishop's palace, where he was received with a completely paternal kindness. One of the lesser priests of the palace wrote to the mayor who personally hastened to bring a passport, signed, but with the space for the traveler's name left blank.

Before midnight that evening, Julien was with Fouqué, whose rational mind was more astonished than delighted at the future that seemed to be awaiting his friend.

"It will end up," that liberal elector said, "with a government post for you which will force you into some action that will be vilified in the newspapers. It's through your disgrace that I'll have news of you. Remember, even speaking financially, it's better to earn a hundred louis in an honest timber business where you're the master, than to receive four thousand francs from a government, even if it were King Solomon's."

Julien saw all this merely as the narrow-mindness of a middle-class yokel. He was at last about to appear in the theater of great events. The joy of going to Paris, which he imagined to be populated by a brilliant race, vastly intriguing, vastly hypocritical but as mannerly as the Bishop of Agde, eclipsed all else in his eyes. To his friend he represented himself as having been deprived of his free will by the Abbé Pirard's letter.

He arrived in Verrières the next day at noon, the happiest of men; he was anticipating seeing Madame de Rênal again. He went first to the home of his first protector, the good Abbé Chélan. He met with a stern reception.

"Do you believe that you are under some obligation to me?" Monsieur Chélan said, without returning his greeting. "You are going to have lunch with me, meanwhile someone will go and hire another horse for you and you will leave Verrières *without seeing anyone*."

"To hear is to obey," Julien answered with his seminary expression; and the talk turned to theology and fine Latin phrases.

He mounted his horse and rode a mile, after which, catching sight of a woods and nobody about to see him enter it, he plunged in. At sunset he sent the horse back to the town in care of a passing laborer. Later he came to the house of a peasant who agreed to sell him a ladder and to carry it for him to the small woods that overlooks the Cours de la Fidélité in Verrières.

"This makes me a poor devil of a deserter—or a smuggler," the peasant said, bidding him good-by, "but what's the difference? My ladder is well paid for, and I haven't lived a whole life without getting in trouble once or twice, myself."

The night was very black. At one o'clock in the morning Julien, burdened with his ladder, entered Verrières. He moved as quickly as he could down the bed of mountain stream which cuts through Monsieur de Rênal's magnificent gardens at a depth of six feet, and confined between walls. Julien easily climbed them with his ladder. What sort of welcome will the watchdogs give me? he wondered. Everything depends upon that. The dogs barked and came racing toward him, but he whistled softly and they licked his hands.

Clambering up, then, from terrace to terrace, although all the gates were locked, it was easy for him to reach a spot beneath the window of Madame de Rênal's bedroom which, on the garden side, was no more than eight or ten feet above the ground.

On each shutter was a small heart-shaped opening which Julien knew well. To his great disappointment, these little openings were not illuminated from within by a night light.

Good God! he thought. Tonight, of all times, Madame de Rênal is not in that room. Where can she be sleeping? The family is in Verrières, since I saw the dogs; but in this room without a night light I may find Monsieur de Rênal himself, or some stranger, and then what a scandal!

The most prudent thing would have been to beat a retreat, but this course was abhorrent to Julien. If it's a stranger, I'll run at top speed, leaving my ladder behind; but if it is she, what sort of reception is waiting for me? She has dedicated herself to remorse and to the most extreme piety, there's no doubt of that; but then, she still has some memory of me, since she has just written to me.

That reasoning decided him. With a quaking heart, but nevertheless determined to see her or to perish, he flung some small pebbles up against the shutter; no response. He propped the ladder beside the window and rapped with his hand on the shutter, gently at first, then more loudly. Even as dark as it is, Julien thought, someone could still shoot at me. This thought reduced the insane enterprise to a matter of courage.

That room is not being used tonight, he thought; otherwise whoever was sleeping there would be awake by now. So there's no more need to worry about that; all I have to do is try not to be heard by the people who are sleeping in the other rooms.

He climbed down, set the top of his ladder against one of the shutters, mounted it again and, slipping his hand through the heart-shaped opening, was fortunate in finding quite quickly the wire attached to the window latch. He pulled the wire; it was with inexpressible relief that he found that the shutter was no longer latched and was yielding to his efforts. I must open it little by little, and let her recognize my voice. He pulled the shutter wide enough to admit his head, repeating in a low voice; "It is a friend."

Straining his ears, he assured himself that nothing stirred in the deep silence of the room. But there most certainly was no night light, even half burned out on the mantel; that was a bad sign.

Beware of a shot! He reflected a moment, then, with his finger, made bold to tap on the pane: no response; he rapped more loudly. Even if I have to break the window, I must go through with it. As he was knocking very loudly, he thought he glimpsed in the midst of the utter blackness something like a white shadow crossing the room. Presently there was no more doubt: he did see a shadow which seemed to move forward with the utmost reluctance. Suddenly he saw a cheek pressed against the pane to which he had set his eye.

He shivered and drew back a little. But the night was so black that even at that distance he could not distinguish whether it was Madame de Rênal. He dreaded an involuntary cry of alarm; he heard the dogs prowling and grumbling about the foot of the ladder. "It's I," he repeated somewhat more loudly, "a friend." No response; the white phantom had disappeared. "Please, open the window, I must speak to you, I'm too miserable!" And he knocked as if to shatter the glass.

A small sharp sound was heard; the catch of the window yielded; he pushed up the sash and sprang lightly into the room.

The white phantom moved away; he caught its arms; it was a woman. All his notions of bravery failed him. If it is she, what will she say? His state of mind was indescribable when he realized, from a little cry, that it was Madame de Rênal.

He crushed her in his arms; she was trembling, and had scarcely the strength to push him away.

"What are you doing, you wretched creature?"

Her convulsive voice was barely able to articulate the words. Julien recognized in it the most genuine outrage.

"I'm coming to see you, after fourteen months of cruel separation."

"Go away, leave me this instant. Oh, Monsieur Chélan, why did you forbid me to write to him? I could have prevented this horrible thing!" She pushed at him with really extraordinary force. "I repent of my sin; heaven has had the goodness to open my eyes," she kept repeating in a half strangled voice. "Go away! Go away!"

"After fourteen months of misery I am certainly not going to leave without having talked to you. I want to know everything that you have done. Surely I loved you enough to deserve that much confidence. . . . I want to know everything."

The authoritative tone influenced Madame de Rênal in spite of herself.

Julien, who had been holding her in a passionate embrace and resisting her efforts to free herself, ceased pressing her in his arms. This reassured Madame de Rênal to some extent.

"I'm going to pull up the ladder," he said, "so that it won't betray us if one of the servants has been roused by the noise and makes the rounds."

"Oh, no, don't! Go away, instead," she said with real anger. "What are men to me? It's God who is watching this awful scene you're making, and who will punish me for it. You're cowardly, abusing the feeling I used to have for you, but haven't any longer. Do you hear, Monsieur Julien?"

He was pulling up the ladder very slowly in order to make no sound.

"Is your husband in town?" he asked, not in a spirit of defiance but surrendering to an old habit.

"Do not talk to me that way, if you please, or I shall call my husband. I'm only too guilty already, for not having sent you away no matter what might happen. I pity you," she said, trying to hurt his pride, which she knew to be so sensitive.

Her distant tone, the abrupt breaking of so tender a bond, and one upon which he still counted, goaded Julien's access of love to the point of frenzy.

"What! Is it possible that you really don't love me any more?" he asked with that note of heartbroken sincerity which it is so difficult to hear unmoved.

She did not answer; as for him, he wept bitterly. He almost literally had not enough strength left to speak.

"So I'm completely deserted by the only person who has ever loved me! What is the use of living any longer?" All his courage had left him the moment he no longer had to dread meeting with a man; his heart was drained of everything but love.

He wept for a long time in silence. He took her hand; she made an effort to snatch it back, and yet, after a few almost convulsive movements, she left it in his. The darkness was profound; they were sitting side by side on Madame de Rênal's bed.

What a difference between this and fourteen months ago! Julien thought, and his tears came faster. How surely absence destroys all human feelings!

"Please be good enough to tell me what has happened to you," he said at length, embarrassed by his silence, and in a broken voice.

"Of course," Madame de Rênal said in a harsh voice the tone of which sounded sharp and reproachful to Julien, "my misbehavior was known all over town, after you left. You acted so very indiscreetly! Sometime after that, when I was in despair, that good Monsieur Chélan came to see me. He tried for a long time to get me to confess, but I would not. Then one day it occurred to him to take me to the church in Dijon where I made my first Communion. There, he dared to be the first to speak . . ." Madame de Rênal was interrupted by her tears. "What a shameful moment! I admitted everything. He was so good, good enough not to heap all the weight of his anger on me: he grieved with me. In those days I used to write to you every day, letters I didn't dare send you; I hid them carefully, and whenever I was too unhappy I locked myself in my room and read them over.

"In the end Monsieur Chélan persuaded me to give them to him. Some of them, the more discreetly written ones, had been sent to you; you never answered."

"I swear to you, I never received a single letter from you at the seminary."

"Good God, who can have intercepted them?"

"Imagine my suffering: up to the day I saw you in the cathedral, I didn't know if you were still alive."

"God was merciful to me and let me understand how terribly I had sinned against Him, against my children, against my husband," Madame de Rênal went on. "He has never loved me as I used to believe that you loved me . . ."

Julien flung himself into her arms, quite without intention, but beyond coherent thought. But Madame de Rênal pushed him away and continued fairly steadily:

"My friend Monsieur Chélan, whom I respect, made me understand that in marrying Monsieur de Rênal I had pledged all my affections to him, even the ones I knew nothing about and had never experienced before that disastrous love affair . . . Since the great sacrifice of those letters, which were so dear to me, my life has run on, if not happily, at least more or less peacefully. Don't disturb it again; be a friend to me . . . my best friend." Julien covered her hands with kisses; she felt that he was weeping again. "Don't cry, you hurt me so . . . Now you tell me what you have been doing." Julien was unable to speak. "I want to know what sort of life you led at the seminary," she repeated. "Then you must go."

Without thinking of what he was saying, Julien told of the innumerable intrigues and jealousies he had at first encountered, then of the more tranquil life he had led since having been appointed instructor.

"It was then," he added, "that after a long silence which must have been intended to make me understand what I realize only too well today: that you do not love me any more, and that I've become a matter of indifference to you . . ." Madame de Rênal gripped his hands. "It was then that you sent me the five hundred francs."

"Oh, no!"

"It was a letter with a Paris postmark and signed Paul Sorel, to avert suspicion."

A little discussion of the possible origin of the letter ensued. Their mental attitude changed. Without realizing it, Madame de Rênal and Julien had abandoned the solemn tone; they had returned to that of affectionate friendship. They could not see each other at all, the darkness was so complete, but the sound of their voices said everything. Julien slipped his arm about his mistress' waist; it was a very hazardous gesture. She tried to put his arm away but Julien, cleverly enough, diverted her attention at that moment to an interesting point in his story. The arm seemed to be forgotten and remained in the position it had assumed.

After many conjectures as to the origin of the letter with the five hundred francs, Julien had resumed his story; he was recovering his composure somewhat in speaking of his past life, which, in comparison to what was happening at the moment, interested him so little. His attention was entirely concentrated on the manner in which he was going to end his visit. "You must go," she kept saying to him from time to time, and in a short tone of voice.

What a disgrace for me if I'm refused! A shame like that would poison my whole life, he thought, and she will never write to me. God knows when I shall return to this part of the country. From that moment, all that was blissful in Julien's mood rapidly faded from his spirit. Seated beside a woman he adored, all but holding her in his arms in that room where he had been so happy, in the midst of impenetrable darkness, realizing quite well that for the last moment or two she had been weeping, feeling by the rise and fall of her breast that she was shaking with sobs, he had the misfortune to turn into a cold politician, almost as calculating and as cold as when, in the seminary courtyard, he found himself the butt of some malicious joke on the part of one of his classmates stronger than himself. Julien spun out his story, telling of the wretched life he had led since leaving Verrières. So, Madame de Rênal thought, after a year's absence, almost completely without any sign of remembrance, while I was learning to forget him, he was thinking only of the happy times he had known at Vergy. Her sobs redoubled. Julien saw the successful effect of his story. He realized that he must try the last resort: He came abruptly to the letter he had just received from Paris.

"I have seen the last of the bishop."

"What! You're not going back to Besançon? You're leaving us forever?"

"Yes," Julien answered in a resolute tone. "Yes, I'm forsaking the place where I have been forgotten even by the one I loved most in my life, and I'm leaving it never to return. I am going to Paris . . ."

"You're going to Paris!" Madame de Rênal cried aloud.

Her voice was all but strangled by tears, and showed the full extent of her distress. Julien had need of this encouragement; he was about to try an expedient that might turn everything against him; and before that exclamation, uncertain of his position, he had absolutely no idea of what effect he might succeed in producing. He hesitated no longer; dread of self-reproach gave him complete mastery of himself; rising to his feet, he added coldly:

"Yes, Madame, I am leaving you forever. Be happy. Good-by."

He strode to the window; he was already opening it. Madame de Rênal sprang after him and flung herself into his arms.

So, after three hours of conversation, Julien achieved what he had so passionately desired during the first two. A little earlier, Madame de Rênal's return to tender sentiment, the eclipse of her remorse, would have been heavenly rapture; obtained thus, by artifice, it was no more than a pleasure. Julien absolutely insisted, against his mistress' protests, upon lighting the night light.

"Do you want me to go away with no memory of having seen you?" he asked her. "Is the love that I know is in those lovely eyes to be lost for me? The whiteness of those pretty hands to be invisible? Remember that I am leaving you, perhaps for a very long time."

Madame de Rênal was unable to resist this consideration, which made her burst into tears. But dawn was beginning to sharpen the outline of the pine trees on the mountain east of Verrières. Instead of taking his departure, Julien, drunk with pleasures, asked Madame de Rênal to let him spend the whole day hidden in her room, and not leave until the following night.

"Why not?" she said. "This second fall from grace has destroyed all my self-respect and will make me miserable for the rest of my life," and she pressed him to her heart. "My husband isn't the same as he used to be, he is suspicious; he thinks that I got him into all this muddle and he shows his anger toward me. If he hears the slightest sound, I am ruined; he'll drive me out like the wicked woman I am."

"Ah, that's one of Monsieur Chélan's phrases," Julien said. "You wouldn't have talked to me that way before my cruel separation from you, at the seminary; you loved me then!"

Julien was rewarded for the coolness which he put into this remark: he saw his mistress promptly forget the danger her husband's presence made her run to think of the far greater danger of seeing Julien doubt her love. The daylight was rapidly strengthening and lighting the room brightly; Julien rediscovered all the delights of vanity when he could once more see in his arms, and all but at his feet, this charming woman, the only one whom he had ever loved and who, a few hours before, had been wholly given over to fear of a wrathful God and to devotion to her duty. Resolutions fortified by a year of constancy had been unable to withstand his courageous attack.

Presently sounds of life were heard about the house; one thing which had not occurred to her before made Madame de Rênal uneasy.

"That horrid Elisa is going to come into the room; what are we to do with that enormous ladder?" she said to her lover. "Where can we hide it? I'm going to take it to the attic," she cried suddenly with a sort of gaiety.

"But you'll have to go through the servant's room," Julien said, astonished.

"I'll leave the ladder in the hall, call the man and send him on an errand."

"Be sure you have an answer ready in case he notices the ladder, passing it in the hall."

"Yes, my darling," Madame de Rênal said, giving him a kiss. "As for you, you be ready to hide very quickly under the bed if Elisa comes in here while I'm gone."

Julien was amazed by this sudden light-heartedness. So, he thought, the approach of actual danger, far from depressing her, restores her gaiety because she forgets her remorse! A really superior woman. Oh, there's the sort of heart in which it's glorious to reign. Julien was enraptured.

Madame de Rênal took up the ladder; it was obviously too heavy for her. Julien went to her assistance; he was admiring that graceful figure, so remote from any suggestion of physical strength when suddenly, with no help, she grasped the ladder and carried it off as if it had been a chair. She took it quickly up to the third-floor hall where she laid it down along the wall. She called the manservant and, to give him time to dress, went up to the dovecote. Five minutes later, on her return to the hall, she could not find the ladder again. What had become of it? If Julien had been out of the house, this danger would not have disturbed her in the least. But if her husband should see that ladder just now! That could have appalling results. Madame de Rênal searched everywhere. At length she discovered the ladder under the roof where the servant had taken it and hidden it himself. It was a singular occurrence; at any other time it would have alarmed her.

What does it matter to me, she thought, what may happen in twenty-four hours, when Julien will be gone? Then won't everything be horror and remorse for me?

She had a sort of vague notion that she ought to destroy herself, but no matter! After a separation which she believed eternal, he was restored to her, she was seeing him again, and what he had gone through in order to reach her showed so much love!

In telling Julien about the episode of the ladder:

"What shall I answer my husband," she said, "if the man tells him he has found that ladder?" She reflected a moment. "It will take them twenty-four hours to find the peasant who sold it to you." And, flinging herself into Julien's arms, clasping him with convulsive strength: "Oh, to die, to die like this!" she cried, covering him with kisses. "But you mustn't die of starvation," she added, laughing.

"Come; first I'm going to hide you in Madame Derville's room; it's always locked." She went to stand guard at the end of the hall, and Julien slipped hurriedly to the other room. "Be sure not to open, if anybody knocks," she instructed him, locking him in. "In any case, it will only be the children playing some game among themselves."

"Have them come into the garden, under the window," Julien said, "so that I can have the pleasure of seeing them. Get them to talk."

"Yes, yes," Madame de Rênal cried, going out.

She returned promptly with oranges, biscuits and a bottle of Malaga; it had been impossible for her to steal any bread.

"What is your husband doing?" Julien asked.

"Writing out plans for business deals with some peasants."

But eight o'clock had struck, there was a great deal of activity in the house. If Madame de Rênal was not in evidence, they would search everywhere for her; she was obliged to leave him. Presently she reappeared, against all prudence, bringing him a cup of coffee; she was in terror that he might die of hunger. After breakfast she succeeded in bringing the children under Madame Derville's window. Julien found them much taller, but they had acquired a common manner, or else his attitude had changed.

Madame de Rênal talked to them about Julien. The eldest responded with friendliness and regret for their former tutor; but he felt that the younger boys had almost forgotten him.

Monsieur de Rênal did not leave the house that morning, and kept going up and down stairs, engaged in bargaining with the peasants to whom he was selling his potato crop. Until dinner time Madame de Rênal had not a moment to spare for her prisoner. Dinner announced and served, it occurred to her to steal a plate of hot soup for him. As she was soundlessly approaching the door of the room he was in, carrying the plate with great care, she found herself face to face with the servant who had hidden the ladder that morning. At that moment he too was walking noiselessly down the hall, and seemed to be listening. Probably Julien had made more noise than was prudent, in walking about. The servant moved away, a little embarrassed. Madame de Rênal boldly entered Julien's room; the meeting made him shudder.

"You are afraid," she said. "As for me, I'd face all the dangers in the world without turning a hair. There is only one thing I dread, and that is the moment when I shall be alone, after you go." And she hurried away.

Ah, Julien thought, transfigured, remorse is the only danger that magnificent spirit fears!

Evening came at last. Monsieur de Rênal went to the Casino.

His wife had complained of a frightful migraine; she retired to her room, hastened to dismiss Elisa and immediately rose from her bed to admit Julien.

He found that he actually was dying of hunger. Madame de Rênal went to the pantry to find some bread. Julien heard a loud scream. Madame de Rênal returned and told him that, entering the pantry in the dark and going over to the cupboard where the bread was kept and stretching out her hand, she had touched a woman's arm. It was Elisa who had made the outcry Julien had heard.

"What was she up to there?"

"She was stealing sweets, or else she was spying on us," Madame de Rênal said with complete indifference. "But luckily I found a pie and a big loaf of bread."

"What have you got there, then?" Julien said, pointing to her apron pockets.

Madame de Rênal had forgotten that, since dinner, they had been full of bread.

Julien took her into his arms with the most ardent passion; never had she seemed so beautiful to him. Even in Paris, he thought confusedly, I can never come across a greater character. She had all the awkwardness of a woman little accustomed to this sort of artifice, and at the same time the true courage of a spirit that fears only dangers of another kind, terrible in quite another way.

While Julien hungrily ate his supper and his mistress joked about the simplicity of the meal, for she shrank from serious speech, the door of the room was suddenly and violently shaken. It was Monsieur de Rênal.

"Why is your door locked?" he called out.

Julien had just time to slide under the couch.

"Why, you're all dressed," Monsieur de Rênal said as he came in. "You're having supper and you locked your door?"

On any ordinary day this question, put with all conjugal sharpness, would have upset Madame de Rênal, but she realized that her husband had only to lower his eyes to catch sight of Julien; for Monsieur de Rênal had dropped into the chair which Julien had occupied a moment before, opposite the couch.

A sick headache excuses all things. While her husband, in turn, was relating at great length the details of the pool he had won in the billiard room of the Casino—"a pool of nineteen francs, by God!" he added—

she noticed on a chair not three feet away from them, Julien's hat. Her composure only increased; she began to undress and, when the time came, passing rapidly behind her husband, flung her gown over the chair with the hat.

Eventually Monsieur de Rênal left her. She begged Julien to tell her again about his life at the seminary. "Yesterday I wasn't listening; all the time you were talking I was thinking only about forcing myself to send you away."

She was indiscretion itself. They spoke quite loudly, and it must have been two o'clock in the morning when they were interrupted by a violent blow on the door. It was Monsieur de Rênal again.

"Open this door at once, there are burglars in the house!" he shouted. "Saint-Jean found their ladder this morning."

"This is the end of everything," Madame de Rênal cried, flinging herself into Julien's arms. "He's going to kill us both, he doesn't believe in that burglar story; I am going to die in your arms, happier in my death than I ever was in my life." She made no answer to her husband who was becoming angry; she embraced Julien passionately.

"You must save Stanislaus' mother," he said to her with a commanding glance. "I am going to jump down into the courtyard from the closet window and escape through the garden, the dogs recognized me. Make a bundle of my clothes and throw it into the garden as soon as you can. In the meantime, let them force the door. Above all, no admissions, I forbid it; better let him have suspicions than certainties."

"You'll kill yourself, jumping!" was her only answer and her only cause for concern.

She went with him to the closet window; then she took the time to hide his clothes. At last she opened the door to her husband, who was seething with rage. He peered about the room and into the closet without a word, and disappeared. Julien's clothes were thrown down to him, he snatched them up and ran swiftly toward the lower end of the garden and the Doubs.

As he ran he heard a bullet sing, and at the same time the sound of a rifle shot.

That's not Monsieur de Rênal, he thought, he's too bad a shot for that. The dogs ran mute beside him; a second shot apparently wounded the paw of one of the dogs, for he began to howl plaintively. Julien leaped a terrace wall, ran under cover for fifty yards and then set off in another direction. He heard voices calling back and forth, and distinctly saw his enemy the manservant fire a shot; a farmer joined the shooting from the other side of the garden, but by that time Julien had reached the bank of the Doubs, where he put on his clothes.

An hour later he was a league from Verrières on the road to Geneva. If they suspect, Julien thought, it's on the road to Paris that they'll look for me.

Volume Two

CHAPTER 1
Country Pleasures

HE WAS little moved by his first view of Paris, seen in the distance. The castles in air of his future destiny had to contend with the still-present memory of the forty-eight hours he had just spent in Verrières.

What would have happened, the night of his arrival in Verrières, if just as he was resting his ladder against Madame de Rênal's bedroom window, he had discovered that the room was occupied by a stranger, or by Monsieur de Rênal?

But then, too, what delights in those first two hours when his mistress was genuinely trying to send him away, while he pleaded his cause, sitting beside her in the darkness! A spirit such as Julien's is haunted by such memories throughout life. The rest of the episode was already becoming confused in his mind with the first days of their love, fourteen months before.

Julien was roused from his profound reverie, for the coach stopped. It had just entered the posthouse courtyard, in the Rue Jean-Jacques Rousseau. "I want to go to Malmaison," he told the driver of a hired carriage which came up to him.

"At this time of day, Monsieur, and what for?"

"What's that to you? Go ahead."

Any true passion thinks only of itself. That, it seems to me, is why passions are so ridiculous in Paris, where one's neighbor always expects that one think a great deal of him. I shall refrain from describing Julien's exaltation at Malmaison. He wept. What! In spite of the hideous white walls built that year, which chopped the park into pieces? Yes, Monsieur: for Julien, as for posterity, Arcole, Saint Helena and Malmaison were all one.

That evening Julien hesitated long before entering a theater; he had strange ideas about that path to perdition.

A deep distrust prevented him from admiring the living Paris; he was moved only by the monuments his hero had left.

So here I am in the center of intrigue and hypocrisy! Here rule the protectors of the Abbé de Frilair.

The evening of the third day curiosity diverted him from the project of seeing everything before presenting himself to the Abbé Pirard. The abbé explained to him, in a chilly tone, the nature of the life that was awaiting him in Monsieur de la Mole's home.

"If at the end of a few months you have not proved useful, you will go back to the seminary, but by the front door. You are going to live in the home of the marquis, one of the greatest noblemen in France. You will wear black, but like a man in mourning, not like a clergyman. I require that you go three times a week to keep up with your studies in theology at a seminary to which I'll have you admitted. Every day at noon you will report to Monsieur de la Mole's library, where you will be expected to write letters regarding lawsuits and other business matters. To put it briefly, the marquis will write in the margin of each letter he receives the nature of the reply that is to be written. I have assured him that at the end of three months you will be so proficient at composing these replies that, out of every twelve you offer for his signature, he will be able to sign eight or nine. At eight in the evening you will tidy your desk, and at ten you will be free.

"It may be," the Abbé Pirard continued, "that some old lady or some persuasive-mannered man will hint to you about immense advantages to be had, or will quite crudely offer you money for showing him the letters the marquis receives . . . "

"Oh, Monsieur!" Julien cried, flushing.

"It is odd," the abbé said with a wry smile, "that poor as you are, and after a year of seminary life, you still retain these virtuous indignations. You must have been extremely blind!

"Can it be the influence of heredity?" the abbé wondered half aloud, and as if speaking to himself. "The strange thing is," he added, looking at Julien, "that the marquis knows of you . . . I can't think how. He is giving you a salary of a hundred louis, to start. He is a man who acts only upon whim, that is his failing; he'll squabble with you over childish trifles. If he is pleased with you, your salary might later be raised as high as eight thousand francs.

"But you certainly realize," the abbé went on in a sharp tone, "that he is not giving you all that money because he likes your looks. You'll have to be useful. In your place, I should speak very little, and above all I should never talk about things I did not understand.

"Oh!" the abbé added, "I made some inquiries for you; I almost forgot Monsieur de la Mole's family. He has two children, a daughter and a nineteen-year-old son, extremely elegant, a sort of madman who never knows at noon what he will be doing at two o'clock. He has intelligence and courage; he fought in Spain. The marquis hopes—I don't know why—that you will become young Count Norbert's friend. I've said that you were an accomplished Latinist, perhaps he is counting on your teaching his son a few ready-made phrases in Cicero and Virgil.

"If I were you, I shouldn't ever let this fine young fellow make a laughingstock of me; and, before responding to his perfectly courteous but rather too ironical approaches, I'd have them repeated more than once.

"I'm not going to hide it from you that the young Count de la Mole is likely to be scornful of you at first because you're only of common stock. One of his own ancestors was at Court, and had the honor of having his head cut off in the Place de Grève on the twenty-sixth of April, 1574, for a political intrigue. As for you, you're the son of a Verrières carpenter, and in his father's pay besides. Weigh these differences well, and study the family's history in Moreri; all the toadies who dine at their house make what they call delicate allusions to it from time to time.

"Be careful how you answer any jokes made by Monsieur le Comte Norbert de la Mole, Squadron Commander of Hussars and future Peer of France, and don't come complaining to me about the consequences."

"It sounds to me," Julien said, flushing hotly, "as though I were not even to answer a man who disparages me."

"You have no idea of that kind of disparagement; it is shown only by means of exaggerated compliments. If you were a fool, you might be taken in by it; if you wanted to make a fortune, you would have to let yourself be taken in by it."

"If a time comes when I can no longer put up with all that," Julien said, "will I be considered an ingrate if I go back to my little cell number 103?"

"All the household hangers-on will undoubtedly vilify you," the abbé said, "but then I will step forward. *Adsum qui feci.* I shall say that I am the author of that decision."

Julien was bewildered by the bitter and almost threatening tone he noticed in Monsieur Pirard; that tone utterly spoiled his reply.

The fact was that the abbé was feeling conscience-stricken over his partiality to Julien, and it was with a sort of religious terror that he intervened so directly in another's destiny.

"You will also meet," he added with the same ill grace, and as if accomplishing a disagreeable duty, "you will meet Madame la Marquise de la Mole. She is a tall blond woman, devout, aloof, perfectly polite and even more insignificant. She is a daughter of the old Duke de Chaulnes, so noted for his aristocratic prejudices. This great lady is a sort of summary, in high relief, of all the basic elements of character in women of her rank. She makes no secret of the fact that, as far as she is concerned, having had ancestors who went to the Crusades is the only advantage worth respecting. Money is only a far smaller consideration: that surprises you? We aren't in the provinces any more, my friend.

"In her drawing-room you will hear many great noblemen speak of our princes in a tone of extreme flippancy. Madame de la Mole, herself, lowers her voice in respect every time she mentions a prince, and more particularly a princess. I should advise you not to say in her presence that Philip II or Henry VIII was a monster. They were KINGS, which gives them inalienable rights to everyone's respect, and especially to the respect of lowborn creatures like you and me. However," Monsieur Pirard added, "we are priests, for she will consider you one; by that token she regards us as servants essential to her salvation."

"Monsieur," Julien said, "it does not look to me as if I would be in Paris very long."

"If the marquise's arrogance or her son's bad jokes make that house definitely unendurable to you, I advise you to complete your studies in some seminary ninety miles from Paris, and in the north rather than in the south. In the north there is more civilization and less injustice, and," he added, lowering his voice, "I must admit it, the proximity of the Paris newspapers frightens petty tyrants.

"If we continue to find pleasure in each other's company, and if the marquis' house is uncomfortable for you, I'll offer to make you my vicar, and share equally with you whatever the living brings in."

The abbé had abandoned his cruel tone of voice. To his great shame, Julien felt tears in his eyes; he yearned to throw himself into his friend's arms: he was unable to prevent himself from saying, in the most manly air of which he was capable:

"I was hated by my father from the cradle on; that was one of my great sorrows; but I shall never complain of circumstances again, I have found another father in you, Monsieur."

"Good, good," the abbé said, embarrassed; then, resorting most aptly to a seminary director's phrase: "You should never say circumstance, my son, always say Providence."

The hired carriage came to a stop; the driver raised the bronze knocker of an immense gate: it was the HÔTEL DE LA MOLE; and, lest passers-by go in ignorance of it, the words were cut in a black marble slab above the gate.

This ostentation displeased Julien. They're so afraid of Jacobins! They see a Robespierre and his tumbrel behind every hedge; often the way they act is enough to make one die laughing, and yet they advertise their house this way so that the mob can't fail to recognize it in case of an uprising, and loot it. He communicated his thought to the Abbé Pirard.

"Oh, poor child, you'll soon be my vicar. What a horrible idea you've got there."

"To my mind there's nothing more obvious," Julien said.

The solemnity of the gatekeeper and particularly the cleanliness of the courtyard had moved him to admiration. The sun was shining splendidly.

"What magnificent architecture!" he said to his friend.

It was one of those excessively dull-faced mansions of the Faubourg Saint-Germain, built in the time of Voltaire's death. Never were fashion and beauty so far removed from one another.

CHAPTER 2
Introduction to Society

J ULIEN paused open-mouthed in the middle of the courtyard.

"Try to look intelligent," the Abbé Pirard said. "You get these horrible ideas, and then you act like a child! Where is Horace's *nil mirari?* [Never show admiration.] Remember that all these servants, seeing you installed here, are going to try to make a mock of you; they'll regard you as an equal unjustly set above them. Under the pretense of friendliness, good advice, a desire to guide you, they are going to try to push you into some gross blunder."

"I defy them to do it," Julien said, biting his lip, and he recovered all his distrust.

The first-floor drawing-rooms, through which these gentlemen passed in order to reach the marquis' study, would have seemed to you, my reader, as gloomy as they were magnificent. If they had been offered to you just as they stood, you would have refused to live in them; they were the native territory of the yawn and the dreary argument. They redoubled Julien's enchantment. How can one be unhappy, he thought, living in so splendid a mansion?

At length the gentlemen came to the ugliest of the rooms in this superb suite: daylight scarcely penetrated there; there they found a thin little man with a sharp eye and a blond periwig. The abbé turned to Julien and presented him. It was the marquis. Julien had great difficulty in recognizing him, he found his manner so courteous. He was no longer the great nobleman, with so arrogant an expression, of the Bray-le-Haut abbey. It seemed to Julien that his wig contained far too much hair. Sustained by this observation, he was not in the least intimidated.

The interview lasted no more than three minutes. As they left, the abbé said to Julien: "You stared at the marquis the way you would at a picture. I'm no great authority on what these people call politeness, you'll soon know more about it than I do, but even so, the boldness of your stare seemed hardly polite to me."

They had reëntered the carriage; the coachman pulled up near the boulevard; the abbé led Julien into a suite of vast rooms. Julien noticed that there was no furniture. He was looking at a handsome gilded clock, representing a subject which he considered highly indecent, when a very elegant gentleman approached with a cordial expression. Julien half bowed.

The gentleman smiled and laid his hand on Julien's shoulder. Julien quivered and leaped back. He grew red with anger. The abbé Pirard, despite his gravity, laughed until tears stood in his eyes. The gentleman was a tailor.

"I am setting you free for two days," the abbé said as they left, "you can't be presented to Madame de la Mole until then. Anyone else would guard you like a young girl in these first moments of your visit to this new Babylon. If you must ruin yourself, do it at once, and I shall be relieved of this weakness I have of caring for you. Day after tomorrow morning that tailor will bring you two suits; give five francs to the fitter. Aside from that, don't let those Parisians hear the sound of your voice. If you say one word, they will discover the secret of making you look foolish. It's their talent. Be at my house at noon on the day after to-morrow. . . . Go along now, ruin yourself. . . . Oh, I was forgetting: go and order boots, shirts and a hat at these addresses."

Julien glanced at the handwriting of the addresses.

"That's the marquis' writing," the abbé said; "he is an active man who foresees everything and prefers doing to commanding. He is taking you into his employ to spare him this sort of trouble. Will you be clever enough to carry out accurately all the things that agile man will suggest to you in less than a word? The future will tell; be careful!"

Julien went into the shops indicated on the list without saying a word; he noticed that the tradesmen received him with respect, and the boot-maker, entering his name in the books, wrote Monsieur Julien Sorel.

At the cemetery of Père-Lachaise a gentleman, most obliging and even more liberal in his conversation, offered to show Julien the tomb of Marshal Ney, whom a foresighted administrative policy had deprived of the honor of an epitaph. But after parting from this liberal who, with tears in his eyes, all but clasped him in his arms, Julien no longer had a watch. Enriched by this experience he presented himself the next day to the Abbé Pirard, who eyed him narrowly.

"It seems you're going to become a fop," the abbé said with a stern look. Julien had the appearance of a very young man in deep mourning; he did actually look very well, but the good abbé was too provincial himself to see that Julien still retained that swaggering motion of the shoulders which, in the provinces, expresses both elegance and importance. Seeing Julien, the marquis formed so different an opinion of his graces from that of the good abbé that he asked:

"Would you have any objection to Monsieur Sorel's taking dancing lessons?"

The abbé stood frozen.

"No," he said at last. "Julien is not a priest."

The marquis, taking a small back staircase two steps at a time, went himself to settle our hero in a fine attic room that looked out over the vast garden of the house. He asked him how many shirts he had bought at the haberdasher's.

"Two," Julien said, overawed at seeing so great a gentleman condescend to such details.

"Very well," the marquis said with a serious expression and in a brief, imperative tone which caught Julien's attention, "very well! Get twenty-two more. Here is your first quarter's salary."

Descending from the attic, the marquis summoned an elderly manservant: "Arsène," he said to him, "you will look after Monsieur Sorel." A few minutes later Julien found himself alone in a magnificent library; this was a moment of delight. In order not to be taken unawares in his emotion, he went and hid himself in a small dark corner; from there he gazed with rapture at the gleaming backs of the books: I'll be able to read them all, he thought. How could I be dissatisfied here? Monsieur de Rênal would have thought himself eternally dishonored by the hundredth part of what the Marquis de la Mole has just done for me.

But let's see the copying that's to be done. . . . That task completed, Julien ventured to approach the books; he all but went wild with joy on finding an edition of Voltaire. He hurried to open the library door, in order not to be surprised. Then he gave himself the pleasure of opening each of the eighty volumes. They were magnificently bound, the set was the masterpiece of the best London bookbinder. This was all that was needed to raise Julien's admiration to the highest pitch.

An hour later the marquis entered, glanced over the copied letters and noticed with amazement that Julien wrote *cela* with two l's: *cella*. All the abbé told me about his learning must have been just a fairy tale! The marquis, vastly disappointed, said gently:

"You're not sure of your spelling?"

"That's true," Julien said, without the slightest notion of the harm he was doing himself; he was touched by the marquis' kindness, which reminded him of Monsieur de Rênal's contemptuous manner.

It's a waste of time, all this experiment with a little provincial priest, the marquis thought; but I had such need of a man I could trust!

"*Cela* has only one *l*," he said. "When you've finished your letters, look up all the words you are not sure of in the dictionary."

At six o'clock the marquis sent for him; he looked with evident consternation at Julien's boots. "I must apologize, I didn't tell you that you must dress every evening at half past five."

Julien looked at him, uncomprehending.

"I mean put on dinner clothes. Arsène will remind you; this evening I'll make your excuses."

As he finished speaking, Monsieur de la Mole showed Julien into a drawing-room resplendent with gilding. On similar occasions, Monsieur de Rênal never failed to lengthen his stride in order to have the advantage of going first through the door. The petty vanity of his former employer caused Julien to step on the marquis' toes and give him a great deal of pain because of his gout. Clumsy into the bargain! the marquis said to himself. He presented Julien to a tall woman of imposing appearance. This was the marquise. Somewhat confused by the extreme opulence of the drawing-room, Julien did not hear what Monsieur de la Mole was saying. The marquise scarcely condescended to look at him.

The men assembled in this drawing-room seemed to Julien to have an atmosphere of melancholy and constraint; in Paris one speaks low and does not exaggerate minor matters.

A handsome young man with a mustache, very white-skinned and very slender, came in at about six-thirty; he had an extremely small head.

"You always keep us waiting," the marquise said as he kissed her hand.

Julien realized that this was the Count de la Mole. At first meeting he found him charming.

Is it possible, he wondered, that this is the man whose offensive mockery was supposed to drive me from the house!

Examining Count Norbert, Julien noticed that he was wearing boots and spurs; and I'm supposed to be in evening slippers, apparently as a badge of inferiority. They sat down at table. Julien heard the marquise speak severely, raising her voice a little. Almost at the same time he caught sight of a young woman, extremely fair and beautifully proportioned, who came in and sat down across from him. She did not appeal to him at all; however, after studying her intently he decided that he had never seen such beautiful eyes, but they reflected great frigidity of spirit. Later Julien came to the conclusion that they expressed the sort of boredom which is alert but cannot forget the obligation to be impressive. Madame de Rênal had very lovely eyes, too, he thought, people complimented her on them; but they had nothing in common with these.

Julien had not enough experience to perceive that it was a flash of humor that sparkled from time to time in the eyes of Mademoiselle Mathilde, as he heard her called. When Madame de Rênal's eyes flashed, it was with passion, or with the response of generous indignation to the story of some unjust action. Toward the end of the meal, Julien found the word to express the nature of the beauty of Mademoiselle de la Mole's eyes: They are scintillating, he thought. Aside from that she painfully resembled her mother, who continued to seem more and more disagreeable to him, and he stopped looking at her. As compensation, Count Norbert struck him as admirable in every way. Julien was so taken with him that it did not occur to him to be jealous and hate him for being wealthier and more aristocratic than himself.

Julien thought the marquis looked bored. During the second course he said to his son: "Norbert, I want you to be nice to Monsieur Sorel, whom I'm adding to my staff and whom I intend to make into a man, if it can be done.

"He's my secretary," the marquis added to his neighbor, "and he spells *cela* with two *l's!*"

Everyone looked at Julien, who nodded a little too exaggeratedly to Norbert; but on the whole they were pleased with his appearance.

The marquis must have spoken of the kind of education Julien had received, for one of the guests challenged him on the subject of Horace. From that instant, he was in command of himself. This reaction was facilitated by his just having come to the conclusion that Mademoiselle de la Mole would never be a woman in his eyes. Since his seminary experience, he was defiant of men and rarely let himself be intimidated by them. He would have been in complete possession of his self-confidence had the dining room been less magnificently furnished. To be exact, it was two mirrors, each eight feet tall, in which he caught occasional glimpses of his interlocutor speaking of Horace, that still awed him. For a provincial, his speech was not too voluble. He had fine eyes, in which apprehensive shyness or, when he had answered well, happiness accentuated the glow. They found him attractive. This sort of examination added a bit of interest to a solemn dinner. By a sign, the marquis urged Julien's questioner to ply him further. Is it possible that he does know something! he thought.

Julien answered, extemporizing ideas, and losing enough of his timidity not to display wit—an impossible achievement to one unfamiliar with Parisian turns of speech—but he had interpretations that were new, although presented without grace or relevance, and it was plain that he knew Latin perfectly.

Julien's adversary was a member of the Academy of Inscriptions who happened to know Latin; he found in Julien an excellent humanist, had no further fear of making him blush, and set out to confuse him in earnest. In the heat of combat Julien at length forgot the magnificent furnishings of the dining room; he went so far as to advance theories on the Latin poets that his questioner had never read anywhere. As an honest man, he gave the young secretary full credit. This discussion seemed to draw the marquis out of the state of torpor into which boredom had plunged him at the beginning of the dinner.

When they tired of talking about the poets the marquise, who made it a law to admire anything which amused her husband, condescended to look at Julien. "That young abbé's awkward manners may conceal an educated man," the academician, who sat near her, said to the marquise; and Julien overheard something of this. Ready-made phrases rather appealed to the mistress of the house; she adopted this one for using about Julien and was pleased with herself for having invited the academician to dinner. He entertains Monsieur de la Mole, she thought.

CHAPTER 3
First Steps

V ᴇʀʏ early the next day, Julien was copying letters in the library
when Mademoiselle Mathilde came in by a small private door
disguised with bookshelves. While Julien admired this ingenious arrangement, Mademoiselle Mathilde seemed highly astonished and
somewhat displeased at finding him there. Julien thought she looked
hard, arrogant and almost masculine in her curl-papers. It was Mademoiselle de la Mole's secret habit to steal books from her father's
library without anyone's knowledge. Julien's presence made her visit
this morning futile.

At three o'clock Count Norbert appeared in the library; he came to
peruse the newspaper in order to be able to talk politics that evening,
and was delighted to see Julien, whose existence he had forgotten. His
manner was full of charm; he invited Julien to go riding.

"My father has let us off until dinnertime."

Julien understood that *us* and thought it charming.

"Lord, Monsieur le Comte," he said, "if you wanted me to cut down
an eight-foot tree, square it up and make boards out of it, I daresay I
could do a good job of it; but when it comes to horseback riding, I
haven't done that more than six times in my life."

"Well, then, this will be the seventh," Norbert said.

Privately, Julien remembered the king's visit to Verrières and thought that he rode exceptionally well. But as they were returning from the Bois de Boulogne, precisely in the middle of the Rue du Bac, he fell, in a precipitate effort to avoid a carriage, and covered himself with mud. He was relieved to think that he had two suits. At dinner the marquis, wishing to say something to him, asked for an account of his ride; Norbert quickly and generously answered for him.

"Monsieur le Comte is more than kind to me," Julien said. "I appreciate it, and I'm grateful to him. He was good enough to have them give me the gentlest and the handsomest horse, but he couldn't tie me on and, lacking that precaution, I fell off right in the middle of that very long street near the bridge."

Mademoiselle Mathilde tried in vain to stifle a shout of laughter; then her curiosity demanded details. Julien responded with perfect simplicity; he had grace without being aware of it.

"I predict that this little priest will turn out well," the marquis said to the academician. "A simple provincial in such a predicament! It's never been seen before and never will be again, and yet he tells of his accident before *ladies!*"

Julien set his audience so much at their ease over his misadventure that at the end of dinner, when the conversation had turned to other channels, Mademoiselle Mathilde questioned her brother about the details of the unfortunate occurrence. Her inquiry was prolonged and Julien, catching her eyes upon him several times, ventured to answer directly, although the questions were not addressed to him, and in the end all three were laughing quite like three young backwoods villagers.

The following day Julien attended two theology lectures and afterwards returned to transcribe a score or so of letters.

At four o'clock, after some hesitation, Julien ventured to seek out Count Norbert. The count was about to go riding and was embarrassed, for he was exquisitely polite.

"I think," he said to Julien, "that very soon you are to take riding lessons, and after a few weeks I'll be delighted to ride with you."

"I wanted to have the honor of thanking you for the kindness you've shown me. Believe me, Monsieur," Julien added very soberly, "I realize how much I owe you. If your horse wasn't injured by my clumsiness yesterday, and if he isn't being ridden, I should like to ride him this afternoon."

"Why, of course, my dear Sorel, at your own risk. Let's take it that

I've made all the objections prudence requires; the fact is, it's four o'clock, we've no time to waste."

Once mounted: "What should I do to keep from falling?" Julien asked the young count.

"A lot of things," Norbert answered, shouting with laughter. "For one, sit well back in the saddle."

Julien set off at a fast trot. They were in the Place Louis XVI.

"Oh, look here, don't be rash!" Norbert said. "There are too many carriages, and with reckless drivers besides. If you did fall off, their tilburies would run over you; they're not going to risk hurting their horses' mouths by stopping short."

A score of times Norbert saw Julien on the point of falling, but eventually the ride ended without accident. Returning to the house, the young count said to his sister:

"May I present a daring roughrider?"

At dinner, speaking to his father from one end of the table to the other, he praised Julien's courage: that was all that could be praised about his fashion of riding. That afternoon the count had heard the grooms taking Julien's fall as an occasion for making outrageous fun of him.

In spite of such graciousness, Julien soon felt completely isolated in the midst of that family. All the customs seemed foreign to him, and he was forever making mistakes. His blunders were a source of delight to the footmen.

The Abbé Pirard had left for his parish. If Julien is a frail reed, let him be destroyed; if he's a sound-hearted man, let him make his way alone, he thought.

CHAPTER 4

The Hôtel de la Mole

I F EVERYTHING seemed strange to Julien in the noble drawing-room of the Hôtel de la Mole, this young man, pale of face and dressed in black, seemed in his turn very odd to the persons who troubled to notice him. Madame de la Mole suggested to her husband that he send him away on some errand the days when certain important people came to dinner.

"I want to complete the experiment," the marquis answered. "The Abbé Pirard claims that we are wrong to injure the self-respect of the people we take into our service. . . . The only bothersome thing about this young fellow is his unfamiliar face. Aside from that, he could be a deaf-mute."

In order to keep them straight in his mind, Julien thought, I must write down the names and a word or two about the personalities of the people I see in this drawing-room.

At the top he listed five or six friends of the family who never failed to be very attentive to him, believing him to be especially favored by some whim of the marquis. These were poor creatures, all more or less lacking in spirit; but it must be said in defense of this species of man, as they are found today in aristocratic salons, they were not equally spineless to everyone. Certain of them would have allowed themselves to be bullied by the marquis, but would have revolted against a harsh word spoken to them by Madame de la Mole.

There was too much pride and too much boredom underlying the characters of the masters of the house; they were too much accustomed to amusing themselves by abusing others to hope to have genuine friends. But except on rainy days or in moments of unspeakable boredom, which were rare, one found them exquisitely courteous at all times.

If the five or six sycophants who evidenced so paternal a friendship for Julien had forsaken the Hôtel de la Mole, the marquise would have been delivered over to great periods of solitude, and to women of her position solitude is horrible: it is the emblem of disgrace.

One morning when the Abbé Pirard was working with Julien, in the marquis' library, over the eternal lawsuit with Frilair:

"Monsieur," Julien said abruptly, "is dining every evening with Madame la Marquise one of my duties, or is it a privilege they're giving me?"

"It's a signal honor!" the abbé said, shocked.

"To me, Monsieur, it's the most unpleasant part of my job. I used to be less bored at the seminary. I even see Mademoiselle de la Mole yawn sometimes, and yet she ought to be used to the loving attentions of friends of the family. I'm afraid of falling asleep. Please, get permission for me to go and eat a two-franc dinner in some humble inn."

The abbé, a true parvenu, was very conscious of the honor of dining with a great nobleman. While he was endeavoring to make Julien understand this point of view, a slight noise made them turn their heads. Julien saw Mademoiselle de la Mole listening. He flushed. She had come in search of a book and had heard everything; Julien rose in her estimation. That one wasn't born kneeling, she thought, like the old abbé. God, how ugly he is!

At dinner Julien did not dare look at Mademoiselle de la Mole, but she was kind enough to speak to him. That evening a large number of guests was expected; she urged him not to leave.

Mademoiselle de la Mole was the center of a small group who met almost every evening behind the marquise's immense armchair. Among them were the Marquis de Croisenois, the Count de Caylus, the Viscount de Luz and two or three other young officers, friends of Norbert or of his sister. These gentlemen sat upon a long blue couch. At the far end of the couch, opposite to that occupied by the brilliant Mathilde, Julien was seated in silence on a small, rather low wicker chair. This unassuming position was envied by all the sycophants; Norbert kept his father's young secretary at ease there by speaking to him or mentioning his name once or twice during the evening. On this occasion, Mademoiselle de la Mole asked him what might be the height of the mountain upon which the citadel of Besançon stood. Julien was completely unable to say whether this mountain was higher or lower than Montmartre. Often he laughed wholeheartedly at what was said in this little group, but he felt himself incapable of concocting similar remarks. It was like a foreign language which he understood but could not speak.

Stern Monsieur Pirard was grimacing in a corner of the drawing-room, hearing the servants announce arrivals.

"What a face that Abbé Pirard has!" Mademoiselle de la Mole was saying as Julien came over to the couch.

Julien felt irritated, but still she was right. Monsieur Pirard was beyond a shadow of doubt the most honest man in the room, but his blotched face, convulsed by the torments of his conscience, made him hideous at that moment. After this, put your trust in expressive faces, Julien thought; it's when the Abbé Pirard's conscience is reproaching him for some peccadillo that he looks hideous, while on the face of this Napier, whom everyone knows for a spy, one reads pure and serene happiness. The Abbé Pirard had, nevertheless, made great concessions to his new way of life, he had hired a servant, he was very well dressed.

Monsieur Pirard moved into the adjoining drawing-room; Julien followed him:

"The marquis does not like scribblers, I warn you; it's his one antipathy. Know Latin, Greek, if you can, the history of the Egyptians, the Persians and the rest, and he'll honor you as a learned man and give you his protection. But don't go and write one page in French, particularly on serious subjects above your position in the world: he'll call you a scribbler and take an aversion to you. What, living in a nobleman's mansion, don't you know the Duke de Castries' remark about d'Alembert and Rousseau: That kind of man wants to argue about everything and hasn't a thousand écus a year?"

Everything becomes known, Julien thought, here as in the seminary! He had written eight or ten rather vehement pages: a sort of historical eulogy of the old surgeon-major who had, he said, made a man of him. And that little notebook, Julien reflected, had always been kept locked up! He went up to his room, burned the manuscript and returned to the salon.

CHAPTER 5

Sensibility and a Devout Lady

AFTER several months on trial, this is the position to which Julien had attained by the time the household steward presented him with his third quarter's salary. Monsieur de la Mole had intrusted him with supervising the administration of his estates in Brittany and Normandy. Julien made frequent journeys there. Further, he was wholly responsible for the correspondence regarding the famous lawsuit with the Abbé de Frilair. Monsieur Pirard had instructed him.

From the brief notes the marquis scrawled in the margins of all sorts of papers addressed to him, Julien composed letters almost all of which were signed.

At the theological seminary his professors complained of his lack of industry, but nevertheless considered him one of their most distinguished students.

These various labors, undertaken with all the ardor of tormented ambition, had quickly divested Julien of the fresh complexion he had brought with him from the provinces. His pallor was a credit to him in the eyes of the young theology students, his classmates; he found them far less malicious, far less inclined to genuflect before an écu than those of Besançon; they believed him to be tubercular. The marquis had given him a saddle horse.

There was a coolness between Julien and the young count. Norbert had felt that he replied too sharply to the pleasantries of one or two of his friends. Julien, having failed once or twice in decorum, had been forbidden ever to address a word to Mademoiselle Mathilde. Everyone was always perfectly polite to him at the Hôtel de la Mole, but he felt that he had lost standing. His provincial common sense explained this reaction with the well-known proverb: Familiarity breeds contempt.

We pass in silence over a host of minor episodes that would have resulted in ridicule for Julien had he not been in a sense beneath ridicule. An exaggerated sensibility caused him to commit a thousand blunders. All his recreations were of a precautionary nature: he practiced every day with a pistol, he was among the best students of the most famous fencing masters. Whenever he had a moment to himself, instead of spending it in reading as he used to do, he hurried to the stables and demanded the most vicious horses. During rides with the riding master, he was almost infallibly thrown.

The marquis found him useful because of his unremitting work, his silence, his intelligence, and little by little turned over to him the management of all his more complicated affairs. At times when his overweening ambition allowed him some relaxation, the marquis conducted his affairs with shrewdness; in a position to receive information, he played the stock market successfully. He bought houses, forests; but he took offense easily. He gave away hundreds of louis and went to court over matters of a hundred francs. Rich men with generous spirits look for recreation, not results, in business deals. The marquis needed a chief of staff capable of putting his money matters in clear and comprehensible order.

Madame de la Mole, although so circumspect in character, frequently made fun of Julien. The *unforeseen*, resulting from self-consciousness, is a source of horror to great ladies; it is the antipode of convention. Two or three times the marquis defended him: "He may be ridiculous in your drawing-room, but he excels in his office."

CHAPTER 6
Pronunciation

For a new arrival who, out of arrogance, refuses to ask questions, Julien did not fall into any really great errors. One day when he was forced by a sudden shower to take shelter in a café in the Rue Saint-Honoré, a tall man in a beaver coat, astonished by his moody stare, stared at him in turn, precisely as Amanda's lover had done, long ago in Besançon.

Julien had too often reproached himself for having let that first insult pass, to endure this stare. He demanded an explanation. At once the man in the greatcoat heaped him with the foulest abuse: everyone in the café gathered about them; passers-by began to pause in front of the door. With typical provincial caution, Julien always carried a pair of small pistols; his hand gripped them in his pockets with convulsive fingers. He used restraint, however, and forced himself to repeat over and over to his man: "Your address, Monsieur? I despise you."

The constancy with which he confined himself to these six words at length impressed the crowd.

"By God, that one that's talking all by himself ought to give the other one his address." The man in the greatcoat, hearing this verdict often repeated, flung five or six cards at Julien's face. Fortunately none of them reached its destination, for he had promised himself not to make use of the pistols unless he was touched. The man went out, not without turning from time to time to shake a threatening fist and utter further insults.

Julien found himself drenched with sweat. So it's in the power of the lowest of men to upset me to this extent! he thought in rage. How can I eradicate this shameful sensibility?

Where was he to find a second? He had not one friend. He had had several acquaintances, but inevitably all of them, at the end of six weeks' acquaintance, drifted away from him. I'm unsociable, and now I'm being cruelly punished for it, he thought. At length it occurred to him to seek out a retired lieutenant of the 96th, named Liéven, a poor devil with whom he sometimes practiced fencing. Julien was frank with him.

"I'm willing to be your second," Liéven said, "but on one condition: If you don't hit your man, you'll fight me, on the spot."

"Very well," Julien said, delighted; and they went to call upon Monsieur C. de Beauvoisis at the address indicated on his cards, in the heart of the Faubourg Saint-Germain.

It was seven o'clock in the morning. Julien handed one of the cards flung at him yesterday and one of his own to a tall footman.

They were kept waiting, he and his second, for a full three-quarters of an hour; at last they were shown into an extremely elegant apartment. They found a tall young man dressed up as fastidiously as a doll; his features displayed the perfection and the insignificance of Grecian beauty. His head, remarkably narrow, supported a pyramid of the most beautiful fair hair. It had been curled with the utmost care, not one hair was out of place. It was to get himself curled up like that, the lieutenant of the 96th thought, that this damned fop kept us waiting. The striped dressing gown, the morning trousers, everything, even down to the embroidered slippers, was correct and exquisitely neat. His features, aristocratic and empty, gave indication of ideas both conventional and infrequent: the ideal of the amiable man, horror of the unexpected and of levity, a vast solemnity.

Julien, to whom his lieutenant had explained that keeping him waiting so long, after having rudely thrown his card in his face, was an added insult, entered Monsieur de Beauvoisis' apartment forcefully. He intended to be insolent, but at the same time he would have liked to act well-bred.

He was so much impressed by the gentleness of Monsieur de Beauvoisis' manner, by his air at once formal, important and self-satisfied, by the extreme elegance which surrounded him that he lost in an instant all idea of being insolent. This was not his man of the previous day. His amazement at meeting so distinguished a man in place of the gross character encountered at the café was such that he could not utter a word. He presented one of the cards that had been flung at him.

"This is my name," said the man of fashion, in whom Julien's black suit, at seven o'clock in the morning, inspired little respect, "but upon my honor I fail to see . . ."

The inflection of the last words restored something of Julien's rage.

"I have come to fight with you, Monsieur," And, in one breath, he explained the whole affair.

Monsieur Charles de Beauvoisis, having considered it minutely, was not dissatisfied with the cut of Julien's black suit. It's from Staub's, that's obvious, he was thinking as he listened; that waistcoat is in good taste, the boots are all right; but on the other hand, a black suit at this hour of the morning! . . . It must be to make it harder for me to aim, the Chevalier de Beauvoisis thought to himself.

As soon as he had thought of this explanation he resumed his completely courteous manner toward Julien, almost as though speaking to an equal. The conversation was rather long, it was a delicate matter; but in the end Julien could not deny the evidence. This aristocratic young man before him bore not the slightest resemblance to the coarse person who had insulted him the day before.

Julien felt an irresistible reluctance to leave, he spun out the explanation. He observed the complacence of the Chevalier de Beauvoisis: it was thus that he spoke of himself, shocked by Julien's calling him simply Monsieur.

He admired his gravity, mingled with an occasional mild levity, but never entirely abandoned. He was astonished by his singular way of moving his tongue in pronouncing words. . . . But after all there was not the slightest excuse, in all this, for seeking a quarrel with him.

The young diplomat offered most graciously to fight, but the exlieutenant of the 96th, who for the last hour had been sitting with his legs apart, his hands on his thighs and his elbows thrust out, came to the conclusion that his friend Monsieur Sorel was not the sort to pick a quarrel with a man, in the German fashion, because someone had stolen that man's calling cards.

Julien left in a very bad humor. The Chevalier de Beauvoisis' carriage was waiting in the courtyard, in front of the step; Julien chanced to look up and recognized the coachman as his man of the previous day.

To see him, to lay hold of his coattail, to drag him down from his seat and thrash him soundly with his own whip was the work of no more than a moment. Two footmen tried to defend their fellow servant; Julien was struck by their fists: instantly he drew one of his pistols and fired on them; they took to their heels. All this in less than a minute.

The Chevalier de Beauvoisis came down the stairs with the most engaging solemnity, repeating in his aristocratic accent: "What's this? What's this?" He was obviously very curious, but his diplomatic importance would not permit him to show any further interest. When he understood what the matter was, arrogance still conflicted in his expression with the slightly mocking composure which must never be absent from a diplomat's face.

The lieutenant of the 96th realized that Monsieur de Beauvoisis longed to fight: at the same time, diplomatically, he wanted to preserve the advantage of the initiative for his friend. "This time," he shouted, "there's cause for a duel!"

"I'm inclined to agree," the diplomat returned.

"That beggar is discharged," he told his servants. "One of you drive." The door of the carriage was opened: the chevalier insisted upon Julien and his second entering first. They went in search of one of Monsieur de Beauvoisis' friends, who directed them to an unfrequented spot. The conversation as they drove along was genuinely pleasant. The only singular circumstance was the diplomat in dressing gown.

These gentlemen, noble as they are, Julien thought, aren't a bit boring like the people who come to dine with Monsieur de la Mole; and I see why, he added after a moment: they don't mind being indecent. There was talk of some dancers whom the public had received very favorably in a ballet given the evening before. The gentlemen made allusions to certain pungent anecdotes of which Julien and his second, the lieutenant of the 96th, were entirely ignorant. Julien was not so stupid as to pretend to understand; he admitted his ignorance with good grace. This frankness pleased the chevalier's friend; he told him the anecdotes in the greatest detail, and told them well.

The duel was over in an instant: Julien received a bullet in the arm; they bound it up with handkerchiefs moistened with brandy, and the

Chevalier de Beauvoisis most politely begged Julien to allow him to drive him home in the same carriage which had brought him to this place. When Julien mentioned the Hôtel de la Mole, the young diplomat and his friend exchanged glances.

Scarcely had they parted when the Chevalier de Beauvoisis hastened in search of information: it was not plentiful.

He was curious to know more about his man: Could he decently pay him a visit? The few facts he had been able to discover were not of an encouraging nature.

"The whole thing is frightful!" he said to his second. "I simply cannot admit having had a duel with a nobody who is Monsieur de la Mole's secretary, and because my coachman stole my calling cards, besides."

"There's certainly some possibility of ridicule in it."

The same evening, the Chevalier de Beauvoisis and his friend began to spread the story that Monsieur Sorel—a perfectly delightful young man, by the way—was the illegitimate son of one of the Marquis de la Mole's intimate friends. This fact was accepted without difficulty. Once it was established, the young diplomat and his friend were kind enough to pay Julien several visits during the fortnight he was confined to his room. Julien confessed to them that he had been to the Opera but once in his life.

"That's dreadful," they said. "Nobody goes anywhere else; the first time you go out, it must be to hear *Count Ory*."

Julien all but paid court to the chevalier; that blend of self-respect, mysterious importance and youthful vanity enchanted him. For example, the chevalier stammered slightly because he had the honor of associating frequently with a great nobleman who had that affliction. Julien had never before found, in one single person, that sort of entertaining absurdity combined with the perfection of manners which a poor provincial should try to imitate.

He was seen at the opera with the Chevalier de Beauvoisis; the association got him talked about.

"Well!" Monsieur de la Mole said to him one day, "so you're the illegitimate son of a wealthy gentleman in Franche-Comté, who is my intimate friend?"

The marquis cut Julien short when he would have explained that he had in no way contributed to the acceptance of this rumor.

"Monsieur de Beauvoisis didn't want to have fought with a carpenter's son."

"I know, I know," Monsieur de la Mole said. "Now it's up to me to give some substance to the story, which suits my purpose. But I've one favor to ask you: every opera evening, at half past eleven, go and stand in the vestibule and watch the society people come out. I see that you still have a few provincial mannerisms, you must get rid of them; besides, it does no harm to know, at least by sight, some of the important people to whom I may send you someday on an errand. Stop at the box office to let them know who you are; they have a note that you're to be admitted."

CHAPTER 7
An Attack of Gout

For the past six weeks the marquis had been confined to the house by an attack of gout. Mademoiselle de le Mole and her mother were in Hyères with the marquise's mother. Count Norbert came to see his father only at odd moments; their relationship was very pleasant, but they had little to say to one another. Monsieur de la Mole, reduced to Julien for companionship, was amazed to find him full of ideas.

One day the marquis said in the tone of excessive courtesy that frequently antagonized Julien:

"My dear Sorel, permit me to make you the gift of a blue suit: whenever you find it convenient to put it on and come to see me, you will be, in my eyes, the Count de Chaulne's younger brother, that is to say, the son of my old friend the duke."

Julien did not entirely understand what this was all about; that very evening he tried paying a visit in his blue suit. The marquis treated him as an equal. Julien had a spirit capable of appreciating genuine courtesy, but he had no conception of subtleties. Before this whim of the marquis, he would have sworn that it was impossible to be received more cordially by him. What remarkable talent! Julien thought. When he rose to go, the marquis apologized for being unable to accompany him to the door, because of his gout.

This curious idea obsessed Julien: Can he be making fun of me? he wondered. He went to ask advice of the Abbé Pirard who, less polite than the marquis, answered only by wheezing and speaking of something else. The next morning Julien presented himself before the marquis in his black suit, with his portfolio and his letters to be signed. He was received in the old manner. That evening, dressed in blue, it was in an utterly different tone, and quite as polite as the evening before.

"Since you aren't too bored by these visits you're kind enough to pay an old invalid," the marquis said, "you might tell him about all the little events of your life, but frankly and with no other thought than speaking clearly and in an amusing manner. For one must be amused," the marquis went on. "That is the only real thing in life."

Since he had been asked for the truth, Julien resolved to tell everything, but holding back two things: his fanatical admiration for a name that aroused the marquis' anger, and the complete lack of belief that was not too becoming to a future priest. The little episode with the Chevalier de Beauvoisis came in very opportunely. The marquis laughed until tears stood in his eyes over the scene in the Rue Saint-Honoré café with the coachman mouthing vile epithets. This was a time of perfect frankness in the relationship between the master and the protégé.

The attack of gout was prolonged by the severe winter cold and lasted for some months.

One becomes very much attached to a fine spaniel, the marquis thought, why am I so ashamed of becoming attached to this little abbé? He is unusual. I treat him like a son; well, where is the harm in that? This whim of mine, if it lasts, will cost me a diamond worth five hundred louis in my will.

Once the marquis had recognized the protégé's firm character, he intrusted him with new responsibilities every day.

One day, at the end of the morning interview, Julien, dressed in black for business, amused the marquis who detained him for two hours and insisted upon giving him a few banknotes which his broker had just brought him from the stock exchange.

"Monsieur le Marquis, I hope I won't be failing in the great respect I owe you if I ask permission to say something."

"Say it, my friend."

"Will Monsieur le Marquis be so kind as to let me refuse this gift?

It isn't given to the man in black, and it would altogether spoil the relationship he is good enough to tolerate with the man in blue." He bowed most respectfully and left the room without another glance.

This episode amused the marquis. He told the Abbé Pirard about it that evening.

"I must finally confess one thing to you, my dear abbé. I know about Julien's birth, and I authorize you not to keep this confidence secret."

His behavior this morning was noble, the marquis thought, and I am going to ennoble him.

Some time later the marquis was at last able to leave the house.

"Go and spend two months in London," he said to Julien. "Special messengers and others will bring you the letters I receive, along with my notes. You will write the answers and send them back to me, inclosing each letter with its answer. I've estimated that it won't mean more than five days delay."

Riding post on the road to Calais, Julien was amazed at the futility of the alleged business upon which he was being sent.

We will not dwell upon the feeling of hatred, almost of horror, with which he set foot on English soil. His insane passion for Bonaparte is known. In every officer he saw a Sir Hudson Lowe, in every nobleman a Lord Bathurst ordering the infamies of Saint Helena and receiving in return ten years of office.

In London he encountered at last the height of empty vanity. He became associated with some young Russian noblemen who initiated him into it.

"You're bound to be a success, my dear Sorel," they said. "You have naturally that expression, cold and a thousand leagues removed from present sensation that we are all trying to develop."

"You don't understand your century," Prince Korasoff told him: "*Always do the opposite of what's expected of you.* On my honor, that's the only religion of our age. Don't be mad or affected, because then madness and affectation will be expected of you and the precept will never be fulfilled."

Julien covered himself with glory one evening in the drawing-room of the Duke of Fitz-Folke who had invited him to dine, along with Prince Korasoff. They were kept waiting an hour. The manner in which Julien conducted himself in the midst of the twenty persons who were waiting is still referred to among young embassy secretaries in London. His expression was inimitable.

Upon his return: "What amusing idea have you brought from England?" Monsieur de la Mole asked him. He remained silent.

"What idea have you brought, amusing or otherwise?" the marquis said sharply.

"One doesn't know how to act, talking to our great diplomats," Julien said. "They have a mania for starting serious discussions. If one confines oneself to the commonplaces of the newspapers, one is taken for a fool. If one goes so far as to say something new and true, they're astonished, don't know how to answer and send you word at seven o'clock the next morning that you were improper."

"Not bad!" the marquis said, laughing. "Aside from that, I'll wager, Monsieur Thinker, that you have no idea what it was you were sent to do in England."

"Pardon me," Julien said. "I went there to dine once a week with the King's Ambassador, who is the most courteous man in the world."

"You went to get this cross," the marquis said. "I don't want to make you leave off your black clothes, and I am accustomed to the more entertaining tone I've adopted with the man in blue. For the time being, understand this: when I see this cross, you will be the younger son of my friend the Duke de Chaulnes who, without suspecting it, has been employed in diplomacy for the past six months. Remember," the marquis added with a very serious air, cutting short Julien's thanks, "that I do not want to raise you above your station. That is always a mistake, and a misfortune for the benefactor as well as for the protégé. When my lawsuits bore you, or when you no longer suit me, I'll ask for a good parish like our friend the Abbé Pirard's for you, and *nothing more*," the marquis added in an extremely dry voice.

This cross soothed Julien's pride; he spoke far more. He took offense less often and received in a better spirit those remarks, capable of some impolite interpretation, which anyone can let slip in the midst of an animated conversation.

The cross earned him a strange visit; it was from Monsieur le Baron de Valenod, who came to Paris to thank the minister for his barony and to come to an understanding with him. He was about to be appointed mayor of Verrières, replacing Monsieur de Rênal.

Inwardly Julien burst out laughing when Monsieur de Valenod gave him to understand that it had just been discovered that Monsieur de Rênal was a Jacobin. The fact was that, in the election which was about to be held, the new baron was the Ministry's candidate and it was Monsieur de Rênal who was supported by the liberals.

In vain Julien tried to find out something about Madame de Rênal; the baron appeared to remember their former rivalry and became inscrutable. In the end he asked Julien for his father's vote in the elections which were about to take place. Julien promised to write.

"You really ought to present me to Monsieur de la Mole, Monsieur le Chevalier."

I certainly *ought*, Julien thought; but a scoundrel like him! . . .

"As a matter of fact," he said, "I'm too obscure a member of the de la Mole household to take it upon myself to present anybody."

Julien told the marquis everything: that evening he recounted Valenod's expectations, as well as his actions and exploits since 1814.

"Not only will you introduce the new baron to me tomorrow," Monsieur de la Mole returned with a serious expression "but I shall invite him to dine the day after. He will be one of our new prefects."

"In that case," Julien said coldly, "I'd like to ask for the position of poorhouse director for my father."

"Good enough!" the marquis said, resuming his air of gaiety. "I was expecting a sermon. You're shaping up."

CHAPTER 8
What Decoration Is a Distinction?

ONE day Julien returned from the charming estate of Villequier, on the banks of the Seine, which Monsieur de la Mole regarded with particular interest because, of all his properties, it was the only one that had belonged to the famous Boniface de la Mole. He found the marquise and her daughter at the town house, just returned from Hyères.

Julien was a dandy now, and versed in the art of living in Paris. He maintained a perfect coolness toward Mademoiselle de la Mole. He seemed to have retained no memory whatever of the times when she used to ask so gaily for details of his manner of falling off a horse.

Mademoiselle de la Mole found him taller and paler. His figure, his garments no longer had anything provincial about them; the same could not be said of his conversation: it was still noticeable that he was too serious, too emphatic. In spite of these uninspiring qualities, thanks to his pride there was nothing servile about it; one merely received the impression that he still considered too many things important. But it could be seen that he was a man to defend his opinions.

"He lacks lightness, but not wit," Mademoiselle de la Mole said to her father, joking with him about the cross he had given Julien. "My brother has been asking for one for a year and a half, and he's a de la Mole!"

"Yes; but Julien has a gift for the unexpected, which is more than you can say for the de la Mole you are talking about."

Mathilde felt an irresistible impulse to yawn. Those lovely eyes, in which dwelt the most profound boredom and, worse yet, despair of ever finding pleasure, lingered on Julien. At least he was not exactly like everybody else.

"Monsieur Sorel," she said in that high short voice with no trace of femininity which young women of the upper class affect, "are you going to Monsieur de Retz's ball tonight?"

"I have not had the honor of being presented to Monsieur le Duc, Mademoiselle." (One would have thought that these words and the title scorched the proud provincial's mouth.)

"He urged my brother to bring you; and if you would come, you could tell me all about the Villequier estate; it's a question of going there this coming spring. I'd like to know if the château is habitable and if the surroundings are as lovely as people say. So many reputations are unwarranted!"

Julien did not answer.

"Come to the ball with my brother," she added in a very sharp tone.

Julien bowed respectfully. So even in the midst of a ball I'm supposed to give an accounting to all members of the family. Am I not paid to be a businessman? His resentment added: Besides, God knows whether what I tell the daughter will upset the father's plans, or the mother's, or the brother's. It's a regular reigning prince's court. You have to be an absolute cipher and yet not give anyone grounds for complaint.

How I dislike that big girl, he thought, watching Mademoiselle de la Mole move away, summoned by her mother to be presented to several of her friends' wives. She exaggerates all the fashions, her gown is falling off her shoulders . . . She is even paler than before the trip . . . What colorless hair, it's so light. It looks as though daylight could show through it! . . . What arrogance in that way of greeting people, in that glance! What queenly gestures!

Mademoiselle de la Mole had just called to her brother as he was leaving the drawing-room.

Count Norbert came up to Julien:

"My dear Sorel," he said, "where do you want me to call for you at midnight, for Monsieur de Retz's ball? He expressly directed me to bring you."

"I know very well to whom I owe all these kindnesses," Julien said, bowing deeply.

His ill humor, finding nothing to resent in the tone of courtesy and even of interest with which Norbert had spoken to him, began to vent himself upon the reply he himself had made to that cordial remark. He found a note of baseness in it.

That evening, arriving at the ball, he was impressed by the magnificence of the Hôtel de Retz. The courtyard was covered by a vast crimson awning with gold stars: nothing could have been more elegant. Beneath this awning the courtyard had been transformed into a grove of orange trees and blossoming oleanders. Everyone was hurrying toward the door, and the crowd was so dense that it was impossible to move. The drawing-room was decorated to represent the Alhambra of Granada.

"She's the queen of the ball, you've got to agree," said a young man with a mustache, whose shoulder was digging into Julien's chest.

"Mademoiselle Fourmont, who has been the prettiest all winter," his neighbor answered, "sees that she has to take second place: look at her queer expression."

"Mademoiselle de la Mole looks to be controlling the pleasure her triumph is giving her, although she's perfectly aware of it. You'd think she was afraid to be pleasant to the people who speak to her."

"Well, that's the art of seduction."

"There's plenty of coquetry in that aristocratic coolness," the young man with the mustache went on.

"And those big blue eyes that turn down so slowly just when you think they're on the point of giving her away," his neighbor added. "Lord, I've never seen anything so expert."

"See how common the beautiful Fourmont girl looks next to her," a third said.

The doorway was cleared, Julien was able to enter.

Since she seems so remarkable to these dressed-up dolls, it's worth my taking the trouble to study her, he thought. I shall understand what perfection is to these people.

As he was searching for her with his eyes, Mathilde glanced at him. Duty calls me, Julien thought; but his ill humor was now only in his expression. Curiosity impelled him forward with a pleasure that Mathilde's gown, cut very low off the shoulders, quickly stimulated in a manner, to be sure, somewhat unflattering to his self-esteem. Her beauty is partly because of youth, he thought. Five or six men, among whom Julien recognized those he had overheard at the doorway, stood between her and himself.

"You, Monsieur, you were here all winter," she said to him. "Isn't it true that this is the loveliest ball of the season?"

The young men turned to see what lucky mortal it was from whom she so evidently desired an answer. It was not encouraging.

"I could hardly be much of a judge, Mademoiselle; I spend my life writing: this is the first ball of such magnificent proportions I've ever seen."

The young men in their mustaches were scandalized.

"You're a wise man, Monsieur Sorel," she returned. "You see all these balls, all these parties as a philosopher, as Jean-Jacques Rousseau would."

An idle remark had just extinguished Julien's imagination and driven all illusion from his heart. His mouth assumed a somewhat exaggerated expression of disdain.

"To my mind," he answered, "Jean-Jacques Rousseau was nothing but a fool, since he took it upon himself to criticize society; he didn't understand it, and he approached it with the spirit of an upstart footman."

"He wrote the *Contrat Social*," Mathilde said in a reverent tone.

"All the while he was preaching democracy and the overthrow of monarchial privilege, the upstart was drunk with joy if a duke changed the direction of his after-dinner walk to accompany one of his friends."

"Oh, yes, the Duke de Luxembourg, in Montmorency, accompanies a Monsieur Coindet part way to Paris . . ." Mademoiselle de la Mole said with the pleasure and enthusiasm of the first indulgence in pedantry. Julien's eye remained penetrating and stern. Mathilde had had a moment of genuine ardor; her partner's coolness greatly disconcerted her. She was all the more astonished because she was accustomed to being the one who had that effect upon others.

Just then, the Marquis de Croisenois strode eagerly over to Mademoiselle de la Mole.

What could be duller, she thought, than all this group! Here's Croisenois who wants to marry me; he is gentle, polite, he has perfect manners. If they weren't so boring, these men would all be quite attractive. He, too, will follow me about at balls with that small satisfied look. A year after the wedding my carriage, my horses, my gowns, my country mansion outside Paris will all be as fine as can be, just the thing to make a social climber, a Countess de Roiville for example, die of envy, and after that . . . ?

The Marquis de Croisenois succeeded in reaching her side and was speaking to her, but she continued to meditate, not listening. She followed Julien with her eye, mechanically, after he had moved away with a respectful, but aloof and dissatisfied air. In a corner, withdrawn from the circling crowd, she caught sight of Count Altamira, condemned to death in his own country.

"Do you know Count Altamira?" she asked Monsieur de Croisenois.

"Who doesn't know poor Altamira?" He told her the story of his ridiculous, absurd, abortive conspiracy.

"Very absurd!" Mathilde said as if speaking to herself, "but as least he did something. I want to meet a man. Bring him to me," she directed the greatly shocked marquis.

Count Altamira was one of the most open admirers of Mademoiselle de la Mole's lofty and almost impertinent manner; according to him, she was one of the most exquisite creatures in Paris.

"How perfect she'd be for a throne!" he said to Monsieur de Croisenois, and allowed himself to be taken to her without difficulty.

A conspirator at a ball, that's an interesting contrast, she was thinking. She thought that this one, with his black mustache, had the face of a resting lion; but she soon discovered that his mind had but one attitude: admiration for what is *useful*.

Aside from what might secure for his country a form of government by two Houses, the young count considered nothing worthy of his attention. He willingly left Mathilde, the most attractive woman at the ball, because he saw a Peruvian general come in. She yielded to the persistence of the Marquis de Croisenois, who for the past hour had been begging for a dance.

But neither the dance nor the desire to please one of the handsomest men of the Court nor anything else could distract Mathilde. A greater success would have been impossible. She was queen of the ball; she realized it, but coldly.

What a blank life I am going to lead with a creature like Croisenois, she thought as he escorted her back to her seat an hour later. . . . What is pleasure for me, she added sorrowfully, if after six months of absence I do not find it in the midst of a ball that is rousing the envy of every woman in Paris? And yet I'm surrounded by the homage of the best-constructed society I can imagine. There is nothing middle class here except a few of the peers and one or two Juliens, perhaps. And besides, she added with growing melancholy, think of all the advantages chance has given me: birth, wealth, youth—everything, alas, except happiness!

The most doubtful of my advantages, on the other hand, are the ones they've been telling me about this evening. Intellect, I believe that, for I obviously frighten them all. If they venture to embark upon a serious subject, they arrive all out of breath and as if they were making a great discovery, at a conclusion I've been repeating for an hour. I am beautiful, I have that advantage for which Madame de Staël would have sacrificed everything, and yet the fact is I'm dying of boredom. Is there any reason why I should be less bored when I've changed my name to that of the Marquis de Croisenois?

But dear God! she added, almost on the point of tears, isn't he a perfect man? He's the masterpiece of our modern education; you can't even look at him without his finding something pleasant, and even witty, to say; he is brave. . . . But this Sorel is odd, she thought, and her eyes abandoned their dismal expression for an angry one. I let him know that I had something to talk to him about, and he doesn't take the trouble to come back!

CHAPTER 9
The Ball

Y OU'RE in a temper," the Marquise de la Mole said to her, "I warn you, that's poor taste at a ball."

"I have a headache," Mathilde said with her scornful air. "It's too warm in here."

And Monsieur Sorel still doesn't come, she said to herself after she had danced again. She was all but searching for him with her eyes when she caught sight of him in another salon. An astonishing thing: he seemed to have lost that air of impenetrable frigidity which was so natural to him; he no longer looked English.

He is talking with the Count Altamira, my condemned man! Mathilde realized. His eye is full of brooding fire; he looks like a prince in disguise; his glance is prouder than ever.

Julien moved nearer the place where she was sitting, still talking with Altamira; she gazed at him intently, studying his features, seeking those lofty characteristics which earn a man the honor of being condemned to death.

As he passed her:

"Yes," he was saying to the Comte Altamira, "Danton was a man!"

Oh, heavens! Mathilde thought. Is he going to be another Danton? But he has such a noble face, and that Danton was so horribly ugly, a butcher, I believe. Julien was still quite close to her and she did not hesitate to call to him; she was aware of asking an extraordinary question, for a young girl, and proud of it.

"Wasn't Danton a butcher?" she said.

"Yes, in certain people's estimation," Julien answered with an air of barely concealed contempt and his eye still alight from his conversation with Altamira, "but unfortunately for well-born people, he was a lawyer in Méry-sur-Seine; which means, Mademoiselle," he added maliciously, "that he started out like several of the peers I see here. It is true that Danton had one tremendous disadvantage in the eyes of beauty: he was very ugly."

These last words were spoken rapidly in a manner certainly extraordinary and not particularly polite.

Julien waited a moment, his body slightly inclined from the waist and with a proudly humble expression. He seemed to say: "I am paid to answer you, and I live on my pay." He did not condescend to raise his eyes to Mathilde. She, with her lovely eyes abnormally wide open and fixed upon him, looked like his slave. At length, as the silence continued, he glanced at her as a manservant looks at his master, to receive his orders. Although his eyes met Mathilde's fully, still fixed upon him with a strange expression, he moved away with ostentatious alacrity.

He, who is really so handsome, Mathilde reflected, emerging at length from her abstraction, to eulogize ugliness that way! Never a selfish consideration! He is not like Caylus or Croisenois. This Sorel has something of the manner my father assumes when he imitates Napoleon at a ball. She had completely forgotten Danton. Positively, I am bored this evening. She reached out for her brother's arm and, to his great discomfiture, forced him to make the circle of the ballroom with her. She had an impulse to follow the conversation of the condemned man and Julien.

The crowd was enormous. Nevertheless, she succeeded in catching up with them just as Altamira, two paces in front of her, paused beside a tray to take an ice. He was talking to Julien, his back half turned.

Mademoiselle de la Mole, quite forgetting her duty toward herself, stepped forward almost directly between Altamira and Julien. Her brother, with her hand upon his arm, being accustomed to obey her, glanced about the room and, to keep himself in countenance, pretended to have been held up by the crowd.

"You're right," Altamira was saying, "they do everything without pleasure and without recollection, even their crimes. I can show you perhaps ten men at this very ball who should be condemned as murderers. They have forgotten about it, and the world has too."

"How true!" Mademoiselle de la Mole said.

Altamira looked at her in astonishment; Julien did not even condescend to glance at her.

"Observe that the revolution of which I found myself leader," Altamira went on, "did not succeed, solely because I was unwilling to order the deaths of three men and distribute to our partisans the seven or eight millions that were in a chest to which I held the key. My king, who is now in a fever to have me hanged and who, before the revolt, used to be more than friendly with me, would have given me his most coveted decoration if I had ordered those three deaths and distributed the money in that chest, because I would have achieved at least a half-success and my country would have had a constitution of some sort. . . . That's the way the world goes, it's a game of checkers."

"At that time," Julien returned, his eyes on fire, "you didn't know the game. Now . . ."

"I'd order the deaths, you mean, and not be a Girondin as you explained it to me the other day? . . . I'll answer you," Altamira said with a grim look, "when you have killed a man in a duel, which is still far less ugly than having him beheaded by an executioner."

"Lord!" Julien said, "any means to an end. If, instead of being a nonentity, I had some power, I'd have three men hanged to save the lives of four."

His eyes reflected the fires of conscience and scorn for the empty judgments of men; they met those of Mademoiselle de la Mole, standing close beside him, and this scorn, far from changing to a cordial and polite expression, seemed to be accentuated.

She was profoundly shocked by it, but it was no longer in her power to put Julien out of her mind; she moved away, vexed, drawing her brother with her.

I must have some punch and dance a great deal, she thought. I want to pick out the best of everything, and make an effect at all costs. She danced until daybreak and at last left the ball, terribly exhausted. But in her carriage, the little strength that remained to her was still concentrated upon making her sad and miserable. She had been scorned by Julien, and was unable to scorn him.

The next day, writing his letters in the library, Julien could still think of nothing but his conversation with the Count Altamira.

As a matter of fact, he thought after long meditation, if these Spanish Liberals had compromised the people by committing crimes they could not have been swept aside so readily. They were conceited babbling children . . . like me! Julien realized suddenly, as if waking with a start.

What difficult thing have I ever done to give me the right to criticize men who at least, once in their lives, did something daring, began to act? . . . This lofty train of thought was interrupted by the unexpected appearance of Mademoiselle de la Mole, who came into the library. He was so thoroughly obsessed by his admiration for the great virtues of Danton, of Mirabeau, of Carnot who had never known what it was to be conquered, that his eyes rested on Mademoiselle de la Mole without recognition, without thought of her, almost without seeing her. When at length his wide fixed eyes took notice of her presence, the light in them went out. Mademoiselle de la Mole observed this with bitterness.

In vain she asked him for a volume of Vély's *Histoire de France*, which stood on the highest shelf, obliging Julien to go and get the larger of the two ladders. Julien brought the ladder; he picked out the volume, he handed it to her, still without being able to fix his mind on her. As he was putting the ladder away, in his preoccupation he struck one of the glass panes of a bookcase with his elbow; the slivers of glass, falling on the floor, at last aroused him. He hastened to apologize to Mademoiselle de la Mole. He tried to be polite, but he was no more than polite. Mathilde saw plainly that she had disturbed him, and that he would have preferred to think about whatever had been engrossing him before her arrival rather than talk to her. After having looked closely at him, she went out slowly. Julien watched her move away. He enjoyed the contrast between the simplicity of the gown she was wearing with the extravagant elegance of the one she had worn the evening before. The difference between the two facial expressions was almost equally striking. That young girl, so arrogant at the Duke de Retz's ball, had just now an almost appealing look. Really, Julien thought, that black dress sets off the beauty of her figure even better. She carries herself like a queen; but why is she in mourning? If I ask someone the cause of this mourning, I'll probably just be committing another error.

Julien had entirely emerged from the profundities of his enthusiasm. I'll have to read over all the letters I've written this morning; God knows the blunders I'll find, and the words left out. As he was reading the first of the letters with forced concentration, he heard the rustle of a silk dress quite close to him; he turned rapidly; Mademoiselle de la Mole was standing not two steps from his table; she was laughing. This second interruption irritated Julien.

As for Mathilde, she had just become acutely aware that she was nothing to this young man; her laughter was to disguise her embarrassment, in which it succeeded.

"Evidently you're thinking about something very absorbing, Monsieur Sorel. Is it some odd anecdote about the conspiracy that sent Monsieur le Comte Altamira to us here in Paris? Tell me about it, I'm dying to know; I'll be discreet, I swear I will!" She was astonished by the words she heard herself saying. Why, she was begging a favor from an underling! Her embarrassment increased, she added lightly:

"What can have made you, who are ordinarily so cold, into an inspired creature, a sort of prophet like one of Michelangelo's?"

This shrewd and indiscreet questioning, hurting Julien deeply, restored the full force of his obsession.

"Was Danton right to steal?" he asked her abruptly, and in a manner that became more and more savage. "Ought the revolutionaries of Piedmont, of Spain, to compromise the people by committing crimes? In short, Mademoiselle," he said, approaching her with a terrifying air, "should the man who wishes to abolish ignorance and crime on earth sweep over it like the hurricane and do evil as if at random?"

Mathilde was frightened, could not sustain his glance, and fell back two steps. She stared at him for an instant; then, ashamed of her fear, left the library with a light step.

CHAPTER 10
Queen Marguerite

Entering the dining room, Julien was distracted from his ill temper by Mademoiselle de la Mole's deep mourning, which struck him the more forcibly since no other member of the family was in black.

By the end of dinner he found himself wholly rid of the access of enthusiasm that had obsessed him all day. By good fortune, the academician who knew Latin dined at the house that evening. There is the man who will be least inclined to make fun of me, Julien thought, if, as I assume, my question about Mademoiselle de la Mole's mourning is a blunder.

Mathilde was watching him with a curious expression. There's a good example of the coquetry of this country's women, as Madame de Rênal described it to me, Julien reflected. I wasn't nice to her this morning, I didn't fall in with her fancy to have a talk. That way I increased my value in her eyes.

The company was leaving the table. I mustn't let my academician get involved in a conversation, Julien thought. He approached him as they were going out into the garden, assumed a gentle and submissive air and agreed with his fury at the success of *Hernani*. After which, in the most indifferent manner: "I suppose," he said, "that Mademoiselle de la Mole has fallen heir to some uncle for whom she's in mourning."

"What!" the academician said, stopping short. "You're one of the household and you don't know about her obsession? As a matter of fact, it's strange that her mother permits such behavior; but just between ourselves, strength of character is not precisely the shining virtue of this household. Mademoiselle Mathilde has enough for all of them, and leads them about by the nose. Today is the thirtieth of April!" The academician paused and glanced slyly at Julien. Julien smiled as intelligently as he could.

What connection could there be between leading a whole family by the nose, wearing a black dress and the thirtieth of April? he wondered. I must be even more ignorant than I thought.

"I must confess . . ." he said to the academician, and his eyes continued to ask questions.

"Let's take a turn around the garden," the academician said, glimpsing with delight the opportunity of making a long elegant speech. "What, is it possible that you do not know what happened on April 30, 1574?"

"Where?" Julien asked, bewildered.

"In the Place de Grève."

Julien was so astonished that the words did not enlighten him. Curiosity, expectation of some absorbing tragedy, so in keeping with his character, gave him those gleaming eyes which a narrator so loves to see in his listener. The academician, enchanted at finding a virgin ear, told Julien at great length of how, on April 30, 1574, the finest young fellow of those times, Boniface de la Mole, and Annibal Coconasso, his friend, a Piedmontese gentleman, had lost their heads in the Place de Grève. "La Mole was the adored lover of Queen Marguerite of Navarre, and don't forget," the academician added, "that Mademoiselle de la Mole's full name is Mathilde-Marguerite. La Mole was also the favorite of the Duke d'Alençon and the intimate friend of the King of Navarre, his mistress' husband who later became Henri IV. On Shrove Tuesday in that year of 1574, the Court was at Saint-Germain with poor King Charles IX who was dying. La Mole tried to rescue his friends the princes whom Queen Catherine de Medici was holding prisoner at Court. He sent two hundred cavalry troops against the walls of Saint-Germain, the Duke d'Alençon took fright, and La Mole was flung to the executioner.

"But what affected Mademoiselle Mathilde, what she admitted to me herself, seven or eight years ago when she was twelve—for she has a mind, a mind of her own! . . ." and the academician raised his eyes to heaven. "The thing that impressed her in that political catastrophe was that Queen Marguerite of Navarre, hidden in a house on the Place de Grève, dared to send a message to the executioner demanding her lover's head. And the following night, at midnight, she took that head in her carriage and went to bury it with her own hands in a chapel at the foot of Montmartre."

"Is it possible?" Julien cried, moved.

"Mademoiselle Mathilde is contemptuous of her brother, because, as you've noticed, he doesn't give a thought to all this ancient history and wears no mourning on April 30. It's since this famous retribution, and in memory of the intimate friendship between de la Mole and Coconasso—which Coconasso, like the Italian he was, was called Annibal—that all the men of this family bear that name. And," the academician added, lowering his voice, "this Coconasso was, according to Charles IX himself, one of the most ruthless assassins of August 24, 1572. But how is it possible, my dear Sorel, that you don't know these things, you, an intimate of the household?"

"Then that's why Mademoiselle de la Mole called her brother Annibal twice at dinner. I thought I had misunderstood."

That evening Mademoiselle de la Mole's little maid, who was courting Julien as Elisa had once done, gave him to understand that her mistress' mourning was not worn for the purpose of attracting attention. The eccentricity was rooted deep in her character. She genuinely loved that de la Mole, the adored lover of his century's most intellectual queen, who died for having tried to restore their liberty to his friends. And what friends! The first prince of the blood and Henri IV.

Accustomed to the complete lack of affectation that graced all of Madame de Rênal's behavior, Julien saw only artificiality in all Parisian women; and, little as he was inclined to melancholy, found nothing to say to them. Mademoiselle de la Mole was an exception.

He began by no longer considering that sort of beauty which is inherent in nobility of bearing as evidence of a barren heart. He had long conversations with Mademoiselle de la Mole, who sometimes walked with him after dinner in the garden beneath the open windows of the drawing-room. She told him one day that she was reading the histories of d'Aubigné and Brantôme. Singular reading matter, Julien thought; and the marquise does not permit her to read Walter Scott's novels!

Gradually his conversations with this young girl of so imposing, and at the same time so easy, a demeanor became more interesting.

He forgot his gloomy rôle as a mutinous plebeian. He found her well-read and even intelligent. Her opinions in the garden were quite different from those she expressed in the drawing-room. Sometimes she displayed with him an enthusiasm and a frankness that were in complete contrast with her ordinary manner, so aloof and so cold.

"The Wars of the League were France's heroic times," she said to him one day, her eyes sparkling with intelligence and ardor. "Then everyone fought to secure one certain thing that he wanted, for the triumph of his party, and not just for the sake of winning some old decoration, as in the times of your emperor. Admit that there was less egotism and meanness then. I love that century."

"And Boniface de la Mole was the hero of it," he said.

"At least he was loved as it must be sweet to be loved. What woman living today wouldn't be horrified at touching her lover's severed head?"

Madame de la Mole called her daughter. Hypocrisy, to be of any use, must be concealed; and Julien, as can be seen, had made Mademoiselle de la Mole a half-confidence of his admiration for Napoleon.

There's the vast advantage they have over us, Julien thought, remaining alone in the garden. The history of their ancestors raises them above vulgar sentiments, and they need not be forever thinking of earning their bread! What miserable considerations! he added bitterly. I am unworthy to have opinions about these weighty matters. My life is nothing but a series of hypocrisies because I haven't a thousand francs a year to live on.

"What are you dreaming about now, Monsieur?" Mathilde asked running back to him.

Julien was tired of feeling contempt for himself. Out of pride he spoke his thought frankly. He blushed deeply, speaking of his poverty to so wealthy a person. He tried to make it quite clear, by his proud tone, that he was not asking for anything. Never had he seemed so appealing to Mathilde; she found in him an indication of sensibility and frankness which he often lacked.

Less than a month later, Julien was walking, deep in thought, in the garden of the de la Mole mansion; but his face no longer had the hardness, the philosophical disdain that formerly expressed the unremitting consciousness of his inferiority. He had just escorted Mademoiselle de la Mole to the drawing-room door, as she maintained that she had hurt her foot, racing with her brother.

She leaned on my arm in a very odd manner! Julien thought. Am I being conceited, or can it be true that she has a liking for me? She listens to me with so sympathetic an air, even when I'm confessing to her all the torments of my pride! She who shows so much pride with everyone! The people in the salon would really be astonished if they could see her with that expression. It's quite certain that she does not have that kind and gentle manner with anyone else.

Julien tried not to exaggerate that curious friendship. Privately he thought of it as an armed truce. Every day when they met, before resuming the almost intimate tone of the day before, they seemed to ask: Shall we be friends today, or enemies? Julien realized that to allow himself to be insulted even once by this arrogant girl without retaliating would be to ruin everything. If I must quarrel, wouldn't it be better to start it myself, in defense of my pride's just rights, rather than in response to the indications of contempt that would promptly follow the slightest departure from what I owe to my personal dignity?

Several times, on days when she was out of humor, Mathilde tried to take a great lady tone with him; she devoted extraordinary subtlety to these attacks, but Julien thrust them rudely aside.

One day he interrupted her bluntly: "Has Mademoiselle de la Mole some order to give her father's secretary?" he asked. "It is his duty to listen to her orders and execute them with respect, but aside from that he has nothing to say to her. He is not paid to share his thoughts with her."

These circumstances, and the singular suspicions Julien had, dissipated the boredom he normally found in that magnificent drawing-room where it was improper to be amusing on any subject.

It would be amusing if she loved me! Whether she loves me or not, Julien continued, I have as an intimate friend an intelligent girl before whom I see the whole household tremble, and the Marquis de Croisenois most of all. This young man, so polite, so mild-mannered, so brave, who is the embodiment of all the advantages of birth and wealth, even one of which would be such a source of comfort to me! He is madly in love with her, he is supposed to marry her. How many letters Monsieur de la Mole has had me write to the two lawyers, to arrange the contract! And I, so lowly with my pen in my hand, two hours later, here in the garden, I triumph over that very attractive man: for preferences, after all, are direct, striking. Perhaps, too, she hates the future husband in the man. She is independent enough for that. And the kindness she has for me I earn for being an inferior in whom she can confide!

No, either I am out of my mind or she is making advances to me; the more cold and respectful I act to her, the more she seeks me out. This must be a deliberate action, an affectation; but I see her eyes light up when I appear unexpectedly. Can women of Paris counterfeit that reaction? No matter! Appearances are with me, let's make the most of appearances. My God, how beautiful she is! How appealing her great blue eyes are, seen close, and looking at me the way they often do! What a difference between this spring and last year's, when I was living wretchedly in the midst of those three hundred wicked, dirty hypocrites, and holding out by sheer will power. I was almost as wicked as they were.

On days of mistrust: That girl is making fun of me, Julien would think. She's in league with her brother to hoax me. But she seems so scornful of that brother's lack of energy! "He's brave, and that's all," she tells me. "He has not one thought that dares to deviate from the fashion." I'm always the one who is obliged to undertake his defense. A girl of nineteen! At that age can anyone be faithful every instant of the day to the hypocrisy one has prescribed for oneself?

On the other hand, when Mademoiselle de la Mole fixes her great blue eyes on me with a certain curious expression, Count Norbert always goes away. This seems suspicious to me; shouldn't he become indignant over his sister's attentions to one of the household *servants?*— for I heard the Duke de Chaulnes speak of me in those terms. At this memory, anger drove out all other emotion. Was it that eccentric duke's love of antique phraseology?

Well, she is lovely, Julien continued, glaring like a tiger. I shall have her, and then I shall go away, and heaven help anyone who hinders me in my flight!

This idea became an obsession with Julien; he could not think of anything else. His days passed like hours.

At any moment, while he was trying to concentrate upon some serious matter, his mind would go blank, and he would rouse himself a quarter of an hour later, his heart beating eccentrically, his head swimming, and pondering the question: Does she love me?

CHAPTER 11
A Young Girl's Influence

I F JULIEN had devoted to studying what went on in the drawing-room, the time he expended in exaggerating Mathilde's beauty or rousing himself to fury over the arrogance natural to her family, which she abandoned for him, he would have understood the nature of her influence over all about her. Whenever anyone displeased Mademoiselle de la Mole, she contrived to punish him with a pleasantry so subtle, so well-chosen, so apparently appropriate, so casually delivered, that the hurt of it grew by the instant, the more one thought it over. Little by little she was becoming unbearable to sensitive vanity.

It was perhaps in order to have victims a little more amusing than her grandparents, the academician and the five or six other lower-class mortals who courted their favor that she had given some encouragement to the Marquis de Croisenois, the Count de Caylus and two or three other young men of the utmost distinction. For her, they were no more than new objects for an epigram.

"They're all the same perfect figure of a man, ready to leave for Palestine," she said to her cousin. "Can you think of anything duller? They must have been less colorless in the time of the Empire. In those days all the young men of the aristocratic world had seen or performed

210

actions that *really* had some greatness. My uncle the Duke de N . . . was at Wagram."

"What intelligence does it take to give a saber thrust? And once they've done that, they talk about it so often!" Mademoiselle de Saint-Hérédité, Mathilde's cousin, said, "Oh, well, stories like that give me pleasure. To have been in a *real* battle, one of Napoleon's battles, where ten thousand soldiers were killed, that's a proof of courage. Being exposed to danger rouses the spirit and saves it from the boredom into which my poor admirers seem to be plunged; and it's contagious, that boredom. Which one of them has any idea of doing anything extraordinary? They're trying to get possession of my hand; a splendid contest! I am rich, and my father will see to it that his son-in-law gets advancement. Oh, if he could only find one that might be a little bit amusing!"

Such were the thoughts of the most envied heiress of the Faubourg Saint-Germain when she began to find pleasure in walking with Julien. She was amazed at his pride; she admired the subtlety of this little bourgeois. He'll find a way to make a bishop of himself, like the Abbé Maury, she thought.

Presently that sincere and unfeigned resistance with which our hero met several of her ideas caught her interest; she thought about it; she repeated the least details of his conversation to her friend, and discovered that she was never able to describe them accurately in every respect.

Suddenly enlightenment came to her: I have the good fortune to be in love, she thought one day with a spasm of incredulous joy. I am in love, I am in love, that's evident. At my age, where can a young, beautiful, intelligent girl find sensations, if not in love? No matter what I do I'll never be able to love Croisenois, Caylus and *tutti quanti*. They are perfect, too perfect perhaps; anyway, they bore me.

She reviewed in her mind all the descriptions of passion she had read in *Manon Lescaut*, the *Nouvelle Héloïse*, the *Letters of a Portuguese Nun*, and all the rest. There was no question, of course, of anything but a great passion; frivolous love was unworthy of a girl of her age and rank. She gave the name of love only to that heroic emotion which was to be encountered in France in the times of Henri III and Bassompierre. That love never meanly gave way before obstacles but, far from that, led to the accomplishment of great feats. What a misfortune for me that there is no real Court, like Catherine de Medici's or Louis XIII's!

I feel that I am on the same plane with all that is bravest and greatest. What could I not do with a great-hearted king like Louis XIII sighing at my feet! I'd take him to the Vendée, as the Baron de Tolly so often says, and from there he would reconquer his kingdom; then no more Charter . . . and Julien would help me. What does he lack? A name and a fortune. He would make his name, he would acquire a fortune.

Between Julien and me there is no signing a contract, no legal business; everything is on a heroic level, everything shall be born of chance. Aside from noble rank, which he lacks, it is Marguerite de Valois' love for the young La Mole, the most distinguished man of his times. Is it my fault that the young men of Court circles are such great adherents to the *proper* and turn pale at the bare thought of any slightly unconventional episode? A little trip to Greece or Africa is the height of daring to them, and the only way they know how to go from one place to another is in a flock. The moment they find themselves alone, they are afraid, not of the Bedouin's lance but of ridicule, and that fear makes imbeciles of them.

My little Julien, on the other hand, likes to act only by himself. Never, in that gifted spirit, the slightest inclination to seek support and encouragement in others! He scorns others, that is why I do not scorn him.

If, along with his poverty, Julien were of noble blood, my love would be no more than a vulgar piece of stupidity, a dull misalliance; I should want nothing to do with it; it would have none of the attributes of great passions: the immensity of the obstacles to be overcome, and the black uncertainty of the outcome.

Mademoiselle de la Mole was so preoccupied with this delightful train of thought that on the following day, she inadvertently praised Julien to the Marquis de Croisenois and to her brother. Her eloquence went to such lengths that it irritated them.

"Watch out for that young man with all his energy," her brother cried. "If the Revolution begins again, he'll have us all guillotined."

She refrained from answering and quickly began to tease her brother and the Marquis de Croisenois about the fear with which energy inspired them. "At bottom, it's no more than the fear of meeting with the unexpected, the fear of being brought up short in the face of the unexpected . . . Always and forever the fear of ridicule, a monster which, unfortunately, gentlemen, died in 1816."

There is no ridicule, Monsieur de la Mole sometimes said, in a country where there are two political parties.

His daughter had understood this conception.

"So, gentlemen," she said to Julien's enemies, "you will have been deathly afraid all your lives, and afterwards they'll say to you:

" '*That was not a wolf, that was but a shadow.*' "

Mathilde left them very soon. Her brother's remark horrified her, it disturbed her greatly; but by the following day she considered it the highest praise.

In this era, when all energy is dead, his energy frightens them. I shall tell him what my brother said, I want to see what answer he will make to it. But I'll choose one of those moments when his eyes are shining. Then he can't lie to me.

From the moment she had decided that she was in love with Julien, she was no longer bored. Daily she congratulated herself upon the course she had taken in providing herself with a great passion. That amusement has many dangers, she thought. So much the better! A thousand times so much the better.

Without a great passion I was pining away with boredom at the finest period of life, from sixteen to twenty. I've already lost my best years, obliged, for my sole diversion, to listen to the nonsensical talk of my mother's friends, who were not, it seems, quite as strict at Coblenz in 1792 as their words are today.

It was while these great uncertainties were troubling Mathilde that Julien was unable to decipher her long glances which rested on him. He did notice an increase of coolness in Count Norbert's attitude, and a new access of insolence in those of Messieurs de Caylus, de Luz and de Croisenois. He was accustomed to that. It was a misfortune that sometimes overtook him following an evening when he had spoken more brilliantly than was suitable to his position. If it had not been for the particular cordiality Mathilde showed him and the curiosity with which the whole group inspired him, he would have avoided following those elegant young men with their mustaches to the garden when they accompanied Mademoiselle de la Mole there after dinner.

Yes, it's impossible not to recognize it, Julien thought, Mademoiselle de la Mole does look at me in an extraordinary manner. But even when her lovely blue eyes, fixed upon me, are gazing at me with the utmost unrestraint, I always read in their depths something calculating, cold-blooded and malicious. Is it possible that that is love? How different from Madame de Rênal's glances!

One evening after dinner, Julien, who had followed Monsieur de la Mole to his study, returned quickly to the garden. As he casually joined the group around Mathilde, he overheard a few words spoken quite loudly. She was tormenting her brother. Julien heard his own name pronounced distinctly twice. His presence was noticed; a deep silence fell abruptly, and there were one or two vain efforts to break it. Mademoiselle de la Mole and her brother were too intent to find another subject of conversation. Messieurs de Caylus, de Luz and de Croisenois seemed cold as ice to Julien. He moved away.

CHAPTER 12
A Plot

THE next day he again surprised Norbert and his sister talking about him. At his appearance a deathly silence fell, as it had the evening before. His suspicions now had no limit. Have these pleasant young people undertaken to make a fool of me? It must be confessed that that seems much more likely than a supposed passion on Mademoiselle de la Mole's part for a poor devil of a secretary. In the first place, do these people have passions? Mockery is their strong point. They are jealous of my poor little gift of speech. Being jealous is another of their weaknesses. This point of view explains everything. Mademoiselle de la Mole is trying to convince me that she favors me, simply in order to make a spectacle of me for the amusement of her future husband.

This cruel suspicion changed Julien's whole mental attitude. The idea found in Julien's heart a first stirring of love, which it had no trouble in destroying. That love was based purely upon Mathilde's rare beauty, or rather upon her queenly demeanor and her exquisite clothes. In that, Julien was still a parvenu. A beautiful society woman, we are assured, is what most astonishes the intelligent peasant when he attains to the upper circles of the social world. It was certainly not Mathilde's character that had set Julien to dreaming, these past days. He had enough sense to realize that he knew nothing about her character. All that he saw of it might be no more than an affectation.

Resolved though he was not to be taken in by Mathilde s demonstrations of interest, they were so marked on certain days, and Julien, whose eyes were beginning to open, found her so attractive that he was sometimes embarrassed by them.

The subtlety and patience of these young aristocrats is eventually going to triumph over my inexperience, he thought; I should go away and put an end to all this. The marquis had recently intrusted him with the administration of small estates and houses he owned in the southern part of Languedoc. A trip there was essential: Monsieur de la Mole reluctantly consented to it. Except upon matters of high ambition, Julien had become another self to him.

When all is said and done, they haven't caught me, Julien reflected, preparing for his departure. Whether Mademoiselle de la Mole's sarcasms to those gentlemen were genuine or simply designed to inspire me with confidence, they amused me.

If there's no conspiracy against the carpenter's son, Mademoiselle de la Mole's behavior is inexplicable, but it's as much so to the Marquis de Croisenois as to me. Yesterday, for instance, her temper was quite real, and I had the pleasure of seeing a young man, as aristocratic and as rich as I am poor and lowborn, forced to give way in my favor. That is the finest of my triumphs; it will cheer me in my post-chaise, riding the plains of Languedoc.

He had made a secret of his departure, but Mathilde knew better than he that he was going to leave Paris on the morrow, and for a long absence. She had recourse to a frightful headache which was aggravated by the stuffy air of the drawing-room. She walked long in the garden, and so tormented the Marquis de Croisenois, Caylus, de Luz, and several other young men who had dined at the de la Mole mansion, with her biting sarcasms that she forced them to leave.

They were left alone; the conversation was obviously flagging. No, Julien has no feeling for me, Mathilde thought, genuinely distressed.

As he was taking leave of her, she clasped his arm urgently: "This evening you'll receive a letter from me," she said in a voice so altered that the sound of it was unrecognizable.

This detail instantly softened Julien.

"My father," she went on, "has due appreciation for the services you perform for him. You *must not* go tomorrow; find some excuse." And she left him, running.

Her waist was exquisite. It would have been impossible to have a prettier foot, she ran with a grace that enchanted Julien; but can one guess what his second thought was, after she was quite out of sight? He was offended by the imperious tone in which she had said the words *you must*. Louis XV, too, at the moment of his death, was violently angered by the words *you must*, clumsily used by his chief physician, and Louis XV was no upstart.

An hour later a servant handed Julien a letter; it was nothing more nor less than a declaration of love.

There's not too much affectation in the style, Julien observed, trying by means of literary observations to contain the joy that pulled at his cheek muscles and forced him to laugh in spite of himself.

"And so I," he cried suddenly, emotion becoming too strong to be contained, "I, a poor peasant, have received a declaration of love from a great lady!

"From my own point of view, I haven't done badly," he went on, suppressing his joy as far as possible. "I've been able to preserve the dignity of my character. I've never said that I loved her." He began to study the formation of the letters. Mademoiselle de le Mole had decorative small handwriting in the English fashion. He needed physical occupation to distract him from joy which approached the point of frenzy.

"Your departure forces me to speak. . . . It would be more than I could endure, not to see you again."

A thought came to strike Julien with the force of a discovery, interrupt his examination of Mathilde's letter and augment his delight. I'm taking her away from the Marquis de Croisenois, he thought, I, who never say other than serious things! And he such a handsome man! He has a mustache, a fine uniform; he always finds something witty and apt to say just at the right moment.

It was a delightful moment for Julien; he wandered about the garden, distracted with happiness.

Later he went upstairs to his office and sought an interview with the Marquis de la Mole, who fortunately had not gone out. He easily demonstrated, by showing him some papers marked as newly arrived from Normandy, that for the sake of the Norman lawsuits he would be obliged to put off his trip to Languedoc.

"I'm very happy that you are not going," the marquis said when they had finished talking business. "I like your company." Julien left the room; the remark embarrassed him.

And I am going to seduce his daughter, perhaps make impossible her marriage to the Marquis de Croisenois, which is the chief thing he looks forward to: if he never becomes a duke, at least his daughter would have a footstool near the throne. It occurred to Julien to leave for Languedoc in spite of Mathilde's letter, in spite of the excuses given the marquis. This impulse of virtue quickly subsided.

How good I am, he thought; I, a commoner, taking pity on a family of this rank! I, whom the Duke de Chaulnes calls a servant. How does the marquis keep adding to his immense fortune? By selling securities when he finds out at Court that there is to be an apparent change in State policy the next day. And I, flung by a malign Providence into the lowest class, I who have been endowed with a noble heart and not even a thousand francs a year: that is, not enough for bread, *literally speaking, bread;* I, refuse an offered pleasure! A clear spring that comes to quench my thirst in the scorching desert of mediocrity across which I am so painfully making my way! Lord, I'm not that much of a fool. Every man for himself in this desert of egotism which is called life.

And he recalled several glances brimming with disdain directed at him by Madame de la Mole and, more particularly, by the *ladies*, her friends.

The pleasure of triumphing over the Marquis de Croisenois came to complete the overthrow of the virtuous impulse.

How I'd like it if he got angry! Julien thought. With what assurance I could give him a sword thrust now! And he made the gesture of a fencer's lunge. Up to now I have been a vulgar fellow with some learning, basely imposing because of a little courage. After this letter, I'm his equal.

Yes, he thought with infinite gratification, the words forming deliberately in his mind, our merits, the marquis' and mine, have been weighed, and the poor carpenter's son from the Jura wins.

Good! he thought suddenly. There's the signature for my reply, ready-made. Do not imagine, Mademoiselle de la Mole, that I am forgetting my position. I will make you realize and feel deeply the fact that it is for a carpenter's son that you are betraying a descendant of the famous Guy de Croisenois who followed Saint Louis to the Crusades.

Yes, but then suppose four of Monsieur de Croisenois' footmen set upon me and snatch the original letter from me?

No, for I'm well armed and it is my habit, as everyone knows, to open fire on lackeys.

Well, then: say one of them has some courage: he jumps on me. He's been promised a hundred napoleons. I kill him or wound him; fine! That's just what they want. I'm thrown into prison quite legally; I appear in police court and am sent, with all justice and equity on the part of the judges, to keep Messieurs Fontan and Magalon company in Poissy. There, I sleep all huddled together with four hundred miserable beggars. . . . And I'm supposed to have some pity for these people! he cried to himself, springing up impetuously. Have they any for fellows of the third estate when they get hold of them? These words were the last gasp of his gratitude to Monsieur de la Mole, which, in spite of himself, had been tormenting him until then.

One moment, gentlemen. I am going to send the crucial letter in a well-sealed packet to Monsieur Pirard to hold for me. He is an honest man, a Jansenist, and by that token not exposed to the seductions of the Budget. Yes, but he opens letters. . . . I'll send this one to Fouqué.

It must be admitted that Julien's glare was shocking, his expression hideous; it was a declaration of unalloyed crime. He was the wretched man at war with all society.

To arms! Julien cried. And he leaped down the steps of the mansion at one bound. He entered the public letter-writer's booth at the street corner; he frightened the man. "Copy it," he said, handing him Mademoiselle de la Mole's letter.

While the letter-writer was working, he himself wrote to Fouqué; he asked him to guard a valuable possession for him. But, he thought, interrupting himself, the secret inspectors at the post office will open my letter and return to you the one you are looking for . . . no, gentlemen! He went and bought an enormous Bible in a Protestant bookseller's, cunningly hid Mathilde's letter in the binding, had the whole thing wrapped, and sent off his package by parcel post, addressed to one of Fouqué's laborers, whose name was known to no one in Paris.

That done, he returned, joyful and energetic, to the Hôtel de la Mole. Now for *us*, he cried, locking the door of his room and flinging off his coat:

"What, Mademoiselle!" he wrote to Mathilde. "Is it Mademoiselle de la Mole who, by the hand of Arsène, her father's footman, had a most seductive letter delivered to a poor carpenter of the Jura, doubtless to make game of his simplicity . . . " And he transcribed the most unequivocal phrases of the letter he had just received.

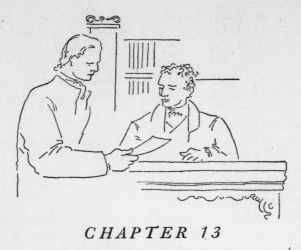

CHAPTER 13
A Girl's Thoughts

I**T WAS** not without conflicts that Mathilde had written. Whatever had been the origin of her interest in Julien, it soon came to overshadow the pride which, ever since she could remember, had been her one dominant emotion. That cold and lofty spirit was for the first time carried away by passionate feeling. But although it overcame pride, it was still faithful to the habits of pride. Two months of conflicts and new sensations had, so to speak, renewed her whole inner being.

A few months before, Mathilde had despaired of meeting anyone at all different from the ordinary pattern. She had found a certain amount of pleasure in going so far as to write to a few young men of her own social circle. That boldness, so improper, so indiscreet in a young woman, could have dishonored her in the eyes of Monsieur de Croisenois, the Duke de Chaulnes, his father and all the de Chaulnes connections who, seeing the wedding plans broken off, would have insisted upon finding out why. In those times she had been unable to sleep at night after having written such a letter. But those letters had merely been replies.

In this case she had boldly declared her love. She had written *first* (terrible word!) to a man in the lowest ranks of the social order.

These circumstances were a guarantee of eternal dishonor, in case of discovery. Which of the women who came to visit her mother would dare to take her part? What phrases could be offered them to repeat, to moderate the effect of the awful contempt of the salons?

Speaking was dreadful enough, but writing! "There are things one does not write down!" Napoleon cried, learning of Baylen's capitulation. And it was Julien who had told her of that remark, as if teaching her a lesson in advance!

But all this by itself was nothing; Mathilde's anguish had other causes. Regardless of the horrible effect upon society, the ineradicable and contemptible disgrace of having outraged her caste, Mathilde was writing to a person of quite another nature than the Croisenois, the de Luz, the Caylus.

The depth, the *unknown* quality of Julien's character would have been terrifying even in undertaking an ordinary relationship with him. And she was about to make him her lover, perhaps her master!

What claims will he not have upon me, if ever I give him complete power over me? Well, then I'll say to myself, like Medea: "In the midst of all these perils, I have still *myself*."

Julien, she believed, had no respect for nobility of blood. Far worse, it was possible that he had no love for her!

(Such characters are fortunately very rare.)

That evening, quite late, Julien was maliciously inspired to have a very heavy trunk brought down to the porter's room; he sent for the footman who was courting Mademoiselle de la Mole's maid to carry it down. This maneuver may have no result, he thought, but if it is successful she will believe that I have gone. He went to sleep highly pleased with this joke. Mathilde did not close an eye.

The next day, very early in the morning, Julien left the house without being seen, but he returned before eight o'clock.

He had no more than reached the library when Mademoiselle de la Mole appeared in the doorway. He handed her his answer. He felt that 't was his duty to speak to her; at least there could have been no more convenient opportunity, but Mademoiselle de la Mole would not listen to him, and vanished. Julien was enchanted at this: he did not know what to say to her.

If all this isn't a game planned with Count Norbert, it is evidently my frigid manner that has stimulated the strange love this high-born girl has decided to feel for me. I should be a bit more of a fool than is necessary if ever I let myself be deluded into feeling any affection for that great blond doll. This left him colder and more calculating than ever before.

In the battle that is about to take place, he added, pride of birth will be like a high hill making a strategic position between her and me. It's on that basis that we must maneuver. I made a bad mistake by remaining in Paris; this postponement of my departure debases me and makes me vulnerable, if all this is not just a trick. What danger was there in leaving? I should have been mocking them, if they are making a mock of me. If there is any reality in her feeling for me, I should have been multiplying that feeling a hundred times.

Mademoiselle de la Mole's letter had given Julien so acute a spur to vanity that even while laughing over what had happened to him, he had forgotten to consider seriously the expediency of departure.

It was one of the flaws in his character to be extremely sensitive about his own errors. He was highly displeased with this one, and gave almost no further consideration to the incredible victory that had preceded this small reverse, when, at nine o'clock, Mademoiselle de la Mole appeared in the library door, flung him a letter and fled.

It seems that this is to be a literary romance, he thought, picking it up. The enemy makes a false move, now I am going to summon up coldness and virtue.

He was asked for a definite answer, with an arrogance that added to his inner amusement. He gave himself the pleasure of spending two pages in mystification, for the benefit of those who were trying to make game of him, and it was in the form of a joke that he announced, near the end of his reply, that his departure was set for the following morning.

This letter finished: The garden will serve for giving it to her, he thought, and went there. He looked up at Mademoiselle de la Mole's bedroom window.

It was on the second floor, next to her mother's rooms, but there was a large entresol.

This second floor was so high above the ground that, walking in the linden alley, his letter in his hand, Julien could not be seen from Mademoiselle de la Mole's window. The arch formed by the shapely branches of the lindens interrupted the view. But what am I doing? Julien thought. Another indiscretion! If they've undertaken to make fun of me, letting myself be seen with a letter in my hand is playing into my enemies' hands.

Norbert's room was directly above his sister's, and if Julien emerged from the arch formed by the intertwined branches of the lindens, the count and his friends could follow his every move.

Mademoiselle de la Mole appeared behind her window; he half indicated his letter; she nodded. At once Julien ran upstairs to his room, and on the staircase, as if by chance, met the beautiful Mathilde, who took his letter with perfect composure and laughing eyes.

What passion there used to be in the eyes of that poor Madame de Rênal, Julien thought, when—even after six months of intimate relations—she found courage to accept a letter from me! Never in her life, I believe, did she look at me with laughter in her eyes.

He did not express the rest of his reaction so clearly to himself; was he ashamed of the futility of his motives? But then, his thought added, what a difference in the elegance of their morning dress, the elegance of their whole appearance! Catching sight of Mademoiselle de la Mole thirty paces away, a man of any discrimination could guess the position she occupies in society. That is something that can be called a definite talent.

At five o'clock Julien received a third letter; it was thrown to him from the library door. Again Mademoiselle de la Mole fled. What a mania for writing, he thought, laughing, when we could so conveniently talk to one another! The enemy wants letters from me, that's plain enough; and more than one. He was in no haste to open this one. More elegant phrases, he thought; but he lost color while reading. There were but eight lines:

"I must talk to you: I must talk to you this evening; be in the garden at the moment when one o'clock strikes. Take the gardener's big ladder from beside the well, place it against my window and climb up to my room. It's full moon: no matter."

CHAPTER 14

Is This a Plot?

THIS is getting to be serious, Julien thought . . . and a bit too obvious, he added on second thought. What! That fine young lady can talk to me in the library with a freedom which, thank God, is complete; the marquis never comes there, for fear I might talk to him about his accounts. Why, Monsieur de la Mole and Count Norbert, the only people who enter this room, are out of the house almost all day long; it would be easy to observe the moment of their return to the house, and yet the sublime Mathilde, for whose hand a reigning prince would not be too noble, wants me to commit an abominable folly!

Obviously they want to destroy me, or at the very least to make a fool of me. First they wanted to destroy me with my own letters; those turned out to be discreet; well, what these folk need is an action plainer than daylight. These handsome young gentlemen think that I too am too stupid or too conceited to be true. The devil! To climb up by the brightest moonlight in the world to a second floor twenty-five feet above the ground! They'd have time to see me even from the house next door! What a fine sight I'll be on my ladder! Julien went up to his room and began to pack his trunk, whistling. He was resolved to leave without even answering.

But this wise resolution did not give him peace of mind. If by any chance, he thought suddenly after he had closed his trunk, Mathilde was in earnest! In that case I'm playing the part of a complete coward in her eyes. I have none of the advantages of birth, so I must have great characteristics ready to hand, proved by eloquent action, not obliging suppositions . . .

He spent a quarter of an hour deep in thought. What is the use of denying it? he thought at last; I shall be a coward in her eyes. I lose not only the most brilliant woman in high society, as everyone said at the Duke de Retz's ball, but also the divine pleasure of seeing the Marquis de Croisenois, a duke's son who will be a duke himself, sacrificed to me. A charming young man who has all the qualities I lack: ready wit, birth, fortune. . . .

This regret would follow me all my life. Not for her: there are so many mistresses!

. . . *But there is just one honor!* old **Don Diego** says, and here I am, obviously and flatly shrinking from the first peril that is offered me; for that duel with Monsieur de Beauvoisis turned out to be more of a joke. This is utterly different. I may be shot at point blank range by a servant, but that's the lesser danger; I may be dishonored.

This is getting serious, my boy, he added with a Gascon merriment and accent. Honor's involved. A poor devil cast down as low as I am by circumstance will never find an opportunity like this again; I'll have strokes of luck, but inferior ones.

He pondered long, he strode precipitately up and down, stopping short from time to time. There had been placed in his room a magnificent marble bust of Cardinal Richelieu, which drew his gaze in spite of himself. This bust seemed to watch him with a stern manner, as if reproaching him for his lack of that audacity which should be so natural to the French character. In your times, great man, would I have hesitated?

Let's suppose the worst, Julien thought at length, that this is a trap; it's a very black one and very compromising for a young lady. Everyone knows that I'm not a man to hold my tongue. So they'll have to kill me. That was all very well in 1574, in the days of Boniface de la Mole, but today's de la Mole would never dare. These people are no longer the same. Mademoiselle de la Mole is so envied! Four hundred drawing-rooms would ring with her shame tomorrow, and with what satisfaction!

The servants gabble among themselves about the marked preference I receive, I know that, I've heard them. . . .

On the other hand, her letters! . . . They may think I have them on me. Catching me in her room, they'll take them away from me. I'll have to deal with two, three, four men—how do I know? But where will they find such men? Where does one get discreet hirelings in Paris? Justice scares them. . . . Oh, Lord! The Caylus, the Croisenois and the de Luz themselves. That moment, and the stupid figure I'll cut in their midst must be what has tempted them to it. Beware of Abelard's fate, Monsieur Secretary!

Well then, the devil, gentlemen! You'll bear the marks of my fists, I'll hit for the face, like Cæsar's soldiers at Pharsalia. . . . As for the letters, I can put them in a safe place.

Julien made copies of the two last, hid them in a volume of the handsome Voltaire in the library, and himself took the originals to the post office.

There were still many hours to wait; to pass the time, Julien wrote to Fouqué: "My friend, open the inclosed letter only in case of accident, if you hear that something strange has happened to me. In that case, erase the proper names in the manuscript I'm sending you, make eight copies of it and send them to the newspapers of Marseilles, Bordeaux, Lyon, Brussels, and so forth; ten days later, have this manuscript printed, send the first copy to Monsieur le Marquis de la Mole; two weeks later scatter the other copies at night in the streets of Verrières."

In this brief self-vindicating statement made in the form of a story, which Fouqué was to open only in case of accident, Julien compromised Mademoiselle de la Mole as little as possible, but in all other respects it described his position very accurately.

Carried away by his own story, like a dramatic author, Julien was genuinely afraid when he entered the dining room. He looked at all the servants in their full livery. He studied their features. Which are the ones who have been chosen for tonight's expedition? he wondered. In this family, the memories of Henri III's Court are so immediate, so frequently recalled that, believing themselves outraged, they would be more decisive than others of their rank. He glanced at Mademoiselle de la Mole, trying to read her family's plans in her eyes; she was pale and wore an utterly medieval expression. Never had he thought her appearance so noble; she was really beautiful and imposing. He almost began to love her. *Pallida morte futura*, he reflected; her pallor betrays her great designs.

In vain, after dinner, did he make a point of walking long in the garden; Mademoiselle de la Mole did not appear. Talking to her just then would have relieved his spirit of a great weight.

Why not admit it? He was afraid. As he was resolved to act, he gave himself up without shame to his emotion. As long as I find the courage when it comes time to act, he thought, what do my feelings matter right now? He went to explore the situation and try the weight of the ladder.

This is an instrument, he told himself, laughing, that it's my destiny to make use of, here as in Verrières! What a difference! Then, he added with a sigh, I wasn't obliged to distrust the person for whom I risked my life. What a difference, too, in the danger.

I could have been killed in Monsieur de Rênal's gardens without dishonor to myself. They would easily have made my death inexplicable. Here, what abominable stories won't they tell in the drawing-rooms of the de Chaulnes mansion, the de Caylus, the de Retz—in fact everywhere. I shall be a monster to posterity.

For two or three years, he went on, laughing and mocking himself. But that idea depressed him. And what about me, how can I be vindicated? Even supposing that Fouqué prints my posthumous manuscript, it will only be an added infamy. What, I was received into this house, and as payment for the hospitality shown me, the kindness with which I am overwhelmed, I print a pamphlet on what goes on here! I attack the ladies' honor! Oh, a thousand times better to be tricked!

It was a horrible evening.

CHAPTER 15

One O'Clock in the Morning

HE WAS about to write countermanding his order to Fouqué when eleven o'clock struck. He noisily manipulated the lock of his bedroom door as if locking himself in. He prowled about on soft feet, observing what was going on in every part of the house, particularly on the fourth floor, where the servants had their rooms. There was nothing out of the ordinary. One of Madame de la Mole's chambermaids was entertaining, the servants were merrily drinking punch. People who are laughing like that, Julien thought, aren't due to take part in a nocturnal expedition. They would be more serious.

At length he went to take up a position in a dark corner of the garden. If it's their plan to avoid being seen by the house servants, they'll have the men who are supposed to take me by surprise come over the garden walls.

If Monsieur de Croisenois is maintaining any of his presence of mind through all this, he should realize that it would be less compromising for the young person he wants to marry if I were caught before I had entered her room.

He made a military and very minute reconnaissance. It's for my honor's sake, he told himself; if I fall into some silly blunder it won't be an excuse in my own eyes to say: I didn't think of that.

The weather was provokingly serene. At eleven o'clock the moon rose, by half past twelve it shone full upon the side of the house overlooking the garden.

She is mad, Julien thought. When one o'clock struck, there was still light in Count Norbert's windows. Julien had never in his life been so frightened, he saw only the dangers of the adventure, and had no enthusiasm whatever.

He went to get the big ladder, waited five minutes to leave time for a countermand, and at five minutes past one placed the ladder against Mathilde's window. He climbed silently, his pistol in his hand, astonished not to be attacked. As he was nearing the window it opened soundlessly:

"You're here, Monsieur!" Mathilde said with much emotion. "I have been watching you for an hour."

Julien was deeply embarrassed, he did not know how to act, he felt no love at all. In his confusion, he thought that he must be bold, he tried to embrace Mathilde.

"No, stop it!" she said, pushing him away.

Quite content to be put off, he glanced hastily about him: the moonlight was so brilliant that the shadows it made in Mademoiselle de la Mole's bedroom were black. There might very well be men hidden here without my seeing them, he thought.

"What have you in the side pocket of your coat?" Mathilde asked, enchanted to have found a subject for conversation. She was extremely uncomfortable; all the feelings of reserve and timidity so natural to a well-bred girl had regained their hold over her and put her in torment.

"All sorts of weapons and a pair of pistols," Julien answered, no less pleased at having something to say.

"You must pull up the ladder," Mathilde said.

"It's tremendous; it may break the windows downstairs in the drawing-room or the entresol."

"It mustn't break windows," Mathilde said, trying in vain to achieve an ordinary conversational note. "It seems to me you could let the ladder down by means of a cord tied to the top rung. I always keep a supply of cord in my room."

And that's a woman in love! Julien thought. She dares to say that she loves me! So much coolness, so much wise precaution is proof enough for me that I'm not triumphing over Monsieur de Croisenois as I stupidly believed, but am quite simply supplanting him. Well,

229

what does that matter; do I love her? I'm triumphing over the marquis in this sense: he will be quite displeased at having a successor, and even more displeased that this successor should be me. How arrogantly he looked at me yesterday evening in the Tortoni café, pretending not to recognize me! How disagreeably he greeted me afterwards, when he could no longer avoid it!

Julien had tied the cord to the top rung of the ladder, he let it down slowly, leaning far out over the balcony to see to it that it did not touch the windows. A fine opportunity for killing me, he thought, if there is anyone hidden in Mathilde's room; but a profound silence continued to reign everywhere.

The ladder touched earth. Julien succeeded in guiding it into the border of exotic flowers along the wall.

"What is Mother going to say when she sees her precious plants all crushed!" Mathilde said. "You had better throw the cord down," she added with vast composure. "If it is seen leading up to the balcony, it will be difficult to explain."

"And how I gonna git out?" Julien asked in a light tone, imitating the Creole accent. (One of the housemaids had been born in San Domingo.)

"You gonna git out by de do'," Mathilde said, delighted with this idea.

Oh, how worthy this man is of all my love! she thought.

Julien had just let the cord fall into the garden; Mathilde grasped his arm. He thought he had been gripped by an enemy and turned swiftly, drawing a dagger. She had thought she heard a window open. They stood immobile, not breathing. The moonlight fell full upon them. The noise was not repeated, their alarm subsided.

Then embarrassment returned, pronounced on both parts. Julien made certain that the door was thoroughly bolted; he was much tempted to look under the bed but did not dare; one or two hirelings might have been posted there. But he dreaded a future reproach from his prudent nature, and at last did look.

Mathilde was plunged into all the torments of extreme timidity. She was horrified by her position.

"What have you done with my letter?" she said at length.

"The first is hidden in a big Protestant Bible which last night's mail is taking far from here."

He spoke very distinctly, entering into these details, and in a manner

230

to be understood by any persons who might be hidden in two great mahogany wardrobes which he had not dared open.

"The two others are in the post and going the same way as the first."

"Good heavens! Why all these precautions?" Mathilde asked, astonished.

What reason have I to lie to her? Julien thought, and confessed all his suspicions.

"Then that's why your letters were so cold, my dear!" Mathilde cried, with an accent rather of nervous excitement than of tenderness.

Julien did not perceive this distinction. The endearment caused him to lose his head, or at least his suspicions evaporated; he ventured to clasp in his arms this beautiful girl who inspired him with so much respect. He was only half repulsed.

He had recourse to his memory, as he had done once before in Besançon, with Amanda Binet, and recited a number of the more graceful passages from the *Nouvelle Héloïse*.

"You have a man's heart," she answered, hardly listening to his phrases. "I wanted to test your courage, I admit it, my dear. Your first suspicions and your resolution show you to be even more courageous than I thought."

Mathilde made an effort to speak tenderly, she was evidently more attentive to this strange affectionate way of speaking than to the sense of what she was saying. The "my dear," stripped of any note of deep feeling, gave Julien no pleasure; he was amazed at his own lack of happiness. At last, in order to feel anything at all, he had recourse to his reason. He took note of the fact that he was respected by this very proud young woman who never granted unreserved praise to anyone; by means of this conscious reasoning he achieved a kind of pleasure through vanity.

It was not, certainly, that spiritual delight that he had sometimes found with Madame de Rênal. There was nothing affectionate in his emotions during these first moments. There was the liveliest gratification of ambition, and Julien was ambitious above all else. He spoke again of the men he had suspected, and of the precautions he had devised. While speaking he was thinking of how to profit by his victory.

Mathilde, still violently embarrassed, and with an air of being overwhelmed by her own action, seemed enchanted at finding a subject for conversation. They discussed means of meeting again. Julien reveled in the spirit and courage of which he once more gave proof during this discussion.

What could be easier than to meet in the library to arrange everything?

"I can go anywhere in the house without exciting suspicion," Julien added, "even into Madame de la Mole's bedroom, almost." Passing through her room was absolutely the only way of reaching her daughter's. If Mathilde preferred that he always come by ladder, it was with a heart drunk with joy that he would expose himself to this slight danger.

Listening to him, Mathilde was shocked by that air of triumph. So he is my master! she thought. Already she was assailed by remorse. Her reason was appalled by the extraordinary folly she had just committed. If she could, she would have annihilated herself and Julien. When, occasionally, her will power was able to silence remorse, sentiments of timidity and suffering modesty made her almost as wretched. She had in no way foreseen the frightful state of mind in which she found herself.

Just the same I've got to talk to him, she thought at last. That's one of the conventions: one talks to one's lover. And then, by way of accomplishing a duty, and with a tenderness that lay far more in the words she used than in her voice, she told him of the various resolutions she had made about him during these last few days.

She had decided that if he was bold enough to come to her with the aid of the gardener's ladder, as she had directed him, she would be his. But never have such tender things been uttered in a colder, more formal tone. So far, it was a frozen meeting. It was enough to make one hate love. What a moral lesson for an imprudent young woman! Was it worth losing one's whole future for such a moment?

After long uncertainty, which might have seemed to a superficial observer to be the effect of the most determined hatred, so difficult was it for the sentiments a woman owes to herself to yield even to so firm a will, Mathilde at last became a charming mistress for him.

To tell the truth, their ardors were somewhat forced. Passionate love was still rather a model to be imitated than a reality.

Mademoiselle de la Mole believed that she was fulfilling a duty toward herself and toward her lover. The poor boy, she thought, has been phenomenally brave, he should be rewarded, or else I am lacking in character. But she would gladly have paid with eternal suffering to be relieved of the cruel necessity with which she found herself faced.

In spite of the appalling violence she was doing herself, she remained perfectly in command of her speech.

No regret, no reproach came to mar this night which seemed more strange than happy to Julien. What a difference, good God! between this and his last twenty-four hours in Verrières. These fine Parisian manners have found the secret of spoiling everything, even love, he thought in his extreme injustice.

He gave himself up to these reflections, standing in one of the great mahogany wardrobes where she had hidden him at the first sounds heard from the adjoining room, which was Madame de la Mole's. Mathilde accompanied her mother to Mass, the maids soon left the apartment, and Julien escaped before they returned to finish their work.

He mounted a horse and sought out the most solitary paths of one of the forests near Paris. He was astonished rather than happy.

If there was no affection in his attitude, it was because, strange as the word may seem, Mathilde, in all her conduct with him, had been accomplishing a duty. There was nothing unexpected for her in all the events of that night except the sorrow and the shame she had felt in place of the utter felicity described in novels.

Have I made a mistake, don't I love him after all? she wondered.

CHAPTER 16
An Antique Sword

THE next day and the day following, coldness again on Mathilde's part; she did not glance at him, she was unaware of his existence. Julien, consumed by the most acute uneasiness, was a thousand leagues from the sensation of triumph which had been his only reaction the first day. Could this by any chance be a return to virtue? he wondered. But it was a very bourgeois expression for referring to the haughty Mathilde.

While Julien, full of prejudices borrowed from books and from his memories of Verrières, was pursuing the chimera of a tender mistress who no longer gives a thought to her own existence after having made her lover happy, Mathilde's vanity was rousing to fury against him.

As she had not been bored for the past two months, she no longer feared boredom; so, without in the least suspecting it, Julien had lost his greatest advantage.

I have given myself a master! Mademoiselle de la Mole kept repeating to herself, gripped by the blackest self-reproach. He is completely honorable, fortunately, but if I try his vanity too far he will take revenge by letting the nature of our relationship be known. Mathilde had never had a lover, and now, in those circumstances of life which give some tender illusions even to the most barren spirits, she was given over to the bitterest reflections.

He has a tremendous power over me, since he reigns by means of terror and can punish me with appalling torment if I push him too far. This thought alone was enough to induce Mademoiselle de la Mole to behave outrageously to him. Courage was the outstanding attribute of her character.

The third day, as Mademoiselle de la Mole persisted in refusing to look at him, Julien followed her, evidently against her will, into the billiard room after dinner.

"Well, Monsieur, so you think that you've acquired some very strong rights over me," she said with barely restrained anger, "since against my quite obviously stated will you insist on talking to me? . . . Do you realize that nobody in the world has ever been so presumptuous?"

Nothing could have been more amusing than the conversation of these two lovers; without being at all aware of it, each of them was inspired by the liveliest hatred for the other. As neither had a tenacious character and as, in addition, both were accustomed to the habits of good society, they soon arrived at the point of declaring incontrovertibly that they were through with one another forever.

"I swear eternal secrecy to you," Julien said. "I would even add that I would never speak to you again if it were not that your reputation might suffer as a result of too obvious a change." He bowed respectfully and left her.

He was accomplishing without much pain what he thought to be his duty; he was far from imagining himself to be deeply in love with Mademoiselle de la Mole. Certainly he had not been in love with her three days earlier when she had hidden him in the great mahogany wardrobe. But all his spiritual values altered rapidly from the moment he saw himself finished with her forever.

His relentless memory began to reëxplore the most minute circumstances of that night which had in reality left him so unmoved.

During the very night that followed their declaration of eternal separation, Julien all but went mad when he was obliged to admit to himself that he loved Mademoiselle de la Mole.

Unbearable conflicts followed this discovery: all his emotions were flung into disorder.

Two days later, rather than standing on pride with Monsieur de Croisenois, he would almost have embraced him and burst into tears.

The habit of being miserable gave him a gleam of good sense: he decided to leave for Languedoc, packed his trunk and went to the stagecoach office.

He felt almost faint when, at the stagecoach office, he was informed that, by a singular chance, there was a seat vacant in the mailcoach to Toulouse the next day. He reserved it and returned to the de la Mole house to announce his departure to the marquis.

Monsieur de la Mole had gone out. More dead than alive, Julien went to wait for him in the library. What were his feelings upon finding Mademoiselle de la Mole there!

Seeing him appear, she assumed a look of spitefulness which he could not possibly have misunderstood.

Beside himself with misery, distracted by surprise, Julien was so weak as to say to her, in the tenderest of tones that came straight from his heart: "So you don't love me any more?"

"I'm horrified at having given myself to the first man who offered," Mathilde said, weeping with fury against herself.

"*To the first man who offered!*" Julien cried, and hurled himself at an old medieval sword that was kept in the library as a curiosity.

His suffering, which he had thought extreme at the moment he spoke to Mademoiselle de la Mole, had just been heightened a hundredfold by the tears of shame he saw her shed. To have been able to kill her would have made him the happiest of men.

Just as he drew the sword, not without some difficulty, from its antique scabbard, Mathilde, reveling in so novel a sensation, advanced proudly to meet him; her tears had stopped.

The thought of the Marquis de la Mole, his benefactor, came vividly to Julien's mind. I should be killing his daughter, he thought. What a hideous thing! He made a gesture as if to fling the sword away. Certainly, he thought, she is going to burst out laughing at this melodramatic behavior: to this realization he owed the return of all his self-possession. He glanced curiously at the blade of the old sword, as if seeking possible rust spots, then replaced it in its scabbard and, with the utmost serenity, hung it back on the gilded bronze stud which supported it.

This whole action, quite deliberate at the end, took a full minute; Mademoiselle de la Mole watched him, dumfounded. So I was on the point of being killed by my lover! she thought.

This thought carried her back to the noblest times of Charles IX's and Henri III's century.

She was standing motionless in front of Julien, who had just replaced the sword; she looked at him out of eyes in which there was no longer any hatred. It must be admitted that she was extremely attractive at that moment, certainly no woman had ever borne less resemblance to a "Parisian doll."

I'm going to relapse into weakness for him, Mathilde thought; he would have a perfect right to consider himself my lord and master after another fall at the precise moment when I have just spoken so harshly to him. She fled.

My God, how beautiful she is! Julien said to himself, seeing her take flight: that is the woman who flung herself into my arms with such frenzy not a week ago. . . . And those moments will never come again, and it is my fault! And at the moment of so extraordinary, so advantageous an occurrence, I was not alive to it! It must be admitted that I was born with a very dull, very unfortunate character.

The marquis came in; Julien hastened to inform him of his departure.

"Where to?" Monsieur de la Mole said.

"To Languedoc."

"No. If you have no objection, you are being reserved for greater things, if you go anywhere it will be North . . . . To use military terms, I'm confining you to the house. You will oblige me by never being absent more than two or three hours, I may have need of you at any moment."

Julien bowed and withdrew, leaving the marquis vastly astonished; he was in no condition to talk; he locked himself in his room. There he could freely exaggerate all the hideousness of his lot.

So, he thought, I cannot even go away! God knows how long the marquis is going to keep me in Paris; good God! what is going to become of me? And not a friend I can ask for advice: the Abbé Pirard wouldn't let me finish the first sentence; Count Altamira would suggest that I join some conspiracy.

And yet I am going mad, I feel it; I am mad!

Who will be able to guide me, what is to become of me?

CHAPTER 17
Cruel Moments

MADEMOISELLE de la Mole, enchanted, could think of nothing but the joy of having been upon the point of being killed. She even went so far as to think: He is worthy to be my master, since he came close to killing me.

At that instant, had some respectable excuse for resuming the relationship offered, she would have seized it with pleasure. Julien, locked and bolted into his room, was assailed by the most violent despair. In his distraction he had the mad notion of flinging himself at her feet. If, rather than keeping himself hidden in an inaccessible spot, he had wandered about the house and garden in such a manner as to stay within reach of opportunity, he might in a single moment have changed his frightful suffering into the most ardent delight.

After dinner, Mademoiselle de la Mole, far from avoiding Julien, spoke to him and by her manner invited him to accompany her to the garden; he obeyed. He was unable to resist. Mathilde was giving way almost without realizing it to the love she was beginning once more to feel for him. She took the greatest pleasure in walking at his side; it was with curiosity that she studied the hands which, that morning, had grasped the sword to kill her.

After such a gesture, after all that had happened, there could no longer be any question of conversing as they once had.

Little by little Mathilde began to speak with confiding intimacy about the state of her heart. She found a singular gratification in this sort of conversation; she went so far as to describe to him the transient impulses of ardor she had felt for Monsieur de Croisenois, for Monsieur de Caylus . . .

"What, for Monsieur de Caylus too!" Julien cried; and all the bitter jealousy of a forsaken lover burst forth in the words. Mathilde recognized it as such, and was not in the least offended by it.

She continued to torture Julien, describing minutely and in the most picturesque terms her former emotions, with an accent of profoundest truth. He saw that she was describing something that she could actually see. It hurt him to notice that while speaking she was making discoveries about her own heart.

The torment of jealousy can go no farther.

To suspect that a rival is loved is bitter enough to start with, but to hear the love he inspires confessed in detail by the woman one adores is undoubtedly the utmost height of suffering.

Mathilde seemed adorable to him, words are impotent to describe the extravagance of his admiration. Walking beside her, he stole glances at her hands, her arms, her queenly carriage. He was ready to fall at her feet, overwhelmed by love and grief, crying: "Pity!"

And this woman, so beautiful, so superior to all others, who was once in love with me, will soon be loving Monsieur de Caylus, very likely.

There is no way of expressing Julien's anguish. He was hearing detailed confidences of the love she had felt for others, in that same linden alley where only a few days before he had waited for one o'clock to strike so that he might climb up to her room. No human being can sustain a higher degree of suffering.

This sort of cruel intimacy continued for an entire week. Mathilde seemed now to seek, now simply not to avoid, opportunities of talking to him; and the subject of their conversation to which they both seemed to return with a kind of relentless gratification, was the account of emotions she had felt for others: she told him about the letters she had written, she remembered them down to the last words, she recited whole sentences to him. During the last days of that week she seemed to contemplate Julien with a sort of malignant joy. His agony was a lively satisfaction to her.

It is plain to be seen that Julien had had no experience of life; he had not even read novels; if he had been a little less awkward and had said with some assurance to this young woman whom he so adored and who made such strange confidences to him: "Admit that although I don't measure up to all those gentlemen, it's still I whom you love . . . "

Perhaps she would have been happy to be found out; at least success would have depended entirely upon the grace with which Julien expressed this idea, and the moment he chose for it. In any case he emerged neatly, and with advantage to himself, from a situation which was about to become monotonous in Mathilde's opinion.

"And you don't love me any longer, when I adore you!" he said to her one day, bewildered by love and sorrow. It was almost the stupidest blunder he could have committed.

These words, so frank but so foolish, changed everything instantly: Mathilde, sure of being loved, scorned him completely.

She was strolling with him at the moment when he made the clumsy remark; she left him, and her last glance was expressive of the most appalling scorn. Returning to the drawing-room, she did not look at him again all evening. The next day contempt for him was in full possession of her heart; there was no further question of the impulse which, for the past week, had led her to find such satisfaction in treating Julien like a most intimate friend; the sight of him was disagreeable to her. Mathilde's reaction amounted almost to disgust; there is no way of expressing the overwhelming scorn she felt when she looked at him.

Julien had understood nothing of what had been going on, during the past week, in Mathilde's heart, but he perceived this contempt. He had the good sense to appear before her only as infrequently as possible, and never looked at her.

But it was not without mortal anguish that he deprived himself in this way of her company. He thought that he could feel his misery aggravated even further. A man's spiritual courage can go no farther, he thought. He spent his life at a small window in one of the gables; its Venetian blind was carefully closed, and from there he could at least catch a glimpse of Mademoiselle de la Mole when she appeared in the garden.

CHAPTER 18
The Opera Bouffe

Absorbed in the future and in the singular part she hoped to play, Mathilde soon reached the point of regretting the dry and metaphysical discussions she often used to have with Julien. Sometimes, wearied of such lofty thinking, she also regretted the moments of happiness she had found with him; these last memories never returned without remorse, at certain instants she was overwhelmed by it.

She watched Julien; she found a charming grace in his slightest actions.

I have undoubtedly succeeded, she thought, in destroying every last trace of an idea that he has any rights.

Besides, the air of melancholy and deep passion with which the poor boy said those words of love, a week ago, proves it; it must be admitted that it was extraordinary of me to become angry over a remark that glowed with so much respect, so much passion. Am I not his wife? What he said was quite natural and, I must confess, it was very pleasant to hear. Julien still loved me after interminable conversations in which I spoke to him—and very cruelly, I admit it—of nothing but the imaginary love that boredom with the life I lead caused me to feel for those young aristocrats of whom he is so jealous. Oh, if he knew how little dangerous they are for me, how pallid and all exactly alike they seem, compared to him!

While these reflections passed through her mind, Mathilde was making random pencil sketches of faces on a leaf of her portfolio. One of the profiles she had just finished amazed and delighted her: it bore a striking resemblance to Julien. It's the voice of heaven! It is one of those miracles of love, she exclaimed to herself ecstatically: without any conscious thought I drew his portrait.

She hurried to her room, locked herself in, made a determined effort, tried seriously to draw a likeness of Julien, but she was unable to do so; the profile sketched by chance remained more like him. Mathilde was enchanted by this: she saw in it an obvious proof of great passion.

She did not leave her portfolio until quite late, when the marquise called her to go to the Italian Opera. She had but one idea, to encounter Julien in order to induce her mother to invite him to go with them.

He did not appear; the ladies had only common mortals as guests in their box. During the entire first act of the opera, Mathilde dreamed with the most intense ecstasy of passion about the man she loved; but in the second act a maxim of love, sung, it must be added, to a melody worthy of Cimarosa, touched her heart. The heroine of the opera was saying: I must punish myself for the excessive adoration I feel for him, I love him too much!

When they returned home, in spite of anything Madame de la Mole could say, Mathilde pretended to be suffering from a fever and spent most of the evening playing the air over and over on her piano. She sang the words of the well-known melody that had charmed her:

> *Devo punirimi, devo punirimi,*
> *Se troppo amai.*

The result of that night of madness was that she believed herself to have triumphed over her love.

Now that it is thoroughly understood that Mathilde's character is impossible in our era, no less prudent than virtuous, I am less afraid of irritating by continuing the tale of that charming girl's follies.

During the whole of the following day she lay in wait for opportunities of assuring herself of her triumph over her insane passion. Her primary object was to displease Julien in every way; but nothing he did escaped her.

Julien was too unhappy and, further, too agitated to analyze so complicated a maneuver of passion, still less could he see all that was favorable in it for him: he was the victim of it; never, perhaps, had his misery been so excessive.

He saw Mathilde walk for a long time in the garden; when at last she had left it, he went down; he went over to a rose bush from which she had picked a flower.

The night was dark, he could give himself up to his desolation without fear of being seen. It was evident to him that Mademoiselle de la Mole loved one of those young officers with whom she had just been talking so gaily. She had loved him, but she had discovered how limited his merits were.

And it's true they are very limited; Julien said to himself with full conviction; on the whole I am quite dull, quite common, quite boring for others, quite unbearable for myself. He was hopelessly disgusted with all his good qualities, with all the things he had once loved enthusiastically; and in this state of inverted values, he undertook to judge life by those values. This is the error of a superior man.

The thought of suicide presented itself more than once; that image was full of charms, it was like a delightful serenity; it was the glass of icy water offered to the wretched man dying of thirst and heat in the desert.

Death would aggravate the contempt she has for me! he thought. What a memory I should be leaving behind!

Plunged into this lowest abyss of misery, a human being has no resource but courage. Julien had not enough intelligence to say to himself: One must dare; but as he was gazing at Mathilde's window he saw through the blinds that she was putting out her light; he pictured to himself that charming room which he had seen, alas! but once in his life. His imagination went no farther.

One o'clock struck; scarcely an instant elapsed between hearing the sound of the bell and thinking: I am going to climb up with the ladder.

It was like a ray of light upon his mind; a host of sound reasons followed. Can I be any more wretched than I am? he thought. He ran to the ladder, the gardener had secured it with a chain. With the help of the grip of one of his pistols, which he broke, Julien, possessed at that moment of superhuman strength, twisted open one of the links of the chain that held the ladder; in a matter of minutes he had hold of it and placed it against Mathilde's window.

She is going to be angry, heap me with scorn, what does that matter? I will give her a kiss, one last kiss, I will go up to my room and kill myself. . . . My lips will touch her cheek before I die!

He flew up the ladder, he tapped on the blind; after a few moments Mathilde heard him, she tried to open the blind, the ladder was in the way: Julien clung to the iron hook designed to hold the shutter open and, at the risk of falling a thousand times over, gave the ladder a violent shake and moved it a little to one side. Mathilde was able to open the shutter.

He fell into the room more dead than alive.

"It's you!" she cried, flinging herself into his arms . . .

* * *

Who could describe the intensity of Julien's happiness? Mathilde's was almost as great.

She reproached herself to him, she denounced herself.

"Punish me for my outrageous pride," she said, clasping him in her arms almost to the point of suffocating him. "You are my master, I am your slave, I should go down on my knees and beg your pardon for having tried to rebel." She slipped out of his arms to fall at his feet. "Yes, you are my master," she said again, intoxicated with happiness and love. "Rule over me forever, punish your slave severely when she tries to rebel."

At another moment she tore herself from his arms, lighted a candle, and Julien had the utmost difficulty in restraining her from cutting all the hair from one side of her head.

"I want to remind myself that I am your servant," she said. "If ever my deplorable pride returns to lead me astray, show me this hair and say: It's not a question of love any longer, it's not a matter of whatever emotion you may be feeling right now, you have sworn obedience, obey as a matter of honor."

But it is wiser to avoid describing such a degree of frenzy and felicity.

Julien's chivalry was equal to his happiness. "I must go down by the ladder," he said to Mathilde when he saw the first daylight touch the distant chimneys in the east, beyond the gardens. "The sacrifice I am setting myself is worthy of you: I'm depriving myself of a few hours of the most overwhelming happiness a human soul can experience, this is the sacrifice I am making to your reputation; if you know what is in my heart, you understand the violence I am doing myself. Will you always be to me what you are right now? But honor speaks, that is enough. Did you know that, after our first meeting, all suspicion wasn't directed against thieves? Monsieur de la Mole has had a guard posted in the garden. Monsieur de Croisenois is surrounded by spies, they know what he is doing every night . . . "

At this idea, Mathilde burst out laughing. Her mother and one of the chambermaids were awakened; suddenly one of them called out to her through the closed door. Julien looked at her; she grew pale as she scolded the maid and refused to answer a word to her mother.

"But if they take it into their heads to open the window, they'll see the ladder!" Julien said.

He clasped her once more in his arms, sprang to the ladder and slid rather than climbed down it; in a moment he was on the ground.

Three seconds later the ladder was in the linden alley and Mathilde's honor saved. Julien, when he recovered his senses, found himself covered with blood and almost naked: he had hurt himself sliding down so recklessly.

Extravagant happiness had restored all the energy of his character: had twenty men appeared just then, to fall upon them single-handed would have been but a further pleasure. Fortunately his military prowess was not put to the test: he stretched the ladder out in its usual place; he replaced the chain that held it; he did not forget to obliterate the marks the ladder had made in the border of exotic flowers below Mathilde's window.

As he was feeling about on the soft earth in the darkness to assure himself that the marks were entirely obliterated, he felt something fall on his hands; it was all the hair from one side of Mathilde's head which she had cut off and thrown down to him.

She was at her window.

"See what your servant sends you," she said quite loudly; "it's a token of eternal obedience. I renounce the right of thinking for myself. Be my master."

Julien, overcome, was upon the point of going for the ladder again and returning to her room. Eventually reason prevailed.

To reënter the house from the garden was not easy. He succeeded in forcing a cellar door; once inside, he was obliged to break open the door of his room as silently as possible. In his excitement he had left behind, in that small room which he had just abandoned so precipitately, even his key which was in the pocket of his coat. It's to be hoped, he thought, that she remembers to hide all those mortal remains!

At last fatigue triumphed over happiness, and as the sun was rising he fell into a profound sleep.

The breakfast bell was barely able to arouse him; he went to the dining room. Soon after, Mathilde came in. Julien's pride had a moment of intense gratification, seeing the love that glowed in the eyes of that young woman, so beautiful and surrounded by such deference; but presently his prudence had cause for alarm.

Upon pretext of having had too little time to dress her hair carefully, Mathilde had arranged it in such a fashion that Julien could see at first glance the extent of the sacrifice she had made for him by cutting it off the night before. If so beautiful a face could have been marred by anything, Mathilde would have succeeded in doing so; one whole side of her exquisite ash-blonde hair had been cut off a half inch from her head.

At breakfast, Mathilde's entire conduct was in keeping with this first indiscretion. One might have thought that she was making a deliberate effort to let everyone know of her mad passion for Julien. Fortunately Monsieur de la Mole and the marquise were absorbed, that day, with a promotions list of Cordons Bleus which were about to appear and in which Monsieur de Chaulnes was not included. Toward the end of the meal Mathilde, speaking to Julien, took it into her head to call him *my master*. He blushed up to the whites of his eyes.

Whether by chance or by intention on Madame de la Mole's part, Mathilde was not left alone an instant that day. In the evening, moving from the dining room to the salon, she nevertheless found an opportunity to say to Julien:

"Are you going to think this is just an excuse I'm making? Mother has just decided that one of her maids is to stay in my room at night."

That day passed like lightning. Julien was on a pinnacle of happiness. At seven o'clock the next morning he was established in the library; he hoped that Mademoiselle de la Mole would have the kindness to come there; he had written her an interminable letter.

He did not see her until many hours later, at luncheon. That day her hair was dressed with the utmost care; a marvelous artistry had contrived to hide the shorn spot. She glanced at Julien once or twice, but with courteous, placid eyes. There was no further question of calling him *master*.

Julien's astonishment prevented him from breathing. . . . Mathilde was reproaching herself for almost everything she had done for him.

Upon mature reflection she had decided that he was a person, if not precisely ordinary, at least not sufficiently distinguished from the rank and file to deserve the extraordinary follies she had ventured into for his sake. On the whole, she was not considering love at all; that day she was tired of loving.

As for Julien, the emotions that stirred in his heart were those of a sixteen-year-old boy. Tormenting doubt, astonishment and despair took possession of him in turn during that luncheon which seemed interminable.

As soon as he could decently rise from the table, he bounded rather than ran to the stable, saddled his horse himself and set off at a gallop; he was afraid of disgracing himself by some manifestation of weakness. I must kill my heart with sheer physical exhaustion, he thought, cantering through the Meudon woods. What have I done, what have I said to deserve such loss of favor?

I must do nothing, say nothing today, he thought, returning to the house, I must be dead in the physical sense as I am in the moral. Julien lives no longer, only his corpse still stirs.

He devoted the following day to killing himself and his horse with fatigue. In the evening he made no further effort to approach the blue couch, to which Mathilde remained faithful. He noticed that Count Norbert did not even condescend to look at him, meeting him about the house. It must be uncommonly disagreeable for him, he thought; he's normally so polite.

For Julien, sleep would have been a blessing. In spite of physical exhaustion, his irresistible memories were beginning to usurp his whole imagination. He had not the sense to realize that his long rides about the woods near Paris reacted only upon himself and not in the least upon Mathilde's heart or spirit. He was leaving the disposition of his destiny to chance.

It seemed to him that one thing would bring infinite relief to his suffering: and that would be to talk with Mathilde. But on the other hand, what could he dare say to her?

He was deep in meditation upon this point one morning at seven o'clock when suddenly he saw her enter the library.

"I know that you want to talk to me, Monsieur."

"Good God! Who told you?"

247

"What does that matter? I know it. If you're lacking in honor, you can destroy me, or at least try to; but this danger, which I don't believe is real, will certainly not prevent me from being sincere. I no longer love you, Monsieur, my foolish imagination misled me . . . "

At this terrible blow, Julien, overcome by love and grief, made an effort to justify himself. It was the most ridiculous thing he could have done. Justify oneself for failing to please? But reason had no longer any control over his actions. A blind instinct impelled him to delay the determining of his fate. It seemed to him that so long as he kept on talking, everything was not over. Mathilde did not listen to his words, the sound of them irritated her, she could not understand his having the audacity to interrupt her.

The remorse of virtue and that of pride were tormenting her equally that morning. She was in a way aghast at the very idea of having given an insignificant abbé, the son of a peasant, rights over herself. It's almost as if I had to reproach myself with a fondness for one of the footmen.

In proud and resolute characters it is but a step from anger with one-self to rage against others; the transports of fury, in this case, are an acute pleasure.

In an instant Mademoiselle de la Mole reached the point of heaping Julien with the most exaggerated marks of contempt. She was infinitely quick-witted, and her wit triumphed in the art of torturing self-esteem and inflicting cruel wounds upon it.

Each word enhanced Julien's terrible suffering a hundredfold. He would have run away, Mademoiselle de la Mole firmly restrained him, by the arm.

"Have the goodness to notice," he said to her, "that you are talking very loudly, they'll hear you in the next room."

"No matter," Mademoiselle de la Mole returned haughtily. "Who will dare tell me that I've been overheard? I want to cure your little conceit once and for all of any ideas it may have conceived about me."

When Julien was able to escape from the library, he was so dumfounded that he felt his unhappiness less because of it. Well, she doesn't love me any more! he kept repeating out loud, as if to inform himself of his position. It seems she loved me for a week or so, and I shall love her all my life.

Is it really possible that she was nothing, nothing at all to me such a short time ago!

Gratified pride flooded Mathilde's heart; so she had been able to break with him permanently! To have triumphed so completely over so potent an inclination made her perfectly happy. So this young man will understand, once and for all, that he has not and never will have any hold over me. She was so happy that actually, at that moment, she was not in love any longer.

After so appalling, so humiliating a scene, love would have become impossible in anyone less enamored than Julien. Without departing for a single instant from the conduct she owed herself, Mademoiselle de la Mole had made some extremely disagreeable statements, so well calculated that they had the semblance of truth even when recollected in cold blood.

The conclusion that Julien drew in the first moment of so extraordinary a scene was that Mathilde had an illimitable pride. He firmly believed that everything was over between them forever, and yet the next morning at breakfast he was awkward and timid in her presence. This was one fault with which he could not have been reproached up to that time. In small things as well as in great, he usually knew clearly what he should and would do, and did it.

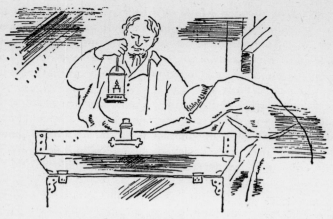

CHAPTER 19
The Secret Note

THE marquis sent for him; Monsieur de la Mole seemed to have recovered his youth, his eye was gleaming.

"Let's talk a little bit about your memory," he said to Julien. "They tell me it's prodigious! Would you be able to memorize four pages and go and recite them in London . . . but without altering a word?"

The marquis was leafing irritably through the day's *Quotidienne*, making a futile effort to disguise a very serious air which Julien had never seen him wear before, even when the Frilair lawsuit was under discussion.

Julien was already experienced enough to realize that he ought to seem to be deceived by the light tone which was being used toward him.

"This issue of *La Quotidienne* may not be particularly entertaining, but if Monsieur le Marquis will permit me, tomorrow morning I shall have the honor of reciting it to him word for word."

"What, even the advertisements?"

"Absolutely, and without missing one word."

"You give me your word for that?" the marquis asked with sudden gravity.

"Yes, Monsieur. The only thing that might impair my memory is the fear of failing to keep it."

"It won't be a boring trip for you, because between Paris and the minister's residence there will be certain men who will ask for nothing better than to have a shot at Monsieur l'Abbé Sorel. And if that happens, his mission is over, and I am faced with a great delay; for, my dear boy, how will we be informed of your death? Your zeal can scarcely go to the lengths of letting us know about that."

"It would be better," Julien said, "to go ninety miles out of the way and not take the direct route. It's Rome that is in question, I suppose . . ."

The marquis assumed an air of haughtiness and displeasure that Julien had not seen so marked since Bray-le-Haut.

"You will be informed of that, Monsieur, when I consider it the proper time to tell you. I do not like questions."

"This was not a question," Julien returned earnestly. "I swear to you, Monsieur, I was thinking aloud; in my mind I was considering the safest route."

"Yes, it's obvious that your mind was far away. Never forget that an ambassador, particularly one of your age, must never seem to be forcing confidences."

Julien was greatly mortified, he was in the wrong. His self-esteem sought for an excuse and found none.

"Now understand," Monsieur de la Mole added, "one always appeals to one's heart after having made a foolish mistake."

If this young man betrays me, Monsieur de la Mole was thinking, whom can I trust? And yet to accomplish anything one must trust someone. My son and his brilliant friends of the same class have courage enough, loyalty enough for a hundred thousand men; if it came to fighting, they would die on the steps of the throne. They know everything . . . except what is essential right now. The devil take me if I know one among them who could learn four pages by heart and travel three hundred miles without getting caught. Norbert would know how to get himself killed like his ancestors; that's also a conscript's merit . . .

The marquis lapsed into profound meditation: Still, as far as getting killed goes, he thought with a sigh, perhaps this Sorel will be as good at it as Norbert.

The next day the Marquis took Julien to a lonely château some distance from Paris. There were assembled several curious guests whom Julien took to be priests. He was given a passport that bore a fictitious name but at last made known the actual goal of his journey of which he had faithfully been pretending to be unaware. Alone, he stepped into a carriage.

The marquis had no uneasiness about his memory. Julien had recited the secret message to him several times, but he was greatly afraid that Julien might be intercepted.

"The most important thing is to look like a fop traveling to kill time," he said with a friendly air, just as he was leaving the drawing-room.

The journey was swift and extremely dreary. Almost before he was out of sight of the marquis he had forgotten both the secret note and the mission, to think only of Mathilde's scorn.

In a village some miles beyond Metz, the man in charge of the posthouse came to tell him that there were no horses. It was six o'clock in the evening; Julien, highly displeased, asked for supper. He walked up and down before the door and very gradually, without ostentation, slipped into the stable yard. He did not see any horses there.

There was nothing to do but have supper and spend the night. Julien was still in his first sleep when he was awakened with a start by the voices of two persons who were talking in his room without bothering to keep their tone low.

He recognized the postmaster, armed with a dark lantern. The light was directed upon the box from the carriage, which Julien had had brought up to his room. Beside the postmaster was a man who was tranquilly rummaging in the open box. Julien could distinguish only the sleeves of his coat, which were black and very tight-fitting.

It's a cassock, he thought, and quietly laid hold of the small pistols that he had placed under his pillow.

"Don't be afraid of his waking up, Monsieur le Curé," the postmaster was saying. "The wine that was served him was what you yourself prepared."

"I don't find any trace of papers," the priest answered. "Plenty of linen, scent, pomade, fripperies; he's a typical young man of our age, absorbed in pleasure."

The men came over to Julien to feel in the pockets of his traveling coat. He was strongly tempted to kill them as thieves. There would be no dangerous consequences. He longed to do it. . . . I should be nothing but a fool, he reflected, I'd jeopardize my mission.

Having felt through his coat: "This is no diplomat," the priest said.

He moved away, and it was as well for him that he did. The curé and his acolyte left the room.

Julien left alone the next day and reached the presence of the Great Personage without other incident. He lost a whole morning vainly seeking an audience. By fool luck, at four o'clock the duke wanted a breath of air. Julien saw him set off on foot; he had no hesitation in approaching him and begging for a word. Two paces from the Great Personage he drew out the Marquis de la Mole's watch and ostentatiously displayed it. "Follow me at a distance," he was told, without a glance.

About a mile farther on, the duke abruptly turned into a small *Kaffeehaus*. It was in a room of this humblest of inns that Julien had the honor of reciting his four pages. When he had finished: "Begin again and speak more slowly," he was told.

The prince took notes. "Go on foot to the next posthouse. Leave your belongings and your carriage here. Go to Strasbourg as best you can, and the twenty-second of this month (it was now the tenth) come to this same *Kaffeehaus* one half-hour past midday. Wait half an hour before you leave here. Silence!"

Such were the only words Julien heard. They were enough to inspire him with the highest admiration. That, he thought, is how one deals with great affairs.

CHAPTER 20
Strasbourg

FORCED to spend a week in Strasbourg, Julien tried to find diversion in thoughts of military glory and patriotic devotion. Was he, then, in love? He had no idea, he only knew that in his tormented soul Mathilde was absolute mistress of his happiness as of his imagination. It required all the strength of his character to keep from lapsing into despair. To concentrate upon anything that bore no relation to Mademoiselle de la Mole was beyond his power.

He rode gloomily about the outskirts of Kehl, a town on the banks of the Rhine, immortalized by Desaix and Gouvion Saint-Cyr. One day an exclamation of pleasure made him raise his head.

It was Prince Korasoff, his friend from London who, some months before, had initiated him into the primary rules of foppery.

Lucky fellow! he thought. How well his breeches fit; how elegantly his hair is cut! If I had only been like him, perhaps she would not have taken a dislike to me after having loved me for three days.

The prince found him decidedly melancholy. "Look here, my dear fellow," he said as they returned to Strasbourg, "have you lost all your money or fallen in love with some little actress?"

Such jokes about love brought tears to Julien's eyes. Why shouldn't I ask this pleasant chap for advice? he wondered suddenly.

"Well, yes, my friend," he said to the prince. "Here I am in Strasbourg, very much in love and just as much forsaken. A charming woman who lives in a near-by town has turned away from me after three days of passion, and the change is killing me."

He described Mathilde's character and behavior to the prince, using a fictitious name.

"Don't say any more," Korasoff said. "To give you confidence in your doctor, I'm going to finish the story for you. This young woman's husband is enormously wealthy—or, rather, she herself belongs to the country's great nobility. She must be proud of something."

Julien nodded; he no longer had the courage to speak.

"Very well," the prince said, "here are three fairly bitter medicines you are going to take without delay:

"First, go every day to see Madame . . . what do you call her?"

"Madame de Dubois."

"What a name!" the prince said with a shout of laughter. "But forgive me, to you it's divine. You must see Madame de Dubois every day, and be particularly sure not to seem cold and hurt with her; remember the great maxim of our age: be the opposite of what's expected of you. Show yourself precisely as you were a week before having been honored by her favors."

"Oh, then I was at peace!" Julien cried in despair. "I thought I felt sorry for her. . . ."

"The moth gets burned by the flame," the prince went on. "The oldest comparison in the world. First, you're to see her every day. Second, you're to pay a great deal of attention to one of the women she associates with, but without letting yourself seem passionately in love, do you understand? I won't hide from you that your rôle is a difficult one. You will be acting a part, and if anyone discovers that you are acting, you're lost."

"She is so quick-witted, and I am so slow! I'm lost to start with," Julien said mournfully.

"No, you're simply more in love than I thought. Madame de Dubois is deeply absorbed in herself, like all women whom heaven has gifted with too much breeding or too much money. She watches herself instead of watching you, so she doesn't know you. During the two or three fits of love which she worked herself up to feeling for you, by a great effort of the imagination, she was seeing in you her dream hero and not what you really are. . . .

"But what the devil, these things are elementary, my dear Sorel. Are you a complete neophyte?

"By the Lord! Let's go into this shop; there's a handsome black cravat, you'd think it was made by John Anderson of Burlington

Street. Do me the pleasure of buying it and getting rid of that shocking black string you have on.

"That's better," the prince continued as they left the shop of Strasbourg's leading haberdasher. "What sort of society does Madame de Dubois keep? Good God, what a name! Don't be angry, my dear Sorel, I can't help it. . . . To whom will you make advances?"

"To a complete prude, the daughter of an immensely wealthy hosier. She has the finest eyes in the world, infinitely attractive to me. She undoubtedly holds the highest social position in this vicinity, but in the midst of all her great advantages, she blushes to the point of embarrassing herself if anyone happens to mention trade and shops. And unfortunately her father is one of the best-known merchants in Strasbourg."

"So if there is talk of *industry*," the prince said, laughing, "you can be sure that your lovely lady is thinking of herself and not of you. A divine absurdity, and a very useful one. It will prevent you from losing your head even for a moment over her fine eyes. Success is certain."

Julien was thinking of Madame la Maréchale de Fervaques, who frequently visited the de la Mole mansion. She was a beautiful foreigner who had married the marshal a year before his death. Her whole life seemed to have no other object than to make people forget that she was the daughter of an *industrialist*, and in order to amount to something in Paris she had established herself as a leading light of virtue.

Julien sincerely admired the prince; he would have given anything to have his ridiculous manners. The conversation between the two friends was endless; Korasoff was enchanted: never had a Frenchman listened to him for so long a time.

"Now it's quite understood," he repeated to Julien for the tenth time, "not a hint of passion when you speak to the young beauty, the Strasbourg hosier's daughter, in Madame de Dubois' presence. On the other hand, burning passion when you write. Reading a well-written love letter is the height of pleasure for a prude; it's a moment of relaxation. She isn't acting a part, she dares to listen to her heart; so two letters a day."

"Never, never!" Julien said, discouraged. "I'd rather be crushed to a pulp in a mortar than compose three sentences. I am a corpse, my dear fellow, don't expect anything more of me. Let me die by the roadside."

"And who is talking about composing sentences? In my dressing case

I have six volumes of handwritten love letters. There are some for every feminine character, I even have some for the most lofty virtue. Didn't Kalisky court the most attractive Quakeress in England at Richmond Terrace—you know the place, not far from London?"

Julien was feeling less wretched when he left his friend at two o'clock in the morning.

The next day the prince sent for a copyist, and two days later Julien had fifty-three love letters, carefully numbered, designed for the most sublime and morbid virtue.

"The reason there aren't fifty-four," the prince said, "is because Kalisky got himself thrown out; but why should you mind being ill-used by a hosier's daughter, since it's only Madame de Dubois' heart you are trying to affect?"

They rode horseback every day: the prince was enchanted with Julien. Not knowing how to express his sudden friendliness, he finally offered him the hand of one of his cousins, a wealthy Moscow heiress. "And once married," he added, "my influence and that cross of yours will make you a colonel in two years."

"But this cross wasn't given me by Napoleon; quite the opposite."

"What does that matter?" the prince said. "He invented it, didn't he? It's still far and away the most outstanding decoration in Europe."

Julien was upon the point of accepting, but his duty recalled him to the Great Personage; leaving Korasoff, he promised to write. He received the reply to the secret note he had brought and hastened back toward Paris; but he had been alone no more than two days in a row before leaving France and Mathilde began to seem a worse torment than death. I will not marry the millions Korasoff is offering me, he thought, but I will follow his advice.

After all, the art of seduction is his vocation. He has thought of nothing else for more than fifteen years, for he's thirty now. It can't be said that he lacks cleverness; he is shrewd and crafty; enthusiasm and poetry are out of the question in his character: he's a procurator: all the more reason why he should not be mistaken.

I must do it, I am going to court Madame de Fervaques.

She may well bore me a little, but I shall look at those beautiful eyes, which are so like the ones that loved me most in the world.

She is a foreigner; that will be a new character to observe.

I am mad, I'm at the end of my tether; I must follow a friend's advice and not trust to myself.

CHAPTER 21

The Ministry of Virtue

IMMEDIATELY after his return to Paris, and upon leaving the office of the Marquis de la Mole, who seemed highly disconcerted by the dispatches brought to him, our hero dressed himself with great care.

First blunder, he reflected, going downstairs; I must follow the prince's commandments to the letter.

He went up to his room again and put on the plainest possible traveling clothes.

Now, he thought, it's a question of controlling my eyes. It was only half past five, and dinner was at six. He decided to go down to the drawing-room and found it deserted. At sight of the blue couch he was moved to the point of tears; presently his cheeks began to burn. I must expend this foolish sensibility, he thought angrily; it will betray me. He picked up a newspaper for the sake of appearances, and walked back and forth two or three times between the drawing-room and the garden. Gradually the guests assembled in the drawing-room; the door did not once open without causing Julien a spasm of mortal terror.

They sat down at table. At last Mademoiselle de la Mole appeared, ever faithful to her habit of keeping others waiting. She flushed deeply upon seeing Julien; she had not been informed of his return. Obedient to Prince Korasoff's injunction, Julien looked at her hands; they were trembling.

Monsieur de la Mole sang his praises. A moment later the marquise spoke to him and complimented him upon his look of fatigue. From instant to instant Julien kept telling himself: I must not look too often at Mademoiselle de la Mole, but neither should my glances avoid her. I must seem to be exactly as I was a week before my misfortune. . . .

At eight o'clock Madame la Maréchale de Fervaques was announced. Julien slipped out of the room and reappeared a little later, dressed with the greatest care. Madame de la Mole felt vastly pleased with him for this mark of respect, and tried to express her gratification by speaking to Madame de Fervaques about his journey. Julien sat down near the maréchale in such a position that his eyes could not be seen by Mathilde. Placed thus, according to all the rules of the art, Madame de Fervaques was to him the object of the most spellbound admiration.

Mathilde had all but forgotten him during his journey. After all, he is nothing but a common creature, she had thought; his name will always remind me of the greatest mistake of my life. I must return in good faith to vulgar standards of discretion and honor; a woman has everything to lose by forgetting them. She had indicated her willingness at last to permit the final arrangements with the Marquis de Croisenois, so long in preparation. He was distracted with joy; he would have been greatly astonished to learn that resignation lay at the bottom of this attitude of Mathilde's which made him so proud.

All Mademoiselle de la Mole's ideas changed upon seeing Julien. He is my husband, in the true sense, she thought; if I am to return in good faith to standards of chaste behavior, it is he that I must marry.

She was expecting importunities, melancholy looks from Julien; she was preparing her answers: for undoubtedly upon leaving the dining room, he would try to speak a few words to her. Far from doing so, he remained planted in the drawing-room, his eyes—with God alone knows what difficulty—refrained from even turning toward the garden. It would be best to have this out right away, Mademoiselle de la Mole thought; she went alone into the garden, Julien did not appear. Mathilde went to stroll in front of the French doors to the drawing-room; she saw him engrossed in describing to Madame de Fervaques the ancient ruined castles that crown the hills beside the Rhine and give them so picturesque a look. He was beginning to acquire some command of the sentimental and artistic phrasing that is called *wit* in certain salons.

Prince Korasoff, had he been in Paris, would have been quite proud: that evening was precisely as he had foretold.

CHAPTER 22
Moral Love

THERE is something a little mad about this whole family's attitude, the maréchale was thinking; they are all infatuated with their young abbé, who can't do anything but stare and listen—with rather fine eyes, it is true.

Julien was aware of the place which, because of the arrangement of the lights, was best suited to Madame de Fervaques' type of beauty. He was there before her every evening, but taking great care to turn his chair so that he could not see Mathilde. Astounded by this persistence in avoiding her, she abandoned the blue couch one evening and went to work at a little table near the maréchale's armchair. Julien saw her quite close, beneath the brim of Madame de Fervaques' hat. Those eyes, which were to determine his fate, at first terrified him, then jolted him violently out of his habitual apathy; he began to talk, and talked very well.

Since he has the poor taste, Mademoiselle de la Mole thought, to speak at such length and so ardently to Madame de Fervaques, I shan't listen any more. For the entire remainder of the evening she kept her word, although not without difficulty.

At midnight, when she took up her mother's candlestick to accompany her to her room, Madame de la Mole paused on the stairs to praise Julien unreservedly. Mathilde lost her temper altogether; she was unable to fall asleep. One idea soothed her: A characteristic that I despise may still be a great credit to a man in the maréchale's eyes.

As for Julien, he had begun to act, he felt less miserable; his eyes happened to fall upon the Russian leather portfolio in which Prince Korasoff had placed the fifty-three love letters he had given him. Julien saw noted at the foot of the first letter: *Send number 1 a week after first seeing her*.

I'm late! Julien thought, for I've been seeing Madame de Fervaques for a long time. He began at once to copy that first love letter; it was a homily larded with phrases about virtue, and insufferably boring: Julien was so fortunate as to fall asleep over the second page.

A few hours later, broad daylight found him slumped over his table. One of the most painful moments of his life was the one in which he woke in the morning and became conscious of his misery. That day he finished the copy of his letter almost laughing. Is it possible, he wondered, that there could have been a young man who wrote like this! He counted several sentences of nine lines each. At the end of the original he found a note in pencil:

These letters are delivered in person: on horseback, black cravat, blue coat. Hand the letter to the porter with a contrite look; profound melancholy in the gaze. Upon seeing a lady's maid, dry the eyes furtively. Speak to the maid.

All this was faithfully executed.

What I am doing is very audacious, Julien thought, leaving the de Fervaques mansion, but so much the worse for Korasoff. Daring to write to so celebrated a virtue! As a result, I'm going to be treated with the utmost contempt, and nothing will amuse me more. When you come down to it, that is the only comedy to which I can be susceptible. Yes, to cover with ridicule this revolting creature I call *me* will amuse me. If I followed my own inclinations, I'd commit a few crimes as a diversion.

For the past month, the happiest moment of Julien's life had been the one when he returned his horse to the stable. Korasoff had expressly forbidden him, upon any pretext whatsoever, to glance at the mistress who had deserted him. But the horse's step, which was so familiar to her, the manner in which Julien rapped with his whiphandle on the stable door to summon a groom sometimes drew Mathilde to her window, behind the curtain. The muslin was so sheer that Julien could see through it. Glancing in a certain way under the brim of his hat, he could glimpse Mathilde's figure without seeing her eyes. Consequently, he thought, she cannot see mine, and so that is not looking at her.

Falling asleep while transcribing a sort of commentary on the Apocalypse, going the next day to deliver a letter with a melancholy air, returning the horse to the stable in the hope of catching a glimpse of Mathilde's gown, working, attending the Opera on the evenings when Madame de Fervaques was not coming to the de la Mole house, such were the monotonous events of Julien's life. There was more interest in it when Madame de Fervaques came to visit the marquise; then he could steal glances at Mathilde's eyes under the edge of the maréchale's hat brim.

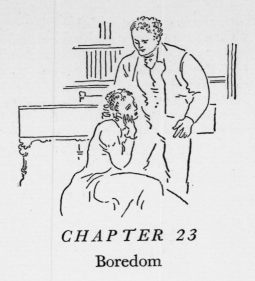

CHAPTER 23

Boredom

AFTER having read Julien's long letters, without pleasure at first, Madame de Fervaques was beginning to be very much interested in them; but one thing made her disconsolate. What a pity Monsieur Sorel isn't actually a priest! He could be admitted to a sort of intimacy. With that cross and his layman's costume, one lays oneself open to unkind questions, and what can one answer? She did not complete her thought: some malicious friend might assume and even spread the rumor that he is an obscure young cousin, a relative of my father, some merchant decorated by the National Guard.

Until she had met Julien, Madame de Fervaques' greatest pleasure had been writing the word *maréchale* in front of her name. Afterwards, a parvenue's vanity, unhealthy and alert for insult, conflicted with a budding interest.

It would be so easy for me, the maréchale thought, to make him a grand vicar in some diocese near Paris. But plain Monsieur Sorel, and Monsieur de la Mole's little secretary besides! It's deplorable.

For the first time this spirit, whose guiding motivation was fear, was stirred by an interest foreign to its social pretensions and superiority of caste. Her old porter noticed that when he brought a letter from that fine young man who had so gloomy an air, he was sure of seeing that absent and dissatisfied look, which the maréchale was always careful to assume at the approach of one of her servants, disappear.

One day, after having asked three times if any letters had come, Madame de Fervaques suddenly decided to answer Julien. This was boredom's victory. At the second letter, the maréchale was almost dissuaded by the impropriety of writing so vulgar an address with her hand: *To Monsieur Sorel, in care of Monsieur le Marquis de la Mole.*

That evening she said to Julien in a very short tone, "You must send me some envelopes with your address written on them."

So that makes me the footman-lover, Julien thought, and he bowed, taking pleasure in making himself look like Arsène, the marquis' old manservant.

That same evening he took her some envelopes, and the next morning, at a very early hour, he received a third letter: he read the first five or six lines of it, and two or three at the end. There were four pages in a small cramped handwriting.

Little by little she formed the pleasant habit of writing practically every day. Julien answered with faithful copies of the Russian letters and, such is the advantage of a forceful style, Madame de Fervaques was not in the least surprised at the lack of connection between the answers and her letters.

One morning the porter brought a letter from the maréchale to Julien in the library; Mathilde met the man, saw the letter and the address in Julien's handwriting. She entered the library as the porter left it; the letter was still lying on the edge of the table; Julien, engrossed in writing, had not placed it in his drawer.

"This is something I cannot tolerate," Mathilde cried, seizing the letter. "You're forgetting me altogether, me, your wife. Your conduct is outrageous, Monsieur."

At these words her pride, overwhelmed by the appalling impropriety of her behavior, strangled her; she burst into tears and in a very short time seemed to Julien to be unable to breathe.

Surprised, bewildered, Julien was not fully aware of the happy and auspicious aspects this scene had for him. He helped Mathilde to a chair; she all but abandoned herself to his arms.

The first instant in which he realized this was one of acute joy. The second was a thought for Korasoff: I may ruin everything with a single word.

His arms stiffened, so painful was the effort imposed by prudence. I

"I AM NOT AN ANGEL. . . . I HAVE SERVED YOU WELL."

must not even allow myself to press this slender and charming body to my heart, or she will despise me and abuse me. What a loathsome character!

And, cursing Mathilde's character, he loved her a hundred times the more for it; he seemed to be holding a queen in his arms.

Julien's imperturbable coolness aggravated the torments of pride that were tearing Mademoiselle de la Mole's heart. She was far from having sufficient composure to try to read in his eyes what he felt for her in that moment. She could not bring herself to look at him; she shuddered at the thought of meeting a look of scorn.

Sitting on the library couch, motionless, her head turned away from Julien, she was assailed by the most acute suffering that pride and love can inflict upon a human soul. What a horrible position she had just stumbled into!

It was reserved for me, miserable woman that I am, to see the most indecent advances rejected! And rejected by whom? pride added, driven mad by suffering. By one of my father's servants!

"That is what I will not tolerate," she said aloud.

And, rising in fury, she opened the drawer of Julien's desk, which stood a few feet from her. She remained as if frozen with horror at seeing in it eight or nine unopened letters identical with the one the porter had just shown her. On all of them she recognized Julien's handwriting, more or less disguised.

"So!" she cried, quite beside herself. "Not only have you ingratiated yourself with her, but you despise her too. You, a nobody, despising Madame la Maréchale de Fervaques!

"Oh, forgive me, my dear," she added, dropping to her knees. "Despise me if you will, but love me, I can't live without your love." And she lost consciousness completely.

So there she is, that proud woman, at my feet! Julien thought.

CHAPTER 24
A Box at the Opera

IN THE midst of all these great events, Julien was more astonished than happy. Mathilde's insults showed him how wise was the Russian policy. *Say little, do little*, that is my only safe course.

He lifted Mathilde and, without saying a word, helped her back to the couch. Little by little tears overcame her.

To keep in countenance, she took up Madame de Fervaques' letters, she opened them slowly. She made a quite noticeable nervous gesture when she recognized the maréchale's writing. She turned the pages of the letters without reading them; most of them ran to six pages.

"At least answer me," Mathilde said at length in the most pleading tone of voice, but without venturing to look at Julien. "You know very well that I am proud; it's the misfortune of my position and of my character, too, I admit it. So Madame de Fervaques has taken your heart from me. . . . Has she made the sacrifices for you that this ill-fated love led me to make?"

A grim silence was Julien's only answer. By what right, he was thinking, does she ask me to commit an indiscretion unworthy of a man of honor?

Mathilde tried to read the letters; her tear-filled eyes made it impossible.

For a month she had been miserable, but that haughty spirit was far from admitting its emotions even to itself. Chance alone had brought on this explosion. For an instant jealousy and love had overcome pride. She was seated on the couch, very close to him. He saw her hair and her alabaster throat; for a moment he forgot all that he owed himself; he slipped his arm about her waist and almost clasped her to his breast.

She turned her head slowly toward him: he was amazed by the excessive sorrow in her eyes, so different from their normal expression that they were almost unrecognizable.

Julien felt his strength forsake him, so agonizing was the courageous course he had set himself.

If I let myself be enticed into the happiness of making love to her, Julien thought, those eyes will soon reflect nothing but the coldest disdain. Meanwhile, in a faint voice and with words which she had barely strength enough to utter, she was repeating her protestations of all her regret for the actions that exaggerated pride had led her into.

"I too have pride," Julien said in a barely audible voice, and his features displayed the utmost limit of physical exhaustion.

Mathilde quickly turned toward him again. Hearing his voice was a happiness of which she had almost given up hope. At that moment she remembered her arrogance only to curse it, she would have been delighted to invent unheard-of, incredible gestures to prove to him how much she adored him and loathed herself.

"It was probably because of that pride," Julien went on, "that you favored me for a little while; it is certainly because of that courageous firmness befitting a man that you respect me just now. I may love the maréchale . . . "

Mathilde shuddered; her eyes took on a strange expression. She was about to hear her sentence pronounced. This movement did not escape Julien; he felt his determination weaken.

Oh, he thought, listening to the sound of the empty words his mouth uttered as if he were making alien sounds; if only I could cover those pale cheeks with kisses without your being aware of it!

"Even leaving out any other sentiment, gratitude alone would be enough to attach me to the maréchale; she was indulgent with me, she consoled me when others scorned me. . . . I can't be expected to have unlimited faith in certain evidences, very flattering, no doubt, but also, perhaps, very short-lived."

"Oh, dear God!" Mathilde cried.

"Well, what guarantee will you give me?" Julien returned with a sharp firm accent which seemed for the moment to abandon the discreet forms of diplomacy. "What guarantee, what god will assure me that the position you seem inclined to restore to me right now will last more than two days?"

"The strength of my love, and of my grief if you no longer love me," she said, seizing his hands and turning to him.

The passionate gesture she had just made had displaced her scarf a little: Julien caught a glimpse of her exquisite shoulders. Her hair, somewhat disordered, recalled a delightful memory. . . .

He was about to yield. One careless word, he thought, and I make that long succession of days spent in despair begin again. Madame de Rênal found reasons for doing what her heart urged: this young society woman lets her heart be moved only after she has given herself good reasons to prove that it ought to be moved.

This truth came to him in the twinkling of an eye, and in the twinkling of an eye he recovered his determination.

He disengaged his hands, which Mathilde was clasping in hers, and with ostentatious respect moved a little away from her. A man's courage can go no further. Then he set about gathering up all Madame de Fervaques' letters, which were scattered about the couch, and it was with every appearance of courtesy—excessive and, at that moment, so cruel— that he added:

"Mademoiselle de la Mole will be so kind as to let me think all this over." He walked rapidly away and left the library; she heard him close all the doors, one after the other.

The monster isn't even ruffled, she thought. . . .

But what am I saying, monster! He is wise, prudent, kind. I am the one who has more faults than are conceivable.

This attitude remained constant. Mathilde was almost happy that day, for she was utterly dedicated to love; one would have said that her spirit could never have been troubled by pride, and such pride!

She shivered with horror when, that evening in the drawing-room, a servant announced Madame de Fervaques; to her the man's voice had a sinister sound. She could not endure the sight of the maréchale, and quickly withdrew. Julien, but little elated over his painful victory, had been afraid to trust his own glances and had not dined at the house.

His love and his rejoicing increased rapidly in proportion as he left the moment of conflict behind; he had already reached the point of blaming himself. How could I have resisted her? he wondered. Suppose she stopped loving me now! A moment is enough to change the attitude of that lofty spirit, and it must be admitted that I treated her in a shocking fashion.

That evening he was well aware that he positively must appear in Madame de Fervaques' box at the Opera. She had expressly invited him, and Mathilde could not fail to hear of his presence or his discourteous absence. In spite of this logical reasoning he had not the strength, in the early part of the evening, to force himself out into society. By speaking, he would lose half of his happiness.

Ten o'clock struck: he must absolutely put in an appearance.

Fortunately he found the maréchale's box crowded with ladies and was relegated to a seat near the door and completely concealed by hat brims. This position saved him from making a ridiculous figure of himself: the divine accents of Caroline's despair in *Il Matrimonio Segreto* brought tears to his eyes. Madame de Fervaque saw these tears; they were in such contrast with the masculine firmness of his habitual expression that this haughty spirit, long saturated with all that is most corrosive in a parvenu's vanity, was touched by them. The small amount of womanly feeling that was left to her led her to speak. She wanted the pleasure of hearing his voice at that moment.

"Have you seen the de la Mole ladies?" she asked him. "They're in the third tier." Instantly Julien bent forward, leaning somewhat discourteously on the railing of the box. He saw Mathilde; her eyes were brilliant with tears.

And yet it's not their day for the Opera, Julien thought. What assiduity!

Mathilde had persuaded her mother to come to the Bouffes in spite of the inferior position of the box that one of the family's sycophants had eagerly offered them. She wanted to know if Julien would spend that evening with the maréchale.

CHAPTER 25

Cause for Alarm

JULIEN hurried to Madame de la Mole's box. His eyes first met the tear-filled eyes of Mathilde; she was weeping without the slightest restraint: only unimportant persons were present, the friend who had invited them to share her box and some men of her acquaintance. Mathilde laid her hand on Julien's; it was as if she had forgotten all fear of her mother. Almost choked by tears, she said only the one word: "Guarantees!"

At least I must not speak to her, Julien thought, deeply stirred himself, and hiding his eyes with his hand as well as he could, using as pretext the chandelier that dazzled the eyes in the third tier of boxes. If I speak, she can no longer doubt the extremity of my emotion, and the sound of my voice will betray me, everything may still be lost.

His inner conflict was a great deal more painful than that of the morning, his spirit had had time to become fully aroused. He dreaded seeing Mathilde's vanity irritated. Intoxicated with love and pleasure, he pledged himself not to speak to her.

Mademoiselle de la Mole insisted upon taking Julien back to the house. Fortunately it was pouring rain. But the marquise saw to it that he was seated directly opposite herself, kept up a constant flow of talk and prevented him from saying a single word to her daughter. One would have thought that it was the marquise who was concerned for Julien's happiness.

Dare I mention that, upon returning to his room, Julien dropped to his knees and covered the love letters given him by Prince Korasoff with kisses?

He was perfectly aware that Mathilde would be in the library before eight o'clock the next morning; he did not go there until nine, burning with love, but with his head in command of his heart. Possibly not a single minute passed without his saying to himself: Keep her constantly in the grip of this great doubt: Does he love me? Her brilliant social position, the flatteries of everyone who speaks to her make her a bit too much inclined to be sure of herself.

He found her seated on the couch, pale, quiet, but apparently incapable of moving. She held out her hand to him:

"My friend, I've offended you, it is true; perhaps you're angry with me? . . ."

Julien was not expecting this utterly simple tone; he was upon the point of betraying himself.

"You want guarantees, my friend," she added after a silence which she had hoped to hear broken. "That is only right. Take me away, let us go to London. . . . I shall be ruined forever, disgraced . . ." She plucked up the courage to withdraw her hand from Julien's in order to cover her eyes with it. All the impulses of restraint and feminine virtue had returned to her spirit. . . . "Well, disgrace me," she said at length with a sigh. "That's a *guarantee*."

Yesterday I was happy because I had the courage to be severe with myself, Julien thought. After a brief silence he regained sufficient control over his emotions to say in a frigid tone:

"Once on the way to London, once you're disgraced—to use your own expression—what assurance have I that you will love me, that my presence in the postchaise won't seem unwelcome to you? I am not a monster; to have ruined your reputation publicly will only be an added sorrow to me. Unfortunately it is not your social position that is the obstacle; it's your character. Can you answer for it that you'll love me for a week?"

(Oh, let her love me for a week, only a week, Julien murmured to himself, and I shall die of happiness. What does the future matter to me, what does life matter? And this miraculous happiness can begin right now if I choose, it depends only upon me!)

Mathilde saw that he was thinking deeply.

"Then I'm utterly unworthy of you," she said, taking his hand.

Julien embraced her, but instantly the iron hand of duty clamped upon his heart. If she sees how much I adore her, I will lose her. And before leaving her arms he had regained all the dignity befitting a man.

That day and the days that followed he was able to conceal the extent of his rapture; there were moments when he refused himself even the pleasure of clasping her in his arms. At other times the frenzy of happiness prevailed over all the counsels of prudence.

It was beside a trellised honeysuckle vine designed to conceal the ladder in the garden that he habitually went to gaze from a distance at Mathilde's window blinds and to grieve over her inconstancy. A huge oak grew close by, and the trunk of this tree prevented his being seen by inquisitive eyes.

Strolling one day with Mathilde past this same spot which reminded him so vividly of the violence of his anguish, he found the contrast between past despair and present delight too strong for his determination; tears flooded his eyes, and raising his mistress' hand to his lips: "Right here, I used to live on thoughts of you; from here I stared at that shutter, I waited for hours on end for the wonderful moment when I would see this hand open it. . . ."

He broke down completely. He described to her in true colors, that cannot be invented, the acuteness of his former despair. Brief interjections testified to his present happiness which had put an end to that hideous suffering. . . .

Good God, what am I doing? Julien thought, coming abruptly to his senses. I'm ruining everything.

In the extremity of his alarm he thought that he could already see less affection in Mademoiselle de la Mole's eyes. It was an illusion, but Julien's face changed expression swiftly and was covered with a deathly pallor. The light in his eyes went out for an instant, and an expression of arrogance not untouched by malice replaced that of the most genuine, most abandoned love.

"What is the matter, my dear?" Mathilde asked, affectionate and disturbed.

"I am lying," Julien said angrily, "and I am lying to you. I reproach myself for it, and yet I have enough respect for you not to lie to you. You love me, you are devoted to me, there is no need for me to make pretty speeches to please you."

"Dear God! Were all the wonderful things you
for the last two minutes just pretty speeches?"

"I reproach myself bitterly for them, my dear friend.
them a long time ago for a woman who loved me, and bored n
It's the fault of my character, I confess it, forgive me."

Bitter tears flowed over Mathilde's cheeks.

"The moment I'm set thinking about some little occurrence that has
shocked me," Julien continued, "my deplorable memory, which I am
cursing right now, offers me a way out and I take advantage of it."

"Then I've just unknowingly done something to displease you?"
Mathilde asked with charming artlessness.

"I remember one day, passing by this honeysuckle vine, you picked
a flower, Monsieur de Luz took it from you and you let him keep it.
I was right there."

"Monsieur de Luz? That's impossible," Mathilde said with the lofty
air which was so natural to her. "I don't do such things."

"I am sure of it," Julien answered sharply.

"Well, then, it is true, my dear," Mathilde said, sadly lowering her
eyes. She knew beyond question that for a number of months past she
had permitted no such action on Monsieur de Luz's part.

Julien gazed at her with inexpressible tenderness: No, he thought,
she doesn't love me any less.

That evening she reproached him, laughing, for his fondness for
Madame de Fervaques: "A bourgeois in love with a parvenue! Perhaps
the hearts of that type are the only ones my Julien can't arouse. She is
making a real dandy of you," she said, playing with his hair.

During the time when he had thought himself despised by Mathilde,
Julien had become one of the best-dressed men in Paris. But he still
retained one advantage over men of that sort: once his clothes were on,
he thought no more about them.

One thing infuriated Mathilde: Julien continued to copy the Russian
letters and to send them to the maréchale.

CHAPTER 26
The Tiger

F OR the first time Mathilde was in love.

Life, which for her had always dragged along at a snail's pace, now flew.

However, since pride must find some outlet, she wanted to expose herself recklessly to all the dangers her love could make her run. It was Julien who had prudence; and it was only when danger was in question that she was not obedient to his will; but, docile and almost humble with him, she displayed all the more arrogance toward any other member of the household, relative or servant, who approached her.

After dinner in the drawing-room, in the midst of sixty persons, she would summon Julien to talk privately and at length to him.

Her conduct toward Messieurs de Croisenois, de Luz and the rest, perfectly polite on the surface, was hardly less provoking in substance. Now, one of these gentlemen could speak to her for no more than a few moments before she would discover that she had a question to ask Julien, and that was a pretext to keep him at her side.

She found that she was pregnant, and told Julien with joy.

"Now can you doubt me? Isn't this a guarantee? I am your wife forever."

This news struck Julien with profound astonishment. He was upon the point of forgetting the principle of his behavior. How can I be deliberately cold and insulting to this poor young girl who is ruining herself for me? If she seemed the least bit indisposed, even on days when caution raised its terrible voice, he no longer found the courage to address to her one of those cruel remarks so indispensable, according to his experience, to the continued existence of their love.

"I want to write to my father," Mathilde said one day. "He is more than a father to me, he's a friend: and as such I'd consider it unworthy of you and of me to try to deceive him even for a moment."

"Good God, what are you going to do?" Julien asked, startled.

"My duty," she answered, her eyes gleaming with joy.

She thought herself more magnanimous than her lover.

"But he'll turn me out in disgrace!"

"That is his right, we must respect it. I'll take your arm and we will walk out by the front door in broad daylight."

Julien, aghast, begged her to wait a week.

"I cannot," she said. "Honor speaks. I have seen my duty, I must obey it, and at once."

"Well, then, I order you to wait," Julien said at last. "Your honor is protected, I am your husband. Both our positions are going to be changed by this drastic step. I, too, am within my rights. Today is Tuesday; next Tuesday is the Duke de Retz's party. That evening, when Monsieur de la Mole comes in, the porter will hand him the fatal letter. . . . He thinks of nothing but making you a duchess, I'm certain of that. Imagine his grief!"

"Do you mean: imagine his revenge?"

"I may pity my benefactor and be overcome at the thought of hurting him, but I am not afraid and never shall be afraid of anyone."

Mathilde submitted. It was the first time he had spoken authoritatively to her since she had informed him of her condition; never had he loved her so much. It was with delight that the affectionate side of his nature seized upon Mathilde's condition as pretext for sparing himself the obligation of speaking cruelly to her. The thought of confessing to Monsieur de la Mole troubled him deeply. Was he going to be separated from Mathilde? And, whatever the sorrow with which she saw him go, would she give him a thought a month after his departure?

He felt an almost equal dread of the merited reproach the marquis could be expected to offer him.

That evening he admitted this second source of concern to Mathilde and then, distracted with love, he also confessed the first.

She changed color.

"Really?" she said. "Six months away from me would be a sorrow to you?"

"An immense one, the only one in the world that I face with terror."

Mathilde was immeasurably happy. Julien had so assiduously applied himself to his rôle that he had succeeded in convincing her that she was the more in love of the two.

The inevitable Tuesday came. At midnight, returning home, the marquis found a letter addressed so as to insure his opening it himself, and only when he was alone.

"Father.

"All social ties between us are broken, only those of nature remain. Next to my husband, you are and always will be the person dearest to me. My eyes fill with tears as I think of the pain I am causing you, but if my shame is not to become public, if you are to be given time to deliberate and to act, I can no longer put off the confession which I owe you. If your affection for me, which I know to be unbounded, will lead you to grant me a small allowance, I will go and settle wherever you wish—in Switzerland, for example—with my husband. His name is so obscure that no one will recognize your daughter in Madame Sorel, daughter-in-law of a carpenter from Verrières. There is that name which it hurts me so to write. I dread your anger, so apparently righteous, for Julien. I shall not be a duchess, Father; but I knew that when I fell in love with him; for it was I who loved him first, I who seduced him. I inherit from you too lofty a spirit to fix my attention upon anything that is, or seems to me, vulgar. It was in vain that, hoping to please you, I considered Monsieur de Croisenois. Why did you place true merit before my eyes? You told me yourself on my return from Hyères: 'This young Sorel is the only person who amuses me.' The poor boy is as grieved as I am, if possible, over the pain this letter is giving you. I cannot prevent your anger as a father; but love me still as a friend.

"Julien respected me. If sometimes he spoke to me, it was solely because of his profound gratitude to you: for the natural reserve of his character is such that he will never answer other than officially anyone so far above him. He has an acute and innate feeling for differences in social positions. It was I, I blush to admit it to my best friend—and such an admission will never be made to another—it was I who, one day in the garden, pressed his arm.

"After the first twenty-four hours, why should you be angry with him? My fault is irreparable. If you insist, the assurances of his profound respect and his despair at hurting you can come through me. You will not see him at all; but I shall go to him wherever he wishes. That is his right, that is my duty, he is the father of my child. If your kindness is great enough to allow us six thousand francs to live on, I shall receive them gratefully: if not, Julien intends to settle in Besançon where he will set up as a Latin and literature instructor. From whatever lowly position he may start, I am certain that he will go far. With him I have no fear of obscurity. If there should be a revolution, I feel sure that he will have a major rôle in it. Could you say as much for any of the others who have asked for my hand? They have fine estates! I cannot find in that circumstance alone reason for admiring them. My Julien would attain to a high position even under this present régime, if he had a million and my father's protection. . . . "

Mathilde, who knew that the marquis was a man strongly influenced by first reactions, had written eight pages.

What am I to do? Julien was wondering while Monsieur de la Mole read this letter. Where is, first, my duty and, second, my best interest? My debt to him is immense: without him I would have been a second-rate rascal, and not even rascal enough to keep from being hated and persecuted by the others. He has made a man of the world out of me. My unavoidable *rascalities* will be, for one thing, rarer and for another less ignoble. That is more than if he had given me a million. I owe him this cross and the appearance of having performed diplomatic services, which has raised me above the common level.

If he took up his pen to prescribe a course of conduct for me, what would he write? . . .

Julien was abruptly interrupted by Monsieur de la Mole's elderly valet.

"The marquis wants you to come at once, dressed or undressed."

The valet added in a low tone, walking at Julien's side, "Take care, he is in a rage."

CHAPTER 27
The Agony of Weakness

JULIEN found the marquis in a fury: for perhaps the first time in his life that great gentleman showed poor taste: he heaped Julien with every offensive epithet that came to his tongue. Our hero was astounded, antagonized, but his gratitude was not in the least shaken. How many fine plans, long cherished at the back of his mind, the poor man is seeing destroyed in one instant! But I owe it to him to answer, my silence will aggravate his fury. The answer was furnished by a line from Tartufe's rôle.

"*I am not an angel.* . . . I have served you well, you have paid me generously. . . . I was grateful, but I am twenty-two years old. . . . In this household my thoughts were only for you, and for that charming person . . . "

"Monster!" the marquis cried. "Charming! Charming! The day you found her charming you should have gone away."

"I tried to; I asked to go to Languedoc at that time."

Weary of pacing angrily about, the marquis, overcome by grief, flung himself into an armchair. Julien heard him murmur half aloud, "That's certainly not a wicked man."

"No, that I am not, to you," Julien cried, dropping to his knees. But he was violently ashamed of this gesture and quickly stood up again.

The marquis was genuinely distracted. At sight of this action he

278

began once more to heap Julien with appalling insults worthy of a cab driver. The novelty of these oaths was perhaps some relief.

"What, my daughter is to be called Madame Sorel! What, my daughter will not be a duchess!" Each time these two ideas came so coherently to his mind, Monsieur de la Mole suffered tortures, and his reactions were no longer under the control of his will. Julien was afraid of being beaten.

In lucid intervals, after the marquis had begun to resign himself to his misfortune, he reproached Julien in fairly reasonable terms:

"You should have gone away, Monsieur," he said. "Your duty was to go. . . . You are the lowest of men. . . ."

Julien moved to the table and wrote:

"For a long time my life has been unendurable to me, I am ending it. I beg Monsieur le Marquis to accept, with the assurance of my unlimited gratitude, my apologies for any embarrassment which my death in his home may cause him."

"If Monsieur le Marquis will be so kind to glance over this note . . . kill me," Julien said, "or have me killed by your servant. It is one o'clock. I am going to take a walk in the garden, by the lower wall."

"Go to the devil!" the marquis called after him as he left the room.

I understand, Julien thought; he wouldn't be sorry to see me spare his man the responsibility for my death. . . . Let him kill me; all right, it's a satisfaction I'm offering him. . . . But Lord, I love life! . . . I owe it to my son to live. . . .

This idea, which for the first time appeared so concisely in his mind, completely absorbed him after the first minutes of his walk which were given over to the consciousness of danger.

That entirely new interest made a cautious man of him. I need advice on how to behave with that impulsive man. . . . He isn't reasonable, he is capable of anything. Fouqué is too far away, besides, he wouldn't understand the reactions of a nature such as the marquis'. I'm afraid there's nobody left but that gloomy Abbé Pirard. . . .

Very early the next morning Julien was several miles from Paris, knocking at the stern Jansenist's door. He found to his vast astonishment that the abbé was not too much surprised by his confidence.

"Perhaps I should reproach myself somewhat," the abbé reflected, more anxious than irritated. "I did once think that I detected this love affair. My friendship for you, you young scoundrel, prevented me from warning her father. . . . "

"What is he going to do?" Julien asked sharply.

(He loved the abbé at this moment, and a scene would have been most painful to him.)

"I see three possible courses," he went on. "First, Monsieur de la Mole can have me killed." And he described the suicide note he had left with the marquis. "Second, have me shot point blank by Count Norbert, who would challenge me to a duel."

"You would accept?" the abbé said angrily, rising.

"You didn't let me finish. Certainly I'd never fire at my benefactor's son.

"Third, he can send me away. If he tells me: 'Go to Edinburgh—to New York—'I shall obey. Then Mademoiselle de la Mole's situation can be concealed; but I will never endure having my son done away with."

"That, you may be sure, will be the first idea that occurs to that corrupt man. . . . "

In Paris, Mathilde was on the verge of despair. She had seen her father at seven o'clock. He had shown her Julien's note, she trembled for fear that he might have considered it noble to put an end to his life: And without my permission? she asked herself in grief which was at least part anger.

"If he is dead, I shall die. You will rejoice over it, perhaps. . . . But I swear to his spirit that first I'll go into mourning and be the *Widow* Sorel publicly, and I'll send out my announcements, you can count on it. You won't find me cowardly or weak."

Her love approached frenzy. Monsieur de la Mole in his turn was left speechless.

He was beginning to see events in some proportion. At luncheon Mathilde did not appear. The marquis was relieved of an immense burden, and also flattered, when he saw that she had said nothing to her mother.

Julien dismounted. Mathilde sent for him and flung herself into his arms almost in front of her maid. Julien was not particularly grateful for this ardent reception; he had emerged from his long conference with the Abbé Pirard in a highly diplomatic, highly calculating frame of mind. His imagination was deadened by concentration upon possibilities. Mathilde, with tears in her eyes, told him that she had seen his suicide note.

"My father may change his mind. Please, for my sake, leave for

Villequier right this instant. Get back in the saddle, leave the house before they get up from the table."

As Julien did not abandon his surprised and chilly air, she burst into tears.

"Let me manage our affairs," she cried in a frenzy, clasping him in her arms. "You know perfectly well that it's not because I want to that I'm parting from you. Write to me, address your letters to my maid in a strange handwriting. I shall write volumes to you. Good-by, my dear. Go quickly!"

These last words wounded Julien; nevertheless he obeyed. It's inevitable, he thought, that these people, even in their finest moments, should find some way of injuring me.

Mathilde obstinately resisted all her father's prudent plans. She absolutely refused to undertake negotiations upon any other basis than this: She would be Madame Sorel and live in poverty with her husband in Switzerland, or at her father's home in Paris. She flatly rejected the proposal of a clandestine confinement. "For me, that would be the beginning of the possibility of slanderous gossip and disgrace. Two months after the marriage I will go traveling with my husband, and it will be easy for us to claim that our son was born at an appropriate time."

This obstinacy, at first received with outbursts of anger, eventually caused the marquis to waver.

In a moment of tenderness:

"Here," he said to his daughter. "Here is a stock transfer worth ten thousand livres. Send it to your Julien, and have him be quick about making it impossible for me to get it back."

For the sake of *obeying* Mathilde, whose fondness for giving orders was well known to him, Julien had made a futile journey of some hundred miles: he was at Villequier, checking over the farmers' accounts. This generosity on the marquis' part occasioned his return. He went to take refuge with the Abbé Pirard who, during his absence, had become Mathilde's most potent ally. Every time he was questioned by the marquis, he offered proof that any other course than public marriage would be a crime in the eyes of God.

"And luckily," the abbé added, "worldly wisdom is in agreement with religion on this point. Knowing Mademoiselle de la Mole's impetuous nature, could one depend for a moment upon a secrecy which she did not adopt of her own free will? If you don't permit the open step of public marriage, society will gossip all the longer about this odd misalliance. The thing to do is tell everything at once, with neither the appearance nor the actuality of the slightest mystery."

"It's true," the marquis said thoughtfully. "By that system, to speak of this marriage after three days becomes the idle repetition of a man who has no ideas of his own. What we should do is profit by some great anti-Jacobin measure on the government's part and slip in unnoticed right after it."

Two or three of Monsieur de la Mole's friends took the same point of view as the Abbé Pirard. The great obstacle, in their eyes, was Mathilde's stubborn character. But even after so much excellent logic, the marquis could not adjust to giving up the hope of a position near the throne for his daughter.

His memory and his imagination were full of the tricks and deceptions of all sorts which had still been possible in his own youth. To yield to necessity, to fear the law seemed an absurd and dishonorable thing for a man of his rank. He was paying a high price now for those seductive visions of his beloved daughter's future in which he had been indulging for the past ten years.

Who could have foreseen it? he kept asking himself. A daughter of so disdainful a nature, so superior an intellect, even prouder than I am of the name she bears, whose hand was sought in advance by all the most illustrious men of France!

We must give up all prudence. This century is designed for our confusion! We are moving toward chaos.

CHAPTER 28
A Man of Spirit

MADAME de la Mole and the entire household believed that Julien was traveling in the provinces to inspect the properties; he was hidden in the Abbé Pirard's presbytery and saw Mathilde almost every day. She went every morning to spend an hour with her father, but sometimes they went for weeks on end without mentioning the affair that engaged all their thoughts.

"I do not want to know where that man is," the marquis said to her one day. "Send him this letter." Mathilde read:

"The Languedoc estates bring in 20,600 francs. I give 10,600 francs to my daughter, and 10,000 francs to Monsieur Julien Sorel. I give the estates as well, naturally. Instruct the notary to draw up two separate deeds and to bring them to me tomorrow; after which, no further relations between us. Oh, Monsieur, should I have expected all this?"

Le Marquis de la Mole

"Thank you very much," Mathilde said gaily. "We're going to live at the Aiguillon château, between Agen and Marmande. They say the country there is as beautiful as Italy."

This gift was extremely surprising to Julien. He was no longer the stern cold man that we have known. His son's destiny absorbed all his thoughts in anticipation. This unexpected fortune, a rather considerable one for so poor a man, made him ambitious. He saw himself, himself or his wife, possessed of thirty-six thousand livres income. As for Mathilde, all her emotions were devoted to adoration for her husband, for it was thus that her pride referred to Julien. Her great, her sole ambition was to have her marriage recognized.

During the six weeks that had just elaspsed, the marquis, yielding to a momentary impulse, had determined to enrich Julien; poverty seemed ignoble to him, a disgrace to Monsieur de la Mole himself, impossible in his daughter's husband. He lavished money upon him. After having thought long of killing Julien or causing him to disappear, he was now contemplating building him a brilliant fortune. He had him take the name of one of his estates; and why should he not arrange to transfer his title to him? Monsieur le duc de Chaulnes, his father-in-law, had spoken to him several times, since his only son had been killed in Spain, of his desire to pass his title on to Norbert . . .

Monsieur de la Mole saw the necessity of making up his mind: It all comes down to this one great question: did Julien's audacity go to the lengths of undertaking to court my daughter because he knew that I love her above everything, and that I have an income of a hundred thousand écus?

Mathilde protests the opposite . . . No, Monsieur Julien, that's one point upon which I won't be deluded.

Is it a genuine, unpremeditated love, or simply a vulgar desire to raise himself to a fine position? Mathilde is very discerning, she felt from the first that this suspicion could ruin him in my estimation, hence that confession that she was the first to fall in love.

A girl of such high character to forget herself so far as to make definite advances! . . . Squeezing his arm in the garden, in the evening. Horrible! As if she hadn't a hundred less indelicate ways of letting him know that she had a preference for him.

To excuse oneself is to accuse oneself; I don't trust Mathilde. . . . That day the marquis' logic was more conclusive than usual. Nevertheless, influenced by habit, he decided to gain time and to write to his daughter. For they communicated in writing from one side of the house to the other. Monsieur de la Mole had no faith in his ability to discuss matters with his daughter and keep his head. He was afraid of ending everything by a sudden concession.

"Beware of committing new follies," he wrote. "Here is a commission as lieutenant of Hussars for Monsieur le Chevalier Julien Sorel de la Vernaye. You see all that I am doing for him. Do not cross me, do not question me. He is to leave within twenty-four hours to report in Strasbourg, where his regiment is stationed. Here is a draft on my banker; I expect to be obeyed."

Mathilde's love and joy knew no bounds; she wanted to profit by the victory and replied instantly:

"Monsieur de la Vernaye would be at your feet, overwhelmed with gratitude, if he knew all that you are being so kind as to do for him. But in the midst of this generosity, my father has forgotten me; your daughter's honor is in danger. One indiscretion can leave an indelible stain which twenty thousand écus a year could not wipe out. I shall not send the commission to Monsieur de le Vernaye unless you give me your word that during the coming month my marriage will be publicly celebrated, at Villequier. In a very short time from now, which I beg you not to exceed, your daughter will be unable to appear in public without the name of Madame de la Vernaye. How I thank you, dear Papa, for having saved me from the name of Sorel . . ."

The reply was unexpected.

"Obey me, or I will take back everything. Tremble, you reckless young woman. I do not yet know what your Julien is, and you yourself know even less than I. He is to go to Strasbourg and take care to watch his step. I will let my intentions be known a fortnight from now."

The firmness of this reply astonished Mathilde. *I do not know what Julien is;* the words plunged her into meditation that presently arrived at the most enchanting suppositions; but she believed them to be true. My Julien's spirit has not assumed the wretched little *uniform* of the salons, and my father refuses to believe in his superiority precisely because of the very thing that proves it. . . .

In any case, if I don't obey this whim of his, I foresee the possibility of a public scandal; a scandal lowers my position in the world and may make me less desirable in Julien's eyes. After the scandal . . . ten years of poverty; and the folly of choosing a husband for his merit can only be saved from ridicule by the most outstanding wealth. If I live far from my father, at his age, he may forget me. . . . Norbert will marry an admirable, clever woman: the elderly Louis XIV was seduced by the Duchess of Bourgogne . . .

She resolved to obey, but refrained from passing her father's letter on to Julien; his irritable nature might have been impelled into some insane action.

That evening when she informed Julien that he was a lieutenant in the Hussars, his joy was boundless. It can be imagined by his lifetime's ambition and by the passion for his son with which he was now inspired. The change of name struck him with astonishment.

After all, he thought, my story has come to its happy ending, and all the credit is mine. I've been able to make this monster of pride love me, he added, looking at Mathilde. Her father can't live without her, nor she without me.

CHAPTER 29
A Storm

H IS spirit was absorbed; he only half responded to the ardent tenderness she lavished upon him. He remained silent and withdrawn. Never had he seemed so great, so worthy of adoration in Mathilde's eyes. She dreaded some subtlety of his pride that might come to upset the whole situation.

Almost every morning she saw the Abbé Pirard arrive at the house. Could Julien not have found out something about her father's intentions from him? The marquis himself, in a capricious moment, might he not have written to him? After such great good fortune, how was Julien's bleak air to be explained? She dared not question him.

She *dared not*, she, Mathilde! From that moment on there was in her feeling for Julien a vague unprecedented suggestion almost of terror. That barren soul was in the grip of all the passion that a creature brought up in the midst of that excessive civilization which Paris admires is capable of feeling.

Shortly after dawn the next morning Julien was at the Abbé Pirard's presbytery. A pair of post horses were led into the courtyard hitched to a dilapidated chaise, hired at the neighboring office.

"An outfit like that is no longer suitable," the stern abbé told him with a surly air. "Here are twenty thousand francs which Monsieur de la Mole is giving you as a present. His instructions are that you spend them within the year, but making an effort to look as little ridiculous as possible." (In so handsome a sum, poured out on a young man, the priest saw only an opportunity for sinning.)

"The marquis adds: Monsieur Julien de la Vernaye will have received this money from his father, whom it is futile to refer to in any other manner. Monsieur de la Vernaye will perhaps consider it proper to make some gift to Monsieur Sorel, a carpenter in Verrières, who cared for him during his childhood . . . ! I could take charge of that part of the instructions," the abbé added. "I've at last persuaded Monsieur de la Mole to come to terms with that Abbé de Frilair. His credit is decidedly too strong for ours. The tacit recognition of your high birth by that man who rules Besançon is to be one of the unwritten conditions of the agreement."

Julien could no longer contain his rapture, he embraced the abbé, he saw himself accepted.

"Now, now!" Monsieur Pirard said, pushing him away. "What's the meaning of this worldly vanity? . . . As for Sorel and his sons, I shall offer them, in my own name, an annual pension of five hundred francs which will be paid to each of them as long as I continue to be pleased with them."

Already Julien was cold and aloof. He thanked the abbé, but in vague terms which committed him to nothing. Could it actually be possible, he was wondering, that I am the illegitimate son of some great nobleman exiled in our mountains by the terrible Napoleon? From one instant to the next this idea seemed less improbable to him. . . . My hatred for my father should be a proof . . . I'm not a monster after all!

A few days after this monolog the Fifteenth Regiment of Hussars, one of the most brilliant in the army, was drawn up in battle array in the Strasbourg fortress. Monsieur le Chevalier de la Vernaye's mount was the finest of Alsatian horses, which had cost him six thousand francs. He had joined as a lieutenant, without ever having been sublieutenant except on the muster rolls of a regiment of which he had never heard.

His imperturbable air, his eyes, stern and almost cruel, his impervious composure began to make a reputation for him from that first day. Before long his perfect courtesy, subtle as it was, his skill with small arms and saber, which he demonstrated without too much ostentation, disposed of any tendencies to joke aloud at his expense. After five or six days of deliberation, public opinion in the regiment declared in his favor. "This young man has everything," the facetious older officers said, "except youth."

Julien was drunk with ambition, not vanity; at all times he gave a great deal of attention to outward appearance. His mounts, his uniforms, his servants' liveries were maintained with an exactness that would have done credit to the punctiliousness of a great English nobleman. Barely a lieutenant, through influence and for only two days, he was already calculating that in order to be commander-in-chief by thirty at the latest, like all the great generals, one must be better than lieutenant by twenty-three. He thought only of glory and of his son.

It was in the midst of the most unbridled flights of ambition that he was surprised by a young footman from the Hôtel de la Mole who came to him as a messenger.

"All is lost," Mathilde wrote. "Hurry here as quickly as possible, sacrifice everything, desert if necessary. As soon as you arrive, wait for me in a hired carriage near the little garden gate of number . . . in the Rue. . . . I will come to talk to you; perhaps I can get you into the garden. All is lost and, I'm afraid, beyond repair. Count on me, you will find me devoted and staunch in adversity. I love you."

Within a few minutes Julien had secured a leave from his colonel and left Strasbourg at a fast gallop; but the terrible apprehension which was consuming him would not permit him to continue this mode of travel beyond Metz. He flung himself into a postchaise, and it was with almost incredible rapidity that he arrived at the place indicated, by the small garden gate of the de la Mole mansion. This gate opened and instantly Mathilde, without any regard for appearances, threw herself into his arms. Fortunately it was but five o'clock in the morning and the street was still deserted.

"Everything is ruined. My father, afraid of seeing me cry, went away Thursday night. Where? Nobody knows. Here is his letter, read it." She climbed into the carriage with Julien.

"I could forgive everything except the design of seducing you because you are rich. That, my poor daughter, is the horrid truth. I give you my word of honour that I shall never consent to your marrying this man. I will guarantee him ten thousand livres a year if he is willing to live at a distance, beyond the borders of France, or better still in America. Read the letter I have received in response to my request for information. The insolent young man himself proposed that I write to Madame de Rênal. I will never read so much as one line from you if it deals with this man. I have a horror of Paris and of you. I instruct you to conceal what must happen with the greatest secrecy. *Genuinely* renounce that vile man, and you will have a father again."

"Where is Madame de Rênal's letter?" Julien asked coldly.
"Here it is. I didn't want to show it to you until you had been prepared."

"My duty to the sacred cause of religion and morality," the letter ran, "forces me, Monsieur, to take the painful course I am about to carry out for your sake. A rule which must not be transgressed commands me to harm my fellow man now, in order to avoid a greater scandal later. The pain I feel must be subordinated to duty. It is only too true, Monsieur, that the conduct of the person about whom you have asked me for the entire truth may have seemed eccentric or even honorable. It might have been thought proper to conceal or disguise a part of the truth: prudence as well as religion would have it so. But that conduct, which you wish to know about, was in fact extremely culpable, more so than I can say. Poor and grasping, that man employed the most consummate hypocrisy and the seduction of a weak and unhappy woman, as a means to acquiring a position and making something of himself. It is part of my grievous duty to add that I am obliged to believe that Monsieur J. . . . has no religious principles. In all conscience I am forced to conclude that one of his methods of establishing himself in a household is trying to seduce the most influential woman in it. Disguised by an apparent disinterest and by phrases from novels, his great and sole object is to achieve control of the master of the house and of his fortune. He leaves behind him misery and eternal regrets. . . . " And so forth, at great length.

This letter, extremely long and half effaced by tears was indeed written by Madame de Rênal's hand; it was even more carefully written than usual.
"I can't blame Monsieur de la Mole," Julien said after having

finished it. "He is just and cautious. What father would be willing to give his beloved daughter to such a man? Good-by!"

Julien sprang out of the carriage and ran to his postchaise which was waiting at the end of the street. Mathilde, whom he seemed to have forgotten, took a few steps after him; but the glances of storekeepers who came to the doors of their shops, and to whom she was known, forced her to retire precipitately to the garden.

Julien had set out for Verrières. During the rapid journey he was unable to write to Mathilde as he had planned; his hand made only illegible marks on the paper.

He reached Verrières on a Sunday morning. He went into the shop of the local gunsmith, who showered him with compliments on his recent good fortune. It was the talk of the countryside.

Julien had some difficulty in making him understand that he required a pair of small pistols. At his request, the gunsmith loaded the pistols.

The three bells sounded; this is a familiar signal in French villages, announcing the immediate beginning of Mass, after the various morning peals.

Julien entered the new church of Verrières. All the tall windows of the edifice were veiled with crimson draperies. Julien found himself a few feet behind Madame de Rênal's pew. It seemed to him that she was praying with fervor. The sight of that woman whom he had loved so deeply caused Julien's arm to shake so that at first he was unable to fulfil his intention. I cannot do it, he said to himself; physically, I cannot.

At that moment the young clergyman who was conducting the Mass struck the bell for Elevation. Madame de Rênal bowed her head, and for an instant it was almost entirely hidden by the folds of her shawl. Julien no longer found her so familiar; he fired one shot at her and missed. At the second shot, she fell.

CHAPTER 30
Grim Details

H E WAS taken to prison. He was led into a cell, his hands were fettered, he was left alone; the door closed upon him, double-locked; all this was executed very swiftly and he was unaware of it all.

"By heaven, it's all over now," he said aloud, returning to his senses. "Yes, in a fortnight it's the guillotine . . . or suicide between now and then."

His reasoning went no further; his head felt as if it were being violently squeezed. He looked about to see if anyone were holding him. After a few moments he fell into a profound sleep.

Madame de Rênal was not fatally injured. The first shot had gone through her hat; as she was turning around, the second had been fired. The bullet had struck her in the shoulder and—astonishingly—had been deflected out again by the shoulder blade which, however, it fractured, and had then struck a Gothic pillar from which it chipped off a huge fragment of stone.

When, after long and painful treatment, the surgeon, a grave man, said to Madame de Rênal: "I will answer for your life as for my own," she was desperately grieved.

For a long time she had sincerely longed for death. The letter which her present confessor had forced her to write to Monsieur de la Mole had been the final blow to a being drained of strength by a too constant grief. The source of this grief was Julien's absence; she herself referred to it as *remorse*. Her confessor, a young clergyman virtuous and fervent, newly arrived from Dijon, was not deceived.

To die this way, but not by my own hand, that is no sin, Madame de Rênal thought. God will perhaps forgive me for rejoicing in my death. She dared not add: And to die by Julien's hand, that is the height of felicity.

The moment she had got rid of the surgeon and the host of friends who had hurried to her side, she sent for Elisa, her maid.

"The jailer," she said, blushing deeply, "is a cruel man. No doubt he will treat him unkindly, thinking to please me that way. . . . The idea is unbearable to me. Couldn't you go as if of your own accord and take the jailer this little package which has a few louis in it? Tell him that the Church does not countenance his treating him badly. . . . It's especially important that he should not talk about this gift of money."

It was to this circumstance that Julien owed the humanity shown him by the Verrières jailer.

A magistrate visited the prison. "I have committed premeditated murder," Julien said to him. "I bought the pistols and had them loaded at So-and-so, the gunsmith's shop. Article 1342 of the Penal Code is clear, I deserve the death penalty and I expect it." The judge, amazed by this manner of answering, tried to construct his questions in such a manner as to get the accused to incriminate himself.

"But don't you see," Julien said smiling, "that I'm making myself out as guilty as you could desire? Go away, Monsieur. You won't fail to catch the game you're after. You'll have the pleasure of giving me the death sentence. Spare me your presence."

There is one tiresome duty left for me to perform, Julien thought. I've got to write to Mademoiselle de la Mole.

"I have had my revenge," he told her. "Unfortunately my name will appear in the newspapers, and I shall not be able to escape from the world incognito. I shall die within two months. My revenge was hideous, like the agony of being separated from you. From this moment on, I forbid myself to write or to speak your name. Never speak of me, even to my son: silence is the only way of honouring me. For the common run of men I shall be a vulgar murderer . . . In this supreme moment, let me speak the truth: you will forget me. This great catastrophe, about which I advise you never to open your mouth to a living soul, will for several years have exhausted all the overromantic, overadventurous elements I used to see in your character. You were made to live among the heroes of the Middle Ages; now you must show their firmness of character. See to it that what is to happen is done in secret and without compromising yourself. You must take a false name, and confide in no one. If you absolutely must have the help of a friend, I bequeath you the Abbé Pirard.

"Don't speak to anyone else, especially not to people of your own class: the de Luz, the de Caylus.

"One year after my death, marry Monsieur de Croisenois; I ask you to, I order you to as your husband. Do not write to me, I would not answer. Although far less wicked than Iago, or so it seems to me, I am going to say as he did: *From this time forth I never will speak word*.

"I will not be seen to speak or to write; you will have had my last words, as well as my last adoration.

"J. S."

It was after having seen this letter off that Julien, somewhat restored to himself, felt for the first time extremely unhappy. All of his ambitious hopes were destined to be snatched from him, one by one, by the final words: I am going to die. Death in itself was not horrible to him. His whole life had been no more than one long preparation for misfortune, and he had taken no pains to disregard the one that passes for the greatest misfortune of all.

Why, look here, he thought, if I were faced with a duel, sixty days from now, with a very skilful fencer, would I be so weak as to think of it constantly, and with terror in my soul?

He spent more than a hour in an attempt to come to a clear understanding of himself in this respect.

When he had searched his spirit, and when the truth appeared before his eyes as definite in shape as one of the bars of his prison, his thoughts turned to remorse.

Why should I feel any? I've been abused in the most outrageous manner; I have killed, I deserve to die, but that is all. I die after having settled my score with humanity. I leave no obligation unfulfilled, I owe

294

nothing to anyone; there is nothing shameful about my death but the instrument: that alone, it is true, is more than enough to shame me in the eyes of the solid citizens of Verrières; but on the intellectual plane, what could be more contemptible? There is one way left for me to make myself important in their eyes: that is to fling gold pieces to the populace as I go to my execution. My memory, linked with thoughts of *gold*, will forever be bright, as far as they are concerned.

After this reasoning, which a moment later seemed completely logical to him: I have nothing further to do on earth, Julien thought, and fell into a deep sleep.

At nine o'clock that evening the jailer roused him, bringing his supper.

"What do they say in Verrières?"

"Monsieur Julien, the oath I took on the crucifix in the King's court the day I was installed in this position imposes silence on me."

He said nothing further, but remained in the cell. The slight of this vulgar hypocrisy amused Julien. I must make him wait a good long while for the five francs he wants for selling me his conscience, he thought.

When the jailer saw that he had finished his meal with no attempt at bribery:

"My friendship for you, Monsieur Julien," he said with a false and kindly air, "forces me to speak; although they do say it's against the interests of justice, because it might help you arrange your defense. . . . Monsieur Julien, who is a good fellow at heart, will be happy to hear that Madame de Rênal is feeling better."

"What! She isn't dead?" Julien cried, aghast.

"What! Didn't you know?" the jailer said with a stupefied look which quickly gave way to gratified cupidity. "It would only be right for Monsieur to give a little something to the surgeon who, according to the law and to justice, should not speak. But, for Monsieur's benefit, I went to see him and he told me all about it. . . ."

"So the wound wasn't fatal," Julien broke in impatiently. "You answer for that, on your life?"

The jailer, a six-foot giant, was alarmed and retreated toward the door. Julien realized that he was taking the wrong course for arriving at the truth. He sat down and flung a gold coin to Monsieur Noiroud.

As the man's story began to convince Julien that Madame de Rênal's wound was not fatal, he felt overcome by tears. "Go away!" he said harshly.

The jailer obeyed. The instant the door was closed: "Good God! She isn't dead!" Julien cried out; he dropped to his knees and wept passionately.

In this moment of extremity he was a believer. What did the hypocrisies of the priests matter? Could they deprive the concept of God of any of its truth and sublimity?

Only then did Julien begin to repent of the crime he had committed. Through a coincidence that released him from despair, only in that instant was the state of physical irritation bordering on frenzy, in which he had been submerged since his departure from Paris for Verrières, relieved.

His tears had an unselfish origin, he had no doubt of the death sentence that awaited him.

"So she will live!" he said. "She will live to forgive me and to love me."

Late the next morning when the jailer awakened him:

"You must have a wonderful heart, Monsieur Julien," the man said. "I've been here twice and couldn't wake you up. Here are two bottles of excellent wine our curé, Monsieur Maslon, sent you."

"What? That old rascal is still here?" Julien said.

"Yes, Monsieur," the jailer answered, lowering his voice, "but don't talk so loud; it might make trouble for you."

Julien laughed wholeheartedly.

"At the point I've got to, my friend, you're the only one who can make trouble for me, by ceasing to be kind and human. . . . You'll be well paid," Julien added, interrupting himself and resuming his imperious manner. At the moment that manner was justified by the gift of a piece of money.

Monsieur Noiroud repeated once more, and in the greatest detail, all that he had found out about Madame de Rênal, but he said not a word about Mademoiselle Elisa's visit.

The man was as humble and submissive as possible. The thought crossed Julien's mind: This sort of misshapen giant can't earn more than three or four hundred francs, for his prison isn't much frequented; I could offer him ten thousand francs if he'll be willing to run away to Switzerland with me. . . . The difficulty would be to convince him of my good faith . . . The thought of the long discussion he would

SHE PLACED JULIEN'S HEAD ON A SMALL MARBLE TABLE.

have to have with so despicable a creature filled Julien with disgust; he turned his thoughts elsewhere.

By that evening it was too late. A postchaise came for him at midnight. He was quite pleased with the police guards who were his traveling companions. In the morning, upon his arrival at the Besançon prison, they were kind enough to give him a cell on the upper floor of the Gothic dungeon. He judged the architecture to be early fourteenth-century; he admired its grace and pointed delicacy. Through the narrow crevice between two walls on the far side of a deep courtyard he had a magnificent view.

The next day he was questioned, after which he was left in peace for some days. His spirit was calm. He no longer saw his position in any but the simplest terms: I tried to kill, I should be killed.

CHAPTER 31
A Powerful Man

THE doors of the dungeon opened very early one morning. Julien
was awakened with a start.

"Oh, God!" he thought. "Here comes my father. What a disagreeable scene!"

At the same moment a woman dressed as a peasant flung herself
into his arms. He had difficulty in recognizing her. It was Mademoiselle de la Mole.

"You're wicked! It was only by your letter that I knew where you
were. I didn't find out about what you call your crime, which was
really nothing but a noble revenge that shows me all the fineness of the
heart that beats in this breast, until I got to Verrières. . . ."

In spite of his prejudices against Mademoiselle de la Mole, prejudices
which, in any case, he had not defined any too clearly to himself,
Julien found her very attractive. How could he refrain from seeing in
all her manner of speaking and acting a noble and unselfish impulse
far beyond any that a small vulgar spirit would have dared display?
Once more he had the illusion of being in love with a queen, and it
was with a rare nobility of accent and thought that he said to her, after
a moment:

"The future was very clear before my eyes. After my death I saw you remarried to Monsieur de Croisenois, who would have been marrying a widow. The fine but somewhat romantic spirit of this charming widow, shocked and converted to belief in common prudence by a singular occurrence, a great and tragic one for her, would have come to recognize the very real worth of the young marquis. You would have resigned yourself to being happy in the things that bring happiness to ordinary mortals: respect, wealth, social prestige. . . . But dear Mathilde, your coming to Besançon, if it's suspected, will be a fatal blow to Monsieur de la Mole, and that I should never forgive myself. I've caused him so much disappointment! The academician is going to say that he has nursed a viper in his bosom."

"I must confess that I was hardly expecting so much cool logic, so much concern for the future," Mademoiselle de la Mole said, somewhat irritated. "My maid, who is almost as cautious as you are, took out a passport for herself, and it's under the name of Madame Michelet that I've traveled here."

"And was Madame Michelet able to reach me as easily as that?"

"Oh, you're still the superior man, the man I chose! First I offered a hundred francs to a magistrate's secretary who claimed that it was impossible for me to get into this dungeon. But once he had the money, that honest man made me wait, raised objections—I thought that he was considering stealing from me. . . ." she paused.

"Well?" Julien said.

"Don't be angry, darling Julien," she said, putting her arms around him. "I had to give my real name to that secretary, who took me for a young working woman from Paris infatuated with the handsome Julien. . . . Truly, those were his words. I swore to him that I was your wife, and I'm to have a pass to see you every day."

That puts the finishing touch on the folly, Julien thought, I couldn't prevent it. After all, Monsieur de la Mole is so great a gentleman that public opinion will certainly be able to find an excuse for the young colonel who marries this charming widow. My approaching death will cover everything. And he gave himself up with delight to Mathilde's love. It was madness, spiritual grandeur, everything that is most extraordinary in human nature. She seriously suggested killing herself with him.

After these first raptures, and when she had recovered from the joy of seeing Julien, a lively curiosity suddenly took possession of her. She studied her lover and found him even more admirable than she had imagined. It seemed to her that Boniface de la Mole was reincarnated, but in more heroic form.

Mathilde had interviews with the town's foremost lawyers, whom she insulted by offering them rich payment too bluntly; but in the end they accepted.

She rapidly came to the conclusion that, in the case of doubtful and momentous affairs, everything in Besançon depended upon the Abbé de Frilair.

Mathilde went alone, on foot, about the streets of Besançon; she hoped not to be recognized. In any case she felt it would do her cause no harm to make a great impression upon the townspeople. In her distraction she considered arousing them to revolt and save Julien as he strode to his death. Mademoiselle de la Mole thought that she was simply dressed as befits a woman in sorrow; actually she was dressed in such a manner as to catch every eye.

She was the object of all attention in Besançon by the time she secured an audience with Monsieur de Frilair, after a week of solicitation.

Courageous as she was, the conception of an influential congregationalist was so closely associated in her mind with that of far-reaching and deliberate infamy that she trembled, ringing at the door of the bishop's palace. She was barely able to walk when she had to go up the stair that led to the First Grand Vicar's apartment. The emptiness of the episcopal palace chilled her. I may sit down in an armchair, and the armchair seize me by the arms, I'll have vanished. Whom will my maid be able to ask what has happened to me? The police chief will take good care not to act. . . . I am cut off from humanity in this great town!

At her first glance about the apartment, Mademoiselle de la Mole was reassured. To begin with, it was a footman in very elegant livery who opened the door for her. The drawing-room in which she was asked to wait displayed that discriminating and delicate luxury, so different from blatant magnificence, that one finds only in the best Parisian homes. The moment she caught sight of Monsieur de Frilair, who came toward her with a paternal air, all her visions of appalling crime vanished. She did not even find on those handsome features the imprint of that militant and rather savage virtue so distasteful to Parisian society. The half-smile that played over the features of the priest whose word was law in Besançon suggested the good companion, the learned prelate, the skilful administrator. Mathilde thought herself back in Paris.

It took Monsieur de Frilair but a few instants to lead Mathilde to admit that she was the daughter of his powerful adversary, the Marquis de la Mole.

"Actually I am not Madame Michelet," she said, resuming all her natural arrogance of manner, "and this admission costs me little, because I have come to consult you, Monsieur, on the possibility of securing Monsieur de la Vernaye's escape. In the first place he is guilty only of having behaved foolishly; the woman he shot is doing well. In the second place, I can produce fifty thousand francs on the spot, for bribing underlings, and I will guarantee double that. Besides, my gratitude and my family's will consider nothing too great a reward for whoever saves Monsieur de la Vernaye."

Monsieur de Frilair seemed to be surprised by this name. Mathilde showed him several letters from the Minister of War addressed to Monsieur Julien Sorel de la Vernaye.

"You see, Monsieur, my father has been taking an interest in his fortune. I married him secretly, my father's wish was that he should be a higher-ranking officer before we announced a marriage somewhat odd for a la Mole."

Mathilde observed that the expression of kindness and gentle gaiety was rapidly vanishing in proportion as Monsieur de Frilair made these important discoveries. Subtlety blended with profound deceit was portrayed on his face.

The abbé had doubts, he reread the official documents slowly.

What advantage is there for me in these strange confidences? he was wondering. Here I am suddenly on confidential terms with a friend of the well-known Maréchale de Fervaques, the extremely influential niece of Monseigneur the Bishop of . . . . , through whom one becomes a bishop in France.

What I have always thought of as being far in the future has unexpectedly happened. This might be the way to realize all my hopes.

Dazzled by this swift and unhoped for avenue to the episcopate that opened out before his eyes, astonished by Mathilde's intelligent grasp of the situation, Monsieur de Frilair was for an instant off guard. Mademoiselle de la Mole saw him all but at her feet, trembling nervously with ambition and eagerness.

Everything is coming clear, she thought, nothing will be impossible here for Madame de Fervaques' friend. Putting aside a feeling of jealousy that was still exceedingly acute, she summoned the courage to explain that Julien was an intimate friend of the maréchale.

"If a list of thirty-six jurors were drawn by lot four or five times in a row from among the leading citizens of this department," the Grand Vicar said with the avid glance of ambition, and emphasizing his words, "I should consider myself very unlucky if, in each list, I couldn't count eight or ten friends, and the most intelligent of the group. I shall have a majority almost every time, more than is needed to pass sentence; you see, Mademoiselle, how easily I can get an acquittal. . . ."

At last the Abbé Frilair was sure of his influence. He gave Mathilde to understand (he was undoubtedly lying) that he could do as he liked with the prosecutor charged with supporting the accusation against Julien.

After the drawing of lots had determined the thirty-six jurors, he would approach at least thirty of them directly and personally.

If Mathilde had not seemed so attractive to Monsieur de Frilair, he would not have spoken so openly to her until the fifth or sixth interview.

CHAPTER 32

Tranquillity

"I T WAS murder, and premeditated murder," Julien said to the magistrate as to the lawyer. "I'm sorry, gentlemen," he added smiling, "but this makes rather a small matter of your task."

After all, Julien thought when he had succeeded in getting rid of these two, I must be brave, and apparently braver than those two men. They look upon this ill-fated contest, to which I shall give no serious thought until the day comes, as the pinnacle of evil, as the *king of horrors*.

It is because I have known a greater torment, Julien continued, philosophizing for his own benefit. I suffered far more during my first trip to Strasbourg, when I believed that I had been deserted by Mathilde. . . . And to think that I so passionately desired that complete intimacy that leaves me so unmoved today! . . . In fact I'm happier alone than when that lovely girl shares my solitude. . . .

The lawyer, a man of rules and formalities, thought him mad and shared the public opinion that it was jealousy which had put the pistol in his hand. One day he undertook to point out to Julien that this allegation, true or false, would be an excellent defense. But the accused instantly became again a vehement and incisive character.

"On your life, Monsieur," Julien cried, enraged, "remember never

303

to suggest that abominable lie again." For an instant the cautious lawyer was afraid of being assaulted.

He was preparing his brief, for the decisive moment was rapidly approaching. Besançon and the whole department could talk of nothing but the much-publicized case. Julien was not aware of this aspect of the matter; he had insisted that no one ever speak to him of this sort of thing.

He spent these last days pacing the narrow terrace at the top of the prison, smoking the excellent cigars that Mathilde had sent a messenger to fetch from Holland, and never suspecting that his daily appearance was awaited by every telescope in town. His thoughts were in Vergy. He never mentioned Madame de Rênal to Fouqué, but this friend had told him two or three times that she was recovering rapidly, and the words reëchoed in his heart.

While Julien's spirit was almost always immersed in the medium of ideas, Mathilde, engaged with realities as befits an aristocratic nature, had been able to advance the intimacy of direct correspondence between Madame de Fervaques and Monsieur de Frilair to such a point that the potent word *bishopric* had already been spoken.

The venerable prelate responsible for the list of benefices added as a postcript in a letter to his niece, "This poor Sorel has only been foolish, I hope that he will be restored to us."

At sight of these words Monsieur de Frilair was as if transfigured. He had no doubt of being able to save Julien.

"If it weren't for this Jacobin law which prescribes the drawing up of an interminable list of jurors and whose only real purpose is depriving well-born people of all influence," he said to Mathilde the day before the drawing of lots for the panel of thirty-six jurors, "I could have answered for the verdict. I certainly got the Curé N . . . acquitted. . . ."

The next day, it was with pleasure that Monsieur de Frilair found, among the names drawn from the urn, five members of the Besançon congregation and, among the nonresidents of the town, the names of Messieurs de Valenod, de Moirod and de Cholin. "I can answer for those eight jurors without hesitation," he told Mathilde. "The first five are automatons. Valenod is my agent, Moirod owes everything to me, de Cholin is an imbecile who's afraid of everything."

The newspaper circulated the names of the jurors about the department, and Madame de Rênal, to the inexpressible horror of her husband, insisted upon going to Besançon. The only concession Monsieur de Rênal was able to secure was that she would not leave her bed, in order not to have the disagreeable experience of being called as witness. "You don't understand my position," the ex-mayor of Verrières said. "I'm now a Liberal of the *defection*, as they say; there's no doubt that blackguard de Valenod and Monsieur de Frilair could easily get the attorney general and the judges to do anything that might be disagreeable for me."

Madame de Rênal yielded without protest to her husband's orders. If I appeared in court, she thought, it would look as if I were seeking revenge.

Despite all the promises of discretion made to her confessor and to her husband, the moment she arrived in Besançon she wrote personally to each of the thirty-six jurors:

"I shall not appear the day of the trial, Monsieur, because my presence might prejudice Monsieur Sorel's case. There is but one thing in the world that I ardently desire, and that is that he should be saved. Make no doubt about it, the appalling idea that an innocent man had gone to his death because of me would poison the rest of my life and undoubtedly cut it short. How could you sentence him to death, since I am still alive? No, there is no doubt, society has no right to take life, particularly the life of a man such as Julien Sorel. In Verrières, everybody knew him to have moments of aberration. This poor young man has powerful enemies, but even among his enemies (and how many he has!) where is one who can cast doubt upon his admirable gifts and his extensive learning? It is not an ordinary person whom you are about to try, Monsieur. For almost eighteen months we all knew him to be devout, good, earnest; but two or three times a year he is attacked by fits of melancholy which amount almost to distraction. The whole town of Verrières, all our neighbors in Vergy where we spend the summer, my whole family, the subprefect himself, all can testify to his exemplary piety; he knows the entire Holy Bible by heart. Would an impious man have devoted years to learning the holy book? My sons will have the honor of delivering this letter to you: they are children. Be kind enough to question them, Monsieur; they will give you any details about this young man that are yet necessary to convince you of the barbarity it would be to convict him. Far from avenging me, you would be sending me to my death.

"What can his enemies produce in opposition to this fact? The wound that resulted from one of those moments of aberration that even my children noticed in their tutor is so minor that after less than two months it has permitted me to travel post from Verrières to Besançon. If I should hear, Monsieur, that you have the least hesitation about sparing a man the barbarity of the law when he is so little guilty, I shall rise from my bed, where only my husband's order keeps me confined, and come to throw myself at your feet.

"Declare that premeditation was not sustained, Monsieur, and you will not have to reproach yourself with the blood of an innocent man. . . ." And so forth.

CHAPTER 33

The Trial

AT LAST the day so dreaded by Madame de Rênal and by Mathilde arrived.

The strange appearance of the town heightened their terror, and even Fouqué's steadfast spirit was not unmoved by it. The whole province had flocked to Besançon to see this romantic case tried.

For some days past there had been no room left in the inns. The president of the assizes was besieged by requests for tickets of admission; all the ladies of the town wished to be present at the trial; Julien's portrait was sold in the streets, and so on.

Mathilde was holding in reserve for this ultimate moment a letter written entirely by the hand of the Bishop of _____. This prelate, who governed the Church of France and created bishops, was graciously pleased to ask Julien's acquittal. On the eve of the trial, Mathilde took this letter to the omnipotent grand vicar.

At the end of the interview, as she was leaving, drowned in tears: "I will answer for the jury's verdict," Monsieur de Frilair said, emerging at last from his diplomatic reserve, and almost emotionally stirred himself. "Among the dozen men whose duty it will be to determine whether your friend's crime is unquestionable, and particularly whether it was premeditated, I count six friends devoted to my welfare, and I have given them to understand that raising me to the episcopacy depends upon them. The Baron de Valenod, whom I made mayor of Verrières, has complete control of two of his administrators, Messieurs de Moirud and de Cholin."

"And what sort of man is this Monsieur de Valenod?" Mathilde asked uneasily.

"If you knew him, you would have no doubt of success. He's an orator, daring, impudent, coarse, made for influencing fools. 1814 brought him up out of obscurity, and I am going to make a prefect of him. He's quite capable of thrashing the other jurors if they won't vote as he sees fit."

Mathilde was a little reassured.

Another argument was waiting for her that evening. In order not to prolong an unpleasant experience, the outcome of which was unquestionable in his estimation, Julien was determined not to say anything himself.

"My lawyer will speak, that's more than enough," he said to Mathilde. "I'll be exposed as a spectacle for my enemies only too long as it is. These provincials were shocked by the quick rise to fortune which I owe to you, and believe me, there's not one of them who is not hoping for the death sentence, even if he will cry like a fool when they lead me to my execution."

"They want to see you humiliated, that's only too true," Mathilde said, "but I don't believe they are cruel. My presence in Besançon and the sight of my suffering have aroused all the women's sympathy; your handsome face will do the rest. If you so much as open your mouth before the judges, the whole audience will be yours. . . ." And so forth.

The next morning at nine o'clock, when Julien came down from his cell to enter the great courtroom of the Palais de Justice, it was only with the greatest difficulty that the guards were able to make a way through the immense crowd packed into the court. Julien had slept well, he was very calm and felt no emotion but a philosophical pity for that throng of envious persons who, without cruelty, had come to applaud his death sentence. He was greatly surprised when, having been detained for more than a quarter of an hour in the midst of the crowd, he was forced to realize that his presence inspired the people with a tender pity. He did not hear a single unpleasant comment. These provincials are less malicious than I thought, he reflected.

Entering the courtroom, he was struck by the beauty of the architecture. It was true Gothic, with many graceful slender columns cut from stone with the greatest artistry. He thought himself in England.

But presently all his attention was focused upon twelve or fifteen attractive-looking women who, seated opposite the dock, filled the three balconies above the bench and jury box. Turning toward the spectators, he saw that the circular gallery which overhung the amphitheater was crowded with women: most of them were young and looked very lovely to him; their eyes were bright and full of sympathy. In the rest of the court the crowd was enormous; there was fighting at the doors and the bailiffs were unable to impose silence.

When all the eyes that were seeking Julien became aware of his presence, seeing him take the slightly raised seat reserved for the accused, he was greeted by a murmur of astonishment and affectionate interest.

That day one would have thought him no more than twenty; he was dressed very simply but in perfect taste; his hair and his forehead were charming; Mathilde herself had insisted upon supervising his attire. His pallor was accentuated. He was no more than seated in the dock when he heard murmurs on all sides: "Lord, how young he is! . . . Why, he's a child. . . . He's far handsomer than his picture."

"Prisoner," the guard seated at his right hand, "do you see the six women in that balcony?" The guard pointed out a small gallery projecting out over the jurybox. "That is the prefect's wife," he went on, "beside her the Marquise de la M . . . , she's got a soft spot in her heart for you, I heard her talking to the prosecutor. Next is Madame Derville. . . ."

"Madame Derville!" Julien exclaimed, and a fiery color rose to his forehead. When she leaves here, he thought, she will write to Madame de Rênal. He was not aware of Madame de Rênal's presence in Besançon.

The witnesses' testimony was quickly heard. At the first words of the speech for the prosecution, made by the attorney general, two of the ladies seated in the small balcony facing Julien burst into tears. Madame Derville will certainly not be so affected, Julien thought. He noticed, however, that she turned quite red.

He was pleased with the steadfast expression on his lawyer's face. "No rhetoric," he muttered softly to him as he was about to speak.

"All the emphasis stolen from Bossuet that they've brought out against you has really helped you," the lawyer said. As a matter of fact he had been speaking for no more than five minutes before almost all the women had their handkerchiefs out. Encouraged, the lawyer addressed the jury in extremely strong terms. Julien shuddered, and felt himself upon the point of tears. My God, what will my enemies say!

Shortly after, Julien was recalled to himself by signs of approval from the spectators. The lawyer had finished his speech for the defense. Julien remembered that it was proper to shake his hand. The time had passed swiftly.

Refreshments were brought for the lawyer and the defendant. It was only then that Julien was struck by one circumstance: not one woman had left her place to go and have dinner.

"Lord, I'm starving," the lawyer said. "What about you?"

"I am too," Julien answered.

"Look, there's the prefect's wife having her dinner brought in too," the lawyer said, nodding toward the small gallery. "Keep up your courage, everything is going well." The hearing was resumed.

As the presiding judge was summing up, midnight struck. The judge was obliged to pause; in the silence of universal anxiety, the reverberations of the striking clock filled the room.

Now begins the last of my days, Julien thought. Presently he began to feel consumed by the idea of duty. Up to now he had controlled his emotion and adhered to his resolution not to speak a word; but when the presiding judge asked him if he had anything to add, he arose. He saw before him Madame Derville's eyes, they seemed to glitter in the lamplight. Can she by any chance be crying, he wondered.

"Gentlemen of the jury:

"A horror of contempt, which I thought that I could face at the moment of my death, forces me to speak. Gentlemen, I have not the honor of belonging to your class, you see me in a peasant who has rebelled against the humbleness of his destiny.

"I ask no mercy of you," Julien continued, steadying his voice. "I have no illusions about it: death awaits me; that is as it should be. I have made an attempt upon the life of the woman most worthy of every respect, every gratitude. Madame de Rênal was like a mother to me. My crime is monstrous, and it was *premeditated*. So I deserve to die, gentlemen of the jury. But even if I were less guilty, I see men here who, without a thought for the pity my youth might warrant, would like to punish in me and discourage forever that class of young men who, born to an inferior station and all more or less oppressed by poverty, have the good fortune to secure an education and the audacity to mingle with what rich men in their pride call society.

"That was my crime, gentlemen, and it will be punished with all the more severity since in actual fact I am not being judged by my peers. I do not see in the jury box one single peasant who has become rich, but only outraged bourgeois. . . ."

For twenty minutes Julien spoke in this vein; he said all that was in his heart. The attorney general, who aspired to the favor of the aristocracy, leaped in his seat; but in spite of the somewhat abstract note Julien had introduced into the discussion, all the women dissolved in tears. Before closing, Julien returned to premeditation, to his repentance, to respect and the unbounded filial devotion which, in happier times, he had had for Madame de Rênal. . . . Madame Derville cried out and fainted.

One o'clock was striking as the jury retired to their room. Not one woman had left her seat; many men had tears in their eyes. At first conversation was eager; but gradually, as the jury's verdict was delayed, general fatigue began to cast a hush over the assembly. It was a solemn moment; the lights dimmed. Julien, on the verge of exhaustion, heard people about him discussing the question of whether this delay was a good or a bad omen. He saw with pleasure that everyone's hopes were with him: the jury did not return, and still no woman left the courtroom.

Two o'clock had just struck when a great stir was heard. The small door of the jury room opened. Monsieur le Baron de Valenod advanced with a grave, theatrical step, followed by all the jurors. He coughed, then stated that upon his soul and conscience the unanimous decision of the jury was that Julien Sorel was guilty of murder, premeditated murder: a verdict which entailed the death sentence. It was pronounced a moment later. Julien glanced at his watch, it was a quarter past two. Today is Friday, he thought.

Yes, but it's a lucky day for Valenod, who is condemning me to death. . . . I'm too closely watched for Mathilde to be able to save me. So, three days from now, at this same hour, I shall know what to expect of the great *perhaps*.

Just then he heard a cry and was recalled to the things of this world. The women about him were sobbing; he saw that all faces were turned toward a small gallery let into one of the Gothic pilasters. Later he learned that Mathilde had hidden herself there. As the cry was not repeated, everyone turned back to look at Julien, whom the guards were trying to help push through the crowd.

I must try not to give that scoundrel Valenod anything to laugh at, Julien thought. With what a contrite, sniveling air he pronounced the verdict that demands the death penalty! While that poor presiding judge, magistrate though he's been for all these years, had tears in his eye when he sentenced me. What a joy for Valenod to be revenged for our old rivalry over Madame de Rênal! . . . And so I'll never see her again! It's all over . . . One last farewell is impossible for us, I feel it. . . . How happy it would have made me to tell her all the horror I feel for my crime!

Just these words: I think that I am justly sentenced.

CHAPTER 34

UPON being returned to the prison, Julien was placed in the cell reserved for those condemned to death. He, who ordinarily noticed even the most insignificant details, was not aware that he was not being taken back to his dungeon. He was thinking of what he would say to Madame de Rênal if, before the last moment, it might be granted him to see her. He was thinking that she would interrupt him, and wanted to be able to express all his remorse in his first word. After such an action, how can I convince her that I love her alone? For after all it was either ambition or love of Mathilde that made me want to kill her.

Lying down on the bed, he noticed the coarse muslin sheets. His eyes came open. Ah, yes, I'm in the condemned cell, he thought. That's right. . . .

Count Altamira told me once that just before his death Danton said in his harsh voice: "It's an odd thing, the verb to guillotine can't be conjugated in all its tenses; one can say 'I shall be guillotined, thou shalt be guillotined, but one never says 'I have been guillotined.' "

Why not, if there is another life. Julien went on. By the Lord, if I meet the Christians' God, I'm lost; He is a despot, and as such He is full of ideas of vengeance; His Bible speaks only of frightful punishments. I have never loved Him; I have never even been willing to believe that anyone could love Him sincerely. He is pitiless (and he recalled several passages from the Bible). He will punish me in an abominable manner. . . .

But if I meet Fénelon's God! He will say to me, perhaps: "Much will be forgiven you, because you have greatly loved. . . ."

Have I greatly loved? Oh, I loved Madame de Rênal, but I've behaved atrociously. In that, as in other things, simple and modest worth was forsaken for what glittered. . . .

But then, what prospects! Colonel of Hussars, if we had a war; legation secretary during peace time; later on, ambassador—for I should soon have mastered the art—and even if I had never been anything but a fool, has the Marquis de la Mole's son-in-law any rivalry to fear? All my blunders would have been excused, or rather counted as merits. A man of merit, reveling in the most splendid existence in Vienna or in London. . . .

"Not precisely, Monsieur. Guillotined in three days."

Julien laughed wholeheartedly at his own mind's jest. A man must actually have two people in him. Who the devil thought of that malicious observation?

Well then, yes, my friend, guillotined in three days, he answered the interruption. Monsieur de Cholin will rent a window for the occasion, sharing the cost with the Abbé Maslon. Well, for the cost of reserving that window, which of those two worthy characters will rob the other?

Suddenly a passage from Rotrou's *Venceslas* recurred to him:

LADISLAUS: . . . *My soul is ready.*
THE KING (his father): *So is the scaffold; lay your head upon it.*

A good answer! he thought, and fell asleep. In the morning someone wakened him by shaking him vigorously.

"What, already!" Julien said, opening a haggard eye. He thought himself in the hands of the executioner.

It was Mathilde. Fortunately she didn't understand me. This realization restored all his composure. He found Mathilde changed as if by six months of illness: she was actually unrecognizable.

"That villainous Frilair betrayed me," she said, wringing her hands; rage prevented her from crying.

"Wasn't I good yesterday when I spoke?" Julien returned. "I was improvising, and for the first time in my life! Of course, it's to be feared that it was also the last time."

At that moment Julien was playing upon Mathilde's character with all the self-possession of a skilful pianist at the piano. . . . "It is true that I lack the advantages of good birth," he added, "but Mathilde's great soul has raised her lover to her level. Do you believe that Boniface de la Mole could have borne himself any better before the judges?"

That day Mathilde was unaffectedly tender, like a poor girl living in a garret; but she was unable to get him to speak any more simply to her. Unconsciously, he was paying her back all the torment she had so often inflicted upon him.

Mathilde kept repeating in a stifled voice, "He is there, in the next room." At length the words caught his attention. Her voice is faint, he thought, but all her imperious nature is still in its accents. She lowers her voice to keep herself from losing her temper.

"Who is there?" he asked gently.

"The lawyer, with your appeal for you to sign."

"I am not going to appeal."

"What? You're not going to appeal!" she cried, springing to her feet, her eyes blazing with anger. "And why not, if you please?"

"Because right now I feel that I have courage enough to die without making too much of a laughingstock of myself. And who can assure me that in two months, after a long stay in this damp cell, I shall be as well prepared? I foresee interviews with priests, with my father. . . . Nothing in the world could be so disagreeable for me. I'd rather die."

This unexpected stubbornness roused all the high-handed element in Mathilde's character. She had been unable to see the Abbé de Frilair before the hour at which the Besançon prison cells were opened; her rage was vented upon Julien. She adored him, and for a full quarter hour he recognized in her imprecations against his character, in her regrets for ever having loved him, the image of that arrogant spirit which once, in the library of the Mole mansion, had heaped him with such stinging insults.

"For the honor of your race, heaven should have made you a man," he said to her.

But as for me, he thought, I should be an utter fool to go on living another two months in this revolting place, the object of every outrage and humiliation the patrician faction can invent, and with this mad woman's imprecations for my only consolation. . . . Well, day after tomorrow I'll be dueling with a man well known for his composure and for his remarkable skill. . . . . "Very remarkable," his personal devil observed; "he never misses."

Well, all right, so much the better. (Mathilde continued to be eloquent.) By God, no! he thought. I will not appeal.

This resolution made, he fell into abstraction. . . . When the postman goes by, he will bring the six o'clock newspaper as usual; at eight o'clock, after Monsieur de Rênal has read it, Elisa will tiptoe in to leave it on *her* bed. Later, she will wake up: suddenly, reading, she will be upset; her pretty hand will tremble; she will read on to the words . . . *at five minutes past ten he had ceased to exist.*

She will shed hot tears, I know her; even though I tried to murder her, all that will be forgotten. And the person whose life I tried to take will be the only one who will sincerely grieve over my death.

There's a paradox! he thought, and during the entire quarter hour the scene Mathilde was making continued, he thought only of Madame de Rênal. In spite of himself, and even while replying frequently to what Mathilde was saying, he could not free his spirit of the memory of that bedroom in Verrières. He saw the Besançon *Gazette* against the orange taffeta counterpane. He saw that white hand crush it in a convulsive grip; he saw Madame de Rênal weep. . . . He followed the course of each tear down over that lovely face.

Mademoiselle de la Mole, unable to get Julien to agree to anything, asked the lawyer to come in. Fortunately, he was an ex-captain of the Army of Italy, a veteran of 1796, when he had been Manuel's brother-in-arms.

For form's sake he opposed the condemned man's resolution. Julien, wishing to show him respect, explained all his reasons to him.

"Lord, yes, I can see how you feel," Monsieur Felix Vanneau, the lawyer, said in the end. "But you have three full days in which to appeal, and it's my duty to return every day. If a volcano erupted under the prison between now and two months from now, you would be saved. You might die of some illness," he said, looking at Julien.

Julien grasped his hand. "Thank you. You're a fine man. I'll think it over."

And when Mathilde at last went out with the lawyer, he felt more friendly toward the lawyer than toward her.

CHAPTER 35

AN HOUR later he was aroused from a profound sleep by tears which he felt falling on his hand. Oh, Mathilde again! he thought, half awake. Faithful to theory, she comes to attack my resolution with tender emotion. Irritated by the prospect of this new scene in the pathetic medium, he did not open his eyes. Belphegor's lines when in flight from his wife came into his mind.

He heard a curious sigh; he opened his eyes, it was Madame de Rênal.

"Ah, I'm seeing you once more before I die! Is it an illusion?" he cried, springing to his feet.

"But forgive me, Madame, I am only a murderer in your eyes," he added instantly, recollecting himself.

"Monsieur . . . I've come to beg you to appeal, I know that you don't want to . . ." Her sobs overcame her; she could not speak.

"Forgive me."

"If you want me to forgive you," she said, rising and flinging herself into his arms, "appeal from your death sentence at once."

Julien covered her with kisses.

"Will you come to see me every day during these next two months?"

"I swear I will. Every day, unless my husband forbids me."

"I'll sign!" Julien cried. "What, you forgive me! Is it possible?"

He crushed her in his arms; he was distracted; she gave a little cry.

"It's nothing," she said. "You hurt me a little."

"Your shoulder!" Julien cried, bursting into tears. He moved a little away and covered her hand with burning kisses. "Who would have thought it, the last time I saw you, in your room at Verrières?"

"Who would have thought then that I'd write that horrible letter to Monsieur de la Mole?"

"I have always loved you, I love no one but you."

"Is it really possible!" Madame de Rênal cried, overcome in turn. She leaned against Julien, who had dropped to his knees, and for a long time they wept together in silence.

At no time in his life had Julien experienced such a moment.

Sometime later, when they were able to speak:

"This young Madame Michelet," Madame de Rênal said, "or rather, Mademoiselle de la Mole—for I'm really beginning to believe in this strange romance!"

"It is a romance only in appearance," Julien said. "She is my wife, but not my mistress."

Interrupting one another a hundred times, they eventually managed to tell each other all that they had not known. The letter sent to Monsieur de la Mole had been composed by the young priest who was Madame de Rênal's confessor, and then copied by her. "What a hateful thing religion forced me to do!" she said. "And even at that I softened the worst passages of that letter."

Julien's rapturous delight proved to her how freely he forgave her. He had never been so distracted with love.

"And yet I believe that I am devout," Madame de Rênal said to him in the course of the conversation. "I believe sincerely in God; I believe equally, and it has even been proved to me, that the sin I am committing is a frightful one, yet the moment I see you, even after you have fired two shots at me. . . ." Here, in spite of anything she could do, Julien smothered her with kisses.

"Let me go on," she continued. "I want to tell you my reasoning, before I forget it. . . . The moment I see you, all notions of duty disappear, I have no longer anything but love for you—or rather, the word love is too feeble. I feel for you what I ought to feel only for God: a mixture of respect, love, submission. . . . In fact, I don't know what it is you inspire me with. If you should tell me to cut the jailer's throat, the crime would be committed before I even thought about it. Explain that very clearly to me before I leave you, I want to see plainly into my heart; for in two months we will be parted. . . . Or will we be parted?" she asked, smiling.

"I take back my word," Julien cried, leaping to his feet. "I will not appeal my death sentence if by poison, knife, pistol, charcoal fumes or any other means whatsoever, you try to put an end to your life."

Madame de Rênal's expression changed suddenly. The most ardent tenderness gave way to profound contemplation.

"If we died right away?" she asked at length.

"Who knows what we will find in the next life?" Julien answered. "Perhaps torments, perhaps nothing at all. Can't we spend two months together in a wonderful way? Two months, that's a good many days. I shall be happier than I have ever been."

"Happier than you have ever been!"

"Ever!" Julien repeated, carried away. "And I am speaking to you as I speak to myself. God preserve me from exaggerating."

"Talking that way makes it a command," she said with a timid and melancholy smile.

"Well, then, do you swear on your love for me that you will not try to take your life by any means, direct or indirect? . . . Remember," he added, "that you must live for my son, whom Mathilde will abandon to servants as soon as she is the Marquise de Croisenois."

"I swear," she returned coldly, "but I want to take your appeal with me, written and signed by your hand. I'll go myself to the attorney general."

"Be careful, you'll compromise yourself."

"After having gone so far as to come and see you in prison, I shall be the heroine of scandalous stories in Besançon and in all Franche-Comté for the rest of my life," she said with a deeply grieved air. "The bounds of strict modesty have been overstepped . . . I am a woman lost to honor; it is true that it's for your sake. . . ."

Her accent was so sorrowful that Julien embraced her with a happiness that was entirely new to him. It was no longer the intoxication of love; it was the utmost gratitude. He had just glimpsed for the first time the full extent of the sacrifice she had made for him.

Some charitable soul, no doubt, informed Monsieur de Rênal of the long visits his wife was paying Julien in prison, for after three days he sent her his carriage with express orders to return at once to Verrières.

For the first time, death began to seem horrible to Julien. He kept thinking of the state of putrefaction his body would be in, two days after the execution.

CHAPTER 36

JULIEN wept frequently, and wept because he was to die. Little by little he began to tell himself that if Madame de Rênal had been in Besançon he could have confessed his weakness to her. . . .

At the moment when he was most bitterly regretting the absence of that adored woman, he heard Mathilde's step. The most unfortunate thing about prison life, he thought, is not being able to close one's door. All that Mathilde said to him only antagonized him.

She told him that on the day of the trial Monsieur Valenod, with his appointment as prefect in his pocket, had dared to defy Monsieur de Frilair and give himself the satisfaction of sentencing Julien to death.

"Monsieur de Frilair just said: 'What came over your friend, to rise up and attack the petty vanity of this bourgeois aristocracy! Why talk about *caste?* He pointed out to them what they must do to safeguard their own political interests: those imbeciles weren't giving it a thought, they were ready to cry. The thought of caste interest mitigated the horror of condemning a man to death, as far as they were concerned. It must be admitted that Monsieur Sorel is very inexperienced in this sort of affair. If we don't succeed in saving him by appealing for mercy, his death will be a kind of *suicide*. . . .'"

Mathilde had no occasion for telling Julien what she herself did not as yet suspect: that the Abbé Frilair, seeing Julien's cause hopeless, had conceived the profitable ambition of becoming his successor.

Almost beside himself with impotent rage and irritation: "Go and have a Mass said for me," he told Mathilde, "and give me a moment's peace." Mathilde, already violently jealous of Madame de Rênal's visits, and having just learned of her departure, understood the cause of Julien's ill-humor and burst into tears.

Her suffering was genuine; Julien recognized it, and was only the more irritated by it. He had an urgent need of solitude, and how was he to secure it?

At length Mathilde, having tried by every possible device to soften him, left him alone, but almost immediately Fouqué appeared. "I need to be alone," he told this faithful friend; and, seeing him hesitate: "I'm composing a memorandum for my appeal for clemency . . . besides . . . do me a favor, never speak to me of death. If I have need of any particular services on that day, let me be the first to mention them."

When Julien had at last achieved solitude, he found himself more overcome and more unheroic than before. The little strength that had remained to his exhausted spirit had been expended in disguising his state of mind from Mademoiselle de la Mole and Fouqué.

By evening an idea had come to console him:

If they had taken me out for execution this morning, at the moment when death seemed so ugly to me, the eye of the public would have been a spur to honor; perhaps there might have been some rigidity in my bearing, like that of a timid fop entering a drawing-room. Some observant souls—if there are any among these provincials—might have been able to guess my weakness . . . but nobody *would have seen* it.

And he felt relieved of a part of his despair. I am a coward right now, he chanted over and over to himself, but nobody will know it.

He was further troubled by all the memories of that Bible he had learned by heart. . . . But how, whenever *two or three are gathered together*, is one to believe in that majestic name: GOD, after the appalling misuse our priests make of it?

To live in isolation! . . . What torment! . . .

I am going mad, I am unjust, Julien thought, striking his forehead. I am isolated here in this cell; but I did not live a life of isolation on earth; I was obsessed by the potent concept of *duty*. The duty I laid down for myself, right or wrong . . . it was like the trunk of a mighty tree to which I clung throughout the storm. I staggered, I was buffeted about. After all I was but a man . . . but I was not swept away.

It's the dank air of this cell that makes me think of isolation. . . .

And why be still a hypocrite, while cursing hypocrisy? It is neither death, nor the cell, nor the dank air; it is Madame de Rênal's absence that oppresses me so. If, in order to see her, I were forced to live weeks on end hidden in the cellars of her house in Verrières, would I complain?

"The influence of my contemporaries is getting the better of me," he said aloud, with a bitter laugh. "Talking to myself, alone, I am still a hypocrite. . . . Oh, nineteenth century!"

. . . A hunter fires a rifle shot in a forest, his game falls, he springs forward to seize it. His boot strikes an anthill two feet high, destroys the ants' habitation, scatters the ants, their eggs far and wide. . . . The most philosophical of the ants will never be able to understand that huge, black, terrifying body, the hunter's boot, which, without warning, has burst through their home with incredible swiftness, accompanied by sparks of reddish fire. . . .

. . . So it is with death, life, eternity—very simple matters for those with organs vast enough to grasp them. . . .

An ephemeral fly is born at nine o'clock in the morning of a midsummer's day, to die at five o'clock that evening; how could it understand the word *night?*

Give it five more hours of existence, it would see and understand what night is.

So it is for me; I shall die at twenty-three. Give me five more years of life, to live with Madame de Rênal.

He began to laugh like a Mephistopheles. What madness, arguing these vast problems with oneself!

First, I'm being just as hypocritical as if there were someone here listening to me.

Second, I am forgetting to live and to love, when there are so few days left to me for living. . . . Alas, Madame de Rênal is gone; perhaps her husband will not allow her to return to Besançon and continue to disgrace herself.

That is what makes my isolation, and not the absence of a just, kind, omnipotent God, not cruel, not greedy for vengeance. . . .

Oh, if only He existed! . . . I would fall at His feet. "I deserve to die," I would say to Him, "but great God, good God, indulgent God, give me back the one I love!"

The night was far advanced. After an hour or two of tranquil sleep, Fouqué came.

Julien felt strong and resolute, as a man who sees clearly into his own soul.

CHAPTER 37

Thanks to Monsieur de Frilair, Julien in his cell was under the care of the congregation; with a more enterprising spirit he might have been able to escape. But the bad air of the cell had its effect upon him, his mental powers degenerated. He was all the happier for that, upon Madame de Rênal's return.

"My first duty is to you," she said, flinging her arms around him. "I ran away from Verrières. . . ."

Julien had no petty conceit where she was concerned, he told her all his weaknesses. She was gentle and charming with him.

By means of gold, and by using and abusing the name of her aunt, a wealthy woman known for her piety, Madame de Rênal secured the privilege of visiting him twice a day.

Upon hearing of this, Mathilde's jealousy was inflamed to the point of frenzy. Monsieur de Frilair had assured her that all his influence was not sufficient to defy convention to the point of allowing her to visit her lover more than once a day. Mathilde had Madame de Rênal followed in order to be informed of every step she took. Monsieur de Frilair expended every resource of a highly skilful nature in an effort to prove to her that Julien was unworthy of her.

In the midst of all these torments she only loved him the more for them, and almost every day she inflicted a horrible scene upon him.

Above all things, Julien wanted to be honest to the end with this poor girl whom he had so strangely compromised; but from moment to moment the illimitable love he had for Madame de Rênal kept overcoming him. When his illogical arguments failed to convince Mathilde of the innocence of her rival's visits: Anyway, he thought, the end of the drama must be quite close; that is an excuse for me, if I'm unable to act my part better.

Mademoiselle de la Mole learned that the Marquis de Croisenois was dead. Monsieur de Thaler, that immensely wealthy man, had gone so far as to make unpleasant comments upon Mathilde's disappearance; Monsieur de Croisenois had gone to request him to retract them; Monsieur de Thaler had shown him some anonymous letters, addressed to himself, and full of details so artfully assembled that it was impossible for the poor marquis not to have a glimpse of the truth.

Monsieur de Thaler took the liberty of making several extremely outspoken jests. Distracted with rage and grief, Monsieur de Croisenois insisted upon so drastic an apology that the millionaire preferred a duel. Stupidity was victorious; and one of the men most worthy to be loved in all Paris died before the age of twenty-four.

This death made a strange and unhealthy impression upon Julien's weakened spirit.

"Poor Croisenois," he said to Mathilde. "He was really very reasonable and very honorable toward us; he had every right to hate me because of your indiscretions in your mother's drawing-room, and to pick a quarrel with me; for the hatred that comes on the heels of contempt is usually furious."

Monsieur de Croisenois' death changed all Julien's ideas about Mathilde's future; he spent several days demonstrating to her that she ought to accept Monsieur de Luz. "He's a retiring man, not too much of a Jesuit," he said to her, "and one who is undoubtedly going to come up in the world. Having a more serious and more persevering kind of ambition than poor Croisenois, and not having a dukedom in his family, he'll have no objection to marrying Julien Sorel's widow."

"A widow, besides, who distrusts great passions," Mathilde added coldly, "because she has lived long enough to see her lover, after six months, prefer another woman, and a woman who was the source of all their misfortunes."

"You're being unjust; Madame de Rênal's visits are providing extraordinary arguments for the lawyer from Paris who is in charge of my appeal. He will paint a picture of the murderer honored by his victim's solicitude. That may have an effect, and perhaps some day you'll see me as the subject of a melodrama. . . ." And so on.

A furious and impotent jealousy, the persistence of sorrow unrelieved by hope (for even supposing Julien saved, how could she regain his heart?), shame, and the pain of loving this unfaithful lover more than ever before, had plunged Mademoiselle de la Mole into a dismal silence.

As for Julien, except in the moments usurped by Mathilde's presence, he was living for love and almost without thinking of the future. Through some curious effect of that passion, when it is intense and devoid of all pretense, Madame de Rênal was almost able to share his indifference and his gentle gaiety.

"Before," Julien told her, "when I could have been so happy, during our walks through the Vergy woods, intense ambition kept dragging my mind away to imaginary realms. Instead of pressing to my heart the lovely arm that was so near my lips, I let the future drive me away from you; I was obsessed with the endless struggles I should have to undergo in order to build up a huge fortune . . . No, I should have died without knowing the meaning of happiness if you had not come to see me in this prison."

Two incidents occurred to disturb this tranquil life. Julien's confessor, strict Jansenist though he was, was not immune to Jesuit intrigue, and inadvertently became their tool.

He came one day to tell Julien that if he was to avoid committing the monstrous sin of suicide, he must do everything in his power to obtain his pardon. Since the clergy exerted considerable influence at the ministry of justice in Paris, one easy course suggested itself: he must be converted with much ostentation . . .

"With ostentation!" Julien echoed. "Oh, now I catch you, too, Father, play-acting like a missionary."

"Your age," the Jansenist returned soberly, "the appealing face Providence gave you, even the very motive of your crime which remains inexplicable, the heroic endeavors Mademoiselle de la Mole is making in your behalf, in fact everything, including the astonishing kindness your victim is showing you, all these things have contributed to making you the hero of every young woman in Besançon. They have forgotten everything else, even politics, for you. . . .

"Your conversion will strike an answering chord in their hearts, and leave a profound impression. You can be of major service to religion, and should I hesitate on the frivolous grounds that it is the course the Jesuits would follow, given the same opportunity? The tears your conversion will cause to be shed will counteract the corrosive effect of ten editions of the impious works of Voltaire."

"And what is there left for me," Julien answered coldly, "if I despise myself? I was ambitious, I cannot blame myself for that. Then, I acted according to the conventions of the times. Now I live from day to day. But by and large, I should make myself very unhappy if I gave way to some cowardly impulse now. . . ."

The other incident, which touched Julien's most sensitive spot in quite another manner, originated with Madame de Rênal.

Some intriguing friend or other had succeeded in convincing this artless and timid soul that it was her duty to go to Saint-Cloud and fling herself at the feet of King Charles X.

She had made the sacrifice of parting from Julien, and after such a strain the unpleasantness of making a spectacle of herself, which in other times would have seemed worse than death, was nothing to her.

"I'll go to the King, I'll tell him proudly that you are my lover: a man's life, the life of a man such as Julien should come before all other considerations. I shall say that it was out of jealousy that you tried to take my life. There are a lot of examples of poor young men saved, in cases like this, by the jury's humanity, or the King's. . . ."

"I will have nothing more to do with you, I'll have my prison door closed to you," Julien cried, "and I shall certainly kill myself out of sheer despair unless you promise me that you will do nothing to make a public spectacle of us both.

"Let's be happy for the few days that are left of this short life. Let's hide our existence; my crime is only too visible. Mademoiselle de la Mole has great influence in Paris, be sure that she is doing everything humanly possible. Here in the province I have all the rich and respected people against me. Your acting that way would only increase the bitterness of those rich and generally moderate folk for whom life is such an easy matter. . . . Let's not make a laughingstock of ourselves for the Maslons, the Valenods and a thousand more worth-while people."

The foul air of the cell was becoming unbearable to Julien. Fortunately, on the day when he was informed that he was to die, nature was rejoicing in a brilliant sunshine, and Julien was inspired with courage. Walking in the fresh air was a delightful sensation for him, like walking on dry land for the sailor who has been long at sea. There, now, all is well, he thought. My courage hasn't failed me.

Never had that head been so poetic as at the moment when it was about to fall. The most exquisite moments which he had found long ago in the woods of Vergy returned in a multitude to his mind, and with the utmost intensity.

Everything passed simply, with dignity and, on his part, without affectation.

Two days before, he had said to Fouqué:"

"I can't answer for my emotions; this cell, so ugly, so damp, makes me have feverish moments in which I do not recognize myself. But as far as fear goes, no. No one will see me blanch.

He had made arrangements in advance for Fouqué to take Mathilde and Madame de Rênal away the morning of the last day.

"Take them in the same carriage," he had said. "See to it that the post horses keep up a steady gallop. They'll either fall into each other's arms or display mortal hatred. In either case, the poor women will be distracted a little from their terrible grief."

Julien had exacted of Madame de Rênal an oath that she would live to care for Mathilde's son.

"Who knows? Perhaps we do still have sensations after death," he said one day to Fouqué. "I should rather like to rest—since rest is the word—in that little grotto on the great mountain that overlooks Verrières. Many's the time, as I've told you, I have gone up at night to that little cave and, with my eyes far out over the richest provinces of France, felt ambition hot in my heart: that was my passion, then. . . . Anyway, that cave is dear to me, and no one can deny that its location is enough to make a philosopher's soul envious. . . . Well, these good congregationalists of Besançon make money out of everything, if you go about it right they'll sell you what's left of me."

Fouqué was successful in this grim negotiation. He was spending the night alone in his room beside the body of his friend when, to his great surprise, he saw Mathilde enter. Only a few hours earlier he had left her thirty miles from Besançon. There was frenzy in her eyes and glance.

"I want to see him," she said.

Fouqué had not the courage to speak nor to rise. He pointed with his finger to a great blue cape on the floor; in it was wrapped all that remained of Julien.

She dropped to her knees. No doubt it was the memory of Boniface

327

de la Mole and Marguerite of Navarre that gave her superhuman courage. Her shaking hands put aside the cape. Fouqué turned away.

He heard Mathilde moving swiftly about the room. She lighted several candles. When Fouqué summoned strength to look at her, she had placed Julien's head on a small marble table before her, and was kissing its forehead. . . .

Mathilde followed her lover to the grave he had chosen. A great number of priests accompanied the coffin and, unknown to all of them, alone in the carriage, behind drawn curtains, she carried on her knees the head of the man she had so loved.

Arriving thus at the highest point of one of the high Jura mountains, in the middle of the night, in that small cave magnificently lighted by innumerable candles, twenty priests celebrated the Office for the Dead. All the inhabitants of the small mountain villages through which the procession had passed had followed it, drawn by the strangeness of that extraordinary ceremony.

Mathilde appeared in their midst in long mourning garments, and at the end of the ceremony had thousands of five-franc pieces flung among them.

Left alone with Fouqué, she insisted upon burying her lover's head with her own hands. Fouqué all but went mad with grief.

Under Mathilde's care, this wild grotto was adorned with marbles sculptured at great cost in Italy.

Madame de Rênal was faithful to her promise. She did not seek in any way to end her life; but, three days after Julien, died with her children in her arms.

The disadvantage of the vogue for free opinion, which of course insures liberty, is that it meddles in matters which do not concern it; for example: private life. Hence the melancholy of America and England. To avoid infringing upon private life, the author has invented a small town, Verrières, and, when he required a bishop, a jury, a Court of Assizes, he located them all in Besançon, where he has never been.